PRAISE FOR CHRI

"Christi Caldwell's *The Vixen* shows readers a darker, grittier version of Regency London than most romance novels . . . Caldwell's more realistic version of London is a particularly gripping backdrop for this enemies-to-lovers romance, and it's heartening to read a story where love triumphs even in the darkest places."

—NPR on *The Vixen*

"In addition to a strong plot, this story boasts actualized characters whose personal demons are clear and credible. The chemistry between the protagonists is seductive and palpable, with their family history of hatred played against their personal similarities and growing attraction to create an atmospheric and captivating romance."

—*Publishers Weekly* on *The Hellion*

"Christi Caldwell is a master of words and *The Hellion* is so descriptive and vibrant that she redefines high definition. Readers will be left panting, craving, and rooting for their favorite characters as unexpected lovers find their happy ending."

—*RT Book Reviews* on *The Hellion*

"Christi Caldwell is a Must Read."

—*New York Times* bestselling author Mary Balogh

"Two people so very broken in different ways, and their journey to becoming whole again. This is Christi Caldwell at her absolute best!"

—Kathryn Bullivant

"One of [Christi] Caldwell's strengths is creating deep, sympathetic characters, and this book is no exception . . ."

—Courtney Tonokawa

The BLUESTOCKING

The Heart of a Scandal

In Need of a Knight (A Prequel Novella)
Schooling the Duke
A Lady's Guide to a Gentleman's Heart

Lords of Honor

Seduced by a Lady's Heart
Captivated by a Lady's Charm
Rescued by a Lady's Love
Tempted by a Lady's Smile

Scandalous Seasons

Forever Betrothed, Never the Bride
Never Courted, Suddenly Wed
Always Proper, Suddenly Scandalous
Always a Rogue, Forever Her Love
A Marquess for Christmas
Once a Wallflower, At Last His Love

The Theodosia Sword

Only For His Lady
Only For Her Honor
Only For Their Love

Danby

A Season of Hope
Winning a Lady's Heart

The Brethren

The Spy Who Seduced Her
The Lady Who Loved Him
The Rogue Who Rescued Her

Brethren of the Lords

My Lady of Deception
Her Duke of Secrets

A Regency Duet

Rogues Rush In

Nonfiction Works

Uninterrupted Joy: A Memoir

The BLUESTOCKING

CHRISTI CALDWELL

Montlake
Romance

Published by Montlake Romance, Seattle

www.apub.com

Amazon, the Amazon logo, and Montlake Romance are trademarks of Amazon.com, Inc., or its affiliates.

ISBN-13: 9781503904071
ISBN-10: 1503904075

Cover design by Erin Dameron-Hill

Cover illustration by Chris Cocozza

Printed in the United States of America

To my mom:
When money was tight, you made sure I still always
had a romance novel in my hands.
And when, years later, I was a grown woman and a
mom myself with books I'd written just sitting on my
computer, you were the first to tell me I should really
"indie publish" them . . . proving, once more, mothers
always know best!
I love you!

Chapter 1

St. Giles, London
Spring 1826

It was as though someone had died.

And in a way, someone had.

This would be a physical loss felt throughout the club, leaving the unlikely home silent in ways it had never been.

Gertrude Killoran stared blankly at the maids folding shirts and garments and placing them in neat piles upon an immaculate four-poster bed.

Small garments packed up, to be gone forevermore . . . and never returned.

Stacks of fine wool trousers and jackets alongside tattered scraps better fit for a street urchin. Torn cotton shirts. Coarse wool. Muddied shoes.

Her throat spasmed. "I have it." All the while the servants, so very focused on their work, continued on, methodical in their task. Gather. Fold. Pile. Repeat. Her quiet words were less of a command and more of a statement, and their whispery-soft quality lent the order an air of weakness.

The only one to pay her any heed was the grey tabby at her feet. Gus nudged his head against her legs and purred.

All these years, Gertrude had been known as the weak Killoran. Blind in one eye, she was the cripple whom no one saw any true value in—at least, not in the way one was valued in the streets. And in this instance, with her young brother, Stephen, being carted off, away from this household they'd shared to the true home he'd been born to, she confronted the reality of her character. And mayhap she *was* weak.

Because if she were as strong as she'd always considered herself to be, then she'd muster a greater show of strength than this for her brother's benefit.

She'd have packed his garments herself. Offered him words of strength and encouragement. Something. He deserved that. He deserved more in the face of uncertainty. Because of all he'd suffered and the pain he would forever know.

From where she stood at the windows overlooking the streets outside the Devil's Den, the glass panes reflected a pair of footmen behind her, entering her brother's rooms with yet another trunk.

Another one to fill with Stephen's things, taking all with him when he was gone.

Oh, God.

With jerky movements, she rushed over to the unfolded garments. "I have them," she said, her voice slightly pitched, and something in it cut across the bustling activity that had existed in this room throughout the day. The maids looked up with bereaved eyes. Tear-filled ones. Stephen would not see tears. Not today. Not on his final day inside the Devil's Den. "I said I have them," she repeated, agony making her tone sharper than she'd intended. "You may go." Gertrude looked to the four somber servants. "All of you."

The group of servants hesitated.

Even though Gertrude had taken on a greater role at the clubs since her sisters had married, it was still new to the staff. They likely didn't *truly* know what to do with this commanding version of her usually collected self. "Now," she said curtly when they made no move to leave.

The pair of maids relinquished the garments in their hands and filed after the footmen. They closed the door in their wake so that Gertrude was left . . . alone.

Her breath came slow and shallow, straining the constricted walls of her chest as she stared at the oak panel of Stephen's door, nicked and scarred from the tip of the dagger he'd hurled at it, a street game he'd carried with him into the club.

It was just one more physical proof of the wrongness of his having lived here. And of the life he'd been forced to live as a member of their family. They'd brought irrevocable harm to him. In every way. But how were they to have known? She bit hard at her lower lip, scrabbling the flesh. How were they to have known that the young boy brought into their gang, squalling and incoherently inconsolable as he'd wailed for his mum and da, had in fact been a marquess and marchioness's son? How were they to have known Stephen had been kidnapped from the comfortable, exalted folds of the peerage and plunged into the living hell and squalor of St. Giles?

And now . . . he would return. Still, by Polite Society's standards, a boy in years, but in the suffering he'd endured and the hell he'd visited upon others at the behest of their gang leader, Mac Diggory, Stephen was more jaded than a man who'd lived sixty years.

Gertrude slid onto the edge of the mattress, depressing the too-soft feather-down bed he'd insisted on. It had been the one luxury he'd embraced when he'd shunned every other hint of respectability.

Her ears pricked.

And she heard him before he'd even reached the other side of the door.

That heightened sense was a gift that had come after she'd lost vision in one eye and been forced to rely upon all her senses in order to survive on the streets.

Gertrude leapt to her feet. Then, catching a glimpse of her grim pallor in the mirrored wall chest that cased Stephen's weapons, she hurriedly pinched her cheeks and plastered a smile on her lips . . . just as the door opened enough to allow the gaunt boy to slip right through.

Stephen scraped a hate-filled stare over the clutter of his belongings that covered the bed behind her, and then his gaze settled on the large trunks marked with their family name.

His familiar scowl slipped, and in that instant he underwent a rare transformation into a vulnerable, scared child.

Gertrude's heart buckled.

"Hullo," she greeted with false cheer.

His glower deepened. "Are you happy to see me go?"

The muscles of her face froze in a painful mask that strained her cheeks. "What?" How could he . . . ? He was like the child she had never had—and would never have. "How could you dare ask that?"

"Yar grinning like the village lackwit," Stephen muttered, and shoving his heel behind him, he slammed the door, shaking the wood frame. He started past her.

Gertrude slid herself into his path. "Stop." She planted her hands on her hips and gave him a pointed look. "Seven years."

He wrinkled his high, noble brow. A young earl's brow. "Wot?"

"I've been giving you lessons on reading and writing and every other last topic considered polite and respectable. You know how to speak properly, Stephen." And yet despite it, he moved between flawless English tones and Cockney the way a skilled thief slipped through a just-emptying Covent Garden theatre.

Fire flashed in his eyes, and he jutted his chin out. "It doesn't matter how I speak." It did not escape her notice that he'd adopted those perfect tones, the ones she suspected came more readily to him than he'd ever dare admit . . . even to himself.

Gertrude settled her hands on his narrow shoulders and, stooping down so she might meet his gaze, gave her brother a little squeeze. "It does matter. You know that. And you might be angry at"—she struggled to get the words out—"your change in fate," she settled for. "But you know your life will be . . . easier." Or as easy as it could be for a stolen boy reseated at his rightful place. "If you attempt to . . . if you . . ." Words failed.

"Make myself someone I'm not?" he jeered.

"But it *is* who you are," she said quietly, sucking the energy from the room and dousing it with a thick, impenetrable tension.

Stricken eyes met hers, a mark of her brother's vulnerability.

Stephen came to life. "It is not," he cried. He whipped himself out of her arms with a hiss that sent Gus into flight across the chambers and sprinting under the oak side cabinet. "I'm from the streets, just like you and Cleo and Ophelia and Broderick. I've committed the same crimes as all of you." Fury blazed within his too-jaded eyes. "Worse," he reminded her in a chilling whisper that raised the gooseflesh on her arms.

His was more an unnecessary reminder of the crimes he'd committed. Trained by Gertrude's sire, the vile and thankfully dead gang leader Mac Diggory, he had been schooled on how to light fires and had destroyed countless businesses and ruined lives. "That time in your life is over," she said, as much as for him as for herself.

His lower lip trembled, and then with a growl, he stalked to the window overlooking the St. Giles streets.

A sense of helplessness clawed at her heart.

God help her, she had no words. What did one say to a boy who'd been raised as one's brother, only for them to learn together that it had all been a lie? That the ruthless gang leader, whom they'd all hated, hadn't found Stephen in the streets as he had so many other orphans, but had ordered two of his thugs to steal the child? Oh, Cleo and Ophelia would have some words for Stephen. They always had a ready supply of them and invariably hurled them first and worried about any consequences after.

He broke the quiet. "They're loading my things."

"Yes." Gertrude drew in a slow, silent breath and then exhaled through her nose. She strode over to the still messy pile of garments and, with jerky movements, proceeded to fold them. Shirts in one pile. Trousers in another. As long as she'd been alive, organizing the once meager, now great belongings they owned had calmed her. It had proven a distraction that kept her mind from the horrors that had been and always would be her life.

Until now.

Now she was . . . empty and aching.

Desolation swept through her.

"Ophelia would have somethin' to say," Stephen taunted, aiming a fierce glare at her.

She didn't pause in her folding. "Ophelia always has something to say."

Stephen retrained his stare outside. Shoulders hunched and head down, he was an empty shadow of the spitfire she'd always known.

And she didn't know what to do with this agonized version of him.

Gertrude forced herself to stop folding but reflexively drew the threadbare shirt close to her chest. "There will be good in you returning." He belonged there. He had never been one for this place. Not so for Gertrude. The blood of a whore and a street thug flowing in her veins, and with a blind eye to boot, she'd never been destined for anywhere except this place.

"To him?" Stephen chuckled, an empty darkness to his laugh. "He shoulda burnt in the fire beside her."

Oh, God. How could he . . . ?

"Do not say that," she rasped. The "her" in question was the very woman who'd birthed him, who'd been just another of Mac Diggory's victims, pregnant, burnt to death after that same Devil had given the orders and sealed her fate.

"He's a stranger," Stephen said with an indifferent shrug. "And he's proven to be a monster. Believe—"

"What someone shows himself to be," she finished the familiar adage.

My God, how is my voice so steady? How, when I'm splintering apart and breaking up inside?

"Stealing my goodbyes," Stephen whispered, resting his brow against the crystal pane. "Making decisions for me about when I go. Who I'll see. Who I won't . . . s-see."

Gertrude briefly pressed her eyes closed. "He is within his rights." Even as she said it, it rang hollow. "And he has reasons for his resentment toward our family." How could the marquess, who'd had seven years with his son stolen, ever have any warmth or affection or anything less than a deep, abiding loathing for the Killorans? Gertrude cleared her throat. "He'll be expecting us shortly."

That statement, spoken in a hollow voice, brought her brother back around, his usual sneering self restored. "Ain't letting you go."

She cocked her head.

Her brother gave her a once-over. "You or Broderick or Cleo or Ophelia. None of you." He spat in a disgusting habit that she had long despised but now ignored, focused solely on that statement.

"What?" she demanded, stalking over, her arms still filled with his favorite shirt.

"Broderick called me to his office. Explained the Mad Marquess don't want any of my family about. Making me come on my own."

Her mouth moved, but no words were forthcoming. He'd rob them of that final goodbye. And why shouldn't he? The marquess was well within his rights and reasons for his hatred. Why should he allow those who'd served, and shared the blood of, the scourge of St. Giles, a man who had destroyed the marquess's own family, to set a foot near his properties?

Yet . . . he should still consider how the changes would affect his son.

And for the first time that day, some emotion other than despair and pain flared in her chest: anger. Palpable. Biting. Distracting. And she clung to it.

"Ya got nothing to say," Stephen taunted. "And *that* is why you'll never be Cleo or even Ophelia." With that he stormed off. "You. Broderick. You're both weak."

"Stephen," she called after him, but he was already through the door and slamming it once more in his wake, so that only his name echoed around the room for company.

Yes, because over the years, he'd been clear that his affections were reserved for only one of the Killoran girls, and it had always been Cleo. Nor had Gertrude given him, or any of the other Killorans, much reason to believe in her strength—at least in the ways that mattered. Relegated to the role of invisible child after she'd lost partial vision, she had been allowed to remain within the household only because of Broderick's intervention and the care she'd provided for the boys and girls in the gang. Oh, the family had relied upon her to teach the children and staff. But, be it when they'd lived on the streets or in the Devil's Den, none had ever come to her for guidance. She'd never danced with danger as her siblings had. As far as Stephen knew, she had done none of these things, because shortly after he'd come to them, she'd been relegated to the position of caretaker. She'd neither killed nor stabbed nor stolen to protect. Instead, she'd allowed her younger sisters to serve in that role of de facto protector.

Her fingers gripped the shirt in her hands, and she glanced down at the threadbare garment.

"He is right," she whispered. Stephen was right.

Gus trotted out from his place under the cabinet and bounded over. The fat tabby knocked into her lower legs, and his sturdy weight ruffled her skirts.

She sank to the floor and distractedly scratched the beloved place where his tail met his back. He purred loudly and curved into her touch.

With her two younger sisters recently married, Gertrude had taken on greater roles and responsibilities in the club's running, but the role of protector had still escaped her. She'd had an obligation to care for her younger siblings . . . and she'd failed them all.

Gertrude exploded to her feet so quickly Gus hissed and bounded off, rushing this time under the bed.

Fueled by purpose, she stormed from the room.

The wide halls were a bustling space of servants gathering up and carting off Stephen's belongings. Young maids and footmen stepped out of her way, allowing her a path.

A handful of minutes later, Gertrude reached a familiar paneled door. Not bothering with a knock, she tossed the door wide.

From his place at the window, Broderick withdrew his gun and had himself positioned in front of his former assistant and now wife, Regina, with that pistol pointed at Gertrude's chest.

He swallowed a curse. "I could have killed you."

"I need to speak with you," she said, ignoring that worry. Each of them had been trained as better shots than that. They didn't fire or lunge first but rather assessed their opponent.

"What is it?" he asked quietly.

Reggie looked between brother and sister and then cleared her throat. "I'll leave you both."

Gertrude let out a sound of protest. "You don't have to do that." Reggie was as much a member of the family as any of the Killorans, in a bond that went back further and deeper than her marriage and to the years she'd spent like another sister to the Killoran girls.

"I should check on Stephen," the other woman insisted in an indication of just how very much she knew each member of their clan.

Gertrude smoothed her palms over the front of the apron covering her bronze skirts. "That . . . would probably be best." Time and life had proven the perils of leaving a volatile Stephen alone and to his own devices.

On the day he was to leave St. Giles and journey to the fancy end of Mayfair? Shivers dusted her spine. There was no telling what he might do.

Regina offered a slight nod. She very well knew and shared Gertrude's fears. Gathering Broderick's hands, Regina gave them a slight squeeze. Nearly of a same height as her husband, she easily met his gaze.

Some unspoken language passed between them, one where words were neither necessary nor used. Two people whose thoughts moved in a synchronic beat. Gertrude averted her stare, allowing them that shared moment. Theirs was a bond between a man and a woman, so foreign to Gertrude, who'd long ago accepted the fact that blind women were at best pitied and at worst treated with kid gloves. The last thing awaiting a cripple was romantic entanglement.

A floorboard started to creak, and she glanced back.

With a thankful smile, Gertrude waited until the other woman had gone before she spoke. "You aren't going."

Broderick exhaled a long sigh and, reaching inside his jacket, fished out a cheroot. "I cannot," he said simply, fiddling with the small striker he kept in his pocket. He struck one, and the faint glow of the orange flame fizzled to life. "The marquess was clear." Broderick lit the scrap of tobacco and took a long draw. With his other hand, he waved the match, wafting a puff of white smoke as the fire went out.

Gertrude frowned. "You don't accept 'no' from anyone." More stubborn than Lucifer, he'd gone toe to toe with the Devil for control of the underworld and won.

Broderick exhaled a small circle of smoke, his breath faintly shuddering, his hand faintly atremble. "He'll see me hanged."

She opened her mouth and then closed it.

With a sound of frustration, he stalked over to his desk. Grabbing the scrap of paper with a crimson seal broken down the middle, he tossed the page down in invitation.

Her frown deepening, Gertrude joined him. Picking it up, she assessed the wax crest, the imprint of a shield divided into four quadrants, neatly severing the crisscrossed swords.

Gertrude unfolded the note and read.

Killoran,

I owe you nothing. I've spared your life because my son is living. But the minute he returns to my fold, your contact with him is over. You will have no communication with him. You will not see him. You will not even set foot on my stoop to deliver him. Your time in his life will be at an end. Any failure to honor these demands will result in the hanging you deserve. Nor do I expect to see your guttersnipish sisters darkening my doorstep, or I'm fully prepared to see their gracious entrance into Polite Society made far less comfortable.

The Marquess of Maddock

Robbed of the ability to speak, Gertrude looked up from the page. He'd threatened not only Broderick but also all the Killorans.

Broderick took another long, slow inhale of his cheroot. "And so, I cannot bring him . . . b-back." He coughed into a fist in a failed bid to cover up the slight crack in his voice.

"But it is the last time we'll see him . . ."

Her brother offered a sad smile. "We lost him long ago."

Gertrude rocked back on her heels. That he should be so accepting . . . so matter of fact? "Where is your outrage at being denied even a last goodbye?"

"I don't deserve a last goodbye," Broderick said quietly as he tipped his cheroot ashes into a crystal tray.

"It is not about what you deserve or don't," she gritted out through her teeth. "It is not about what any of us deserve." It was only about Stephen. "It is about easing his way from the only life he remembers."

"And you think we're the ones to do that?" he asked in achingly painful tones. "I'm the one who ordered him taken."

Her frown deepened. "Do not say that," she snapped. Gertrude tossed the marquess's threatening note atop her brother's ledgers. "You are the one who tried to save an orphan in the streets." She took a step toward him and jammed a fingertip into the surface of his desk. "It was Diggory's sick fascination with the nobility that led to Stephen's kidnapping. You merely sought to give an orphan boy a home. Walsh and Lucy were the ones who brought a child of the nobility as Diggory always craved."

Through a small circle of smoke, Broderick flashed a wistful smile. "You were the one always capable of forgiveness . . . of seeing goodness where there wasn't any."

Her fingers curled into the sides of her muslin dress. Broderick and her other siblings had always had an inflated sense of her goodness and depth of forgiveness. They had put her on a pedestal that separated her from her origins and sins.

"Cleo needs to go," she said, stating that deliverance as fact.

"Thorne's club would be ruined."

"She won't care," Gertrude shot back, stunned.

"No. But Stephen does."

There it was, yet again. The evidence that the boy was in fact a man with a weight of responsibility upon his narrow shoulders. He'd sacrifice that last opportunity to see his siblings in order to protect them.

"Look at me, Gert," Broderick murmured. "Cleo is not accompanying him," he said when she'd forced her gaze to his.

The sting of tears blurred the whole of her vision. "It cannot be like this," she whispered, blinking furiously to keep those drops from falling.

A hand rested on her shoulder, jerking her attention upward.

Broderick held her gaze. "It is to be like this." His throat muscles worked. With a grimace, he released her and took another pull from his cheroot. "Are his belongings packed?"

That is what he'd ask after? But then, mayhap it was just simpler to speak of garments and impersonal artifacts than the loss of their sibling.

Only they weren't impersonal. They were items Stephen had groused about. Wrinkling his pert nose at the fine wool garments. Clinging to articles that bore rips and hints of faded blood from street fights he'd fought and won.

Yes, it was very nearly done.

A knock sounded at the door.

"Enter," Broderick called out.

MacLeod, the head guard, ducked inside the room. His gaze briefly lingered on Gertrude, and then he doffed his hat. "Pardon the interruption. Mr. Killoran, there's a question regarding the boy's . . . weapons."

Emotion wadded in her throat. Weapons. They weren't just weapons. A Western Great Lakes Pipe Tomahawk. An Indian Bank dagger sickle. The Turkish composite dagger. A jade-and-silver Mongolian eating knife. A Scottish targe.

Aside from the jewel-studded dagger Broderick had insisted upon, the rest of Stephen's collection had all been learning tools she'd used to motivate a child who'd chafed at the lessons Broderick had demanded Stephen be taught.

She hugged her arms around her middle. *Oh, God.* "He'll take them with him."

MacLeod went slack-jawed and looked questioningly at his employer.

Yes, because she'd never been one to publicly challenge Broderick or interject her opinion in front of a crowd. Her cases had been pleaded quietly.

A slight frown puckered between Broderick's brows. "We'll speak on it later, MacLeod."

"Sir. Miss Killoran," the guard murmured and backed out, leaving them alone once more.

Broderick tamped out his cheroot. "Everything is changing, Gertrude. It has to." He paused, staring down at the ashes in the crystal tray. "For all of us."

Everything *was* changing.

Her eyes slid closed.

They were losing Stephen. And nothing could be done to stop it. Nothing.

And before she broke down and revealed the expected weakness in front of her eldest brother, Gertrude stormed off.

What were they going to do without him?

Chapter 2

Mayfair, England

It had been decided long ago, given the mistakes and sins that belonged to him, that the eventual fate of Edwin Ludlow Phineas Shadrack Warwick, the Marquess of Maddock, was to be banished to the fiery pits of hell.

That conflagration, in this instance, was a good deal preferable to the current state of his damned affairs.

"Absolutely not."

And it certainly spoke to the depth of ugliness in his soul, the perverse pleasure he found in delivering that icy whisper.

The silver-haired, regal pair seated opposite his desk shared a look. A long stretch of silence met Edwin's pronouncement.

"Wh-what do you mean, absolutely n-not?"

It had never been a good day when his mother-in-law, the Duchess of Walford, sputtered.

Her husband stretched a hand over, resting it on hers in a gesture that would have been mistaken as one of warmth and affection in most couples.

The duchess smacked His Grace across his gloved fingers with her gilded ivory fan.

He wisely withdrew his hand and, bringing back his broad shoulders, sat more upright in his seat. "What do you mean, absolutely not?" The duke jammed a fingertip toward the floor. "We demand to be here."

Husband and wife wore impressively matching glowers. In fairness, they'd always glowered; the duke and duchess commanded fear in the hearts of nearly all members of the *ton*. Edwin, however, had come to appreciate there were far greater demons and monsters to fear than a pair of overinflated members of the peerage.

Furthermore, their disdain of Edwin went back to long ago, to the moment that he, a young rogue amongst the *ton*, had fallen in love with their late daughter and stated his intention to marry her—with or without their approval.

Edwin spread his palms out. "I mean precisely that. You aren't invited."

The couple launched into a furious tirade, abandoning all veneer of civility and descending into a firestorm of insults and outraged charges against his character.

"We warned her. You were never to be trusted . . ."

"You vile, vile monster," the duchess spat, vitriol pulling that uninventive charge from her.

Edwin settled back in his seat and rested his palms over the muscles of his flat stomach. In fairness, his in-laws had always despised him. The only crack in their otherwise icy disdain had come when he and Lavinia had made them grandparents. And even then, they'd visited but spared barely a word for the son-in-law who'd ultimately eloped with their cherished daughter.

Their palpable loathing had been fully restored the day their daughter perished in a blaze along with their unborn grandchild.

Yes, the family was justified in their hatred of him. And yet, their loathing had managed that which had been impossible while his wife lived—it had freed him from their visits and terse company.

Until now.

"You are likely being played for a fool," the Duke of Walford clipped out. Raising the same monocle that had dangled about his neck when Edwin had first met him, the duke held it to his keen eye and passed his gaze over Edwin. "You've not proven yourself the most reliable with those in your employ or company."

On his lap, Edwin curled his palms tight as the insult slid through him, a well-placed arrow that found its mark and lanced him for the truth of it.

And the duchess, who'd been previously enthusiastic in her diatribe, faltered. "You failed h-her," Her Grace said in a watery echo of the regretful musings that would forever swirl around his tortured mind. A glimmer of tears filled his mother-in-law's eyes, transforming her from one who'd long been his nemesis into a bereaved parent.

It was a familiar suffering, one he knew too well, learned at the merciless hands of Satan's helper.

"I knew you would," she said.

"*We* knew you would," the duke chimed in, resting his hand upon his wife's once more, and this time she did not draw back.

Edwin wanted to look away from her suffering, which he was responsible for, but instead, he forced himself to take ownership of what he'd done . . . and what he'd visited upon this couple.

When he'd met and fallen in love with Lavinia, he'd done nothing to merit their enmity. As the son-in-law who'd failed to protect their beloved daughter, he could appreciate all the ways they were entitled to their hatred of him.

"He will learn precisely the manner of man you are," the duchess tossed at him.

"But not the murderous marquess," he gibed, curving his lips up in a taunting smile, leveling that charge they'd raised all over London in the immediate aftermath of his wife's death.

"*Pfft,*" his mother-in-law scoffed. "You killed her all the same."

Edwin went absolutely still, determined she'd not see this latest barb had pierced that organ he'd believed long dead. For he *had* killed her. The blame, and the responsibility, belonged to him as much as if he'd set the blaze himself.

"He will see that you killed his mother and b-brother or sister. We will be sure of it." She stifled that sob with a clenched fist.

And this was why they'd arrived . . . on the very day *he* was set to return.

Nay, not *he.*

My son.

It is my son who is at last returning, after seven years. Now a stranger. A boy who had dwelled in the bowels of hell and carried scars as deep as the ones Edwin himself bore.

"I fear your plans of sowing the seeds of my son's hatred will have to wait until he attends *ton* events, many years from now," he said coolly as he shoved back his chair. "You'll have no access to him."

The powerful peers opposite him, wholly unaccustomed to having their wishes gainsaid, collapsed back against the folds of his chairs.

A knock sounded at the door before either of them could formulate a response.

Edwin stood. His heart knocked at a jumbled rhythm against his rib cage.

"Enter," he barked.

The door opened, and Quint Marlow, the man who'd served as butler, man-of-affairs, and the closest thing he'd had to a friend since Lavinia's murder, entered. He took in the duke and duchess a moment.

Edwin waved his hand. "Say what it is you'd say," he said impatiently.

"I've received word the carriages are scheduled to depart shortly, my lord."

Out of the corner of his eye, he saw the duchess clutch at her throat with one hand, and this time, she made a grab for her husband's with the other.

August is coming . . .

At last. After what felt like a lifetime apart . . . a child who'd spent just four short years in Edwin's life and almost double that with the most ruthless gang in East London, he was more a stranger than anything. "And has the boy yet been loaded into them?" Edwin spoke in measured, unaffected tones at odds with the jumbled rhythm of his heartbeat.

"He has not."

Runners had been set up at each station, monitoring the boy's . . . *his son's* movements. Nay, monitoring the movements of those rotted street rats. "That will be all."

The man who'd served as his butler these past years made to leave, but not before he shot a pointed glance over the heads of Edwin's in-laws, his meaning clearer than had the offer been spoken: if Edwin so wished it, Marlow would see the pair tossed out on their arses, titles of "duke" and "duchess" be damned. Edwin gave a near-imperceptible shake of his head.

Marlow nodded and, with a final look at the pair of visitors, backed from the room.

The minute the door had clicked shut behind him, the duchess launched into another diatribe. "We told her you were a damned fool, and you continue to prove us correct. Trusting those people to send your son safely on?"

Her husband harrumphed his support. "A father has a responsibility to defend and protect his children."

"As you were so skilled at protecting Lavinia from me?" he jeered.

The color bled from His Grace's cheeks. "Bastard," he whispered. "I should have called you out. Charles should have." The ducal heir . . . and also August's godfather. "All those years he insisted that you were respectable. A loyal friend. And what did you do? Get his sister killed."

Yet another vicious arrow found its mark, square in his chest. "Get out." Edwin clipped that command out and leveled them with the same glower that had sent servants scurrying in the opposite direction.

The duke's monocle slipped from his fingers and twisted in a forlorn back-and-forth dance, and with his Adam's apple bobbing, he jumped up with the speed of a man half his years.

His wife scowled up at him. "Tremaine," she snapped in an impressive display of resilience.

When the duke only gave a shake of his head, her frown deepened. "Well, I am staying. I won't be run off by this monster." At last she turned her attention back to Edwin. "I will see my grandson and . . ." Her words trailed off as her gaze met his.

She paled.

It was "the look." The one he'd perfected over the years in an effort that had come too easily. Everything he was . . . any hint of emotion within him . . . had perished in the blaze with his wife and unborn babe. Regardless of station, men, women, children—they could all recognize madness, and every animal knew to run. Knew that flight was safer than interacting with one such as Edwin.

"You were . . . saying?" Edwin dared her with his eyes to continue.

With fingers that shook, she used the arms of her chair as leverage to push to her feet. "We are not done h-here." That warning was effectively ruined by the quaver to that last syllable.

"Ah." He stretched that word out. "But you see"—he spread his arms wide—"we are. You expected you could shred my reputation, seek to see me hang for the murder of . . ." *Lavinia. My wife.* He struggled to get either out. A word. A sound. Anything. "Your daughter," he at last managed, that slightly divorced connection between his once young bride and her unflinchingly derisive parents far easier. "And you thought there should be no consequences? That I would turn the other cheek and allow you time with my son, poisoning him against me?" As they had so effortlessly managed amongst the *ton*.

Through each word leveled, Her Grace's tall, regal frame became more rigid.

A man mindless with grief, he'd been forced to contend with the venom they'd spread throughout London. Edwin smirked. "For all that . . . I should thank you, still."

Her lips tensed. "Why is that?" she asked, her mouth barely moving as she squeezed that three-word query out.

It did not escape his notice that she made no attempt to apologize, nor did the duke, for labeling him a murderer and enlisting the aid of the king himself to try and see Edwin hang. "You spared me from suffering through unwanted company. And as we are on the topic of 'unwanted company'?" Not taking his gaze from the duchess opposite him, Edwin stretched a finger out, pointing past her husband, to the doorway. "Get the hell out."

His mother-in-law slapped a palm over her mouth and then wrenched it away. "A monster," she spat and stood her ground with a remarkable show of resolve. "We warned her about the manner of man you were."

A rogue. A scoundrel. A rake. All had been insults leveled at him when he'd courted their daughter. And then those less harmful invectives had been replaced with "wife murderer" and "child killer."

"You couldn't even be bothered to gather your own child. You learn he is alive and leave him in the folds of those murderous thieves?"

Edwin's neck went hot. "I'll not answer to you," he warned on a steely whisper. Having lived a solitary life for nearly seven years, with no one except cowering servants underfoot, he'd never had to contend with anyone calling him out . . . or challenging him. But then as a parent himself, albeit a lousy, pathetic excuse of a father, he identified with what it was to fear nothing, not even death, when it pertained to the matter of one's child.

"*Pfft.* As if you ever truly cared about my daughter or August or the other babe you got on her."

As she launched an impressively stoic rant, each insult fell harmlessly off him. There was nothing she could say or hurl that he'd not already felt himself. Nay, he'd long ago grown immune to feeling . . . anything.

At last, she went silent. He winged a single brow up. "Are you done, madam?"

Fire and fury blazed from her eyes.

Edwin flicked an imaginary speck of dust from his crisp coat sleeve. "I do not answer to you, madam. Get out," he repeated, adding layers of ice to his tone that managed to penetrate her earlier confidence.

The duchess's cheeks paled. "Come, Tremaine," she ordered like the queen calling after her terriers. And without waiting to see if her husband followed, she sailed from the room.

The duke lingered at the doorway, his back presented to Edwin, and then, not bothering to close the door in his wake, he left.

The clock ticked off twenty beats while Edwin stood, staring at that entranceway through which his esteemed in-laws had taken their leave.

And when the angry staccato of their footfalls faded from the corridors, he moved.

Cursing roundly, he stalked over to his sideboard and, grabbing a half-empty bottle of whiskey and a glass, splashed himself several fingers full. He thought better of it and then poured until the amber brew challenged the brim of the glass. Edwin tossed back the drink, and it seared a path of fire down his throat.

He grimaced and set the tumbler down with a hard *thunk*.

Tension thrummed inside him, all his nerves coming to life, as they invariably did when the past was visited upon him.

As though he could ever be truly free. In the dead of night, the nightmares were always there. But this . . . this day was different. It wasn't the ghost of his wife, whose death deservedly rested at his feet, that haunted him in this moment. It was the ghost of the living.

Edwin laid his hands on the edge of the sideboard and dug his fingers into the smooth mahogany surface. The layered edge bit sharply into his palms, the sting of discomfort welcome. And yet ultimately, it did little to vanquish the memories dragged forward by his damned in-laws.

How very much their visit had been akin to another long-ago night. Memories trickled in of the morning he'd presented a formal offer to the duke for Lavinia's hand. That offer had been rejected by the duke, who'd sent Edwin off, angry and vowing to marry her anyway.

He stared blankly at the sapphire satin wallpaper.

And that was just what Edwin had done. He'd married her. He'd married her, even though her parents had fought the union . . . and eventually capitulated, but only because of their son's intervention on Edwin's behalf.

He squeezed his eyes shut.

He'd not allowed himself to think of Charles, Lavinia's only sibling and elder brother. Boyhood friends at Eton, Charles and Edwin had been inseparable.

There hadn't been a hell they wouldn't have visited or a woman they wouldn't have seduced . . . until Edwin had fallen head over proverbial heels for the other man's sister. When Edwin and Charles could have become a cliché—their friendship ended because of Edwin's lack of suitability and his intention to wed the other man's sister—Charles had instead only encouraged the match.

A memory slipped in . . . of that same friend after Lavinia had perished. During that faux burial, made up of only garments Lavinia had left at Edwin's country house, Charles had stood there . . . his gaze blank, his stare empty.

Just another person Edwin was responsible for destroying.

Like August.

Edwin sucked in a breath.

The demons, those both living and dead, could no longer be buried.

With his son—Edwin's hands curved hard into the wood, leaving crescent marks upon the once flawless surface—with *August* back in his rightful place, Edwin would be forever reminded of that night . . . and the dark days that followed. August would serve as a visual reminder of loss and pain and suffering . . .

This child, who was, except for the blood they shared, truly a stranger to him in every way.

And in his son, every day, Edwin would see his own failings. *He'll be a mirror in which you can see all the ways you failed him* . . . and Lavinia, her parents, and Charles.

Nearly a quarter of an hour later, footsteps fell outside Edwin's office.

His in-laws forgotten, Edwin turned.

Marlow cleared his throat. "Another Runner arrived recently." His man-of-affairs paused.

"Yes?" Edwin bit out, impatience pulling that query from him.

Color splotched the red-haired servant's freckled cheeks. "He indicated that His Lordship had not yet taken his leave."

Edwin went absolutely still, and with a sharp bark of fury, he slammed his fist onto the sideboard. The crystal decanters jumped under the force of that strike. "Damn it." It had been a mistake to leave him there for any length of time.

So why did you?

Marlow rushed over. "I am confident that my sister will not—"

"Your sister?" he thundered over him. "The sister you've not seen in ten years?" he barked. "The same sister who's been the lover of that Devil's spawn?" he spat.

His man-of-affairs remained wisely silent. Alas, what *could* he say?

Only . . . Edwin's rage was misplaced. Yet again, the blame resided with him.

He began to pace a frenzied path back and forth along the edge of the Aubusson carpet.

He'd been first presented with the truth that August was still alive weeks ago by Connor Steele, the detective Edwin had hired to investigate his son's whereabouts. Only to find that same *detective* had gone and fallen in love with Ophelia Killoran. And when she'd been sent to Newgate, Steele had come to Edwin with the far-fetched tale that the youngest Killoran sibling was in fact Edwin's son. As if Edwin should be grateful. As if he'd help coordinate her release out of . . . gratitude? No, he'd been duped by that family too many times to trust any lie fed him by one of their lovers.

Until Marlow's sister had demanded Edwin hear the truth . . .

And then Edwin had seen it, in the forms of a birthmark and a scar on his son's body. *Only after he'd been injured, because of your failure to get to him . . .*

All Edwin's muscles tensed.

His mother-in-law, God rot her soul, had been proven correct about yet another thing. *I should have taken August with me a week ago, after he was shot trying to protect Marlow's sister. I should have insisted over the pleading and tears that the child make his goodbyes then and there, forevermore.*

It is my fault.

My fault.

Edwin dug his fingertips into his temples.

"I trust they will be here, my lord," Marlow said with the same quiet calm he'd had when he'd first come upon Edwin in those dark days when he had descended into madness.

He stopped abruptly. "You had better hope, Marlow." Because if Killoran and his lover turned wife did not honor the promise to return August, this time Edwin would not hesitate to become the murderer the world took him to be.

Chapter 3

They were late.

And no one had remarked upon the man being kept waiting while Stephen said his parting words to his family at the Devil's Den.

For all intents and purposes, no one except Gertrude had even noted that particular violation of the terms.

She hovered alongside the gargoyle, an interloper of sorts, as the Killorans made their goodbyes to Stephen. Just then, Stephen and Cleo were speaking. Near in height to the boy, though he'd reached only the tender age of eleven, that was where the illusion of Cleo's frailty ended.

Cleo had always possessed more gumption, spirit, and strength than every last member of Diggory's gang rolled into one. And it was no wonder that Stephen . . . and everyone . . . looked to her for guidance as a de facto leader of their once ragtag, now powerful clan.

All around, everyone from Broderick to Ophelia and her husband, Connor, to the guards, who'd been more family than anything else, surrounded that pair.

Periodically, Stephen alternated between nodding at whatever Cleo was saying and jutting his chin up in a usual display of his defiance.

"I don't want . . . t . . ." Whatever was the remainder of those inaudible words was lost as Gertrude damned her one blind eye for obscuring those details that could save a soul in St. Giles . . . or see one destroyed.

Reggie slid into place beside her, and Gertrude glanced over. "He will be all right," Broderick's wife vowed.

Would he? "You don't know that," Gertrude reminded her. But then, living the life of a thief and an arsonist, then dwelling inside a gaming hell, had he truly been all right? What was "safe" after all? In her pocket, Sethos, the mouse tucked away there, wriggled back and forth. She slipped a hand inside her cloak and stroked the unlikely pet until he calmed.

Worry twisted the other woman's freckled features, and troubling her lower lip, she glanced once more at Stephen. "The marquess is his father," she finally said, an unnecessary reminder of where Stephen's place in fact was.

Gertrude faced this woman who'd been more like another sister. "And Diggory was mine."

Reggie winced. "Gertrude—"

"I am merely saying that his status as the marquess's heir does not forge a bond between them. Blood does not a bond make," she said, offering that long-memorized vow spoken to them by Broderick when he'd first joined their family. Ophelia glanced over, a question in her gaze. Mindful of the suspicion there, Gertrude schooled her features and faced Reggie directly, in a way that deliberately cut off Ophelia's view of their mouths moving in speech. "Reggie, the man is rumored to be mad."

"And with *reasons* for his insanity."

She made a sound of impatience. "I am not disputing that." With his wife and unborn child burnt to death at an order given by Mac Diggory, and his only other child, whom the world had believed dead, stolen from him, what fate awaited such a parent other than madness?

"A person does not simply recover from that," she said softly in hushed tones with words that were a reminder for herself. About the place Stephen would soon depart for. And the man he'd live with.

Stephen would be . . . alone. She shivered and gently caressed Sethos, finding some comfort in the white creature's downy softness.

"My brother will be there," Reggie reminded her, as if she'd followed Gertrude's unspoken fears.

Gertrude bit the tip of her tongue to keep from pointing out that until only just days ago, Reggie hadn't seen the man in more than ten years.

"They are strangers, all of them." Gertrude slid her eyes closed. And Stephen would eat the marquess's household for breakfast, lunch, and dinner, and spit out their entrails for dessert. Everyone loved an easy, smiling child. The world didn't have patience or a place for those who were snarling and angry. Except the Killorans. *Only, we inadvertently shaped him into that, too.*

Reggie rested a hand on her shoulder, slashing into those guilty musings. "I will receive updates from my brother."

"And what then?" Gertrude asked calmly. "What if Stephen is harmed or frightened?" Because the world took him for one who was fearless. But there was a vulnerability to him buried under layers of carefully constructed armor. As one who carried her own secrets and fears, Gertrude recognized it in another. "Or what if he sacks your brother? Do you trust His Lordship will embrace having a child who'd rather be studying on weapons and practicing their uses than learning Latin and his familial history?"

This time, Reggie had no false assurances. The other woman hugged herself.

Gertrude's heart quavered, and she wanted to throw herself prostrate and keen like that ancient Irish burial custom she'd read of. One she'd not understood until now. How could they just let him leave?

How can you? You treated him as you would a son born of your own womb, and now you'd bundle him into a carriage and send him on his way alone?

She found Stephen off speaking with Broderick now. While the two brothers conversed, Stephen's little shoulders slumped; he had a defeated air she'd never before seen from the scrappy child. It hit her square in the chest, like a physical blow.

And on the heels of that agony came the stirrings of annoyance. How dare the Killorans simply bow to the marquess's demands. And how dare the man who'd sired him steal that small comfort from the child.

"W-we should make our goodbyes." Reggie's voice broke, showing the first crack in her until-now stoic composure.

"Hmm?" Gertrude said distractedly. "Of course. Right." All the while, her mind continued spinning with thoughts of Stephen huddled in the Killoran carriage for one more ride with nothing but the loud churn of the wheels and his driver for company.

From across the way, Ophelia and Cleo caught her stare. Her younger sisters frowned and made their way to Gertrude's side.

"What is it?" Ophelia prodded.

Gertrude drew in a breath. "I'm accompanying him."

Silence met her avowal.

Ophelia was the first to break it. "What?"

"I've been like a mother to him." Gertrude looked between the shorter pair before her. "I tended his scrapes and readied his meals." And held him as a boy when he'd been haunted by nightmares. "I'll be the last to see him."

Cleo frowned. "You can't. The marquess was clear in stating he didn't want us there."

"He doesn't want *you* there," Gertrude amended, stripping that statement of inflection and offering it as the pragmatic fact it was. Before her sisters could argue, she launched her defense. "You know the terms." Gertrude glanced between Ophelia and Cleo. "You both do."

29

"What is this about?"

Engrossed in their debate, they'd failed to hear Broderick's approach. Arms folded at his chest, he stared expectantly at them, waiting for an answer. "Gert has it in her head to escort Stephen," Ophelia elucidated.

Not allowing Broderick to try and sway her from her course, Gertrude hurried to defend her plan. "*Someone* should be with him. You?" She pointed to Broderick. "You can't. You'll hang. And you?" She looked to Ophelia. "Your situation, if the marquess wishes it, is as untenable as Cleo's. You'll join him for a handful of minutes, deliver him to the marquess, and then see everything your husband built destroyed? Destroyed when I can as easily see to it." Gertrude drew in a deep breath. "I am accompanying him."

Ophelia's brows shot to her hairline. "But Stephen won't . . ." Her words trailed off, color blazing across her cheeks.

"Want me?" Gertrude lifted an eyebrow.

Her middle sister spoke on a rush. "I didn't mean—"

"It's fine," Gertrude said gently. Her feelings weren't hurt by the realization of her place in Stephen's affections. She'd done nothing to protect him when he'd most needed it. Whereas Cleo and Ophelia and Broderick all had. It was why she had to do this, now. "I'm going, and it's time." As it was, they were nearly twenty minutes late.

"Gertrude," Cleo began.

"She'll make the journey with him," Broderick said quietly.

Surprise shot through her, that emotion reflected back in her younger sisters' gazes. It was the first time he'd ever ceded any assignment or role to her in lieu of her younger sisters.

Broderick held her gaze. "You will go."

"I don't need anyone coming with me."

That snarled response came from beyond the circle of their group.

The servants and guards wisely took themselves back inside, leaving the Killorans with the snarling boy.

"Stephen—" Cleo said gently.

"Go to hell," he said, cutting off whatever his elder sister would say. "I'm not a baby."

No, he wasn't. He'd been robbed of that state years earlier.

Tears welling behind the smudged lenses of her spectacles, Cleo drew Stephen close and hugged him.

And despite the fact that life on the streets of London had proven the peril in any displays of weakness, Stephen didn't struggle free of Cleo's embrace. Nor did he fight when Ophelia took him in her arms next.

Gertrude blinked furiously. They would expect her to cry. She, the weakest of the Killorans, would be the one to lose control of her emotions and give over to tears.

He'd never again steal furtive strokes of her many cats when he thought the world wasn't watching.

He'd never join her at the oak breakfast table, long before the rest of the house or world had risen, cleverly but still transparently fishing for any knowledge she possessed on ancient weapons. That had been one bond they'd shared. And never again would they do any of these things together.

Oh, God. It was too much.

Glancing away from the final goodbyes, Gertrude looked to the open doorway. Stephen's favorite of her menagerie, Gus, lingered at the doorstep. She snapped her fingers four times in quick succession.

The tabby bounded down the steps, stopping at her feet.

She bent and scooped him up, hugging him tight. He squirmed in her embrace, attempting to nose around her pocket.

"Do behave," she scolded. Gus squiggled around a bit more before settling into her arms. "It is time," she reminded the group once again.

Wrenching away from Ophelia, Stephen stalked off without a final goodbye for Broderick.

Broderick's face spasmed, and Reggie quickly slid her fingers into his, clutching his hand.

Cleo made to call after Stephen as he rushed to the carriage, but Broderick shook his head, staying her efforts. "Don't," he said hoarsely. "It is better this way."

It wasn't. It wasn't better for any of them, this divide the marquess was forcing upon them.

It didn't matter that Broderick hadn't intentionally ordered the kidnapping of a nobleman's child. It didn't matter that neither Gertrude nor Cleo nor Ophelia had known the truth of his identity until just recently. The only consideration the marquess had taken into account was his own deserved resentment and hatred for all of them.

And I will journey to that household.

Another chill scraped down her spine. Before her courage deserted her, she released Gus. He landed on all fours and sprinted into the carriage Stephen had climbed inside.

"He will be fine," Gertrude promised.

He would be educated as he should have been, and he would never have to worry about a thief on the streets looking for revenge against the boy who'd slighted him or her in the past.

Even telling herself that did little to ease the tension knotting her stomach.

It was time. She looked between her siblings. "I . . . I . . ." And fearing they'd see every last secret she carried, Gertrude coughed into her hand. "I should see to Stephen." And with that, she rushed off after her brother.

MacLeod, standing at the doorway of the carriage, held a hand out. "Miss Killoran," he said in his familiar greeting, that thick Scottish brogue warmly comforting because of its familiarity.

She managed a smile for the loyal guard's benefit. With a word of thanks, she let him help her up.

"Smiling again," Stephen groused in the corner.

Gertrude squinted in the darkened space, struggling to bring her brother into focus. Her lips turned down into a grim line. She settled onto the bench opposite her brother, and Gus leapt over, joining the surly little boy. "I was—"

"Don't care what you were doing or why," he muttered, tugging the brim of his favorite cap lower over his brow, that single article so wholly out of place with the high-quality burgundy jacket, fawn trousers, and gleaming, buckled black shoes Broderick had insisted he don.

MacLeod slammed the door shut, throwing even more shadows upon the velvet upholstery.

If one looked upon the surface, they'd see nothing more than the vitriol Stephen had directed her way, but when one lived life with only partial vision, one viewed the world with greater depth and attention to each detail. Stephen snuck a small hand over, onto the bench beside him, and finding Gus, he stroked the sensitive portion of the cat's back. With a loud purr, the tabby scooted closer and leaned into that touch.

"At least you don't prattle on like Ophelia."

It was the closest he'd ever come to a compliment . . . to anyone she remembered, Cleo included. Her lips twitched.

As if he'd recognized that show of weakness, Stephen growled and quickly drew his palm back. "When in 'ell are we leaving?"

"Not 'ell. Hell," she automatically corrected, then grimaced. "Though neither, whether spoken grammatically correctly or in Cockney, is appropriate."

"I ain't—"

"You aren't."

"Looking for any of your speech sessions," he spoke over her. It didn't escape her notice that he had, however, modified his speech. He directed his gaze down at the floor.

"Stephen, look at me." That quiet directive brought his shoulders back. "I said, look at me," she repeated. "Speaking in your Cockney or cursing . . . It will not get you sent back to the Devil's Den."

His lower lip trembled. "I don't want to go back."

"I don't believe you," she said softly. "And it is all right to be upset and miss everything you kn-knew here." For there had been good. This had been the first place in which they'd had peace and safety and security. And laughter. For all the vices that existed within the Devil's Den, there had been those shared moments of laughter, too. Granted, they had been fleeting moments from individuals who all had learned the peril of expressing any emotion. Leaning over, she covered his hand with her own.

Stephen's big Adam's apple jumped as he looked down at her callused fingers. "The marquess wouldn't ever let me go back, a-anyway."

"No." Because what was there to say? The marquess, by all intents and purposes, had waited longer than any other nobleman would have to retrieve his child. He owed the Killorans not a moment more with his kidnapped son.

A moment later, the carriage lurched forward and began a slow roll through the crowded streets of St. Giles on a journey that would be the last one her brother made from the Devil's Den.

The *clip-clop* of the horse's hooves and the rattle of the wheels as they rumbled over the grimy St. Giles cobbles filled the carriage, accentuating the silence. Hammering home each passing moment that marked their arrival at Stephen's new—and yet, oddly also his first—home.

To give her fingers something to do, Gertrude clutched the corner of the curtain and pulled it back slightly.

In the near distance, the handful of guards and her siblings remained rooted to the pavement, staring after Broderick's black carriage.

"Let it go," Stephen said, his voice wavering.

She started, following his stare to the velvet draperies.

He growled. "I said let it go."

Gertrude released the fabric, and it fluttered into place.

"Broderick said Oi—I couldn't bring my weapons." He spoke like a child deprived of his favorite toy and not the near arsenal he'd amassed over the years. Stephen stuck his index finger out, and Gus lapped at the tip of it several times. And then, giving a shake of his head that revealed his feline displeasure, Gus settled into the other side of the carriage, away from Stephen's reach.

"Yes." She paused. "He believes it essential you begin to acclimate to life amongst Polite Society." Even as she said it, she recognized the inherent impossibility of Stephen . . . or any other member of the Killorans . . . settling easily into the life of the peerage. It wasn't possible.

Stephen's incoherent rumblings of displeasure were lost to her ears.

"I insisted they be packed."

Stephen paused. His eyes went unblinking, his mouth fell open, and then he scrambled forward onto the edge of his seat. "What?" For the first time since he'd come face-to-face with his father again, a sparkle of joy glimmered in his eyes. "Broderick said yes?"

"It required some . . . convincing." The pointed reminder that they could not very well leave Stephen in unfamiliar territory without any means to properly defend himself, should the need arise.

As quickly as that happiness had come, it faded. Stephen's features fell and then returned to the stony mask of indifference.

Gertrude stared across at him, and a sense of desperation ran through her. This need to take away his fears and assure him that all would be well. But they would both know the lie there. Surviving in the bowels of East London had long ago proven the world was ruthless with no true promise for tomorrow except uncertainty.

Sethos squirmed in her pocket and peeked his head out. Gertrude held her palm out, and he jumped into it.

From his seat next to Stephen, Gus sat up, his ears pitched forward and his hind legs poised to pounce.

"Don't." At her stern directive, the tabby hesitated before collapsing onto his belly. With the tip of her index finger, Gertrude stroked the top of the tiny mouse's head.

Not another word was spoken. The carriage continued its slow roll through London, and as they drew farther away from the Devil's Den and Stephen's former life and closer to the posh end of Mayfair where he'd spend the rest of his days, her brother slumped lower and lower in his seat.

And then they stopped.

The carriage rolled to a slow, lurching halt that signaled the end of their journey and the beginning of a new one for Stephen . . . and Gertrude. Hands shaking, she carefully tucked Sethos inside her cloak pocket.

A handful of minutes later, someone knocked on the lacquered door.

"Just a moment," Gertrude called. She waited, straining her ears as MacLeod's familiar heavy-booted footfall receded before she turned back to Stephen.

His gaunt cheeks ashen, he had the same look he'd had when Diggory forced him to drink down a tankard of spirits.

"I know you don't want to be here," she said quietly, those words needing to be spoken because he deserved to feel everything he was feeling in this instance. "And I know we don't truly know what manner of man your father is now." Or who he'd been in the past before his life had been ripped asunder.

Stephen's gaze fell to the gleaming gold buckles affixed atop his shoes.

"But Stephen?" She waited until he reluctantly picked his head up. "He didn't let you go." Tears stuck in her throat, and she struggled to get words out past them. "You were taken."

"I was just an heir."

"You don't know that," she said automatically.

"*Pfft.*" He directed his words at the floor. "That's all a nob's child is."

Gertrude drew in a breath. "It is time."

Leaning forward, she adjusted his crooked cap so it sat straight and then tucked his hair behind his ears. "There."

"You aren't going to take it? Broderick said I couldn't wear it."

"It's part of you, Stephen." Just as his fascination with ancient weaponry was. "I'm not looking for you to present yourself as someone you are not for the marquess. I'm looking for you to be who you are." With all his flaws. And pray the gentleman was not the ruthless madman the papers and society professed him to be.

She stretched a hand up to the ceiling, but he stayed her.

"I didn't appreciate you," he whispered, his voice so threadbare the words were nearly swallowed up by a passing conveyance. "You weren't as bad as I made you out to be."

Oh, God. She was dying inside. Slowly. Piece by piece. Tears flooded her eyes, blurring his beloved and so-often-angry face. "Th-thank you." The driver knocked once. *No! I'm not ready yet.* She'd never be ready. "Just a m-moment." Her voice cracked. Gertrude turned back to Stephen. "I want you to know you're going to have a w-wonderful life."

Stephen's lower lip trembled. "I'm not."

"And one day, you're going to be so very happy." *Rap-Rap.* "I said, just a moment," she cried and then continued on a rush, letting the words fly. Wanting to say so much. There wasn't enough time. There never would be. "You think you won't be . . . but someday you'll marvel, Stephen, that you ever w-wanted to stay." *With us.*

With a sob, Stephen launched himself across the carriage and into her arms.

Gertrude caught him as his small body knocked them both off-balance. "It is going to be all right," she whispered against his temple. Holding her brother. Wanting to hold on to him forever.

"I l-love you," he rasped against her chest.

And as the boy who'd not cried in years wept against her now, she patted his back in the hard, staccato thumps that had always calmed him at night.

Another knock sounded. This one firmer. More impatient.

Stephen stiffened, and she knew the moment her brother had resurrected the barriers he'd so masterfully built up. Angrily swiping the back of his sleeve over his eyes, he growled. "Bloody impatient bastard. Eager to drop me off." He reached for the handle, and agony clutched at her heart.

No.

I cannot let him go. Not without being sure he is safe.

Stephen clasped the handle, and the panic threatened to suck her under.

Be strong . . . for Stephen. She buried her trembling hands in her skirts and forced her features into a mask that strained the muscles and was just a moment away from crumpling.

Her brother tossed a glance over his shoulder. "I will miss you, Gert," he whispered. He flashed his mischievous half grin. "And not just because I'm going to be alone, either."

I will miss you.

That was it.

Before he could press the door handle, Gertrude lunged across the carriage and knocked him off-balance. *"Oomph,"* he grunted, falling into the side of the carriage. "What in hell was—?"

"You're not going to be alone," she said, her words rolling into one another.

He cocked his head. "I'm not?"

No, he was not. Her lips formed a tremulous smile, her first real one since she'd discovered Stephen belonged to another. "You won't be alone, because I'm staying behind with you."

Chapter 4

The evil carried out by the Diggorys through the years proved they were not a people to be trusted. From Broderick Killoran, who'd issued the command that had seen August stolen, to Mac Diggory, who'd given the orders that left Lavinia murdered. Base savages was what they were. Soulless animals.

Standing on the Maddock crest at the center of his office carpet, Edwin stared unblinkingly at the paneled doorway.

They had arrived . . .

He consulted his timepiece once more.

Twelve minutes ago. With a growl, he stuffed the chain back inside his jacket.

"We're sure he's in there?" he barked.

"I . . . I believe so, my lord," Marlow called from beyond his shoulder. "He was seen departing by the Runner, in the same carriage."

That assurance fell on deaf ears. "Killoran?" he gritted out through clenched teeth, that most loathsome of names.

"Was not seen exiting with your son, or any time prior or after."

Hatred pumped furiously through Edwin's veins. That bastard . . . the man who'd served in the role of *father* after Satan's spawn, Mac Diggory, had thankfully been erased from the earth. Edwin balled his hands so tight his wrists strained under the force exerted.

After Diggory, another man had stepped in as a father when that distinction should have only ever belonged to Edwin. Another man had raised August. Reared him. Chased away the occasional nightmare that had once sent his son toddling into Edwin's chambers in the dead of night. Or worse, had not driven back the boy's fears and had allowed him to suffer those terrors alone.

He squeezed his eyes shut.

There had been a certain vicious kind of pain in losing one's child, but having been made to suffer through life when everything that mattered was taken from him, Edwin appreciated there were far worse fates than dying a physical death.

What had August's life been on the streets? What horrors had he seen or been forced to carry out, all in the name of survival?

His stomach pitched.

With jerky movements, he stalked over to the window and tossed back the curtains.

Those three carriages remained motionless below, as they'd been since they first arrived. Nor were they the only ones lining the streets.

Crowds of carriages and onlookers sat in wait, lining the streets of Mayfair.

Strangers made no attempt to conceal their morbid curiosity at the scene unfolding before them. Or the one that would unfold the moment the carriage doors opened and August stepped out.

As if on cue of that truth, several gentlemen with ladies on their arms pointed and gestured to Broderick Killoran's marked, black-lacquered conveyances and then over at Edwin's townhouse.

Fodder is all they were. It's all he'd ever been. First, for reasons he'd visited upon himself as a rogue and scapegrace, causing scandals about society. And then, for the whirlwind love affair and marriage that had set the *ton* to sighing.

And . . . everything that had come after. Death. Murder. Madness.

One of Killoran's thugs, a burly guard with a shock of red hair, folded his arms threateningly at his chest and glared daggers at a pair of portly gents who moved too close to the carriage.

They immediately fell back, darting off to a safer distance where they might take in the grand "show."

Edwin released the gold-fringed curtain. "What in hell are they doing out there?" he growled.

Through the gossamer fabric, Marlow's visage reflected back in the crystal pane, just beyond Edwin's shoulder. It was his man-of-affair's usual telling, introspective silence.

"What, Marlow?"

At that invitation, the younger man spoke. "You might always . . ."

Edwin waited.

And when no further words were forthcoming, he spun about. "What?" he snapped when Marlow made no attempt to speak. "I might what?"

"Greet the boy yourself, my lord."

Under his thin leather gloves, Edwin's palms grew moist, and he reflexively wiped the sides of his pants before he realized what he was doing. He stopped. "Go find out what in hell is keeping him."

"As you wish," Marlow said tightly, his disapproval as transparent as if he'd spoken that disparagement aloud. Clicking his heels together, his man-of-affairs marched off.

As soon as he'd gone, Edwin began pacing. *Greet him.* In the streets with all of Polite Society clogging the thoroughfare, waiting for a hint of their reunion.

He'd not allow those insatiable gossips to feed on the morsels that were his and August's lives. They weren't fodder meant to entertain the lords and ladies of London, and Edwin would be damned if he gave them any more of his life than they'd already taken from him over the years.

Liar. You are nothing but a bloody coward.

He cursed as that taunt throbbed around his mind. Mocking him. Calling him out.

Edwin stood stock still. For there was some truth to that. He didn't know what to do with this child who was his.

The snarling, snappish boy who'd been grazed by a bullet had stared back at Edwin with nothing but hatred. In that instant, kneeling beside him, with blood coating his fingers, Edwin had confronted the realization that the child was, all at the same time, both his son . . . and a stranger.

There'd been no hint of bright-red, cherubic cheeks or a wide, dimpled smile.

There had been a void of coldness and emptiness that was now an inherent part of who Edwin himself was.

That deadness suited to one who'd lived three lifetimes had glimmered back in the eyes of a boy he'd once cradled close as the world slept on. The same boy whom Edwin had tossed at the sky to Lavinia's scolding and August's chortling laughter.

Numb, Edwin gathered the gold enameled timepiece once more and, pressing the button top, opened it with a click.

He stared at the miniature portrait inside of August as he'd once been.

There had been an ease to fatherhood. Made stronger by the uncomplicated, unconditional love that had existed in that tiny, helpless child.

When his in-laws had hated him and his wife had grown melancholy and then angry over the duke and duchess's disapproval, loving his son had been simple.

But that had been before. Back when Edwin had been alive; back when he'd been capable of laughter and smiling and hadn't descended into madness, where he'd dwelled for seven years.

They were both strangers, cold and full of hate, destroyed by life. August's place was here, and yet, Edwin could not offer him the life he deserved. The one he'd once known as a cherished child with a doting mama.

And there was to have been a younger brother or sister for August to look after and guide through life as siblings were expected to do.

And now there was nothing.

He stared grimly down at his son's image.

There was nothing but Edwin, twisted memories, and a house riddled with sadness and horror.

A hesitant rap echoed outside his office.

His heart knocking harder against his chest, Edwin hastily closed the watch and looked up.

Pruitt, one of the Runners whose services he'd enlisted these past days, watching over the Devil's Den to be sure August wasn't stolen out from under him again, stood framed by the doorway with Marlow at his back.

His hat clenched in a white-knuckled grip, the greying man fiddled with the article.

A frisson of dread snaked along Edwin's spine; it was that intuitive sense of knowing that all was not as it should be. Intuition that went back to another, darker, day. "What?" he asked on a steely whisper.

"There's a problem," Marlow announced.

"N-no problems, my lord," Pruitt squawked. "Not truly."

Edwin's loyal man-of-affairs demonstrated the shockingly unexpected fearlessness that he had all those years ago at their first meeting, that fierce command at odds with the bookish, bespectacled man. "Get in there."

Edwin gripped tight the timepiece with that precious portrait contained within. "The boy?" *My son . . . ?*

Pruitt twisted his hat in his hands. "The boy is here, just descended from the carriage. Entered the household."

"That isn't all," Marlow snapped. "Tell him!"

Edwin stalked over, and the Runner shrank back. "What is it?"

"The child was accompanied by . . . someone."

Edwin jerked erect. "You assured me Killoran had not exited his clubs," he seethed.

Pruitt gulped. "It wasn't Killoran." He paused. "That is, it wasn't Broderick Killoran."

"Who?" he asked, that steely whisper measured and in full control.

Marlow nudged the other man between the shoulder blades, and when the Runner made no move to speak, the servant let loose a sound of disgust. "It was *a* Killoran. A Killoran is with him." Marlow pursed his mouth. "And she's refusing to leave."

"And you left them . . . *unattended?*"

Both men exchanged nervous looks.

Marlow's cheeks paled. "The servants are with them," he offered lamely.

"The servants?" Edwin repeated. "You bloody fool, Marlow," he hissed, and with rage snatching him in a manacle-like grip, Edwin stalked past the pair at the entrance of the room, who hurried to step out of his way.

A damned member of Diggory's gang in his home, defying their orders and refusing to leave?

Edwin lengthened his stride.

By God, I'll see them destroyed.

It was too quiet.

And as one who'd developed an overheightened sense of hearing, Gertrude had come to learn that unwavering silence never promised anything good and portended only doom.

Standing in the Marquess of Maddock's foyer with a small contingent of servants all neat in a row like soldiers in His Majesty's army, Gertrude and Stephen had not heard a sound since they'd entered the townhouse. In fact, Gertrude's presence alone had been enough to send Reggie Spark's brother, the marquess's butler, sprinting with a Runner at his side.

Yes, because there could never, would never, be a warm welcome, or any kind of welcome, for any of Diggory's kin.

A chill snaked along Gertrude's spine, tingling ice along it, and she huddled deeper into her cloak.

She was here. She, the daughter of the man who'd as good as killed the mistress of this residence, had stormed the townhouse and intended to put demands to the gentleman. Seek his permission to remain.

Her stomach lurched. How would a man purported to be dicked in the nob respond to such an order? Would he himself toss her out on her buttocks? Or would he launch into a blistering, nonsensical berating?

Feeling Stephen's eyes on her, she glanced over and found him smiling from ear to ear. He gave her a jaunty little wave.

She told her brain to tell her lips to tilt up in a requisite smile. As soon as Stephen glanced away, surveying his . . . their . . . surroundings, she let that false smile fall. Stuffing her trembling hands inside her cloak pocket, she found Sethos there. The mouse nuzzled around at her gloveless fingertips.

His tiny presence did little to ease her nervousness.

Stephen was the one who broke that tense quiet with words that were barely audible.

"You're *staying*."

She forced her lips back up at the corners. Since they'd climbed down from the carriage and strode along the crowded pavement and into the marquess's household, Stephen had put those two words to her thrice.

Each time, they'd been spoken with a different inflection.

You're staying?

A query that suggested Gertrude had been the last of all the Killorans he'd have expected such a showing from.

You're . . . staying?

A hesitant, hopeful child's question that had set Stephen to blushing.

"I'm"—*What have I done?*—"staying," she said from the corner of her mouth. All the while the marquess's servants ogled her and Stephen like they'd come for the household jewels.

Which, in fairness, was a fear that could have been rightly attributed to any one of the Killorans, for the number of treasured heirlooms and valuables they'd filched over the years.

Herself included—before she'd gone and lost her vision.

Stephen's question, however, also seemed to shatter the tense impasse between the Killoran interlopers and the marquess's staff.

A young footman was the first to take a step in their direction. "May I take your cl—?"

Gus hissed and shot an angry paw out, batting at the footman.

The servant blanched and instantly fell back, returning to his place in that neat line that went quiet once more.

"Do behave," Gertrude chided. Drawing her hands out of her pockets, she scooped the tabby into her arms, the soft weight of his body against hers offering some reassurance.

"Pathetic bastard," Stephen mumbled under his breath. "All of them." His gaze went to Gertrude's still trembling arms, and she stiffened, braced for her brother's disdain.

He'd never had any tolerance or use for those who were weak. By St. Giles standards, cowering earned nothing but derision and shame. What did it say about Gertrude's own character, then, this unease snaking around her belly?

Only this time, when Stephen glanced up and held her gaze, he gave a slight, near-imperceptible nod. An assurance that all would be all right. And this from her brother. A child thirteen years her junior, who was being ripped from their family and thrust into a new world and new life.

Shame sat heavy as a rock in her stomach as he turned his focus back to the marquess's servants and the palatial foyer.

Gertrude drew a breath slowly through her nostrils, steadying herself, fixed on that silent intake of air in a strategy she'd used as a child whenever Mac Diggory came near.

Now she used this moment as an opportunity to study her surroundings, as Stephen had wisely done from the start and continued to do even now.

Take in every last detail of unfamiliar grounds . . . or else. It was a hard lesson, ground into a person on the streets of East London. To overlook strangers around one and one's space had seen too many men, women, and children dead before they'd even realized the fatal mistake they'd made.

From the white Italian marble floor to the sweeping red-velvet-carpeted staircase and the crystal chandelier that hung overhead, the entryway to this lair exuded wealth and power.

Double Doric columns drew the eye to arched marble doorways, which offered intersecting pathways to this home.

Reflexively, she ducked deeper inside her wool cloak. Nay, there was nothing homelike about this place. Empty. Cold. The hum of silence and loss pinged off the walls.

Was it the loss the marquess had known that accounted for the palpable misery? Or mayhap Stephen was, in fact, correct, and any place Edwin dwelled would be devoid of love, warmth, or joy. And that lonely fate had come long before Diggory had visited death and darkness upon him. Perhaps the marriage had been cold, a formal arrangement between a pair who honored tradition and rank and gave not a jot for a child, outside of how that babe might have advanced those same traditions.

Impossible . . .

And yet, is it?

You've witnessed the gentlemen who visit your family's clubs. Men who, when prostitution had been allowed within the Devil's Den, had betrayed their wives. Men who'd beaten those women they'd taken as temporary lovers, some for pleasure. Some because their tempers ran as dark as their souls.

And not for the first time since she'd set foot inside the marquess's residence, she took in the nearly two dozen servants stretching the length of the foyer, their line continuing on down a hall. And they all stared at her and Stephen unabashedly.

The male servants all wore pale-gold knee breeches and crimson jackets with gold adornments that ran the length of the high collars to the lapels and down to the tails. Those lavish liveried uniforms stood in an ostentatious contrast to the dark blues and blacks worn by servants at the Devil's Den.

Unable to muster the furtive yet thorough study done by her brother, she stared baldly back with something akin to horror spreading through her. She alternated her stare over to the female staff and housekeeper.

Everyone standing close to Stephen, on down to the most wrinkled of the servants, wore like expressions. Their faces were contorted with fear. That primitive emotion spilled from each pair of eyes.

As if in feline agreement, Gus leapt from her arms and hid behind her skirts.

She glanced down at Stephen, and her heart spasmed.

For it was there, too. In this child who put on such a masterful display of unaffectedness, it was too easy to believe it true.

The white lines at the corner of his tense mouth and pale cheeks all bespoke a boy who was afraid of the uncertainty that awaited him here.

Gertrude slipped a hand into Stephen's.

Her brother stiffened, and then his small, sweaty palm gripped hers. He squeezed so tightly her knuckles cracked from the pressure, thundering loudly around the foyer.

Gus darted under the narrow opening at the base of Lord Maddock's walnut longcase clock, and not for the first time in her life, she envied those creatures for the ease with which they took flight.

Stephen blanched and made to tug free, but she gave a reassuring squeeze and he clung to her still.

Her ears caught the rapid flurry of steps from down the central corridor. Three pairs. Equal in their franticness. Two chasing, one leading.

Gertrude's mouth went dry. For there could be no doubting who was the leader of this sinister household.

She straightened and faced the inevitable storm directly.

And when it came, it was not the raging tempest of lightning, fire, and fury, which would have been safer, as rage and what to do with it had always come far easier to Gertrude.

Rather, it came with more . . . silence.

The Marquess of Maddock.

He strode forward, these steps different from the earlier ones she'd merely heard. These were measured. Practiced. They were steps that belonged to a man in complete control of this moment and impending exchange. Until he stopped, only three paces dividing him from Gertrude and Stephen.

Energy thrummed around the foyer; it bounced off the tension-filled frames of those who answered to this man.

Gertrude cocked her head. She'd not known what she'd expected of the marquess.

Nay, she had.

In her days in St. Giles, she'd known any number of men and women who'd fallen to madness. Garments tattered, their eyes glittering with their lunacy, those unfortunate souls had sat on corners or paced pavements spouting words strung together into a jumble of incoherency.

With unfashionably long, gleaming golden locks, drawn back almost as an afterthought behind his ears, and with the spark of intelligence that lit the marquess's brown gaze, he bore no hint of those hopeless souls in St. Giles.

But still, he was one to be feared, even more than any of those mad men and women.

In her pocket Sethos chirped, the tiny creature darting back and forth, until Gertrude dipped a hand inside her cloak, unsure if she sought to calm herself or the mouse. She swallowed slowly. Or mayhap she sought to soothe the both of them.

The marquess glanced around at his servants. "You are dismissed." He issued that command in slightly graveled tones; they were rough ones belonging to a man unaccustomed to speech.

And while the long row of servants neatly filed out, Gertrude used that distraction as an opportunity to study the man whose wrath her father . . . nay, her entire family . . . had earned, taking in every detail.

Angled as he was, his focus trained on the backs of his staff as they marched off, the marquess presented a powerfully broad profile. With heavy muscles straining the fabric of his coat sleeves, he radiated strength enough to challenge and conquer any London street fighter. In fact, his broad physique was better suited to one of her family's guards than a proper lord, and yet his garments alluded to his wealth and status and marked him as different from the Gertrude Killorans of the world. His midnight-blue wool neckcloth was finer than any garment she'd worn or sewn in the first fifteen years of her life. That double-breasted morning coat accentuated with black satin buttons, those small gleaming articles in the shape of . . . she squinted . . . lions. Lions that were as menacing as the man himself.

And everything down to the long, golden mane shoved haphazardly behind his ears painted him as that primitive beast to be rightly feared.

At last, every servant had gone, so all that remained were the marquess and two others, an eclectic trio: one a burly Runner, the other a bespectacled butler.

"You are also dismissed."

For a glorious instant she believed it was she and Stephen who'd been issued that coveted pardon.

But then the pair sprang into movement, with Lord Maddock's servant ushering off that uniformed figure beside him.

Until no one but the three of them remained.

Gertrude's knees knocked together, and she gave thanks for the heavy fabric of her cloak and gown that muted all sound and obscured all movement.

At last, the marquess glanced at Gertrude, only that penetrating stare, piercing in its intensity, lingered but a moment before he shifted it over to Stephen.

On it went.

An endless study. Meant to unnerve? Or was it that he was as uncertain as Gertrude herself in this moment? And through it, Gertrude searched for a glitter in those dark eyes that spoke to his madness. That unnerving glint she'd seen in too many people on the streets of London who'd either been born with that sickness in their blood . . . or who'd succumbed to the pressures of surviving.

Only . . . the Marquess of Maddock's brown gaze was a direct one, clear and belonging to a man at war with himself and not the demons in his head. Lord Maddock continued to move that stare between the child he'd lost and the woman who'd invaded his home. Again, he glanced briefly at Gertrude, and the vitriol and hatred there stole her breath away. Neither unexpected nor unfamiliar for the number of people in St. Giles who'd been wronged by Mac Diggory. In this man, however, that loathing had a lifelike force of one who wished her gone, not only from his residence but also from this earth altogether.

Do not make the first move. Do not utter the first word.

That lesson, ingrained into her by Mac Diggory, hadn't been doled out from an affectionate father who sought to look after a beloved child. Rather, it had been a rote assignment he'd handed down to each child in his gang, meant to preserve his commodity—boys and girls who built up his coffers.

And here all along she'd believed there'd been no gifts Mac Diggory had given her. But now, those words rolling through her mind in his hated Cockney kept her focused. They kept her from wilting any more than she already had for this stranger.

At the lengthening silence, Stephen moved closer to her, the first time in the whole of his life that he'd sought any support from her.

She took an involuntary step back, toward the door.

Stephen stared at Gertrude, his eyes so stricken that the sight of his fear managed to keep her rooted to the marble foyer when every instinct within screamed for her to flee.

Gertrude managed a feat no other single one of Diggory's descendants could have: she set aside the rules that guided those in the streets and showed the first weakness.

"Say hello to"—Gertrude stumbled—"your father."

Chapter 5

His own son could not even say hello to him.

Nay, the child *would* not offer Edwin a single word.

By the street-hardened glint of his brown eyes, there were any number of words the boy would like to say to him. None of which were warm in nature.

It was at best . . . an inauspicious beginning.

His son's antipathy was also, ironically, a good deal safer a detail to focus on than the fact that Edwin's household had been invaded by Mac Diggory's daughter.

Mac Diggory, the man who'd taken it all. Who'd killed his wife and babe and robbed him of—

The young woman cleared her throat. "Stephen," she prodded. As soon as the last syllable left her lips, the young woman's lips parted on a whispery gasp.

Edwin's entire body recoiled.

She pressed a palm to her mouth, staring over those callused, ink-stained fingertips at Edwin.

Stephen.

A stranger's name, and yet the one he'd been given. By another man who'd served in the role of father. The role that had belonged to Edwin and been taken from him.

It was just a reminder of everything he'd been robbed of . . . and of how complicated every aspect of this reunion, and life, would be from this point onward.

And it stirred the always-fresh embers of his hatred, for the Diggorys and Killorans, or whatever those scourges of the earth chose to call themselves on a given day. They'd taken so much from him, and now this spawn of Satan had also taken away Edwin's first meeting alone with his son.

Awkwardly, Edwin sank to one knee so he could meet August . . . Stephen . . . *his son's* gaze. Wary. Mistrustful. Angry. They were Edwin's eyes, just . . . in a different way.

The space between his son's brows puckered.

Edwin was expected to speak. That was his role as a father . . . to take control of a situation when so much had been wrested away from him years earlier. "Hullo." The muscles of Edwin's mouth pulled. That was the first and best word he could offer the child he'd not seen in seven years. A graveled "hello" roughened with fury and rage for the boy's . . . de facto sister. But then, what words were the right ones in moments such as these?

That lame greeting was met with prolonged silence from the child and a deepening disdain in his eyes.

"I . . ." Nothing. Edwin's mind went blank, and then the past trickled in, happier times, ones that were simpler and safer . . . *As long as you don't tell your mother, you can have one more treat . . .* The babe's laughter pealed around the recesses of Edwin's mind. "There are sugared Shrewsbury cakes prepared," he said hoarsely. "I've had Cook prepare Shrewsbury."

"Are ya offering me treats like Oi'm a child?" his son spat, squeezing the vise about Edwin's heart.

August *was* a child. He was of an age where he should be at Eton, or educated at home with only the finest scholars, but no one in Polite Society would dare take him as anything other than a boy.

His son took a surging step forward, knocking into Edwin and nearly toppling him backward. "I'll tell you what ya can do with yar—"

"Stephen," the young woman clipped out, managing to defuse the child's fury when Edwin had been unable to, and he wanted to toss his head back like the beast he'd become to snarl at the enemy before him, so capable with his child.

August stepped back. Not taking his taunting gaze from Edwin, he folded his arms at his spindly chest.

"Thank His Lordship," Diggory's daughter urged.

His *father.* Not "His Lordship." Not "my lord." *I am the child's father.*

"You needn't thank me." Edwin directed that at his son, ignoring the woman who'd dared to issue that directive. Treats had been the lure he'd used to soothe a child's tears. How did one ease this little stranger's worries? He held his son's gaze. "I would ask for a few moments to speak alone with . . ." Edwin's gaze slid involuntarily over to the proudly silent chit.

"My sister," August snapped.

His true sibling—the only one he would ever have—had been brutally slain by the man he'd called father. Nonetheless, Edwin conceded the point. Fighting him on the alternative history that had been written around his life would accomplish nothing. "I would discuss several matters with her."

August hesitated. Suspicion lit his eyes. "You wanting to get rid of me?" Suspicion and something worse . . . hope.

Edwin didn't know what to do with the boy. Or how to be. Or what to say. But he wanted him here anyway. "No," he said quietly. "I am not trying to get rid of you."

The boy's shoulders sagged.

Miss Killoran touched a hand to August's arm, squeezing slightly. Some unspoken words passed between the pair, a long look that hinted at the bond they'd forged. They were, as he'd claimed earlier, siblings. It was a status she'd imposed, stealing like the thief she and her ilk were.

And while Edwin stood there, an interloper in his own household, hatred burning his tongue like vinegar, all that kept him from hurling epithets and the words of loathing he'd carried for her and all the Killorans was the waif-thin boy beside her.

At last, Miss Killoran drew her hand back. Her lips moved, but whatever she said remained inaudible. Was it a trick of a thief to hone that quiet?

August slid a sideways glance in Edwin's direction. "Fine," he muttered.

It was a capitulation grudgingly given, but Edwin would accept any triumphs, no matter how small, where his son was concerned.

"Marlow," he barked, and then his neck immediately went hot at the sharp stares turned on him.

With his wife's death and son's abduction years earlier, Edwin had lost the veneer of civility ingrained into every nobleman.

Therefore, when Marlow trotted out from the shadows and stopped before him, Edwin measured his tones. "Will you accompany . . . Aug—" Fire gleamed in his son's eyes. A silent dare and battle waged . . . that Edwin would not win. Not like this. "Accompany Stephen to the kitchens."

Marlow turned a smile on the boy. "If you'll follow me?" he offered.

Stubborn as the day he'd entered the world, flipped upside down, refusing to turn, and torturing Lavinia, his son stood there. And then he nodded once. "I'll go." August leveled a finger at Edwin's chest. "You threaten her. You hurt her. You so much as shout at her?" He made a slashing motion at his throat.

This was how August had lived. Violence had been seared into his soul. Agony ripped through Edwin, and in stoic silence, he mourned the child he'd lost all over again.

Marlow glanced uncertainly between his charge and Edwin.

"Stephen," Miss Killoran chided with an affront better suited to a high-end governess than the street rat Edwin knew her to be.

"I meant what I said," the child warned Edwin, touching a finger to the corner of his eye.

And a moment later, that unlikely pairing marched off, Marlow filling the quiet with cheerful questions that went unanswered until they disappeared, silence reigned altogether, and Edwin found himself alone with the enemy.

He flicked a frosty stare up and down her slender frame. Her drab brown hair, drawn back. Brown eyes. One of her eyes peculiarly vacant, the other clever and indicating she was one to be carefully watched. She was . . . the forgotten one. The only Diggory daughter who'd not had a formal London season and therefore had been easy to dismiss as irrelevant. He'd once made the perilous misstep of letting one of society's dregs inside his residence. He'd not make the same mistake again. He'd already faltered too many times where this stubborn chit was concerned. "My offices." Sweeping one arm out, he urged her onward.

Miss Killoran hesitated, and then smoothing her palms along her muslin cloak, she started down the hall.

Edwin followed, close enough to have an eye on the Devil's daughter while also setting her on the correct path to his offices. To a place where he could meet her, away from his son's threatening stare and without worry over judgment.

"You would renege upon an agreement I reached with that bastard; I should see him hanged for your failure to respect the terms," he hissed close to her ear.

She drew her shoulders back. Prouder and more fearless than Joan of Arc being marched to her own fiery fate, she said nothing. Rather, she moved with steps most ladies of the *ton* could not so effortlessly affect.

And his ire only climbed. How dare she be so coolly composed?

Edwin stepped into her path, and reaching past the chit, he pressed the door handle. "Get inside," he whispered. "Now," he added at her hesitation. When she still made no move to heed that order, he leaned close. "Have you realized too late that you've entered the lair of a madman?" he whispered against her ear.

A hint of apple blossoms and lilac filled his nostrils, the scent of her unexpectedly sweet and maddeningly appealing.

The young woman angled her chin up a notch. "I'm less worried about myself than I am about my brother."

Edwin reeled. He should have learned the moment he'd set foot in his foyer and found her there waiting that she'd not be cowed into anything.

The whole world reviled him. Everyone feared him. Even his loyal servant Quint Marlow did.

Of course the only bloody person in the damned kingdom who'd spit his madness in his face was Broderick Killoran's sister. Edwin sought and found his footing once more. "Your . . . *brother*?" He stretched those two syllables out, letting the icy disdain drip into them.

"Yes, my brother," she said evenly, not taking his bait. Rather, she assessed him, sizing him up. "Furthermore, I should point out, I violated nothing. With regard to your terms?" She wrapped that last word in a derisive sneer. "I'd suggest you place more attention upon the verbiage you use—or in this case, did *not* use." With a toss of her head, she swept into his offices, taking up a position at the center of the room.

Edwin flared his nostrils, glowering after her.

Had she been any other woman, he'd have been impressed by her show of bravery and spirit. But she was not. She was the offspring of the man who'd dismantled Edwin's life.

Battling for control of the quagmire of emotions roiling within him, he followed. Not taking his gaze off her, not offering her his back, Edwin reached behind him and pushed the door quietly closed.

The young woman blinked, then squinted as if she struggled to follow his every movement.

"Miss *Diggory*," he said, stretching that silken whisper out, elongating those hated syllables. He propped a shoulder against the heavily paneled oak door and studied her.

The young woman dipped a graceful curtsy, flawless in its ease. "My lord," she murmured.

Edwin sharpened his gaze on her. Where was the street-roughened Cockney accent the papers and gossip claimed clung to the Killorans still? For all intents and purposes, London's finest, proudest lady might as well have stood before him.

Who was this . . . daughter of Diggory? The one few spoke of and about whom little was known.

He pushed himself away from the door, and folding his arms at his chest, he took slow, predatory steps closer, walking a path around her. His earlier assessment in the darkened foyer of the woman had proven correct. Drab brown hair. Nondescript brown eyes. Of medium height, and in possession of a slender frame that left her cloak hanging unflatteringly upon her, there was nothing extraordinary about the last unwed Killoran. Which was no doubt why she'd not snagged herself a wealthy or powerful husband as her sisters had already done. At his lengthy scrutiny, she dared him with her eyes. And yet for her . . . ordinariness, there was a strength of spirit that radiated, casting a soft blush upon cream-white cheeks, that marked her as . . . interesting. She was *interesting*. He stopped abruptly. Seeing this woman in any light except the darkened one was a betrayal to his late wife and his children, both living and dead . . . and himself.

"I was clear with my demands. Get out now, Miss Diggory."

The stubborn chit pursed her slightly too-full lips. "As I said earlier, you were less clear than you give yourself credit for," she challenged, ignoring the latter part of his directive. *My God, she is an insolent bit of baggage*. "And my name is Killoran."

The names were synonymous and interchangeable.

Edwin stopped before her so only a pace divided them. "And tell me, where was I not clear?" he purred. "Was it the part about making sure Broderick Diggory hangs, as he deserves, that was not clear?" The color bled from her cheeks. "Or was it my stated intentions for your sisters . . . what are their names? Ophelia? *Cleopatra?*" he asked, mocking that Shakespearean queen's name, and the woman in front of him frowned deeper. "How . . . unfortunate it would be if their business ventures were both to fail."

The young woman curled and uncurled her coarse hands at her sides. "Do *not* threaten my family," she said coolly.

He'd hand it to her. She remained undaunted.

"Or *what*, Miss Diggory?" A muscle ticked at the corner of her right eye, but she did not rise to the bait, either. "Will you set my townhouse afire and attempt to steal my son . . . *again?*"

Her features leached even more of their color, leaving those previously blushing cheeks a ghastly grey-white. And for her earlier brave show, it was her turn to falter. "I didn't . . ." And he celebrated that triumph over his enemy.

"What was that?" he barked, cupping a hand around his ear. "You didn't what?" *Destroy my life? Shatter my family?* "Kidnap my son?" he settled for, refusing to voice aloud his greatest agonies before this of all women.

She flinched.

"Now leave, and tell your *real* brother if he violates our arrangement once more, using you or another one of your . . . sisters or his henchmen to do his work for him, I'll take you all down." His in-laws' earlier recriminations flooded forward. It was just something else they'd been right about.

Edwin had stomped over to his desk when he registered the absolute silence—more specifically, the lack of retreating footfalls.

He turned back.

Miss Diggory jutted her chin up defiantly. "No one *sent* me, my lord. I am here of my own volition."

He chuckled, that rusty, ill-used laugh more a growl than anything that could ever be confused with a real expression of mirth. No one came here of their own volition. As a rule, the world avoided him.

Shifting direction, he returned to the stubborn chit's side, and leaning down, he placed his mouth close to her temple once more and fought the maddening pull of whatever damned perfume she dabbed behind her ears. "Do you think I'm foolish enough all these years later to believe a lie dripping off a Diggory's lips?"

The young woman's back moved up and down, an indication of her rapid breath. Of her fear. A lifetime ago, he'd have sooner chopped off his left hand than deliberately taunt a woman and take pleasure in her fear. No longer. That pathetic excuse of a man who'd gotten his wife and babe killed, and the other son snatched, reveled in this woman's unease. "Hmm?" he prodded, and she jumped.

"I have no reason to lie to you, my lord," she said calmly, and as she spoke, her breath, containing a whispery trace of honey, filtered from her lips and fanned his mouth. Another unexpectedly sweet scent, at odds with her past and name and sins. It enticed, drawing his gaze to her mouth and holding his focus there, mesmerized. "There is nothing I want, need, or desire." She darted her tongue out and traced the plump seam of her lips. And God forgive him, his gut clenched. For even as self-loathing spiraled through him, something far worse, far more perilous and viler and more treacherous, held him in its snare: *desire*. "The only reason I've come . . . the only worry I had . . . was for Stephen."

Stephen.

That single name, spoken aloud, snapped whatever siren's trap she'd sucked him momentarily into. "August." Had there ever been a doubt as to his insanity, this quixotic fascination with the woman's slightly too-full mouth as she spoke was evidence enough of it.

She tipped her head, and one of the few brown strands that had managed a curl bounced at her shoulder.

Edwin flared his nostrils. "His name is August Rudolph Thadeus Stephen Warren, the Earl of Greyley." He flicked a stare over her face. "You've no relation to him. He is His Lordship to you." Stalking over to the front of the room, he pulled the door open. "Now that you've seen him"—he peeled his lip in a mocking sneer—"safely delivered to his rightful home, you are dismissed. You may leave now."

Gertrude Killoran drew in a breath. "I am afraid I cannot do that."

He narrowed his eyes. "And whyever not?"

"I'm not leaving."

"I beg your pardon?" What more could she possibly want or expect of him?

The young woman clasped her palms before her, like a nun at the abbey. "I'm staying."

Confusion rooted around his mind. "Staying?" he repeated. "Staying *where?*"

"Here." She settled her features into a serene expression he'd have believed impossible for a Diggory. *"Indefinitely,"* she clarified.

Edwin rocked back on his heels.

My God, I've finally found someone madder than myself.

Chapter 6

Silence met Gertrude's pronouncement.

Given the vitriol in the Marquess of Maddock's gaze since the moment he'd caught sight of her, one might believe the gentleman was taking her announcement a good deal more calmly than one might expect.

And yet . . .

A memory trickled in, tugging at the corner of her remaining vision, tunneling her sight.

I lost the purse.

She squeezed her eyes shut and reflexively hunched her shoulders against that vicious strike, willing the remembrance gone. Willing Diggory back into the bowels of hell where he belonged. And yet, being here before the marquess and answering for crimes carried out by her father, Gertrude could not simply thrust aside thoughts of the man who'd sired her. Instead, she was forced to think of him . . . and the wrath he'd unleashed on her . . .

Moisture beaded on her brow. It slicked her palms.

Get out . . . leave me . . . leave me . . .

A faint whistle pealed around her ears, not an unfamiliar call in the streets of East London. This whistle, however, wasn't the practiced warning amongst a den of thieves or the alarm raised when a constable was close. "You're mad."

That awed invective brought her gaze open and reality rushing back in the form of the marquess.

The Marquess of Maddock.

Not Diggory.

"I'm not mad," she croaked, cursing her weakness once more. Cleo would neither croak, choke, tremble, nor sweat in the face of a threat. She'd take it on and own it. That reminder of her youngest sister sent strength back into her spine. "I am the woman who came to view your son as my brother over the years, and as such, I cannot simply sever my affections because of . . . what happened."

Lord Maddock flicked a speck of imagined lint from his immaculate sapphire-colored sleeve. "Whatever affections or feelings you have or don't have for my son matter not at all."

"Not to you," she conceded. She'd never make him see her as anything other than the enemy. But this, his deserved resentment for her and her family, wasn't about Gertrude or her siblings or the marquess himself. "They matter to Stephen."

She may as well have run him through with her dagger.

The marquess jerked.

But said nothing. Those men and women she'd known and witnessed in East London who'd been afflicted by madness had been incoherent; their gazes had darted around, and their words had often been rendered nonsensical gibberish. Lord Maddock was measured with his speech. Encouraged by that and his silence, Gertrude found her strength and trudged on with her plans.

"Banishing me and my family from Stephen's life does not make his life as it has been these past years without you just go away." Gertrude moved deeper into his office and set up a position in the middle of the carpet. "It does not diminish the feelings he has for us or take away the fear he knows being here."

A muscle at the powerful, square set of his jaw jumped.

He was a proud man. He wore it in his granite, chiseled, slightly-too-broad-to-ever-be-considered-handsome features.

"What are your intentions? Have you found a governess for him?" she pressed. "Tutors?"

"I don't answer to you," he said brusquely.

"No, you do not," she agreed. "But I'm not asking you to answer to me for your decisions or actions; rather, I'm raising questions as to how your plans might affect"—*my brother*—"Stephen." A terrifying idea settled around her brain. "Or do you intend to send him away to Eton?" It was the common way for the nobility, and yet Stephen, being scuttled off and thrust amidst a sea of proper, gently bred boys? Gertrude shivered as dread snaked down her spine for the peril that would come to Stephen and any noble boys he'd be forced to live and attend school with.

Crimson splotches of color suffused Lord Maddock's cheeks.

Gertrude opened and closed her mouth. "You haven't yet decided what to do."

His go-to-hell silence spoke volumes. Her eyes widened. "You've hired no one." Oh, dear, this was even more dire than she'd considered.

The marquess ground his teeth so loudly he was going to give himself a devilish headache. "Nor do I need advice from you in how to care for my son."

"I wouldn't presume to," she lied.

Within her pocket Sethos chirped and squirmed about as if calling her out for the liar she was.

The marquess sharpened his gaze on Gertrude. "What was that?" he barked.

She slipped her hands into her pocket and pressed her palms gently to the tiny creature darting back and forth in panic, seeking escape. *I well know the feeling.* Gertrude kept her features smooth. "I'm afraid I don't know what you are talking about," she lied with an ease that had saved her skin countless times from a Diggory beating. Gertrude made a show of glancing about the room.

With a growl, the marquess slashed a hand in her direction, and Gertrude flinched. He wouldn't put his hands upon her. Her earlier confidence in this man called mad, feared by so many, evaporated. *And why wouldn't he?* Why, when his hatred was even stronger than the antipathy her father had carried for her?

"Get on with whatever it is you'd say," he gritted out.

The perils of her leaving now, with Stephen's fate even more uncertain than it had been at her arrival, set off a new wave of determination that outweighed any fears over what he might do to her. "Steph—His Lordship . . ." Her heart twisted at that correct form of address for the boy who had been and always would be her brother. "He cannot be unattended." Gertrude removed her hands from her pocket and turned the palms up, needing him to see. Willing him to understand. "His Lordship's life has been such that he requires structure and . . . surveillance."

"He'll have it."

"Does he have a tutor or governess in place?" she rebutted. At the marquess's silence, she pounced. "Because if he does not, then you . . ." She shook her head. "You do not know the failure you'll set him up for."

The air hissed between Lord Maddock's teeth. "You would presume to call me out as one setting him up for failure." His voice dripped with a mocking derision. And then he tossed back that golden lion's mane and shouted his empty amusement to the rafters. Gertrude huddled deep within her cloak, borrowing the little comfort she could from Sethos. For in this instance, she was proven so very wrong: from the marquess's glittering eyes down to those unruly, overly long strands, he bore the look of a man who'd gone mad . . . and embraced it.

"You, of all people? Your family taught him to thieve and set fires and shoot guns and . . ." As he spoke, he slashed a large hand angrily through the air, and she carefully followed each wave of his erratic palm. The marquess's stinging diatribe drifted in and out of focus. A humming rang in her ears as those oldest, darkest of memories fought their way back to the surface. *I'll show you wot 'appens, ya stupid chit . . .* "Keeping company with the vilest thugs." The marquess's voice came roaring back, even with his rage, safer than the demons that threatened still. "Whatever other crimes you've forced him to commit."

Those accurately leveled charges landed a decisive mark at the corner of her chest where her heart beat. He was right. Gertrude had lived a life steeped in logic, and she was not so proud that she could not see the veracity of the marquess's heated accusations.

Even correct as he was, she still had to make him see reason. For Stephen. "His Lordship's lessons cannot be delivered the way a governess or tutor would for a typical charge."

Lord Maddock flattened his lips into an unyielding line.

At his silence, Gertrude continued. "He's resisted his studies, and therefore, instruction has to be carefully tailored to meet his interests." As it should for any child.

The marquess eyed her for a long while before moving to his desk and taking up a seat in an Empire-style, gilded chair, a king in charge of this kingdom. She braced for him to order her gone once more. This time, he simply sat back in his seat. "You have experience with how a child should be instructed."

Unable to make sense out of the meaning to his deadened tones, Gertrude ventured forward. And without waiting or asking permission, she claimed the seat opposite him, perching herself on the edge. "I have experience working with him."

"You?"

She frowned at the heavy skepticism there. Her pride smarted, and yet her own feelings were irrelevant, too. "I have," she repeated.

Gertrude placed her palm on the edge of his immaculate desk. "It is why I know the manner of instructor and education he needs."

"He requires an education for a marquisate."

"Yes, that much is true." She paused. "But you cannot simply shift him away from everything he's known and over to the life that awaits him now."

Any other man, regardless of station, would take umbrage to being challenged and refuse to concede the point. It was therefore a mark in Lord Maddock's favor when he steepled his fingers, resting them under his chin, and contemplated her—*the enemy's*—advice.

That gaze, all frosted ice, was emptier and hollower than those of the most street-hardened criminals in St. Giles. He drummed his fingertips together in a slow one-two-three-four pattern. "What are you proposing then? To stay here as his"—the marquess curled his lips up in an equally cold, small grin—"governess?"

As Stephen's sister. That was what she'd been. It was a role she could not and would not divorce herself from simply because they'd all been deceived in the cruelest way possible. Their bond was too strong and was one that would only further stir the embers of this man's resentment. "Yes," she settled for in quiet tones. "That is precisely what I'm proposing."

The marquess abruptly ceased that tapping. "No."

Her heart sank. "No," she echoed dumbly, falling back in her chair at the abrupt rejection. *You fool. Did you truly believe he was actually considering what you'd put to him?*

Lord Maddock dropped his elbows onto his desk and leaned forward. "One of the last times I had someone linked to your family in my household, it was left in a pile of ash." A spasm of pain twisted his features, and her heart wrenched anew for altogether different reasons. Ones that had to do with his tangible suffering. The marquess narrowed his gaze on hers, and as soon as that brief expression of grief had come, it was gone, replaced by hardened, hate-filled emotions. He seethed. "I'd sooner trust my soul to Satan than allow you to reside here." With that, he shoved back his chair; the legs of that thronelike seat scraped along the hardwood floor, certain to leave marks upon the surface.

Panic setting in, Gertrude jumped up, her muslin skirts swishing noisily. "But—"

"You have my answer. The answer, regardless of your pleading, pathetic attempt at reasoning or begging—"

"I do not beg."

"Miss Diggory."

She gritted her teeth, and she dropped her palms onto his desktop. "My *name* is Miss Killoran." *And I will beg . . . for Stephen. For any member of my family.*

He matched her pose. "My answer remains, and will remain, no. Now we are officially done here."

The door exploded open with such force, it slammed back against the plaster wall and bounced forward, nearly hitting the face of the angry observer on the other side. *August.*

"You send her away, you might as well send me, too," the young boy hurled. "Because I'll be damned if I stay here without Gertrude."

———— ❦ ————

Goddamn Gertrude Diggory.

With her presence and terms, she'd pit Edwin and his son into a battle that Edwin would always come out on the losing side of.

"Is there something wrong with your hearing?" August shouted, waving a tiny fist as he stalked over. "*And* your mind?"

Edwin jerked.

"Stephen, that is *enough*," Miss Diggory said sharply. Sliding herself in front of the boy hurtling himself across the office, she gripped him by the right arm. "Do not speak so."

"But he *is* mad."

While August proceeded to quarrel with the young woman who called herself August's sister, Edwin stared on dumbly.

His son was correct. Edwin was insane. He hadn't always been. His madness, however, hadn't been a disease passed on through rotten blood; rather, his mind had been poisoned by the memories of all he had lost.

The boy wrestled against her hold. "Let me go!"

Edwin snapped back to the moment. He schooled his features into the mask he'd worn so long for protection. "It appears you've overestimated your *abilities*, madam," he taunted.

That managed to quiet the feral boy's frenetic movements.

Color rushed to the stubborn chit's cheeks.

"What's that supposed to mean?" August glanced back and forth between Edwin and Miss Killoran.

It meant no one, not even this woman who'd stormed Edwin's household, could tame the child that had been returned to him. That realization hit Edwin square in the chest.

He was saved from answering by the harried footsteps pounding outside his office. Hopping out from behind Miss Diggory, August yanked a jewel-studded dagger from his boot and had it pointed at the door just as Marlow stumbled inside. "I cannot find . . . ," he rasped, and then his gaze found the boy he'd been tasked with watching and the vicious tip of the dagger pointed at him. Marlow's eyes bulged, and he took a hasty step back. "Oh." Breathless and his face flushed red from his exertions, the servant stared past the boy to Edwin, his features a blend of fear, horror, and remorse.

"It is fine." Edwin waved off that silent apology, damning this day. Damning his life. Damning the chit with steely determination for being proven correct in this instance. August didn't require just anyone watching over him. He required someone capable and prepared for a charge who could sneak off and—Edwin's gut clenched—brandish weapons like a seasoned military man. "Shut the door behind you."

With a jerky nod, Marlow backed out of the room and closed the panel with a faint click, leaving Edwin alone with two strangers. Just one of whom shared his blood.

Desperate to regain some foothold, Edwin gestured for the ragtag pair to sit. "If you would?" he urged, calling forth every lesson ingrained in him long ago about politeness and self-control. They were sentiments he'd had no use for after his wife's death. It hadn't mattered what the world thought or didn't think of him. He had become the monster everyone took him to be: a madman tortured by the memories of a fire that had stolen everything from him. But now . . . it *did* matter. Not for anyone other than the eleven-year-old boy with hatred brimming in his eyes.

When they'd all claimed chairs, August was the first to speak in another explosion of fury and resentment. "If you send her away, I'm leaving, too."

"That is not your call to make," the young woman murmured, resting a hand on the boy's knee.

August shoved her touch off him. "You *said* you weren't leaving."

She'd made *that* promise to his son? Edwin made himself look at this obstinate wench who'd turned his life and world upside down . . . again.

For one given to a life of crime and treachery, Gertrude Diggory did a rubbish job of hiding her feelings. Rather, she was an open book with her every thought and emotion parading over her diamond-shaped face. The lady warred with herself. She wanted to go toe to toe with Edwin still. "It might be for the best," she finally said in solemn tones. "If you begin again without me here."

There should be a swell of triumph at having her falter, at besting her, despite the demands she'd put to him.

"Says who? You?" His son finally looked over at Edwin. "Or *him?*"

Except it was impossible to be victorious when one's own son looked at one the way he might a slug crawling upon the earth.

"Miss Diggory cannot remain here forever," Edwin finally said diplomatically. "She has her own life." Doing whatever it was thieves and sinners did. And he'd be damned if she remained here, ready to pounce like the last vile thug of Mac Diggory's who'd lived here.

The woman shifted then, falling to a knee alongside August's chair. Taking his hands in her own, she squeezed them and said something.

With his lips pursed, August shook his head.

She nodded; whatever words she spoke to the child were so hushed they barely qualified as sound.

August's lower lip trembled, that first mark of vulnerability, and it wrenched at that organ in Edwin's chest that he had believed dead long, long ago. Catching Edwin's stare, all hint of weakness immediately lifted. "I ain't staying."

"You are," the young woman repeated. "And you will be fine. You will be better than fine."

While the pair resumed their nearly inaudible discussion, August stole several glances at him. Edwin sat still, the recipient of his own child's flagrant animosity.

The villain in his own household . . . because of this woman.

She'd seen to it that when she left, his son would have nothing but resentment for the one who'd sent her away. It had been a neat, clever trap that Edwin could not find his way out of. Not without forever damaging his new beginning with August. For with her demands and Edwin's insistence that she take herself off to whichever hole the Diggorys resided in at the given moment, she'd managed to shred him in his son's eyes—again.

Bloody, bloody hell on Sunday.

"If you will excuse Miss Diggory and me for a moment?" Edwin clipped out, and the sibling-like pair across from him both glanced up, shocked, as if they'd forgotten his presence.

August set his chin at a mutinous angle in a gesture so resembling the woman next to him that in the moment, Edwin could almost be deceived into believing the two were in fact brother and sister who shared blood.

The young woman leaned forward and whispered something into the boy's ear.

August lingered there, defiant.

But then he climbed to his feet. Holding Edwin's eyes with his own, the boy turned his knife menacingly in Edwin's direction. He swirled the tip of that gleaming blade, motioning to the neckcloth at Edwin's throat. The irony of that silent, threatening exchange was not lost on Edwin. How many times had he silently prayed for such a fate? A swift, decisive end to his miserable existence.

"Stephen," the young woman scolded with such horror and shock a less jaded person than Edwin might believe she was capable of such emotions.

All the while grief battered at him. His longing for death had belonged to a man who'd lost his family . . . mourning this boy who stood before him. The same boy who now issued a threat against his life—one Edwin didn't believe was at all empty.

The boy abruptly stopped, his knife and gaze all trained on the gold pin at Edwin's throat. August's arm faltered, and for a moment Edwin believed he recognized the piece. Remembered it.

Until he shifted his focus up and there was only nothingness there.

"I said, put your knife away, Stephen," she admonished.

"Fine," the boy mumbled. He jammed his dagger back inside a clever strap attached to the point just above his ankle. Backing slowly toward the front of the room, August watched them both, and reaching the door, the boy shot a hand behind him and pressed the handle.

Quint Marlow stood there in loyal wait, as he'd done so many other times before this one.

August spared him a quick look, sizing him up and down. "You again." By the derisive smile on his lips, he found the other man wanting.

Edwin's man-of-affairs now assessed the boy with a proper degree of wariness and mistrust. "Why don't I show you to your rooms now, Lord August."

And this time, after a moment's hesitation, August continued on. Marlow quickly drew the door shut once more.

"I don't want you here," Edwin said without preamble. "I'd rather see you to the Devil where you belong than allow you to reside in my household."

The chit's eyebrows lifted. "And yet?"

She was clever, and he would do well to remember that much. To not forget it. To always assume she was ten steps ahead of him and then plot his way to five and ten past the woman to beat her. He'd not, however, give her the pleasure of being told she was right . . . even as she was. Edwin proceeded to fire off directives, reclaiming control. "You'll remain here until a proper governess or tutor can be found." One who'd not be devoured by the snarling boy who'd just quit Edwin's offices. "You'll continue to oversee his lessons until then. You're not to set foot outside this townhouse with my son unless someone accompanies you, and even then, I want details so I can choose whether or not to give my permission." There wouldn't be a reason for her to leave. He didn't expect it would take more than a fortnight to find a suitable instructor.

The minx pursed her mouth. "You'll make us prisoners, then," she said brusquely. "That is rather an inauspicious beginning to your future with your son."

His ears went hot at having his own unspoken words from a short while ago hurled in his face by this sternly disapproving woman. She of all people would condemn his decisions or actions? Edwin dropped his voice to a rough whisper. "You misunderstand. You are the prisoner here. Not August. *You.*"

Fear flashed within her eyes. It bled her cheeks of color. And it was the first time since she'd invaded his household that she'd shown a hint of weakening. "I'm no man's p-prisoner." That faintest of quivers further evidenced the young woman's unease.

He grinned coldly at the interloper. "If you choose to remain, then yes, that is precisely what you'll be. You will not have any correspondence with your family. You're not to instruct my servants to send word to your family's minions." As he spoke, her thin chestnut eyebrows drew into a line, the only telltale indication she heard—and resented—each order. Resting his palms on his stomach, Edwin reclined in his chair and braced for her to finally take flight.

She scrabbled with her lower lip, worrying that flesh between her slightly crooked front teeth.

"Well?" he purred, arching a single eyebrow.

The young woman glanced over her shoulder a long while. Whether she stayed or left, the decision would be owned by her. August's resentment would be reserved for the one who'd abandoned him. And then Edwin and August could begin their lives anew. Under his palms, his stomach muscles contracted. This woman's leaving still did not make up for the fact that Edwin didn't have a single bloody clue what to do with his son.

"What is it to be, Miss Killoran?"

Her shoulders snapped back as a crackling tension went through her slender frame, and she returned her focus to him. That one clear, clever eye leveled him to his seat. Slowly, she pushed herself upright. "What I said at the outset of our conversation still holds true. I'm remaining as long as it takes for Stephen to acclimate to his place and role here. Now, if you'll excuse me?"

He flared his nostrils, staring after her retreating back. By God, was there no end to the chit's insolence?

"Halt," he commanded. The young woman stopped and did a slow, graceful turn so that they again faced one another. "I have not yet dismissed you, Miss Killoran." Nor was he foolish enough to allow her free rein of his household. *Except . . . you are allowing the chit to reside under the same roof.* What did that say about his logic? He'd allow her to stay, but that did not mean he himself had to have any personal dealings with her. "While you are here, you are not to darken my door. Any communication between us will be carried out through Marlow." Reaching behind him, he tugged the bell pull.

A dutiful, strapping footman nearly eight inches taller than the chit entered a few moments later.

"See Miss Killoran to the guest chambers," Edwin instructed.

The liveried servant bowed and started forward.

"Oh, and Miss Killoran?" Edwin called after her before she could be ushered off.

She eyed him with a proper modicum of wariness. "Yes?"

"You might have won this round"—he thinned his eyes into small slits—"but your days are numbered here. When you do leave, this will have been the last contact you ever have with my son."

And then Edwin would at last be free of her and her cursed siblings.

Chapter 7

"You convinced him."

"Well, it certainly wasn't Cleopatra, Ophelia, or Broderick."
Gertrude directed that mumbled utterance into the back of her brother's new armoire. Pride, however, filled her. She had done it. She'd not only faced down a man rumored to be mad—one who'd tormented her and her siblings over crimes that belonged squarely with their father—but also secured his agreement and inserted her place in his household.

Having been shown to her rooms, Gertrude had quit the bright, sun-filled guest chamber and gone in search of Stephen. Now, several hours since they'd arrived, she saw to tidying and making this new space Stephen's.

She squinted into the darkened armoire and felt around, running her palms along the walls of the mahogany piece. "Oh, no." She made a *tsk*ing sound that echoed off the empty wood closet. No, this would not do at all.

"Yea," Stephen called from behind her. "But I didn't expect that it would be *you* who convinced him."

"Thank you," she muttered. "But it was, in fact, you who changed the marquess's mind." If he'd had his way, Gertrude would have been banished to the fiery flames of hell with her rotted sire.

"Me?" Incredulity filled Stephen's voice.

Pushing herself upright, Gertrude turned, and the words died on her lips.

Stephen sat perched on the edge of an ornate half tester bed; the gigantic, carved piece dwarfed his tiny frame and highlighted just how small her brother in fact was. And for all intents and purposes, with her working as she was and him swinging his legs off the side of that frame, they might as well have been at home in the Devil's Den and not in this foreign place.

Slightly reclined and stroking Gus's back, Stephen went on. "Maddock didn't seem that afraid when I stuck my knife at him."

She laughed softly. "Oh, Stephen." Quitting her place at the opposite end of the room, she joined him at the side of the rosewood rococo bed and, gripping the edges, pulled herself up so that she sat next to him. The moment she was settled on the slightly too-firm mattress, Gus popped up and clawed his way from around Stephen. "It wasn't your knife," she said, stroking the cat's sensitive back.

Stephen's face pulled. "It wasn't?"

"No." She'd known the precise moment the marquess had capitulated. Warmth filled her chest. He'd not allowed Gertrude to stay because of any threat, real or otherwise perceived. It spoke volumes of the gentleman. It spoke of one who wasn't necessarily violent or mad, but who still had compassion in him. Gertrude looked over at Stephen. "He saw that you wanted me here."

Her brother stiffened. "*Pfft*. He doesn't care what I want."

"He does," she returned with an automaticity born of truth. "If he didn't, he'd have tossed me out on my buttocks. Instead, he's allowed me to remain, and that"—she stuck a finger up—"surely says something about your father."

Her brother snorted. "You're defending the madman? You're as crazy as him."

At that hateful insult Stephen continued to hurl about his father, Gertrude frowned. It was one he'd tossed out during their meeting with the man who'd sired him. What must it be like for a man to lose everything he held dear and then go through life, shunned as a lunatic by all . . . including the child he'd so desperately searched for? "He is your father, Stephen," she said gently, adding a firmness to that reminder. "And you shouldn't go about calling him mad."

"He ain't my father," Stephen mumbled.

The marquess, from his obstinate noble jawline down to his clever and harsh gaze, was very much the boy's father. She'd not force Stephen to accept the truth of it. That was something he needed to come to terms with . . . in his own time . . . and couldn't have forced upon him. "Very well. I'll not insist you accept him as your father . . ." After all, she'd learned firsthand that blood did not a father make. The marquess, however, had searched for his son when Gertrude's own father hadn't even bothered to name her at birth. "I *will* ask," she went on, "that you stop insulting him."

"I can't promise that."

Damn his stubbornness. She, however, shared that same obstinacy. "Then try."

They battled in silence. "*Fiiiiine.* I'll try. But I don't see why it matters if I call him 'mad' if he is m—" Gertrude gave him a look. "Fine. Fine," he groused. "Broderick isn't going to be happy with you," he said suddenly.

"He'll understand." *And he's going to be panicked when you fail to return.*

"He's going to worry."

Of course Broderick would worry. She suspected he and the rest of their siblings all doubted Gertrude's abilities. Refusing to let talk or thought of her family's low expectations diminish her earlier triumph, she smiled at her brother. "Enough talk about Broderick." She hopped up, and at that abrupt movement, Gus leapt off the bed, landing with a solid thump on the hardwood floors. "We need to focus first on making this space yours."

Gertrude settled her hands on her hips and did a slow circle, assessing each corner and article. The chambers were made up of matching rosewood rococo furniture; from the three-drawer worktable to a curved writing desk with built-in cases and cubbies, no expense had been spared. Ornate, bronzed, rococo mirror wall sconces hung in pairs throughout the rooms, filled with enough candles that at dark, one could likely be tricked into believing it was daylight still.

"I hate it," Stephen muttered, bringing her gaze away from the furnishings and over to him. His legs folded in a crisscross, he'd made an effective little cage. And by the chirping from within, Sethos was happy at play there.

"It isn't all bad," she said with forced cheer.

"You're a lousy liar. At least Cleo would tell the truth."

Fair turn.

"Very well. Do you want to know what I'm really thinking? It's ornate," she said bluntly. "It exudes wealth and power, and in that appreciation for the finer things, the marquess is not different from Broderick, Stephen." It did, however, mean that the marquess didn't know the boy who'd call this household home.

Because of you and your family . . .

Guilt scissored at her chest. The marquess was right in his hatred and fury.

Stephen carefully stretched his legs out, and Sethos scurried out from under them.

Gus's ears pricked up. "Stop," Gertrude said briskly, snapping her fingers twice, and the tabby sank reluctantly back onto the floral, pink-and-green Aubusson carpet.

"Pink and green and flowers," Stephen groused, shooing Gus away until the cat abandoned his interest in Sethos and took up a spot in the corner of the room.

"I'll speak to the marquess," Gertrude offered, and as soon as those words slipped out, she wanted to pull them back.

Except . . .

Stephen's face brightened. "You will?"

She didn't want to. She wanted to have as few dealings as possible with a man who looked like he wished her dead ten times to Sunday. But *she'd* insisted on remaining. She was determined to be here for Stephen. Gertrude forced a smile that strained every muscle of her face. "I will."

Stephen snorted. "And what are you going to say? 'Burn your fancy furniture'?"

It was the wrong thing to say, and if he realized it, he gave no indication. And whether it had been intentional, Gertrude could not say.

"I'm going to say that you might do better with new . . . décor." Gertrude returned to the side of the bed and pressed her hand on it. She grimaced. "And your mattress. We're going to require your mattress be brought over."

She winced. There was the whole matter of getting that beloved piece from within the Devil's Den, which would be a nigh-impossible feat after the marquess's express orders about her and—

Gertrude groaned. "Bloody, bloody hell," she whispered. How was she going to notify her family? She had to tell them something.

"What?" Stephen piped in.

Gertrude let her hand fall to her side and forced another grin in place. "Nothing. It is nothing at all. We'll simply require a place for you to . . . hide your things." *Later.* She'd just have to convince the marquess to let her send word to her family. For now, Stephen was who mattered and where all her focus needed to be. "Rule one . . . protect your belongings," she reminded her brother, ruffling the top of his head.

He swatted at her hand. "I didn't think you of all people would say that. Thought you'd be, 'Now, Stephen, speak proper, dress proper, and be proper,'" he said in high-pitched tones.

Gertrude wrinkled her nose. "I do not sound like that."

"Yes, you do. Every time you give me a lesson."

Fair enough. "Yes, well, one can speak properly and attain a valuable education while also honoring the lessons we learned on the streets." That philosophical belief, however, had long set her apart from every one of her siblings, except Broderick. He'd seen that it mattered. Gertrude resumed her stroll around Stephen's rooms, exploring the narrow desk drawers and underside of each piece of furniture.

How dreadfully dull and predictable. There were no secret latches. No hidden compartments.

"There's *nowhere* to hide my things."

Gertrude dropped to her knees beside the armoire and peered inside once again. "It will have to be here for now. Until I speak again with His Lordship."

"When's that going to be?"

While you are here, you are not to darken my door.

"Soon," she hedged. Lord Maddock had been abundantly clear in his expectations. Her heart pounded hard. Nay, his demands.

From somewhere within the household, a chiming clock struck the quarter hour.

Gertrude sighed. "Now." Because if she did not, then Broderick would storm the marquess's home, demanding to know just where in blazes she'd gone off to. And then they were doomed. All of them.

But before she spoke to his father, Stephen required a task. He always required something to do. But it had to be something he saw value in, or he sought out trouble—and invariably discovered it. And Stephen's trouble was not the same as that of an innocent young boy's putting ink or frogs in teacups. It was setting fires or picking nobs' pockets or scaling roofs. "Here." Gertrude rushed over to the corner of the room, and catching the crimson-and-orange-painted Mongolian trunk Broderick had commissioned for Stephen, she dragged it over, back hunched and panting from exertion. It scraped loudly over the floor until it snagged the edge of the pink-and-green carpet. With a grunt, Gertrude heaved it over that slight lip and pulled it the remainder of the way to where her brother sat watching her, wide-eyed.

"What—?"

"Your weapons are in here," she explained, slightly breathless. A strand fell free from the tight arrangement Reggie had managed that morning and slipped over her brow. She brushed the errant lock back, tucking it behind her ear. "You'll need to find a place for them, preferably where a chambermaid will not make the mistake of dusting or touching them." Some possessed spikes and notches, all clever designs crafted long ago to trick the person who made the mistake of lifting the weapon that didn't belong to them.

"It would serve them," he said with such ruthless ease she frowned.

He didn't mean that. He wasn't truly like Diggory. He'd merely sought to fill that monster's image. "It would also see them taken away from you for certain," she said, using a logic he could make sense of through his resentment.

"Fine," he groused.

Reaching inside the pocket at the front of her bronze muslin gown, she fished out a small ring of keys. "Here." She tossed them over.

Stephen shot a hand up and caught them effortlessly in a single, fisted grip.

"And when you are done, make sure Sethos and Gus are occupied and safe. I don't need to tell you what would likely happen to them should they be discovered underfoot."

He nodded and, falling to his knees, unlocked the gold latches.

Gertrude started for the door.

"Gertrude?"

She glanced back.

"Thank you," he said softly.

Gertrude smiled. "It will be all right," she promised, lying for him . . . and for herself.

For there could be no doubting that the upcoming meeting with Lord Maddock was even more foolhardy and dangerous than their initial one.

With an impending sense of doom, she wound her way along the same path she'd traveled earlier, to the door she'd been instructed not to darken, hopeful she would be able to establish new terms for her arrangement here.

Chapter 8

Edwin had spent the past years consumed.

For the first four of those seven, it had been grief, heartache, and hatred over the loss of his wife, unborn child, and son.

And for the latter three, he'd been consumed by the fledgling hope and belief that his son had, in fact, survived the fire that had taken everything. He'd committed his days and nights to finding information about the Diggory gang and the child he had lost.

With the passage of time, August wouldn't have been a young boy. But in Edwin's research and countless, sleepless hours, days spent without food and barely water, unshaven, unbathed, he'd not thought of August as a figure who'd aged. Rather, he'd existed in Edwin's mind as the boy he'd been. He'd been un-aging, plump, precocious, smiling. He'd always been smiling.

Edwin stared blankly across the ledgers spread out before him, over to the doorway.

For now, that dream had been realized and his son found . . . and Edwin didn't know what to do with . . . anything.

How did one live life for a single-minded purpose and then simply . . . stop?

A sharp knock cut into his musings.

Edwin quickly sat up, and grabbing a quill with one hand, he dragged the nearest ledger over with the other. "Enter," he boomed, and made a show of studying the numbers scrawled there. He glanced up and found Marlow in the doorway. Edwin's fingers curled into a reflexive fist, the weight of it snapping the pen in half. One scrap fell useless atop the book. "Is there—?"

"No trouble, my lord." The other man neatly slipped in. "I merely sought to update you. Lord August is in his chambers." Some of the unease left Edwin. Marlow paused and coughed into his hand. "With Miss Killoran." And just like that, tension crackled through his frame like the impending energy just before a lightning strike. "His belongings have been sent to his rooms."

It only made sense that she would be with August. That was essentially the capitulation he'd made. Nay, it was what he'd agreed to. *It is a mistake. It is a trap.*

"My lord?"

He snapped his gaze over to Marlow. Worry lined the younger man's features.

"The servant stairways, any entrance and exit to this residence, need to be secured," Edwin instructed.

"I've already taken it upon myself to have footmen directed to those respective locations, my lord."

Since Quint Marlow had discovered him, half mad, stinking from spirits, and praying for death, the butler had come to anticipate what Edwin required. In fact, if he were being truthful with himself, he could acknowledge that the only reason he'd not found himself dead in the streets of St. Giles had been because of the loyal friend-servant-man-of-affairs before him. "Thank you, Marlow. That will be all."

Instead of taking his leave, however, the other man lingered. "I know you question my sister's relationship with the Killoran family, and also question my confidence and trust in my sister, but she possesses a good heart. She speaks with warmth and great affection for Miss Killoran, and therefore, I find some . . . assurance in that."

It was always easier to find assurance before one found oneself made a widower by London's most violent gang leader and kidnapper.

"Thank you. That will be all."

Marlow hesitated and then took himself off.

As soon as the door closed, Edwin dropped his head into his hands. What was he thinking, allowing her to remain? "Because you *are* mad," he whispered into his palms, muffling that utterance. This latest decision was proof enough of the state of his sanity. The damned lady shared the blood of a murderer. By all accounts of information uncovered about the Diggory gang, all those within it were the same: murderers faithfully stealing for him, killing for him, kidnapping for him.

Ice slipped along his spine. *What if I am falling into the same bloody trap?* Edwin jammed his fingertips into his temples and pressed so hard his head throbbed. But the Killorans also had their club now. They had businesses. Surely they knew better than to make another attempt to take August? They'd lose . . . everything.

Or was he simply trying to reassure himself? For telling himself all that, analyzing his decision from every angle did nothing to vanquish his unrest.

Another firm knock sounded at the door. *Damn it.* "What is it n . . . ?" His words trailed off as the door opened. *"You."* My God, she doesn't fear me—or all the tales whispered about my reputation.

The spirited chit didn't bother awaiting an invitation but simply closed the door and admitted herself. "My lord," she said, offering a belated curtsy.

He fell back in his chair. "You want me to throw you out on your arse," he breathed. "There is nothing else to explain it. Did I not make myself clear?"

A proper lady would have blushed red at that crudity.

Gertrude Killoran merely returned a smile, a soft, serene, and gentle one that was belied by only the little crinkles at the corners of her eyes. "Oh, you were *abundantly* clear, my lord. There *is* something else to explain my . . . being here."

"Defying orders," he corrected.

Coming forward, she claimed the seat opposite him with the ease of one who owned this room and all its contents. He froze. For up close . . . her large lips turned up in a smile . . . it rather transformed her, highlighting a face he'd taken at first glance as ordinary in every way. Now he stared on, riveted by the contours of it. It was neither round nor heart-shaped, but rather a pear-shaped diamond, soft and yet regal all at the same time and . . .

Edwin choked, gasping for air.

The young woman came out of her chair. "Are you all—?"

He shot a staying hand up, glowering at her over his fingertips. "D-do not," he strangled out.

Gertrude Killoran hesitated and then reseated herself at the very edge, carefully watching as he struggled for a proper breath. Was she waiting for evidence he needed help? Or sitting and hoping for his slow strangulation?

When he'd managed to gather air into his lungs without dissolving into a paroxysm, he sat back. "I ordered you gone."

"No, you ordered me out of your offices and away from your door. More specifically, you ordered me not to darken your door." And in perfect rote remembrance, she spat out the very directives he'd leveled at her. "Any communication between us will be carried out through Marlow." She gave him a look. "You might have won this round"—she thinned her eyes into small slits—"but your days are numbered here.

When you do leave, this will have been the last contact you ever have with my son."

He blinked. She'd remembered it precisely, both words and inflection. And she'd defied him anyway. "My God, *you* are mad."

"No, I'm really quite sane. I simply have a strong ability to memorize and remember . . ." At catching his horrified stare, she abruptly ceased her ramblings.

Reclined in his chair, immobile, and still contemplating the woman across from him, Edwin didn't know . . . what to make of her. There was a peculiar blend of strength and spirit and . . . innocence. There was that, too. The latter of which didn't fit with the most mysterious of the Killorans, whom investigators had uncovered little about. "We have a problem, Miss Killoran," he murmured, laying his palms on the arms of his chair.

Gertrude Killoran clasped her callused hands and rested them on her lap, a model of piety. "Do we?" she asked, her tone wholly unfazed and almost bored.

"You've proven in just an hour's time here that you're unable to keep your word, and you are very much your father's daughter."

Her body tensed. "You know nothing about me," she said quietly.

He honed his gaze on her flushed cheeks. He could almost believe his insult had struck its intended mark. But that would have to mean she resented Mac Diggory, that vile criminal who'd also seen this woman's pockets lined and provided her with fancy garments. Nay, her loyalty and soul belonged to Satan.

"But I know your father," he returned on a silken purr that he layered with steel. "As such, it was already a folly for me to agree to your being here. It would be even more so to allow you to remain after you've violated our agreement. And so, you've freed me from my pledge."

"I had time to consider your terms," she said, matching his body's movements, "and decided they are not in Stephen's best interest."

He narrowed his eyes. "August. His name is August."

She went on, ignoring that correction. "How can I properly ease his transition into your household if I'm not free to speak to you about his lessons and concerns I might have or the governesses or tutors whom you should consider for hire?"

That gave him pause.

She sat motionless, not pressing her point or the advantage she'd found over him.

Edwin pushed back his chair, measuring his movements, refusing her any satisfaction in seeing she'd confounded him yet again. He felt her gaze follow his path over to the sideboard and linger on his movements as he poured himself a brandy. Edwin splashed several fingers into the crystal glass and then contemplated the amber depths.

Bloody hell. He despised that the chit was right in this matter, as well. Edwin could not have it both ways. He couldn't allow Gertrude Killoran to remain with the intention of seeing August properly settled, while also himself having no contact with her.

So toss her out. No good can come from her being here.

Every instinct he'd honed, every lesson he'd been cruelly handed by her father to be wary of the motives and actions of all, fairly screamed at him to turn her out on his doorstep and never spare her another thought.

But then an image flashed to mind, an unwanted one.

Her kneeling alongside his son, August's lower lip trembling in the boy's only display of vulnerability.

His son would hate him, even more than he already did. There would be no turning those sentiments if Gertrude Killoran was shown the door.

The chit had him there.

Gripping his glass hard, he faced her. "All right." He flicked an icy stare over her. Once again, she remained stoic in the face of his derision, ratcheting up his annoyance . . . and damned appreciation for the courageous minx. "Out with it."

"I want to review his lessons with you and discuss his past." She shot out each command like Wellington himself in his battlefield days. "I want you and I to be able to freely speak about Stephen and how he is or is not adjusting to his time here."

He had opened his mouth to correct her on the usage of his son's name when she said, "And I must have . . . some contact with my family."

That marked the first note of hesitancy in her otherwise impressively stoic list.

"Absolutely not." He tossed back a long swallow.

"They were unaware of my intentions to remain," she said calmly, "and as such, they'll wonder why I've not returned, and then . . ."

And then Broderick Killoran would come here, and God help Edwin, there'd be no stopping him this time from ending that bastard with his bare hands.

Edwin took another sip and then set his glass down hard. "No."

Gertrude stood. "You misunderstand. I was not asking for you to alter the terms involving my siblings." How . . . interesting. And yet . . .

"I don't believe you," he said bluntly. He'd be a fool to trust her. "You expect me to believe you left no word behind? You entrusted not one of your loyal family with your *plan*."

She pursed her mouth. "I didn't."

"Then you're either a liar or the least *skilled* of those thugs in your family's gang."

She winced, and blast and damn, if he didn't feel like a bully who'd kicked the cat. And for telling a woman that she was rot at subterfuge. "Only with a damned Diggory," he mumbled under his breath.

"What was that?"

By the intelligent sparkle in her right eye, he'd wager the last shred he had of his sanity that she'd heard him quite clearly.

The tenacious spitfire took a step closer. "I am not asking you to believe me or trust me," she said in soothing, dulcet tones, ones she

91

might reserve for a skittish animal. And that ploy should grate, and yet her voice washed over him, a dangerous siren's pull. She stopped before him, so close that honeyed scent filled his senses once more, and he swallowed hard, fighting her hold. Nearly six inches smaller than his six-foot, two-inch frame, she had to arch her neck back to meet his eyes. Had he found her eyes common? They were impossibly round and dark, like Belgium's finest chocolate. She smiled gently, sucking him further into that illusion of innocence. "I'm merely telling you that unless you wish my brother and sisters to come knocking at your door, then I have to send them word."

"And then that will be your last communication until you return." Collecting his glass, Edwin stepped around her.

The lady waggled her fingertips. "That will not work, either."

"It wasn't a question, Miss Killoran—it was a statement," he muttered, stomping over to his desk.

"That brings me to the next reason for my being here." With long, brisk strides, she was across the room and in her seat just as he was settling back into his chair for this hellish, never-ending meeting.

Though, if you're being honest with yourself . . . you're also refreshed by it.

When had been the last time anyone had looked upon him with anything but fear and loathing? Why, even Marlow had avoided his gaze more often than he'd held it.

"And that reason, Miss Killoran?"

"Stephen's rooms."

Edwin opened his mouth to again correct her on that incorrect usage of his son's name, but then he stopped. "Is there something wrong with his chambers?" He frowned. He'd given specific orders of which rooms were to be set up, and the furniture—

"Oh, no," she was quick to assure him. "They are fine."

He gave voice to that unspoken word dangling there, unsaid by her. "But?"

"They are fine for another child." Leaning forward, she rested her palms on the edge of his desk. "They are just not . . . fine for Stephen at this moment."

"And whyever not?" he barked. With the exception of a brand-new mattress and an Aubusson carpet he'd had commissioned, every last item in August's room had belonged to him as a young boy in the Cheshire countryside. When he'd speculated his son was still alive, Edwin had specifically ordered those items be brought over and the rooms recreated in the image of his son's own former rooms.

"The bed is too firm. He is . . . accustomed to sleeping on a certain bed." She paused. "His bed."

"This *is* his bed," he gritted.

"Yes. That is correct. But it does not make it the one he feels comfortable in."

Bloody hell. "What do you *advise*?"

If she heard the mocking edge there, she gave no indication. "I would encourage you to allow Stephen's mattress to be delivered."

He was already shaking his head.

"As a sign to him that his comfort and what matters to him are also of value to you," she said solemnly. And had she been chastising or lecturing, it would have been easier to send her and her opinions to the Devil. But she was, once again, putting his son's own needs first.

When you yourself cannot. When you cannot see past the hatred and fury and fear to sort out what August requires.

He thrust aside that damning taunt reverberating around his mind. "One note to your family," he clipped out, "and the damned mattress. What else?"

She settled back in her chair, now entirely too comfortable with her hold on the conversation. And why shouldn't she be? This was yet another time this woman, and the Diggorys as a whole, had bested him. "As I was saying earlier, about the furniture . . ." Miss Killoran chewed at her lower lip, her porcelain-white teeth troubling that plump flesh, drawing his attention where it should not go. "Living in the Dials, one becomes accustomed to . . ." She scrunched her brow.

Tick. Tock. Tick. Tock. Tick. To—

"Accustomed to what?" he snapped.

"Hiding their cherished belongings."

What in blazes was she on about? "I don't understand." Such had been the state of his existence for nearly a decade now.

"There need to be clever compartments and locks and—"

"You are asking me to commission furniture so that my son can hide his belongings? Like a common street thief?"

She beamed. "Precisely."

And blast if she didn't make him feel like the dim-witted student who'd at last mastered his lessons. "It was a damned rhetorical question," he said tightly.

"Well, it is what he was." Edwin went cold at the calmness of that somber deliverance. "He was a pickpocket more years than he was an earl."

"It is what you made him," Edwin thundered, slamming his fist down so hard the half-drunk snifter of brandy jumped, sloshing several drops over the rim and marring the leather surface of his desk.

The young woman jumped up and had a dagger in hand, pointed at him, before the last residual of his accusation echoed around the room.

Edwin smiled coldly at that dagger leveled on his throat. "You fear the madman after all, I see," he jeered.

Gertrude Killoran opened and closed her mouth several times, her stricken gaze alternating quickly between the weapon she wielded and his face. "I did not . . . I would not . . ."

"What?" he mocked. "Harm me or my family?"

With fingers that shook, she leaned down and, edging up her skirts, inserted the blade into a clever strap attached to her ankle, drawing Edwin's gaze there, to the flash of trim, cream-white flesh revealed above the pale-pink silk stockings.

His face hot, Edwin whipped his head up.

He'd been too long without a woman. There was no other accounting for this lusting after a Killoran . . . and a Killoran who'd pulled a weapon on him in his own home, no less.

The young woman finally lifted her eyes once more to his.

"Let us be clear," he said with a restoration of his icy control. "My son has always been an earl."

"I understand that."

"Do you?" he shot back. "Do you know that August has the blood of marquesses that runs more than six hundred years flowing in his veins? Now"—he tipped his chin at her—"say whatever business it is you've sought me out for." So he could be done with her and try to regain control of his senses.

She managed a jerky nod. "Uh—yes. As I was saying . . ."

"My son, the thief." It was a reminder he made for himself. That this woman and her kin had transformed not only his life but also his son's into one of sin and shame.

"People who have lived in the streets cannot ever fully divest themselves of their past."

"And you believe the nobility is able to . . . what? Simply forget *our* past?"

She flinched.

Did he imagine the regret and pain that sparked in her eyes?

"No," she said quietly. "I do not believe . . . they can forget." Gertrude Killoran glanced briefly back at the doorway, and then when she returned her attention forward and again spoke, she did so in hushed tones. Ones belonging to a person who feared there was someone lurking about, listening . . . "Regardless of the wrong done to both you and your son, the fact remains that this has been the life he's lived, and as such, he can no sooner separate himself from who he's become than"—she nudged her head slightly in Edwin's direction—"you can separate from whom you've become."

Bitter. Broken. Angry. Wary. Empty. They were all parts of whom he'd forever be after Diggory's treacherous act. Having August back, reestablishing a life together with the son he'd lost, would never, ever take away . . . everything that had been visited upon them.

Edwin glanced at the floor-length windows, the drapes of which hadn't been drawn for years, only today opened for the first time. "August will have a say in the commissioning of new furniture," he said dismissively.

"I will let my brother know that tomorrow at noon, after his lessons are concluded, we may begin the process."

Her brother. This time Edwin managed to swallow the jeering retort.

Several moments passed, and Gertrude Killoran made no move to leave.

"What. Else?" he enunciated each of those words, stretching them out. Layering a warning within. He'd made all the concessions he intended to this day.

The young woman cleared her throat. "There still remains the reason for my visit."

They still hadn't . . . ? *Bloody hell.* "There's more?"

"There's more," she confirmed with a nod.

There always was with these people. They were collectively determined to steal any and every shred of peace from his existence.

"What?" he clipped out.

He'd hand it to the woman. Most any other lady would have shaken at that sharp command. But then this was no ordinary woman, and certainly no lady.

"With regard to his name," she began, smoothing her palms along her skirts.

"August," he snapped.

"Yes, I understand that is his name, as do you, my lord."

He'd have to be deaf as a post to fail to hear the lingering statement hanging on her sentence. "However?"

Several lines creased Miss Killoran's high brow. "Beg pardon?"

"There was, I trust, a 'however' there, Miss Killoran?"

"Oh, uh . . . yes." She flashed a pleased smile. "There was." She began again. "I understand there has been some confusion in what to call him."

"No," he said flatly. Climbing to his feet, he stalked back over to his sideboard with his snifter in hand. He assessed the row of decanters and grabbed the nearest, fullest bottle. Many times he'd turned to drink. After his townhouse had been burnt down and his wife and unborn babe had perished. Then in the subsequent days when the nightmares came. "There is not," he clarified. "It is quite clear as to what August should"—and more importantly should not—"be called."

"And though I'd not intended to debate the matter of names with you," she went on as though Edwin had not even spoken.

My God, the insolence of the chit. She was breathtaking and infuriating all at once. "Good." Edwin hooded his lashes. "Then don't."

"But," she persisted, "I suggest it would be beneficial if we also speak about forms of address."

"Forms of address," he echoed dumbly.

"Names," she clarified with a perfunctory nod of a noticeably untidy chignon. "For all of us."

Decanter and glass in hand, Edwin sank his hip onto the edge of the mahogany sideboard. Good God, the whole world had been turned upside down. And here he'd believed his life couldn't become any more disordered than it had been these past seven years. He poured himself a healthy glass. Thought better of it and added several more fingers into his snifter.

"You prefer to call him August."

His hand shook, splashing several droplets over the rim. With a curse that would have sent any proper lady to blushing, Edwin slammed his bottle down. "Because it is his name."

This woman, however, remained implacable. Calm when others would have either run off crying or cowered before him. "It is not the name he has gone by these past seven years, my lord," Miss Killoran said quietly in sober tones.

Suspicion darkened the back corner of his mind. "Surely you are not suggesting . . . ?" Unable to finish the rest of that query, he tried again. "Never tell me you expect . . . ?" Again the remainder of that failed him. "What in blazes are you saying?" he snapped.

Gertrude Killoran sailed to her feet, and turning a palm out, she walked closer. "I understand his name is, in fact, August. I understand he is an earl, and your son, and that my family is n-not his." That single trembling syllable was the only indication of weakness she'd otherwise not shown. A quake that wasn't a signal of her fear, but rather her heartbreak.

Do not be fooled by her or any other Killoran. Their skills at deception could rival the most accomplished actor on any London stage.

"Out with it, Miss Killoran," he said coolly.

Only . . .

As she lifted her gaze to his, the pain and regret spilling from within their brown depths made a mockery of his frostiness. And goddamn it if she didn't look like a kicked dog, and he the very bully who'd seen to the kicking. "His name is August. You and I know that. My family knows that." He stilled at that allusion to her equally hated kin. "Even Stephen knows that," she said softly, drifting closer. "And someday he will take ownership of that name and take pride in it as he should."

Some unfamiliar scent clung to her skin. It wafted about his senses, dangerously quixotic for the pull of it, and he fought through the thick haze cast by the unlikeliest of people, to attend her. Tread carefully.

Monitor. Watch her at every turn. It was a litany he clung to; otherwise, she'd win at whatever game she and her kind played.

At last, Gertrude Killoran stopped before him with a few paces between them; it was enough space that with the height difference, they might meet one another's gazes. Or was it distance she herself also craved around him? "But my lord," she finally went on. "That time is not now," she said flatly, effectively killing whatever momentary spell she'd cast and returning them both to the battle they waged. "Now is a time for making Stephen feel comfortable and secure, and you"—she took a step closer and continued coming until only a step separated them—"insisting that he change, insisting that he shed who he's been and the people he has called family, will not endear him to you."

Edwin balled his hands, damning her. Damning her family. Damning his bloody life and the mess it had become. "I don't need to endear myself to him." It was true and yet not at the same time.

He may as well have remarked upon the weather for the casual up-and-down glance Gertrude gave him. "I don't believe you mean that."

"I don't care what you believe," he thundered, slamming his drink down. The delicate stem of his glass splintered and sent the bowl of the snifter tumbling, spraying the drink cart and floor with a steady stream of amber.

Miss Killoran's cheeks went an ashen white, but God help him, she remained rooted before him. Unbending in her courage and unwavering in her determination. That strength she proved herself in full possession of as she was the first to speak after his outburst. "Allowing Stephen the right to a name he feels comfortable with will allow him to see that you do not reject him."

"I do not reject him," he said, her insinuation grating on his nerves. "I'm the one who insisted he return."

"You are also the one who learned of his existence and allowed him to remain with my family and still did not believe he was yours . . . until you saw the proof upon his skin," she corrected, tenacious at every turn.

He winced. For damn if the chit wasn't correct. His mind and soul shied away from the reasons for that decision. "I don't owe you any explanations," he barked.

Miss Killoran lifted her shoulders in a little shrug. "I am not asking for them." She folded her palms before her in that prim abbess's way she had, which was utter rubbish given she'd lived amongst the most ruthless gang in all of London. "I'm merely trying to help ease *August's* return into his new world."

New. Old. Edwin wouldn't debate her on this particular point. Restless, he stalked over to the floor-to-ceiling window that overlooked the streets below. Clasping his hands at his back, he stared out. A sea of passersby lingered upon the pavement, whispering, stealing glances, pointing at the doorway, periodically nodding to one another.

They were lords and ladies dressed in the finest garments, accustomed only to the world of Polite Society.

And then there was August. August, who, as Gertrude Killoran so aptly pointed out, was an outsider. And likely always would be. Scandal would always follow his name. Talks and whispers of August's days in the streets, and the fire that claimed his mother, and the pockets he'd picked, and—

Edwin's eyes slid closed, and he squeezed them shut.

He didn't want to call his son anything other than the name that he'd personally selected for the child. A family name his wife had simply agreed to. Back when everything had been . . . simpler. And yet, at the same time, not. How complicated those earliest days of his marriage, and then fatherhood, had been. "Stephen, then," he said, that concession costing him the remaining piece of his soul he'd not sold along the way to this point. "Now get the hell out."

"I'm afraid there is still one matter I'd discuss with you."

"Never tell me," he boomed, sweeping his arms wide. "My family's silver. The jewels passed down since William the Conqueror."

"I've no need of jewels or silver," she said calmly.

"I was being facetious."

"Well, I was being honest. It is a good deal more useful than"—she flicked a disapproving stare up and down his frame—"facetiousness."

"If you're opting for directness, have out with the remaining favor you'd put to me."

"My name is Gertrude."

Oh, God in heaven. What in blazes was this game? "I know your name, Miss Killoran," he said dismissively.

She shook her head. "No. I'm indicating that you should, as long as I'm living here—"

"A fortnight." He supplied that reminder for himself that her time here was limited, and then he could move on to building a new life with his son. "Until a proper governess is found for my son."

"In that time, however long it may take, you should call me by my Christian name." She paused. "Gertrude," she repeated. "Rather, we should call one another by our Christian names."

Edwin ignored the latter part of that suggestion. "Do spawns of the Devil have Christian names?" he taunted.

Miss Killoran lifted her head, regal like a princess and in possession of heaps more strength and power. "Actually, they do not. My brother Broderick conferred one upon my sisters and me when I was near two and ten years."

That knocked him back, the unexpectedness of that composed revelation hitting him square in the chest. She'd been without a name, the most basic thing passed to a child. It required no coin and only a thought from a parent. Only, she—Gertrude—had been without. This was an unwanted look at how she . . . and his enemies within that gang . . . had lived. It humanized her when that weakening would certainly only set him up for peril. And yet, there it was.

Miss Killoran—Gertrude—lifted her chin in mutinous defiance.

And a kernel of some emotion so very unexpected for this woman pitted low in his gut—guilt.

She continued as if they spoke casually over tea and biscuits. "It would do good for Stephen to see some amicability between us."

Edwin dragged a hand over his brow. "Edwin," he forced out between clenched teeth. "My name is Edwin. I'll call you by your damned name, but I draw the line at any pretend shows of friendship. Now, is there anything else," he said firmly, this time with a warning. This time, resolved to throw her out on her arse before he conceded another proverbial inch.

She shook her head. "No. Thank you . . . Edwin." Gertrude glided over to the doorway, her skirts sweeping about her ankles at the long steps she took. When she had her fingers on the handle of the door, she stopped and glanced back. "That will be all." She paused. "For now."

With that ominous warning, she swept from the room.

Edwin stood there, unease settling in every corner of his life-hardened body, and he was unable to shake the possibility that he'd made a perilous misstep in allowing Gertrude Killoran to call this townhouse home for even a day more.

Chapter 9

For a person unfortunate enough to live in the Dials, timing was everything.

Every fragile piece of a person's existence hung upon the whisper of a second. If one was late or miscalculated one's timing, invariably one fell—to the lord whose pocket one nicked, to the constable there to cart one off, and then ultimately to the noose looped over one's neck as one took that final lesson to the unmarked grave for common street thieves.

Having witnessed enough hangings to haunt her for each day she had remaining on this earth, Gertrude had developed early on an appreciation for punctuality.

And had little patience for those who did not possess a like value and understanding of it.

The following day, standing in the center of the foyer, she stole yet another peek at the walnut longcase clock. She squinted, struggling in the more dimly lit entryway to bring those hands into focus. Unable to make sense of the numbers, she drifted closer until they pulled into focus.

Four and ten minutes past twelve?

Blast and damn. Where in blazes was he?

"Bloody nob," Stephen muttered.

Gertrude yanked her attention away from the clock and looked at the angry little figure sprawled on the first marble step of the marquess's sweeping, winged stairway.

Lying on his back, Stephen drew his dagger on the cherub overhead, then sheathed it. He drew it again, on another.

Reggie's brother hovered off to the side. His cheeks were a stark white as he took in that violent display.

"Put that away, Stephen," she scolded, stalking over. She'd not further feed the ill opinion the world held of the Killorans.

"I'm not doing anything," Stephen protested, leveling the tip of his blade on one particularly cheerful winged angel overhead.

"Stephen," she said, this time nothing more than his name, spoken in the warning tone she'd used on all the children in Diggory's gang through the years.

"Fine, fine," he groused. He propelled himself upright, and in one fluid movement that barely ruffled the cuff of his tan trousers, he sheathed the dagger given him by Broderick.

The clock chimed, marking the quarter hour. Gertrude glanced around in search of Edwin. Arriving late to one's first appointment with his son hardly marked an auspicious beginning for the newly reunited pair. And yet he'd agreed to the appointment. She'd been able to reason with him. He'd put his son's feelings and wants ahead of his own. Those weren't the actions of a madman not in control of his faculties. She chewed at her lower lip. Who *was* the Marquess of Maddock? That question whispered forward once more, needing to be answered. Was he the madman the world accused him of being, a reminder he tossed out at their every meeting? Or was he a devoted father who'd been so riddled by the pain of losing his family that he'd simply come to believe the words spoken about him? *Or mayhap you simply wish to reassure yourself, for Stephen's and your own benefit, that you've not willingly committed to living with a volatile lunatic.*

Mr. Marlow, who'd been lingering in the shadows, spoke for a second time since Gertrude and Stephen had arrived and she'd donned her cloak. "The carriage is readied, Miss Killoran," he said, cutting across her musings.

"Yes, you said as much," she replied absently, doing another search for the marquess.

Nay—Edwin. It was a name that suited him in some ways, conjuring that tale of the great king of Northumbria, exiled.

Do you truly believe that angry, coldhearted man who taunted you at every turn would join you for an outing? Even if it was with his son?

Only, Gertrude's family was responsible for the misery he'd known. Mayhap that hatred was reserved for her, and when she left, he'd again learn to be happy with the son he'd—

Mr. Marlow coughed.

"Is there something wrong with you?" Before the young man could reply, Stephen added, "You don't have consumption, do you?" He backed away from the butler.

"Do not be ridiculous." Splotches of color filled Mr. Marlow's cheeks. "I was merely attempting to gain Miss Killoran's attention."

Stephen scoffed. "*Pfft*, ain't the way to grab anyone's attention. You want her attention, you say, 'I need to talk to you about business.' Or—"

"Stephen," Gertrude warned. "Return to what you were doing before."

The stubborn boy pouted. "I'm not a child to be ordered about."

She skewered him with a glare.

"Fine, fine," he mumbled, but she'd have to be completely blind to fail to note the eagerness in those little fingers as he grabbed his knife and proceeded to point it ominously overhead at the marquess's mural.

Her brother attending his threatening task, Gertrude drifted over to Mr. Marlow. Alas, despite the low opinion of her survival skills, Gertrude was no fool and knew her brother enough to glean his ears were attuned to the exchange taking place without him.

"What is it, Mr. Marlow?" she asked in barely audible tones.

"Miss Killoran, it is—"

"Gertrude, please," she put forward instead. "Given that your sister has been like another sibling to me and is now my sister by marriage, we should dispense with the formalities." She forced a smile for the young man's benefit.

He bowed his head. "Marlow."

Gertrude cast a glance over her shoulder at Stephen, still engrossed in his foreboding study of the painting overhead. When she spoke, she lowered her voice all the more. "You wished to speak with me?"

"It is about your scheduled outing for this afternoon." He leaned closer and said in a pathetically loud whisper: "You are . . . *certain* that His Lordship indicated his intentions to go?"

"Most certain," she said automatically. Reaching inside the pocket sewn along the front of her cloak, she began to draw out the pair of serviceable French leather gloves tucked there. Sethos nosed at her finger, and she gave him a discreet, reassuring pat. "I was quite clear about the time we would be departing." She frowned. "Is he not here?" she asked. Drawing one of the brown leather gloves on, she buttoned it at the wrist.

"No. He is here. In his offices." Marlow wrung his hands together.

Gertrude remained silent, giving the young man the time he required.

"Lord Maddock generally does not leave the townhouse to oversee . . . business." From behind his lenses, regret glimmered in his eyes. "The world has not been so very kind to the marquess."

You fear the madman, after all, I see. The memory of Edwin's taunt brought her up short, and she paused with the other glove in hand, forgotten. She'd been so very focused on her family's loss and Stephen's return to his rightful place and fear over living—and leaving Stephen—with Lord Maddock that she'd simply glossed over what life surely had been like for the marquess . . . before Stephen's return. Branded a murderer of his wife and babe, accused of arson, and scorned by society for those claims, Edwin had lived a life in exile. Not so very different from the king whose name he carried. The suffering he'd endured would have turned most sane men not. Her frown deepened. She and her family had erroneously believed Stephen the most affected, and yet . . . in Edwin's case, one could not simply relegate the seven hellish years that came before as forgotten. She sighed and again glanced at the clock. At the very least, the gentleman required her patience.

"His Lordship indicated he'd come, and he does not strike me as one who'd renege upon his word." In his failure to gather Stephen from the Devil's Den and now to arrive in the foyer for their scheduled appointment, however, he had demonstrated that punctuality was not amongst his strengths.

Still, Quint Marlow hovered. "I'm not certain you are correct, Miss—Gertrude. No offense meant," he said on a rush. "His Lordship tends to avoid Polite Society."

Her heart pulled. Given how the world freely spoke of him and his circumstances? The gentleman was better off. "Wise man," she muttered, shoving her other fingers into the leather scrap.

Mr. Marlow angled his right ear toward her. "I beg your pardon?"

Gertrude patted his arm. "That isolation was before his son's arrival," she substituted instead. "Everything has changed now." For all of them. With determined steps, Gertrude started down the hall.

"Miss . . . Gertrude," Mr. Marlow stammered, rushing after her. "*Where* are you going?"

"To fetch His Lordship." Gertrude didn't break her stride, and even though taller, Reggie's brother struggled to keep pace.

"To fetch . . . ?" By the horror lacing that unfinished echo, she might as well have stated her intentions to gather up the jewels tracing back to the first Marquess of Maddock. "But . . . His Lordship does not welcome intrusions from anybody."

This time, Gertrude stopped so quickly the servant stumbled out of the way to keep from knocking into her. "Ah," she said with a wag of her finger. "But I am *not* just anybody."

Reggie's brother eyed her warily.

She flashed him a reassuring smile. "I'm Stephen's sister."

The other man slapped his palms over his face, muffling the groan that escaped him. "Miss Killoran," he entreated.

"No. No," Gertrude cut him off. "I'd advise you to go watch after Stephen, lest he run . . . off." Quint Marlow was already sprinting in the opposite direction toward her brother.

She gave her head a bemused shake and resumed her march to Edwin's offices. Poor Mr. Marlow. She'd spent all the years lamenting the existence she'd lived in the Dials: a life of fear, poverty, uncertainty. But she'd learned to conquer fear so that it did not serve as master to her. She'd not wish to go back to the life she'd known, but she'd also carried away with her valuable lessons which would never have her stammering and stumbling as Reggie's brother did.

Gertrude reached Edwin's offices and rapped. "Edwin?" she called, leaning into the ornate oak panel.

A faint, muffled cursing reached her ears, followed by the rapid beat of angry footfalls.

She wrinkled her brow. Now, that was hardly a congenial welcome for the person who'd be calling his house home—albeit a temporary one. Why, her speech to him yesterday may as well have fallen on deaf ears. Nonetheless, as he yanked open the door, she swiftly plastered a smile upon her face.

"What in . . . ?" His brusque question trailed off. His penetrating brown gaze went to her mouth and lingered there.

Her heart beat a funny little rhythm. Did she imagine the heated intensity of that stare? For there was something else there. A spark of the desire she'd seen in the eyes of countless patrons in her family's clubs. But never had she been a recipient of it . . .

"What in hell do you want, Miss Kill—" He flushed. "Gertrude," he substituted.

And those frosty, indifferent tones had the same effect as the bucket of freezing rainwater Diggory's men had once doused her with, for no other reason than the cruelty of it.

"You are late," she said evenly. Unfastening the latch at her throat, Gertrude loosened her cloak and displayed the pearl-set brooch watch affixed to the front of her dress. She tapped her index finger against the face of the timepiece. "Now eight and ten minutes late."

Edwin cocked his head. "Late for *what*?"

For what? She opened her mouth to chide him, when Mr. Marlow's words from a short while ago flickered forward.

. . . *Lord Maddock generally does not leave the townhouse to oversee . . . business . . . The world has not been so very kind to the marquess . . .*

How very difficult all this would be for him. He'd gone from widower and father to a murdered child . . . to a father once more.

All her outrage dissolved, and Gertrude resolved to answer his curtness with kindness. "May I enter?" she asked quietly.

She was determined to torture him.

There was nothing else for it. And no other explaining it.

Gertrude, a Killoran or Diggory or whatever she fashioned herself on a given day, one day would see him completely mad.

And by God if it didn't seem that this would be the exchange to put him beyond the point of no return.

"May I enter?" she repeated.

Wordlessly, he stepped aside, allowing Gertrude to sweep forward, her muslin skirts swirling about trim ankles encased in soft-blue silk stockings.

It was an odd detail to note. A dangerous one.

Neck burning, he shoved the door shut, hard. "You have two minutes," he said sharply.

The young woman glanced over at the ledgers laid out upon his desk, and this time, uninvited, she drifted over to his desk.

Edwin stiffened, all his muscles screaming with the urge to demand she stop.

Gertrude paused alongside his desk. "Hmm," she said noncommittally as she took in the leather journals piled around. Books he'd neglected for too long; turning them over to Quint Marlow's expert hand had seen his estates in largely a good place. And yet . . . there had been errors made, too. Just another failure on his part. "Ah. I see," she finally said, glancing back over her shoulder.

And she sounded very much like one who did see, though for the life of him, he didn't have a bloody clue what in blazes she thought she saw. "What?" he snapped, folding his arms defensively at his chest.

This time as she spoke, he detected a layer of gentleness to Gertrude's words. "You were busy with your accounting." She nodded her head, almost approvingly. As if he sought or needed approval from her or anyone else. "*Many* people forget appointments," she said in placating tones. "It happens to everyone at some point or another."

Forget appointments? What in blazes was she talking about?

"If it is a habit you have, Edwin, I would suggest a daily diary." He lowered his brow. What . . . ? "A commercial diary?" she clarified. "A portable account book?" she prodded through his blank confusion. "Oh, you must have one." She gave a firm, finalizing nod. "They are quite popular in the Americas. Their George Washington and Thomas Jefferson insisted upon carrying one."

A strangled choking sound escaped Edwin. "George . . . ?"

"Washington," she stretched out those three syllables like one would when speaking to a slow-witted child.

Edwin closed his eyes and counted to ten, praying for patience. "I know who George Washington is," he said coolly.

"Ah, forgive me." Except she didn't sound *or* appear even remotely apologetic. "I forget you are . . . very . . ." She chewed at that enticingly full lower lip, drawing his gaze there, stirring an awareness that he didn't wish to have of this woman. She dipped her voice to a husked whisper that washed over him, tempting, captivating. *"British."*

And then that word, whispered like an insult she'd sought to hide, sank through the quagmire of inexplicable awareness he had of her. *"You* are also very *British*, madam."

"It is not quite the same, though, is it?"

Do not engage her. Let the matter rest. No good could come in discussing any of this . . . whatever this was . . . with her. Except . . . she looked so very damned knowing. "In what way is your Britishness different from my own?"

Gertrude smoothed her palms down the front of her muslin skirts, warming to her topic. "You are a marquess, and I was born on the streets."

"I know very well the differences between our stations," he said without inflection. She and her family were guttersnipes who'd risen to kings and queens of the underworld. And she'd also been a girl without a name. A vise squeezed at his chest. And he who'd believed himself incapable of feeling anything was proven wrong, and for this woman, no less.

"Given that difference, I expect we do not have the same loyalty to king and country."

He narrowed his eyes. "Most would consider that a hanging admission, madam."

"And *that* is precisely the difference between us." Gertrude shrugged. "Regardless, I'm guiltier of far more crimes than those very true words."

Edwin rocked back on his heels. How very . . . direct and . . . real this woman was. There was no effortful attempt to mask one's true meaning, as had been the way of his late wife and every other proper lady he'd known. It left him disconcerted in ways he'd never been.

"As I was saying," she went on, redirecting them back to whatever nonsense she'd been rambling on about. Gertrude once more tapped the place where her timepiece rested. "Daily diaries are tremendously beneficial to those who struggle with honoring strict schedules."

Edwin ground his teeth, the rows scraping sharply against one another. "I do not forget appointments or meetings, madam."

"To the contrary." She lifted a long ink-stained finger, pointing it at the ceiling. "You are late for one even now."

"With *whom*?"

She released an exasperated sigh, that slight exhalation sending an artfully arranged lone curl dancing back and forth over her brow. "Stephen and me."

He searched his suddenly muddled mind. A mind he'd believed jumbled after his life had fallen apart, only to find he'd been in far stricter control of his thoughts. "What are you talking about?" he asked in pained tones.

"The cabinetmaker."

Oh, so that was what this was all about. At last. Edwin returned to his desk and, with the young woman's attention directed at him, swiftly closed those ledgers that revealed details of his finances for the past four years. "Rest assured, madam—"

"Gertrude," she supplied. "Remember, we've agreed to an amicable relationship as long as I live here."

"Three and ten days," he muttered. And then she'd be gone, and he could return to some semblance of naturalness with his son. Edwin's palms went moist, and he discreetly wiped them along the sides of his trousers.

Gertrude cupped a palm around her right ear and leaned forward. "What was that?"

The insolent minx no more had hearing problems than he had. She knew very well what he'd said. "I said you have an appointment."

Gertrude shook her head. "I've handled the appointment."

Edwin laid his palms on opposite sides of the desk and leaned forward. "Madam, I do not care if you, or I, or Satan himself scheduled a damned meeting. The only relevant detail is that it has been made, and you are in fact late for your meeting with Mr. Seddon." As if on perfect cue, the hall clock chimed the thirtieth minute on the hour.

"No," Gertrude said slowly. "*We* are late for an appointment I've secured, not with your Mr. Seddon but with my fam—" He sharpened his eyes upon her. "My cabinetmaker," she settled for.

Edwin remained frozen with his palms pressed to his desk. "Your meeting is with Mr. Thomas Seddon."

Gertrude wrinkled her nose. "Who is that?"

"He is a cabinetmaker whose late uncle only employed more than four hundred—" A sparkle lit one of her eyes, the other curiously blank. And yet. My God, she was teasing him. The minx. "Thomas Seddon is the nephew of the late George Seddon. Their family has designed every piece within this townhouse." And every piece that had been burnt at her ruthless father's hands. Hatred for the man who'd sired her raced through his veins, burning him with its ferocity.

"I thank you for coordinating the meeting—"

"You are welcome."

"However, you will have to send a cancellation around. Our appointment is scheduled with Mr. Gunner Draven."

Gunner Draven? What kind of name was that? "I've never heard of him," he said flatly.

"No worries," Gertrude said, flashing a wide smile. It dimpled her cheeks and lit her face, transforming her from plain miss . . . into someone quite extraordinary.

He recoiled. "Good God."

"Oh, come. Using a different designer will not be so very bad as all that," she assured, mistaking the reason for his horror.

Then the implications of what she'd said moments ago registered. "Why . . . why . . ." He straightened. "You think I'm *accompanying* you?"

"No." Her dazzling smile widened. "I know you are." Gertrude fiddled with her pocket, searching her fingers around, and as she did, she started for the door. "As it is, we are late."

She'd already opened it and stepped outside—before she noted him inside his office still.

Gertrude ducked back into the rooms.

"I'm not coming," he said flatly. He'd made more concessions than he ought where this family was concerned: Gertrude's presence here, his son's name, the commissioning of new furniture. "That was never part of the discussion." He drew the damned line at joining her and Stephen in broad daylight. Edwin avoided stepping outside during the fashionable hours because invariably stares and whispers followed his every movement. It had simply become . . . easier, following altogether different hours than those set by proper society.

"Hmm," she said vaguely, chewing at the tip of her gloved fingertip, eyeing him like he was an exhibit at the British Museum. She could stare, barter, cajole, or employ whichever trickery she wished—he had no intention of accompanying them or rising to her bait.

"What?" he bit out, proving weak once more.

"It is nothing," she said with a toss of her head. "I just had this silly idea that you'd"—she rolled her eye, the other remaining unaffected under that subtle movement—"insist on accompanying us out of some silly fear because I'm a Killoran." Gertrude laughed, an airy and bell-like expression that pinged around the room. Enthralling as the blasted woman herself was. "Good day, Edwin." With that, she turned on her heel and marched off.

Thank God, she was gone. Striding over, he kicked the panel closed with the heel of his boot. "Accompany her," he muttered. As if he wanted to . . . or could reenter society. He wanted no part of the stares and the whispers that followed his every movement. Why . . . He stopped suddenly. She intended to go alone. Despite the orders he'd given her yesterday. *She insisted you join them, and yet you urged her to go off by herself.* "Over my dead body," he seethed. Cursing roundly, Edwin yanked the door open and let himself out. "Miss Killoran—Gertrude," he thundered.

The young woman stopped and turned back with an infuriating slowness. "Edwin?"

"I'll accompany you."

She smiled once more. "Splendid. Shall we go, then?"

And as he joined her and headed to the foyer to meet his son, Edwin could not help but feel he'd been tricked once more by the scheming young woman.

Chapter 10

The *clip-clop* of the horses' hooves and the rumble of the carriage wall added the only sounds to the otherwise tense carriage ride from Edwin's Grosvenor Square residence to the streets of St. Giles.

Seated on the comfortable gold velvet squabs of the marquess's black conveyance, Gertrude made a show of studying the passing scenery as stucco-and-brick townhouses with handsomely dressed lords and ladies eventually gave way to dilapidated buildings, narrower streets, and the squalor that had marked the whole of her existence. All the while, she attended the pair opposite her: Edwin and a glowering Stephen.

Father and son. They were a pairing of a blond, muscular, hulking bearlike figure of a man and a golden-haired child who was waiflike in his build. To pass them on the streets, even with their similar fine wool garments and gleaming black boots, by the aloofness between them, one would never venture the pair was related in any way.

Edwin and Stephen sat with their backs slightly presented to one another, stiffly impersonal, not touching, not looking at one another. Strangers, in every way.

And Gertrude's heart cracked, broke, and then bled for the both of them.

She was not so very delusional nor naive to believe that a bond automatically existed between a parent and his or her child. She wasn't. Somewhere between her own sire's indifference and the beatings he'd rained down upon her, she'd learned that blood did not a bond make.

No, Mac Diggory could have seen Gertrude cut down in the street and would have stepped over her dead body without a backward glance, for as little as he'd cared about her.

But Edwin . . . he'd proven himself to be different. Oh, he'd been so very determined to be hostile and keep impenetrable walls around himself.

And yet, at every turn, he'd proven himself a man able to set aside his own resentments and hatred in the best interests of his son. That sacrifice for another was one she and her siblings knew all too well. They would have killed or taken the fall for one another. But never had she known a parent capable of that devotion or love.

And something in that . . . in seeing the battle he fought within himself while ultimately always putting Stephen's well-being first, sent warmth spiraling in her chest.

The carriage hit a broken cobble, and Edwin cursed. He finally released the brocade curtain and looked forward. "Where in hell are we going?" As soon as that profanity had left him, he glanced over at Stephen. "I . . ."

For the first time, the child looked upon the marquess with something other than disdain. A blend of curiosity and amusement filled Stephen's eyes. "*You* curse?"

Edwin tugged at his slightly wrinkled cravat. "Occasionally." Stephen's face fell, and he started to look away. "Regularly," the marquess corrected, and his son froze, glancing back. "All the time."

Stephen gave an approving nod, and at that small but meaningful moment of bonding between father and son, a sheen of tears dusted her vision. Gertrude blinked them back. Both Stephen and Edwin would be repulsed by that expression, taking it for weakness, and it would only shatter the moment.

The tension Stephen had been carrying in his small frame eased as he shifted on the bench. "You curse in front of women?" He pointed over at Gertrude. "I mean . . . it is just Gertrude, but my brother says a man shouldn't curse in front of a woman. Says it ain't polite."

Edwin blanched. To his credit, the marquess swiftly schooled his features so that his face remained a careful mask. "*Killoran* . . . was correct. I will strive to use more care in my speech around women."

Stephen sat upright and glared daggers at the man next to him. And just like that the shared moment between father and son . . . was shattered. "That is *Mr.* Killoran to you. Broderick to me. Because he is my brother."

"Stephen," Gertrude warned, giving her head a firm shake. "Enough," she mouthed.

Edwin stiffened.

"Well, he is." Stephen turned tauntingly back to the marquess. "Broderick made his own fortune and protected me and the women he was responsible for." He sneered. "Which is more than I can say for you," he spat.

Edwin's entire body recoiled like he'd been punched in the belly.

Gertrude gasped and sprang forward in her seat. "Stephen," she hissed, at last managing to silence the boy. Belatedly.

With a go-to-hell shrug, Stephen offered his back up toward his father once more and looked out at the now-familiar streets of St. Giles.

Biting the inside of her lip, Gertrude stared hopelessly at the marquess.

His chiseled cheeks a ghastly shade of grey, motionless, he was a man who'd been wounded . . . and badly. Long before this latest vicious verbal assault carried out by his own son, and an inadvertent product of the man the same child now defended. Stephen might not remember the mother or life he'd had ripped from him, but those losses were real and no doubt raw for his father.

Gertrude stared at the mutinously silent pair. *Blast.* This was not the way she'd imagined the day going for Stephen and his father. They were to have come together and slowly begun to learn about one another. Her visions of the day had certainly not included Stephen throwing his mother's death in the widowed marquess's face.

And for the first time since she'd crafted this scheme on her own to join Stephen in his new household and help smooth his way, easing the tense relationship between father and son . . . she wavered.

Ya're nothing but a failure, girl. No reason to keep ya around, ya blind bitch . . . If it weren't for Broderick, I would have knifed ya in yar sleep long ago . . . done ya a favor . . .

Gertrude's fingers twitched with her need to clamp them over her ears and blot out that hated Cockney. She focused on drawing in slow, steadying breaths through her nose. All the while, she fought her past and the oldest insecurities she'd carried about her own self-worth.

Or, rather, the lack thereof.

Gertrude reached inside her pocket and found Sethos there, taking some comfort in that small, soft creature. To no avail. A panicky laugh swelled in her chest and caught in her throat. What had made her think she, of anyone, could help in any way . . . Her, the weak, pathetic, pitiable Gertrude Killoran?

Stop. Do not let him in. Do not let him win. Do not . . .

The carriage slowed, pushing the past out and the present thankfully forward where it belonged.

"We've arrived," Edwin murmured.

"Finally," Stephen muttered. And not even waiting until the conveyance rocked to a complete stop, the boy shoved the door open and leapt out, leaving Gertrude and Edwin . . . *alone.*

From the doorway, she followed his quick steps as he darted along the pavement and up the handful of cracked stone stairs of Mr. Gunner Draven's establishment.

Edwin made no move to climb out. He remained fixed to his bench, his cheeks ashen, the muscles of his face tense. He didn't wish to be here . . . but was his response a product of where they'd gone? Or of a man rumored to have lived in isolation, fearful of reentering the world of the living?

As if he'd followed the questions running through her mind, Edwin stiffened. Without sparing her a look, he started for the doorway.

"I wanted to apologize," she called out, staying him.

He sat back on the bench and arched a cool blond eyebrow.

"For Stephen," she added lamely, her mind still jumbled from her latest haunting by Mac Diggory. She forced herself to focus, owing it to Stephen and this man before her. "Stephen is an angry boy," she explained, braced for the usual—and deserved—blame he'd shower upon her. That this time . . . did not come. Encouraged by his silence, she slipped through the crack he allowed her. "He is angry because of what he's seen and done. And yes," she put in before he could and they dissolved once more into hated foes, "it is my family's fault—even inadvertent though it may have been." Gertrude stretched a hand out. "But there is so very much good in Stephen. He is loyal and loving, even if . . . there is just an odd way in how he shows it. And he's clever, not only in matters of survival but also in his schooling." A wad of emotion stuck in her throat, and she laughed around it. "Though he'd fight anyone for daring to call him a scholar. He'll come 'round," she promised. "Someday." Hopefully soon. But with his streak of Killoran stubbornness, that day might well come when he went on to meet his maker, many, many years from now. An awkward silence met her telling. "I just wanted you to know that," she added, when Edwin still made no attempt to reply.

"Apricot tarts."

Gertrude angled her head and sought to understand that random statement, not even a sentence. "I don't—"

"It was his favorite treat. Cook made it daily for him, and there was always additional left in the kitchens because without fail, August would awaken in the dead of night. Always past two o'clock. Always before five o'clock. He would creep to the side of my bed, and at those times, we'd sneak down to the empty kitchens and eat one together."

Once more, her vision blurred from another sting of tears. From the tale Edwin shared, he presented an image she couldn't understand in life but had always dreamed of . . . a loving father and his cherished child. Not a babe turned over to the care of a nursemaid, but one who'd loved his father so dearly he'd sought him out first when sleep eluded him. And his father had not sent him on his way. Rather, he'd joined him. And in that moment, she had the answer to the question that had riddled her mind since she'd arrived—the marquess hadn't been mad prior to losing his family. She'd venture he wasn't insane now, but instead a man so consumed with grief he'd forgotten how to be around anyone.

"You'll not ask why we should only have one?" he asked, calling her back from that cogitation. Placing his palms on his knees, Edwin leaned over, erasing the space between them in the carriage.

She gave her head a hesitant shake. "I . . ." It wouldn't have come into her head to ask as to why there'd been only one when for her there had been none.

"Because the tray he asked Cook to make . . . wasn't for him. It was for each of the horses in the stables. On those nights, Gertrude," Edwin went on, "we'd visit the stables and pass those treats on to the horses because Stephen insisted they worked so very hard during the day and should be mightily rewarded."

He described a child so unlike Stephen. A stranger, in every way, a boy who'd deserved the life this man painted in heartbreaking strokes with every word that left his lips.

A tear slid down her cheek. Followed by another, and another.

Edwin flicked his gaze over her face, taking in those useless expressions of her misery. "Therefore, do not seek to convince me of the reasons I should love my son." Pain blazed within his eyes, piercing her from the intensity of the emotion there. "I loved him long before you knew him," he said hoarsely. "I loved him when your family ripped him from my life, and I love him even now, angry and hating me as he does."

She slid her eyes closed; his paternal love, his broken heart, and his tangible grief all slammed into her, stealing the air from her lungs.

All along she'd believed she needed to be here with Stephen and Edwin so that she might help the marquess to understand his son and show him all the good that existed within the boy. Only to find that hers wasn't a matter of teaching Edwin to care for Stephen but rather of helping her brother see that he was loved by the marquess. That he always had been and always would be.

Gertrude patted her cheeks. She could do this. She owed it to both Edwin and Stephen, and the task before her was certainly a good deal more favorable than had the marquess proven to be a heartless noble who'd merely wanted his heir back for the sake of lineage.

Fueled with a new purpose, Gertrude gripped the sides of the carriage to hand herself down.

Edwin stood there, a hand stretched out. Even hating her as he did, he was still a gentleman in ways that neither she nor her siblings could understand. The velvet collar of his fine wool overcoat marked him here in the streets of the Seven Dials as a foreigner.

"Miss Killoran?" he urged, alternating his stare between her and the truculent child waiting on the steps.

He feared he'd again lose him.

"Forgive me," she murmured, placing her fingers in his. He curled his palm over hers, enveloping hers. Her glove proved little barrier against a wave of unexpected warmth that sent small shivers of awareness radiating through her.

And this time, not a word passed between them as they found their way over to the steps where Stephen waited.

Chapter 11

Standing in the streets of the Dials with his arms folded before him, Edwin flicked his gaze around the whores and drunkards who cluttered the pavement. He did a continuous sweep, his eyes taking in everything.

Having been burnt every way in which a man could be by the Killorans, he'd be mad to trust there was anything aboveboard in . . . any of this.

"Mayhap he's not here," Stephen muttered as Gertrude knocked for a third time on the door of the establishment.

"I am sure he's here. I sent word 'round yesterday after I spoke with your father," she murmured, a frown in her voice.

Stephen glowered back at Edwin. "You. Are . . . My. Fath . . . ," he mouthed, the clarity of words lost to the length of that statement, but Edwin would wager his title and every property attached to it that the sentence contained the word "not" somewhere in there.

Gertrude shoved an elbow into the boy's side.

"*Oomph.*" Stephen rubbed at the wounded flesh. "What in hell was that for?" he groused.

"Behave," she warned.

"I didn't say anything," the boy whined.

"I know you," she said, not so much as glancing at the boy and earning a blush from Stephen anyway. "Behave," she repeated once more.

How had she . . . ? The young woman had an uncanny ability to gather precisely what the boy was doing, even with his back presented to her. It spoke to her devotion and their relationship, and for the first time, he saw her . . . not as a thief who'd claimed Stephen . . . but as the sister she'd proclaimed herself to be.

An odd tightening squeezed at his chest.

He didn't want to witness any hint of Gertrude's bond with his son. He didn't want to see the maternal side that marked her not as the monster he'd taken her to be but instead a young woman whose family had, by her insistence, made a mistake. It cast shades of grey upon something that had only existed, and should only exist, in black and white.

Gertrude unfastened the clasp at her throat and consulted the pearl timepiece affixed to her dress.

Edwin hooded his lashes, lowering his focus not to the jeweled pendant there but to the small swell of Gertrude's breasts, that cream-white flesh barely on display in her modest décolletage. But enough . . . It was enough to entice. Entrance. And make a man hunger to pull back the fabric and reveal every secret concealed there. Yes. He'd been too long without a woman. Too long. This reaction to Gertrude Killoran was a response he'd have to any female. Edwin swallowed hard and forced his attention away, and his gaze collided with his son's.

Stephen narrowed his eyes, and with slow, methodical movements, he touched his index finger to the corner of his eye. "Careful. There."

Unlike before, this time there could be no confusion or missed meaning in the inaudible—and implied threats.

And bloody hell, he—a grown man—found himself blushing.

"Where in blazes is he?" Gertrude muttered to herself and knocked again on the heavily nicked door that—Edwin peered at the pane—might or might not contain bullet holes.

The door burst open.

Gertrude had a dagger in hand and herself positioned in front of Stephen and . . . Edwin.

Six inches past six feet and at least fourteen stone, which was surely all muscle, the stranger in the door had the look of a street fighter, and Gertrude had placed herself between the monster of a man and Edwin.

"Bloody hell. Step aside, Gertrude Killoran," Edwin gritted out, shuffling to reposition himself. He'd be damned ten times to Sunday before he allowed a woman—any woman, including this one with her Diggory blood—to put herself in danger for him.

"There you are," she called out cheerfully, ignoring Edwin's command.

It was a rare day indeed when a lord found his orders unheeded. The minx.

"Miss Killoran," the man greeted. "Mr. Killoran."

The boy smiled widely, in the first pure, most real expression of genuine happiness, and it cut Edwin to the quick that his joy should be delivered at the hands of this stranger. "Draven."

And then that name registered. *This* was the cabinetmaker Gertrude insisted craft Stephen's furnishings?

Draven spared a glance over at Edwin and then looked to Gertrude. "Oh, he's fine."

With no further assurances needed, Gertrude's having vouched for him apparently enough, Draven stepped aside and allowed them to enter.

Edwin lingered a moment, scanning the streets and then assessing the trio that now moved deeper inside the establishment with his presence seemingly forgotten. He'd be the madman the world professed him to be if he stepped trustingly into this place. The only reason he stepped forward despite his reservations was the son now amicably chatting beside the behemoth of a man. Closing the door, Edwin doffed his hat and followed at a more sedate . . . careful pace behind Gertrude, Stephen, and Gunner Draven.

As he moved deeper and deeper into the establishment, the smells of Draven's workrooms filled his nostrils: a pungent scent of cut wood and fire.

His stomach roiled, and Edwin swallowed the bile fighting its way up his throat.

I am afraid she is . . . dead . . . my lord . . .

That whispered announcement from a servant who'd managed to escape thundered around Edwin's brain. His wife's death—his fault. All of it. Had he been there. But he hadn't, and for his failure to protect them—as Stephen had rightfully charged—Lavinia had lost her life in the cruelest way. Burnt beyond recognition. His body broke into a sweat, and he dug his fingers hard into his temple. *No. No. No. No. No.* "No."

"Something wrong with you?"

His pulse pounding in his ears, Edwin whipped his gaze over to that child's voice that had pulled him back from madness. Nay . . . not any boy's. His son's.

"Fine," Edwin managed to squeeze out, his voice hoarsened. "I'm fine." He let his arms fall to his sides.

For the first time since they'd been reunited, Stephen wandered closer. "You don't look fine."

Which was a statement right on the mark. Edwin didn't feel fine. In fact, he hadn't been right in any way since the night of the fire.

"Shouldn't you be with Gertrude?" he asked, needing to be alone. Needing to fight through the horrors that had intruded and still licked at the corners of his mind.

Stephen's eyebrows went shooting to his hairline. "You called her Gertrude."

"It is her name," he pointed out, pretending to misunderstand the reason for the boy's shock.

"You don't like her," his son said bluntly.

"No." Edwin found the young woman seated alongside a long, rectangular worktable. With a pencil in her hand, she periodically waved it about as she issued some directive or another to the bearlike man at her side. Any other lady, regardless of station, when presented with a stranger as formidable in size as Draven, would have cowered in fear. Gertrude, however, commanded with a greater ease than Wellington. "I do, however, admire her," he murmured to himself.

"She's all right," Stephen gruffly conceded. "Cleo and Ophelia are stronger. My other sisters. Or . . . I used to think they were. I still do, in some ways," he tried to clarify.

And God . . . it felt so very good . . . so very right, to simply be talking again with his son that he didn't care if the boy sang the praises of Diggory or the Devil himself in that instant; Edwin just wanted the moment to stretch out unto forever. And he also wanted to know about Gertrude Killoran. "In what ways is Gertrude different from her . . . your sisters?" he murmured, stealing a glance at his son from the corner of his eye. While also watching the woman they discussed.

"Well, Gert's the bookish one."

They are quite popular in the Americas. Their George Washington and Thomas Jefferson insisted upon carrying one . . .

His lips twisted in a half smile, the muscles of his face strained under the unfamiliar movement of his mouth.

"On account of what happened to her eye," his son was saying.

Edwin's musings snapped, and he grasped on to that statement. "What happened?"

It was too much. Too soon. He'd mistakenly revealed his fascination with Gertrude Killoran.

Stephen instantly shuttered his expression. "Ya tryin' ta get information from me about moi sister?" he demanded in his thick Cockney.

"Ya think ya're goin' ta 'arm 'er in any way, and Oi'll burn yar newest townhouse down, too."

That arrow found the proper mark, surely where the boy had wished to deliver it, right where his heart beat.

"I've no ill intentions toward Gertrude." Two days ago, he had. Two days ago, he'd have gladly escorted her to the gallows, walked her up the parapet, and slid the noose around her neck himself. And yet . . . that had been before she'd revealed herself to be courageous and resolute and devoted to his son.

"Good," Stephen said bluntly. "Don't." Making a slashing motion across his throat, Edwin's son stomped off and joined the pair at work.

Gertrude paused in her discourse and said something to the boy. Stephen ducked his head and gave it a shake. She took his chin gently in hand and guided his gaze up to her own.

Some unspoken exchange passed between them before Stephen offered a reluctant nod. Smiling, she patted the empty chair beside her.

Edwin had known his son fewer years than he'd been lost to him. And yet, he gathered enough about the person he'd become to glean there was no way Stephen would be so commanded to—

Stephen plopped his small frame into the seat and then dragged it between Gertrude and Gunner Draven, and the young woman returned to her earlier work.

Edwin hovered in the background, the interloper time and the Killorans had forced him to be. But in this moment, he didn't watch Gertrude, sister to that bastard Broderick Killoran, with suspicion or rage.

This time, it was with an inexplicable and dangerous fascination for the woman herself. She was a conundrum presented in the form of a riddle. A woman who carried a dagger strapped to her leg and wielded it with masterful efficiency . . . but a woman whose eyes also radiated gentleness. And her every exchange with Stephen revealed a resolve, but also gentleness.

Gertrude chewed at the end of her pencil and then shook her head. Dropping that charcoal scrap, she used her hands to illustrate whatever design innovation she had for Stephen's furniture. Edwin watched on, riveted by the animated way in which she conveyed her desires to Draven. No-nonsense, in command, she picked up her pencil once more and proceeded to draw something else onto that page. There was an endearing color to her cheeks as she worked.

Why could he not look away from her?

This need to watch her had nothing to do with the suspicion and fear that had dogged him for this woman or her family. It was for some other reason he didn't understand and couldn't explain, nor wished to. His mind shied away from whatever pull she had over him.

He gave his head a tight shake. *It is about my son. That is the only reason my hatred doesn't burn as strong.*

Wasn't it?

Chapter 12

Gertrude hadn't always lived on the fringe.

For a short time, she'd been an included, welcomed, and more valued member of her family and the Diggory gang.

Until she hadn't.

Until she'd lost her vision and her role and her rank, and visibility within both of those groups. Oh, she'd never doubted her siblings' love . . . but their earliest years had been spent on survival. And Gertrude had been seen only as a liability that put the group at risk. From then on, she'd always hovered, just on the outside. There. But not. A member, but not in the same capacity as her siblings.

As such, she'd developed a keen awareness of when someone else found themselves so excluded.

And where every other Killoran had developed a hardened exterior that made them immune to empathy—an emotion that might weaken one—it had become an inherent part of who Gertrude herself was. For better or for worse, she could not make herself *not care* about another person's pain or discomfort.

It was why, even as she should be attending Draven's plans, she could focus only on the looming figure that hovered in the shadows. Also on the fringe. Also on the outside.

A man who'd professed his hatred for Gertrude and all she was and represented. But also a man who'd come 'round at every turn, making decisions that went against what he wished and were instead in Stephen's best interests: from calling the boy by his street name to accompanying them even now, Edwin revealed there was far more to him than met the eye.

He was not the emotionless monster jaded by the death of his wife and kidnapping of his son. Rather, he was very much a real man . . . a father, doing the best he could with a situation that was only bad and wrong.

Gertrude set her pencil down, and Draven and Stephen both looked up. "I thought it would be good for Stephen to have a moment of privacy to tell you his thoughts on the design."

Excitement glittered in her brother's eyes as he brought his shoulders back.

Shoving back her chair, Gertrude stood and left the pair to their work. She tucked her palms inside her deep pocket, seeking out the sleeping Sethos. From where Edwin lingered in the corner by an ornate, hand-designed chair, he watched her approach with a wariness in his eyes that she'd have to be completely blind not to see.

Gertrude stopped at the opposite end of the high-backed seat.

Edwin stiffened and rested his hand atop the gilded and inlaid wood.

She also knew what it was to not know how to be around people. What it was to be surrounded by others and yet, all at the same time, lonely. "It is magnificent, is it not?"

He gave her a quizzical look.

Gertrude motioned to the barrier between them. "It was modeled after ancient Egyptian ceremonial chairs."

"You have an appreciation for the history of furniture?" he asked without inflection but with a real curiosity that was a welcome change to his biting suspicion.

"I have an appreciation for everything," she explained. And it was the truth. Having lost her ability to thieve, she'd been forced to occupy her time in different ways. She'd taught herself to read, and an entire world had opened before her. "The Egyptians were the first to use chairs as we know them, and yet ours have become strictly two-dimensional in purpose: comfort, style. There is not the same intricacy put into the design as there was then." She dropped to a knee and ran her fingers down the feline-like legs of that chair. "They incorporated their religion and beliefs into every aspect of their furniture." Gertrude glanced up to find Edwin's hooded gaze on her, taking in her every movement. Unable to read his immobile features but encouraged by his silence, she came to her feet and motioned for him to join her. Not waiting to see if he followed, knowing that if she did he'd likely dig in his heels and remain in his corner, Gertrude continued deeper into Draven's familiar warehouse. "Too often society sees furniture in that one-dimensional light. Furniture serves—"

"A functional purpose."

"Precisely," she said with a nod. "We perform our official business at desks. We slumber in four-poster beds. It is so functional, we too many times fail to appreciate there could be . . . and should be . . . a dynamic need to those articles."

"Like hiding Stephen's *weapons*," he said with a droll edge.

Deliberately ignoring the biting sarcasm underlying that reply, she again nodded. "Exactly." Gertrude brought them to a stop alongside a hammock.

Edwin eyed the piece a long while.

"It's a hammock," she supplied. "They are used by—"

"The navy. Shipmen. I'm familiar with its uses."

His words knocked her briefly off-balance. She'd spent her whole life believing noblemen were indolent lords, not bothering with information that did not pertain to their estates, power, or wealth. "They became popular because there was limited space and it was a way to avoid constructing bunks. It's not simply a matter of convenience for shipmen. Have you ever lain in one?"

"I've not," he clipped out. That austerity was, however, what she'd come to expect from the peerage.

"Lie in it," she urged in gentle tones she usually reserved for Master Brave, the small black barn cat, when he found himself trapped atop the stables at the Devil's Den. It was a challenge, couched as an invitation. Nonetheless, she expected a "Go to hell, Killoran" . . . that did not come.

Edwin hesitated a long while, glancing off to where Stephen and Draven conversed on the design plans.

And then Gertrude struggled not to don a mask of surprise as he sat on the edge and shimmied his muscular frame into the woven netting. It swung back and forth rhythmically under the addition of his weight.

His gaze found hers, and an endearing rush of color suffused his cheeks. "This is foolish," he muttered, making to toss his legs over the side.

Gertrude slid into place along the front of the netting, blocking his attempts. "Only because it is unfamiliar."

"Because there is no purpose in it," he gritted out.

"Everything has a purpose, Edwin." Every object. Every man, woman, or child. Even if society and the world around them failed to see their value.

He stole another look in his son's direction.

Gertrude cocked her head. She'd always believed only the unfortunate souls in the Dials were required to keep a careful guard up, to present one image of indomitability to the world and conceal all vulnerability. This . . . Edwin's diffidence . . . only heightened that most unexpected of links between Gertrude and this man born to an entirely different social universe. "Do you know many sailors would eventually grow so accustomed to the hammocks that even when they were ashore, they carried them and made those hammocks their bedding?"

Edwin went absolutely still.

"Sometimes . . . it is just a matter of something feeling right." She glanced over to her brother, and Edwin followed her stare. "It hardly makes sense for us to sleep in, and yet there are benefits to them. There is a soothing calm to be found in the folds," she murmured.

Edwin stiffened, and this time he did swing his legs over the side of the netting. His gleaming black boots landed with a decisive thwack, cutting into the fleeting peace she'd stolen between them. "You are speaking about Stephen's furniture."

Gertrude tried to make anything out of those empty tones. She lowered herself into the place beside him, sending the swing into a light rock. "It's a lack of familiarity that makes it feel wrong, but there is nothing wrong or right in the comfort we find in one's world. It's just . . . what we know."

Edwin narrowed his gaze on her face; the piercing intensity of it would have shaken most any other woman. And yet, as he opened his mouth to speak, no blistering words came forward. No taunts or jibes. Nothing.

Those enigmatic brown eyes darkened, and all at once energy crackled and sizzled between them. Gertrude became aware of the press of his leg against hers, a muscle-hewn thigh that crushed her skirts and molded the garment to her legs. And the absolute heat that spilled from him.

His throat moved. "I don't want that to make sense." That gruff whisper filtered the air between them, his voice a hoarse baritone that left a mark upon her cheek like a physical caress. Dangerous and tempting, all at once.

Nothing made sense. Somewhere along the way, their discourse on furniture had shifted, taken on a new meaning that only they knew the implication of.

His gaze went to her mouth and remained there.

That glint in his eyes turned molten hot, and had she been innocent, she would have never noted that slight darkening. She would have remained naive to what it meant or signified. But she was neither of those things. Her innocence existed as nothing more than a technicality of a piece of flesh that had been somehow preserved. But she'd been raised first on the streets and then in the gaming hell. There were no secrets or mysteries in terms of lust and passion and desire, and all those sentiments were contained within the heat of his stare.

Gertrude darted her tongue out, trailing it along suddenly dry lips.

Edwin leaned down, bringing his head close to hers.

Her lashes slid closed of their own volition, and she inhaled deeply.

His breath, not the tobacco- and spirit-tinged scents she was accustomed to, but something purer and quixotic. Less overt and wholly enticing: coffee and honey, both bitter and sweet, those warring flavors perfectly suited to this man.

"What in hell are you doing?"

She and Edwin jumped, and the suddenness of that movement sent the hammock tipping back, upending them both.

With a grunt, Edwin landed with a loud thump on the hardwood floor, and with catlike reflexes not even Master Brave could have managed, the marquess shot an arm out and caught Gertrude before she hit the same floor.

Her heart raced.

Stephen stood glowering over them, like a disapproving and rightfully suspicious papa.

"Stephen," she said lamely.

"Yea. Your brother." He shot a hard look at Edwin. "What is going on?"

"We were discussing the history of the hammock," Edwin said with a calm and unaffectedness only a lord could manage. In one fluid movement, he came to his feet and held out a hand to Gertrude.

"You were spouting on with your odd facts," the boy said, his voice and the gaze he still moved back and forth between them not wholly convinced.

"I—"

Edwin spoke, interrupting her response. "You'd do well to focus on the lessons Gertrude has to teach. She was admirably explaining the various purposes of items like the furniture you're having designed today."

Gertrude's lips parted at the unexpectedness of that defense. She'd long been an oddity in the Diggory gang, her family, and the Devil's Den itself. The information she imparted earned peculiar looks or impatient stares from people who either didn't care or didn't have the time to spare for those details.

"All of a sudden you're going to approve of Gert as an instructor?" Stephen stared at his father like he'd sprouted a second head. "You're sending her away when you find me a new governess. Don't seem like you can appreciate her skill *that* much."

And just like that the warmth suffusing her chest dissolved under the weight of reality. They were enemies. Or, by the marquess's determination, they were. Even with that, she'd not have her brother throw his father's decision back in his face. Not when Edwin was within his rights and justified in every way.

Unnerved by the tense wall her brother had unwittingly resurrected, Gertrude focused on the boy. "Why don't we take a trip to Gunter's before we return home."

The color leached from Edwin's cheeks, and a muscle ticked at the corner of his jaw. "I do not—"

With a little whoop, Stephen sprinted to the door. "Come on," he continued over the marquess's protestations as he yanked the door open and rushed off.

Gertrude had started after her brother when she registered that Edwin had made no attempt to join her and Stephen. Frowning, she glanced back and found him motionless, rooted to Draven's floor. Pale. Not unlike the way he'd been upon their arrival here.

He is . . . scared.

Of visiting Gunter's? Or of his son? Or, mayhap, both?

Staggered by that realization, she found her heart aching once more for the unlikeliest person. Or . . . he would have been the unlikeliest recipient. Not anymore. Not since she'd come to acknowledge the Marquess of Maddock's suffering. "Are you all right?" she asked gently.

Red color splotched his cheeks. "I'm fine," he clipped out. He made an angry slashing gesture at the doorway, motioning her forward.

Fool. Do you believe he would accept concern from you, of all people?

Avoiding Edwin's volatile stare, Gertrude made her goodbyes to the builder and braced for another outing with the marquess.

Chapter 13

He'd almost kissed her.

Edwin had been just a moment away from descending into the madness that had become his namesake and claiming Gertrude's mouth. And the only thing that had stopped him from doing so had been his rightfully outraged son's unexpected interruption.

And yet, that near embrace was not the reason for the horror clogging his head in this instance.

Gaze trained forward, Edwin walked along the crowded Curzon Street.

He had ceased moving in society after his wife's death.

Nay, that wasn't completely accurate. After the fire, he'd ventured out only in the dead of night, and only in the most dangerous streets of London. He'd craved death, courting it in the place most likely to deal him that deliverance.

Until a night long ago when Edwin had been dragged from a dank alley by Quint Marlow and had given up on death. Instead, he'd shifted his energies to finding the ones guilty for that act of great treachery. He'd kept company only with the men he'd hired to find out details . . .

any details he could about the fire, the ones who'd set it. And then about his missing son.

He'd not attended balls or sparred with Gentleman Jackson or visited his respectable clubs—all those acts that had been as much a part of his life as his daily ablutions.

And now, walking down the fashionable Curzon Street, he found himself swamped with panic; it choked him and stole his breath. It made him long for the much safer peril that had existed in the Seven Dials.

But there was no salvation this time. This time, there were only the gaping stares of the lords and ladies of London and the unconventional spitfire who spouted off equally unconventional facts that ranged from history to damned furniture making.

The spitfire who now walked several paces ahead, her attention squarely focused on the little boy at her side. The greater the distance between himself and that pair, the more Edwin was sucked into the crowd around him.

Throngs of passersby clogged the pavement, the crush of bodies sending up a raucous din of laughter and discourse that blurred in his ears, innocuous sounds that when wound together rang with a maniacal intent.

His forehead beaded with moisture.

Breathe. Breathe.

These men and women were once your peers. Are your peers. They still were. Except . . . they weren't. They were strangers to whom he could no longer relate. People who gawked and whispered behind their gloved fingertips.

I'm going to be ill.

Tunneling his vision forward, he fixed on the slender woman moving with long-legged strides through the crowds. People rushed out of their way, allowing her and the boy at her side to pass.

A spring wind gusted; it caught several loose curls that hung about her shoulder. How odd: that color he'd taken as nondescript glimmered like warmed chocolate in the sun's rays. Those loose curls bounced with every step she took.

And he fixed on them. He fixed on her. A half-mad chuckle welled in his chest and spilled past his lips before ultimately being lost to the steady stream of carriages passing by.

What bloody irony that a Diggory should prove the lifeline that kept him from giving over to the terror. His feet twitched with the need to bolt in the opposite direction and continue on until he reached his residence. And then shut the door and keep her out. His son. The world. And go back to the empty existence that had not only become familiar but also was the one he so desperately craved.

Then Gertrude stopped. Several inches shy of six feet, Gertrude was taller than most men, and she easily found him. She squinted. Was it the glare of the afternoon sun? The distance between them? Or that one oddly blank eye that accounted for that stare?

She said something to Stephen, and the boy nodded and dashed ahead.

Just days ago, he would have sensed a trap in . . . all this. And mayhap there was. Mayhap he was ultimately to be felled by a Killoran. But right now, his need for her and a connection to . . . something . . . superseded all.

Gertrude started back in Edwin's direction. As she did, lords and ladies cut a wide swath around her, allowing her a direct path. All the while, they looked upon her with derision dripping from their austere, noble gazes.

A young lady in blindingly bright-white skirts yanked them close.

If Gertrude either cared or noted, she gave no indication, and that strength of courage was so breathtaking in the light of his paralysis.

"Is there something wrong?" she asked in hushed tones that reached his ears.

It was the question she'd asked at Draven's. It was also on the tip of his tongue to turn away her and the concern she showed . . . but he couldn't. This time he proved too weak. "I should not be here," he whispered, so quietly the admission barely registered in his own ears.

He should not, even now, be standing in the middle of Curzon Street with all of Polite Society walking a path around Gertrude and him.

She glanced around as if just suddenly realizing they were the focus of every passerby's scrutiny. Gertrude took a step closer. "They don't matter, Edwin." How confident she was in that reassurance. "Their opinions matter even less."

Yes, he'd been of a like opinion. But it was easier for one to hate the world around one when one wasn't really moving amongst it. For as much as he didn't give ten bloody damns what they said of him . . . he cared about the rumors that remained and how they would forever affect his son. *Liar . . . you still care. You hate that all anyone sees when they look at you is madness. Including your son.*

Gertrude settled a delicate but strong palm upon his sleeve. Gasps went up around them, along with whispers to follow. "Come," Gertrude murmured.

Was she a Devil or angel or both, all at the same time? For it was not society that compelled his feet forward, but rather her. A short while later, they entered under the pineapple sign of Gunter's Tea Shop.

That tinny jingle rang out like a shot as the patrons seated throughout the establishment looked up.

Edwin hardened his features against those antipathetic stares—

Before he noted their concentration, not on him but on the pair just ahead of him.

Stephen's eyes flashed fire, and with a cold grin, he swaggered forward like he was himself the owner of this establishment. One by one, each table of ladies and young gentlemen came to their feet and filed out of the shop until all that remained was the faded tinkling of a bell and *thunk* of a door shutting.

And in that instant, the unexpected happened. Rage coursed through him. Not for the likeliest recipient of that ire—Gertrude Killoran—but rather for the gathering of Polite Society who'd treated her like the grime on their boots.

As she and Stephen walked to the counter to look at the ices, disquiet held Edwin frozen.

For he hadn't been any different from every other person who'd judged her and found her wanting. *Isn't that how you've felt toward her and her kind, too? Is that family not deserving of such disdain?*

The answer just days earlier would have been an emphatic, resounding yes with a "go to hell" to anyone who thought the family deserving of even the slightest showing of respect. But that had been before. Before she'd bravely squared off with him on his son's well-being. And before she'd revealed herself to be a bluestocking with an impressive wealth of obscure and interesting facts that made her . . . *real.* That made her not a monster but very much a woman—and now, a woman unfairly judged by people who didn't know her.

An ache throbbed at the back of his head, and he doffed his hat. Edwin rubbed his nape in a bid to right his mind and find stability in how he felt. And how he should feel.

Fact: she was a Killoran. Fact: she was a former member of the Diggory gang.

Fact: despite these past years when he'd felt and lived like less than a human, his annoyance on the young woman's behalf was merely because he was a gentleman. That was all.

To give her credit, to feel badly for her or about her, was dangerous territory that he dared not cross into.

She—

Was just reaching into her pocket and withdrawing several coins.

Springing into motion, Edwin strode over.

Stephen glanced up and shot an elbow into his sister's side, then nodded his little head at Edwin just as he stopped before them.

"I will pay," Edwin said.

"I have it," she said with an easy smile that belied the earlier ugliness that had been directed at her, or the tumult slapping at him.

The delicate thread Edwin had retained over his self-control this day frayed and then snapped. "He is my son, and I will pay," he said sharply.

"I ain't your son," Stephen hissed, taking a jerky step toward Edwin and knocking the coins from his sister's hand. A jingle of silver, they clattered forlornly upon the counter.

"Stephen," Gertrude said on a stern whisper. She took him by his arm, but like an angry, cornered cat, he yanked free. "I'm sorry," she mouthed to Edwin. Pity and sympathy, all emotions he would have once believed her incapable of, directed his way. And he preferred a world in which she was not sensitive to his suffering.

"It's fine." Edwin's lie came, convincing to his own ears. For that was precisely what he did: lie to himself. Stephen's disavowal struck like a well-placed arrow to the heart. For . . . the boy was right. There were different types of fatherhood. Whereas the extent of most gentlemen's interest and role started and stopped with the creation of an heir and a spare, being a parent had meant something altogether more for Edwin. It had been not only siring him but also loving him and playing with him . . . *But then, you lost him.* "I just . . . wanted to pay." To do the smallest of things that fathers did.

"We don't need your money. We got money of our own, Maddock. Gert said she was paying, and she can pay. Unless you have a problem with a woman paying?" A challenge blared from every fiber of the boy's recalcitrant, coiled frame.

Actually . . . he did. It went against the gentlemanly code of conduct that had been ingrained to him early on. A code his son should have memorized long ago, and yet he had been reared altogether differently:

with different norms and beliefs and values. And that discrepancy left father and son existing together, at the same time but on different planets. "I assure you, I do not have a problem with it," he said smoothly, in control once more.

Holding Gertrude's gaze, Edwin made a sweeping gesture to the counter and to the serving lad across from them who could sell the story of the exchange here to any gossip column for a generous payment. And likely would. "As you were, Miss Killoran."

Retrieving the coins from the counter, she scooped them up one at a time and turned her palm up once again.

Edwin's gaze tunneled, not on those coins that had been the source of contention, nor on the callused, ink-stained palms.

A letter had been carved into the inseam of her hand. An inch in length, it stood out, a stark, vivid symbol that marked her origins—*D. Diggory*.

"Find us a seat," she was saying to Stephen. And as the boy bolted off as instructed and Edwin was left alone with Gertrude, he remained transfixed by that scar. Gertrude spoke. "Edwin, I am so sorry about . . ." Her words trailed off, and she followed his stare. She hurriedly yanked her hand back from the counter and lowered it to her side.

Questions, however, swirled around his mind over that marking. Was it one affixed to all that monster's issue? Had she voluntarily taken a knife and etched that mark upon her skin as a testament of her loyalty? Or mayhap it was neither . . . Mayhap it had been as sinister as the heinous acts carried out against Edwin and his kin . . . ?

But suddenly, he had no desire to know the truth . . . for reasons he couldn't understand. They started over to the table Stephen had settled on at the front of the shop. The damned front of the shop. Edwin's palms grew moist. His son was braver than he. At their approach, Stephen hopped up and perused the jars of sweets and fruits.

Edwin drew out Gertrude's chair, and after she'd taken her seat, he claimed the one across from her. "You come here often with him." He put forward that statement to shift them back to safer areas of discourse. The child who united them, and not the villain who divided them.

"I do. I began taking him here when he was . . ." She faltered, abruptly cutting off that look into Stephen's past.

But Edwin wanted it. He wanted all of what she could offer. "Tell me," he urged, his voice faintly entreating. He was a beggar who'd take any scraps into the seconds and minutes and hours and years he'd missed.

"Partially blind, I couldn't steal for him, so he put me to work instead 'instructing' the boys and girls."

"Instructing them?" he asked, coward that he was, not wanting the answer but needing it anyway.

"On the art of stealing. When to commit the acts. Where to commit them. When not to." She peeled her lip back in an unexpected-for-her sneer, that cynical tilt of her lips that offered a clear window into just how she'd felt about serving that monster.

Or mayhap that is all she wishes you to see . . . Mayhap she is playing the role of innocent, just like the nursemaid who kidnapped Stephen . . .

"I would bring Stephen here." She stared out at the kaleidoscope of strangers moving past the shop window, and he knew that was the precise moment she'd ceased speaking to him and begun seeing only the memories of the long-ago days she spoke of. "Under the guise of conducting his lessons on thievery. All the while"—Gertrude dragged her stare from the passersby—"I brought him here, to Gunter's. I'd a fancy change of garments for the both of us. I paid a street rat every week to meet me in the alley and keep track of our garments and belongings." She spoke with the same methodical precision as she must have gone through coordinating those details years ago. "When we were supposed to be thieving, I'd bring him here instead."

And just like that, the great block of ice that had enshrined his heart thawed and cracked, ushering in a forgotten warmth.

This woman loved his son. It was there in her eyes, and in her telling, and could not be feigned by even the greatest Drury Lane actress.

"We'd only have one. His favorite was—"

"Chocolate cream," he whispered.

"Yes. There weren't funds to have an endless sampling, and he insisted it was safer to remain with the flavor he knew he—" Gertrude abruptly stopped. She stared back with stricken eyes. "You took him here."

"Often." While Stephen's mother had been too busy to attend or uninterested or indifferent, Edwin had brought him—alone, without even the nursemaid assigned to his care. "He always had the chocolate."

"And always got it everywhere," Gertrude added, a wistful quality to that remembrance.

"Everywhere." Edwin chuckled, the sound rusty and raw and foreign. Each time, every time, Edwin and Stephen returned home, his son had been sticky from the top of his head to the tips of his toes. "H-he would have it e-everywhere," he squeezed out through his amusement. "H-his cheeks. The t-table. His hands."

Gertrude's laughter joined his, clear and tinkling, like a flawless bell. That fortress he'd resurrected shifted once more, a cataclysmic movement that there would be time enough to panic over. Now there was just her and memories of once joyous times, and both were equally hypnotic. "His eyelids. I would say to him, 'August, y-you manage to get ice cream in places I didn't kn-know one could.'" And as he laughed, the force of that memory proved so very healing and cathartic, and it was made all the more wonderful by the fact that the lost boy who'd spurred those memories now flitted around that very same shop.

Gertrude dusted tears of mirth from her eyes. "H-he insisted on ordering *only* ever chocolate." She dropped her chin atop her palm. "The last time we came here, I promised him that someday we'd have money and I would bring him back." She followed Stephen's darting form with her eyes. "I told him he'd eat every ice so that he learned all the flavors and he could know for certain if chocolate was, in fact, his favorite."

She'd taken time to wonder and worry about Stephen's favorite. *I didn't even do that.* Yet . . . there was one previous statement of all those musings that he clung to. "The last time?"

Gertrude didn't blink for several moments. She let her arms fall to the table. "Beg pardon?"

"You said, 'the last time.'" Edwin searched his gaze over her face. And this time the secrets he sought didn't belong to Stephen. They were this woman's. "Why did you stop bringing him, Gertrude?"

"I don't . . ." She gave her head a dazed shake. "I'm not . . ." Her incoherent replies all went unfinished. And then a shadow fell over her gaze, and an impenetrable barrier went up. "It was no longer safe."

She'd say nothing more on that memory. The truth was there in those clipped syllables.

On the heel of that telling and the silence that fell between them, Edwin was hit square in the chest by the staggering realization: all along his son had still moved in the same world Edwin had once dwelled in. His heart buckled. He might have even seen him . . . had he not given himself over to despair. "Why did you tell me this?" he whispered.

Gertrude toyed with the crisp white napkin. "To the world, most see Stephen as an angry child aged beyond his years."

"Which he is." Edwin attempted to swallow around the wad of misery choking at his throat.

Gertrude stretched a hand across the table, settling it on his, and the air, his fingers, both crackled with that touch of familiarity she wielded so expertly. "This is the one place I see that he's truly a child, still. Here, he is excited about treats and ices and doesn't worry about weapons." Gertrude lightly squeezed his hand. "He is there still, Edwin. The boy you remember. And every day that he remains with you and this world, he will shed more of the hard exterior he's built about himself."

Together, they watched Stephen. Absorbed in his study, Stephen moved along the row of fruits and candies cased within the shelving that lined the side of the window.

"And do you speak as someone who knows?" he asked quietly, a query that had nothing to do with Stephen and came simply from a place of wanting to know who Gertrude Killoran, in fact, was: ruthless emissary of Broderick and Mac Diggory . . . or a once blameless woman who'd also been taken in. "Do you know what it was to have your innocence stolen and eventually find a place back from the anger?" Or mayhap he now spoke of himself. It was all blurred and confused. And mayhap it would always be, because there was no order or clarity for those burnt by evil.

Gertrude went absolutely motionless except for her fingers. Those long digits clasped almost reflexively upon him. A stark, hellish misery, glinting in that one seeing eye, went through him. "I was never innocent," she whispered. "Not like Stephen." A sad smile pried her lips upright in the corners, and he wanted to chase it away. Wanted to drive back that sadness. "Not like any child."

He fought with himself. Her demons were her own. They belonged to her, and he sure as hell shouldn't give a damn what pain ravaged her soul. But God help him, mayhap he was the same pathetic fool who'd trusted when he should not. "You preserved your humanity anyway."

Surprise brought her lips apart. "I . . ."

Neither wanting nor knowing what to do with that softening in her expression and gaze, he dragged his white wrought iron chair closer to her. "You are not what I expected you to be." And he braced for the onslaught of guilt and horror such an admission should cost him—that did not come.

"You are not who I expected you to be, either. But there is always more to a person than we see or expect. It is just too easy to forget as much."

They'd delved into intimate and unsafe territory. They were thankfully saved from any further discussion as an employee came forward with a tray of some ten glasses of ices. No sooner had the crystal-handled glasses been set out than Stephen came bounding over.

And Edwin observed him, not with the regretful eyes he had since the boy's return, but with new ones, opened by Gertrude's admission from moments ago. There was innocence in his son, still. He might not ever wholly recover, but neither had Stephen descended to complete darkness.

And it was because of this woman.

Stephen skidded to a halt, catching the table to right himself.

The crystal glasses clattered. "They're here!" With a childlike zeal, Stephen yanked out the chair opposite Edwin and grabbed for a crystal glass . . . Punch Water. Not chocolate, but Punch Water.

"Mm-mm." Gertrude lifted a staying hand. She stared pointedly at the boy.

And the ever-snappish child flashed a wide, toothy grin. "Fine. Fine."

She lifted a finger. "I thought we might allow Edwin to take part."

"Pfft." Folding his arms at his spindly chest, Stephen kicked back on the legs of his chair. "What's he know about ices?"

Puzzled, like one who'd wandered upon a stage without the benefit of his lines, Edwin looked back and forth between Gertrude and his son. "I know something about ices," he blurted.

It was a child's statement to make, but really, he wasn't so useless that he couldn't enjoy those treats.

Gertrude beamed. "That is precisely what I said, isn't it, Stephen?" Crimson color rushed to her cream cheeks, that bright-cherry hue a match to her full lips, lips he'd come so very close to kissing. "Now, first we'll need . . ." And as she spoke, the lady proved a thief of a different sort, for in that moment, he found himself robbed of a proper breath, wanting to take that mouth. To explore and taste the contours of the plump flesh.

"Shall we?" she went on, jolting him away from wicked thoughts he had no place having.

Seated side by side, Gertrude and Stephen stared back. Edwin shook his head. What in blazes had he missed while he was lusting after the young woman? "Fine?" he ventured, hearing the question in his own response.

Gertrude sighed. "Very well. I'll do it." She shoved back her chair, the wrought iron scraping the marble, and came to her feet. Leaning across the table, she plucked his cravat free.

"Wh—?" She'd already expertly disentangled that scrap of white satin before he could question what she intended. They were a thief's fingers, too quick to see at work.

"What are you doing?" he demanded in hushed tones. Edwin glanced around the shop, taking in the staff working behind the counter . . . and the people strolling on the street outside. Each one who trotted by stole a look inside . . . at him. And his son. Nay, it was really all three of them who garnered that naked interest.

Gertrude followed his stare. "You're trying ices."

As she leaned closer, he recoiled in his seat. "It's not pr—" His son sharpened his gaze on Edwin's face. Stephen expected him to duck out of the challenge. That disgust and disappointment, reserved so often for him, reared once more. "Precisely difficult ascertaining the flavors," he substituted.

Wide-eyed, his son sat upright in his chair . . . and then . . . Stephen smiled.

Edwin had a taste of what it must have felt like for Atlas to have heaved the Earth over his shoulders.

"Splendid," Gertrude praised. Reaching across the table once again, she proceeded to tie his cravat over his eyes. As she made quick work, tying the scrap of finely woven cloth, the tempting scent of her—a hint of apple blossom and lilacs—wafted over his senses. The makeshift blindfold heightened each sense: that faint increase in her respirations, the slight quake to her fingers, the feel of her. The floral scent . . .

"Th-there," she murmured, and his ears, wholly attuned to this woman, went on alert all the more. "Stephen," she encouraged, and this time her voice came steady.

"I ain't feeding him."

"That's the game," she reminded him.

As brother and sister exchanged words in that rapid volley, Edwin moved his head between them, feeling like a bloody arse with his cravat over his eyes. But oddly, that scrap was also . . . unexpectedly welcome, too. It shielded his face and kept him from noting the sea of strangers with their noses likely pressed to the windowpane.

"But they're going to see me feeding him."

"*You* picked the table, Stephen."

"A wager, then?" Edwin suggested.

That quelled the rapid sibling discourse.

"Go on, Maddock?" his son allowed.

"You set the terms."

There was another long pause before Stephen spoke. "Truly?"

"Tru—"

As if the boy feared Edwin might change his mind and pull back those terms, he spoke on a rush. "I get to cancel out a decision you make."

Cancel out . . . ? "I'm afraid I don't understand."

"If I want something, or want to go someplace, and you don't want me to, I get to do it anyway." It was a risky arrangement. Because none of the places his son would wish to go, nor the people he wanted to see, were safe.

"Very well. And if I win, I'm permitted to *cancel out* one request you put to me without any objections on your part."

"Those hardly seem equitable in value," Gertrude murmured, then gasped. "Do not step on my foot, Stephen."

"Fine, Maddock. It's a deal." There was the faint clink of a metal spoon striking crystal and—

Edwin grunted as Stephen shoved that utensil at his lips. "You even know how to properly eat?"

"Proper eating doesn't involve a blindfold," he muttered around the spoonful of cold ice.

Stephen laughed; that abrupt snorting hint of mirth burst from him, and all the tension in Edwin's frame dissipated under that joy-filled, joy-inducing response. God, how he'd missed August's laughter. His smile.

"Well?" Gertrude pressed, forcing him to attend the tasting test she and his son performed.

Nay, it was a game. It had been so very long since he'd played one with Stephen. "Bergamot."

The minx across from him clapped her hands. "Bravo."

"It was an easy one," Stephen groused. *Tinkle-tinkle-clink.* "Here."

This time, Edwin was prepared, and he opened his mouth to sample the next flavored ice. He let the bite melt on his tongue, stretching on the anticipation of the pair beside him. And emotion filled him. *I missed this . . .* Edwin gave thanks again for the coverage provided by that cravat.

How very good this felt. How right. To laugh. And be teased. When he'd thought himself incapable of feeling any of this lightheartedness.

And he wouldn't have known precisely what he'd been missing this day if it had not been for Gertrude. Had he sent her packing as he'd been so determined to do, there would have never been any of this. All the joy of this day would have been lost. He'd have been alone, still futilely attempting to navigate simple pleasantries with his son.

A small foot collided with Edwin's shin, and he grunted. "Well, Maddock?"

"Burnt filbert cream ice."

His son thumped a fist down on the table, and the crystal glasses jumped. "Impossible. You're peeking."

There had been a time when no one had dared question or call out his honor. It had, since his wife's death, however, become a common occurrence. One that he abhorred with every fiber of his being.

"Inspect, Gert," Stephen prodded.

Another whisper of soft floral fragrance filled his nostrils, and he drew a breath in, letting that enthralling scent fill him.

Then Gertrude slipped her fingertips through his hair, and behind the blindfold, he closed his eyes, craving that soothing caress, wanting to know more of it.

"It is secure." Did he imagine the breathless quality to that assurance she gave Stephen? There was a faint gust of air and a noisy whir of muslin skirts as she reclaimed her seat. "His blindfold is secure."

Stephen spooned another bite into Edwin's mouth. "Parmesan cream ice."

"Parmesan cream ice?" Stephen's voice crept up, and then he released a chortling laugh. "Parmesan cream i-ice," he repeated through his levity. "It was muscadine. I told you he wouldn't know." With a wild whoop, Stephen banged a triumphant fist upon the table again. "I won!"

Edwin loosened the knot Gertrude had made with his cravat. "It appears you were correct," he drawled. "I knew less than I credited."

"Always the case with you nobs," Stephen said with a grin, but this time there wasn't the boy's usual antipathy when he spoke of Edwin's station.

With his spare hand, Edwin fished out a small purse and tossed it over. "Here."

With catlike reflexes, his son opened his palm and caught it in a fist.

"Given your triumph, it only seems fair that you choose something else."

Stephen's grin widened, dimpling his cheeks. "Aye. It is fair." Shoving back his chair, he jumped up and darted across the checkered marbled floor to the case, where several workers filled the porcelain ice pails with various creams.

Edwin settled back in his chair and watched on as his son chatted with a young man working there at the counter. The ease with which those two spoke hinted at a familiarity. And then the truth slammed into him. The Gunter's staff who'd stared on with horror hadn't been condemning the pair of Killorans with their gazes the way the lords and ladies in the shop and streets had, but rather . . . Edwin alone. No, Stephen was at home here in ways that he wasn't in his own household.

In all his hellish thoughts of the suffering his son had known during his time living on the streets . . . of all the ruthless, soulless men, women, and children he'd imagined Stephen keeping company with, none of those wonderings had included trips to Gunter's. Once more, it was because of Gertrude. He clenched his fingers around a spoon he'd not realized he was holding.

"You let him win."

He stiffened and looked over. "How . . . ?"

"Did I know?" She lifted a regal dark eyebrow. A twinkle danced in her eye, and she dragged her chair round the table, scooting herself closer, closer still, until their thighs brushed. The muscles there jumped, and his body went on alert with an ever-increasing awareness of Gertrude Killoran. "May I share a secret?" she asked, clearly enunciating each syllable, and God help him for the depraved bastard he was, with his gaze he devoured her mouth.

Nod your head. Say something . . . "What secret?" he managed to croak.

"If you're going to incorrectly guess one, make it the parmesan ice and not muscadine." She followed that with a wink.

His neck heated. Tossing down the forgotten spoon, Edwin grabbed up his cravat and gave it a snap. "I didn't—"

"Edwin, don't forget, I grew up on the streets. I could spot a liar from St. Giles to the Seven Dials." All the muscles of her face froze in a pained mask, and her smile melted, taking with it a light that he'd lost himself within this day. "I'm sorry. I—"

"It's fine." And . . . surprisingly, this time, the reminder of her past *was* fine.

Her features softened, and unsettled by that guile, he turned his focus over to Stephen.

It was a galling capitulation to make, and yet, that two-word assurance had held . . . true. Later, there would be time enough to firm up the walls of wariness around a Killoran. Not in this instance, however. Now he'd not have anything interfere with the perfection of this day.

Gertrude held his gaze; there was an unflinching strength to her directness, one that he'd known in few men and never in any woman. Not even his late wife, a duke's daughter born to great wealth and influence. "Why did you do it?"

Gertrude Killoran was tenacious. However, she also possessed an innate ability to draw forth admissions and secrets a man wished to cling to but simply couldn't where she was concerned.

He was the first to glance away, shifting his attention onto Stephen, still engaged in a lively discourse with the Gunter's worker. "Because I know what it is to feel . . . and to be . . . powerless. To crave some control of one's life and happiness, while all the while having nothing," he said, his voice fading to a whisper.

He'd said too much. Grimacing, Edwin smoothed the fabric of his cravat and then with quick, jerky movements, proceeded to tie a suitable if haphazard knot. Gertrude reached over, covering his hand with hers, staying his movements. Edwin distantly registered that tinny bell announcing another patron, but he couldn't care who walked through that damned door.

For Gertrude didn't offer words or platitudes. She didn't attempt to fill his ears with tales of her own tribulations and struggles, of which there were surely plenty. Her touch indicated greater than any word, however, could: that she heard him, that she understood, and for the first time, he was not alone. He was . . .

"Maddock."

. . . jolted viciously away from that powerful connection by a once familiar, now foreign voice.

My God.

Wordlessly, Edwin sat immobile, the shock in his own gaze reflected back in the eyes of his former best friend, Lord Charles Taylor. Friends since Eton and then at Oxford, they'd once been inseparable . . . until they hadn't been. Guilt. Regret. Shame. Sadness. All of it found a place in his chest, those sentiments roiling together. Ones that would forever be with him.

Under the table, Gertrude nudged Edwin with the tip of her boot.

"Charles," he greeted, and belatedly came to his feet. "Tenwhestle," he amended. They'd lost the right to casual forms of address.

The marquess yanked his hat off as they both recalled the years of propriety drilled into them. They dropped perfectly matching bows.

Mirror images of one another, like the brothers they'd once been.

And now we're greeting as strangers in public.

Tenwhestle's eyes, harder, more cynical, emptier than they'd ever been, found Gertrude. And yet again, Edwin was reminded of all the ways that this man had changed. Nay, they'd both changed. They'd both been forever altered.

Gertrude proved completely in control in ways Edwin was not. She stood and dipped a flawless curtsy.

"Tenwhestle, may I present . . ." Gertrude stared at Edwin, a question in her eyes. Edwin clenched and unclenched his palms and forced himself to complete those introductions. "Miss Killoran. Gert—*Miss Killoran*, the Marquess of Tenwhestle."

All the color bled from Lord Tenwhestle's cheeks, leaving his expression sallow. "I . . ." He shook his head slowly, backing away like he'd stumbled upon a Medusa. "I don't . . ." And without another word, the other man spun on his heel and fled. Tenwhestle slammed the door hard behind him, sending the bell into a feverish jingle.

Edwin stared after that swiftly retreating form, following him as he collected the reins of his mount from a street urchin outside.

And then, he was gone.

What did you expect? He told you precisely what he thought of you long ago. He'd blasted Edwin with a deserved blame that should be heaped on his shoulders, and then, just like the rest of the world, had left Edwin in exile to suffer for mistakes he himself could never forgive.

"Edwin?" Gertrude urged in gentle, calming tones that were so at odds with the tumult left in the marquess's wake.

"I'm fine," he barked, even though she hadn't asked. Even though she was undeserving of those harsh tones he leveled on her.

Gertrude recoiled and took a step away from him, putting the chair between them.

The pit of guilt only intensified in Edwin's belly. He scraped a trembling hand through his hair. "My apologies, Gertrude."

Stephen sidled up next to Edwin. "Is there trouble?" he asked with entirely too much relish, like one spoiling for an altercation.

"There is not," he assured the child beside him, just as the marquess wheeled his black stallion around and caught sight of Stephen.

Tenwhestle's entire face contorted into a paroxysm of grief. And then a moment later, he was racing his mount recklessly down Curzon Street . . . until he was gone.

"Who in hell was that?" his son asked, glancing up at Edwin.

"That was Lord Charles, the Marquess of Tenwhestle," Edwin said quietly. "Your uncle."

Chapter 14

"Meoowwww."

Seated on the Empire-style, carved-and-painted chaise, Gertrude glanced over the lessons she'd designed for her time here with Stephen, then at the grey cat. "Passing judgment, are you?" In a display of his usual feline fickleness, Gus leapt onto the pink, floral-embroidered jacquard upholstery. "But not too proud to seek my attentions, I see." She softened that chastisement by stroking him between his ears.

Closing his eyes, he purred long and low and then stretched out, curling beside her.

"Though in fairness, you are correct," she conceded. "I am deserving of that." Abandoning all attempts at work, Gertrude closed the leather journal on her lap with a decisive click and set it aside.

She, Stephen, and Edwin had returned from Gunter's more than ten hours ago, and Edwin had immediately sought out his library . . . where he'd been closeted away ever since. And she, despite working with Stephen on his lessons and designing future ones, had thought of no one except him—Edwin.

That was Lord Charles, the Marquess of Tenwhestle . . . Your uncle.

Edwin had been a man . . . haunted. Having herself battled—and often been crushed by—her own demons, she easily recognized them in another.

Nor had he been the only one discomposed. The stranger who'd interrupted that all-too-brief moment she and Edwin had shared had possessed a like grimness.

With a groan, Gertrude flung herself back in her seat and glared at the cheerful mural painted overhead. "I've never considered myself self-absorbed." Gus lapped at his right paw with his small, coarse pink tongue. "And that is precisely what I've been," she said into the void, owning that admission. Self-absorbed, singularly focused . . . ultimately, she'd not thought enough of what it would mean, her coming here. Of her forcing herself on this household, and on Edwin.

She had been so insistent on accompanying Stephen to his new residence in Mayfair that she'd not fully considered the implications of her being here on anyone . . . *except Stephen.*

Because truly, no one's happiness or well-being meant more to her—anything to her—except Stephen's. Gertrude, Cleo, Ophelia, Reggie, Broderick . . . they were each grown-ups, capable and able to now take care of themselves. Stephen, however, was just a child. One she yearned to see restored to the innocent child he'd once been. And so she'd forced herself inside Edwin's household and maintained her commitment to remaining until someone suitable could be found for her brother.

"But that was before," she whispered, stroking her fingertips along the silken softness of Gus's fur. That was before the Marquess of Maddock had been . . . a living, breathing man capable of great love and great suffering and hurt. Prior to these past days, Edwin had existed only in her mind.

The extent of her understanding about him as a person had been confined to their family's discourse—he was the madman who'd sent a threatening letter to Broderick that promised their demise. Yes, it had been all too easy to see Edwin as a shadowy figure, more fiction than real.

Until she'd come here. Until he'd agreed to accompany her and Stephen to the cabinetmaker's and Gunter's and allowed himself to be blindfolded in plain sight of all his peers, with Gertrude, a bastard born to the streets.

Nay, she'd not fully registered what her being here would mean to anyone else—until today.

Now there was Edwin. And Stephen's uncle.

And her—Gertrude Diggory. For that's who she truly was—Mac Diggory's daughter. That truth of her birthright could never be scrubbed from her identity. Coming face-to-face with a man whose sister had been killed by orders given by Gertrude's father only served as a reminder of Gertrude's ugly past.

Gertrude forced herself to look at that imprint upon the edge of her palm, that mark worn by every Diggory, one she had, over the years, stopped bringing herself to look at. But not now. Now she owned the mark of her name and birthright. Her father had wrought suffering upon Edwin and his family. Her father had denied Stephen of his mother. And in the wake of that fire set and the series of treacheries enacted that night, lives had been upended.

Stephen was the most important person to her. But others mattered, too. They mattered as much. Yes, it had been wrong to fail to consider how cruel it would be to force her presence upon Edwin. It was even more wrong to remain in his household when he'd proven to be a man who loved his son and yearned for the time they'd lost.

Gertrude trailed a jagged fingertip along the misshapen *D*. It was wrong for her to stay here, but shamefully, she would anyway—for Stephen.

She curled her fingers and ceased that distracted movement.

A faint whirring sounded atop her bureau. A moment later, the makeshift miniature roulette wheel she'd had specially designed began turning. It spun in a quick circle, set to motion by Sethos.

Gus lifted his head. His ears pricked upright, and his small body tensed as he went on alert.

"Enough," she scolded, eventually resting a warning hand atop his back until he again sat beside her.

Gertrude stared absently at that silver wheel spinning in dizzying circles.

With every encounter, she was forced to see Edwin—as a person. He was a gentleman who would have been well within his rights to throw her out on her arse for her relation to Diggory, but who'd allowed her to stay. He was a man who allowed himself to be blindfolded in public and take part in a child's game, all to earn a smile from his lost son. A man who'd purposefully lose a wager, just so that same child might have some manner of control over an untenable world.

Her heart did a little leap in her chest.

For where she was from, people did not willingly relinquish control. Victory was everything and superseded all. But Edwin had willingly done so for Stephen. And that sacrifice, a devotion to the happiness of another, before one's own pride and power, was heady stuff. It was foreign to all she knew and perilous for how it held her so wholly captivated now.

Nor is that all that captivated you . . . You're still thinking of the moment he sat beside you on the hammock, your knees touching, your lips close.

She briefly closed her eyes. So close that for a moment born of madness, she'd believed he intended to kiss her, and she'd wanted it. Craved it. Thought of what it would have been nearly every moment since. "Don't be a blasted fool."

The door burst open, and she gasped as her brother barged in.

With a squeal, Gus jumped down and darted under the chaise.

Brandishing his knife in one hand, Stephen did a sweep of the rooms. "Who you talking to?"

Her cheeks exploded with a mortifying heat. *Calm down. He doesn't know that you've been sitting here mooning over a man who hates you for the blood that flows in your veins.* "No one." Stephen narrowed his eyes in challenge. "Myself," she brought herself to admit. "I was just thinking aloud."

"That's dangerous and stupid," Stephen warned. He sheathed his dagger and then closed the door behind him.

"Yes, well, I trust my peculiar habits aren't what have you visiting my rooms at this hour," she muttered.

"No." Stephen opened his mouth and then did another search. When he spoke, he did so in conspiratorial tones. "It was strange."

Swinging her legs over the side of the chaise, Gertrude stood. "I've already told you. I was—"

"Not *you.*" The boy shot a hand out. "Well, sometimes you. But that's not what I'm talking about. *Him.*"

She shook her head. "Him?"

Her brother tossed his arms to the ceiling. "Bloody hell. Cleo and Ophelia wouldn't be this obtuse. I'm talking about the marquess. I've been thinking all day about the favor I want to put to the nob."

His father. She opened her mouth to correct him but called those words back. Neither she nor Edwin could force him. "And you've decided?" God help Edwin. He couldn't have understood the danger in offering a boy like Stephen a carte blanche favor.

"Something doesn't add up," Stephen said bluntly, misunderstanding her question.

Nothing, to borrow Stephen's terms, added up anymore. "Why don't you tell me what this is about?"

His little, freckled brow creased with confusion, Stephen started across the room and then stopped in front of the roulette wheel. "If it was the parmesan ice he didn't guess? I'd understand that, Gert. But muscadine?" He tossed a glance over his shoulder. *"Muscadine?"* he repeated. "I think he let me win." Stephen stared expectantly back.

Gertrude measured her response by turning a question on him. "Does it matter if he did?"

"Absolutely, it does," he shot back. "You don't do that. *We* don't do that." His jaw hardened. "It's weak."

Yes, that is how Broderick, Cleo, and Ophelia would see it. It was how Gertrude herself would have seen it, as well. But that was before Edwin. Before he'd made that sacrifice on behalf of his son and she'd come to understand what appeared a weak decision hadn't been. For it had brought another person joy and, through it, happiness to Edwin. Therefore, she'd rather say the marquess had the way of it. In fact, the Killorans could learn far more from him in that regard. "Do you know what I think?"

Stephen didn't move for a long moment, and then slowly, he shook his head.

"He didn't hurt you. He didn't belittle you. He took part in a game of which he was an outsider, which is all more than Mac Diggory ever did." *For me, or any of us.* "And so, I'd say whatever his reasons, there was honor to them, and *honor* is something we as Killorans respect."

"I still don't like it if he let me win," he insisted with a grudging obstinacy only he was capable of.

"Ah," she said, stretching out that syllable as she joined Stephen at the roulette wheel. She caught him by the shoulders and squeezed. "But we don't know if he did, so it would be a shame to not relish in your triumph because of something you fear might or might not have occurred."

He wrinkled his small nose. "Fair point. It would be a waste to not call in whichever favor I wish. I mean, after all, it wouldn't be that different from stealing."

It would be more like when they'd stood on corners and begged for coins outside of the London theatres. That more accurate analogy, however, would never sit with the boy more stubborn than the London day was long.

"There's the spirit." Gertrude winked.

He grinned. "I have an idea of what I might ask him for." And as he rubbed his hands with a dangerous slyness, Gertrude groaned.

"Be good," she called after him as he started for the door.

"I always am."

Gertrude snorted.

"I'm jesting. But I will . . . this time." Still, her brother did not leave but hovered at the front of the room.

She waited in silence, not able to bring herself to ask what troubled him, which would only send him fleeing.

After several long moments, he spoke. "He came with us today."

"Yes," she murmured, not pretending to misunderstand.

He pondered the tips of his worn shoes again. "I didn't expect that. For him to join us at Draven's . . . or Gunter's. I mean, I might have expected if he did come to one place, that it would be Gunter's because it's fancy and respectable. I still, however, didn't think he'd come with us there." Stephen brought his ramblings to a cessation.

Gertrude carefully considered her response. "Sometimes, Stephen, people surprise us." She drifted closer to him. If she made too sudden a movement, he'd bolt. "You and I?" Gertrude gestured between them. "And other people born in the Dials? We're *so* accustomed to all the bad ways in which those surprises come that we fail to see the wonderful ways that a person might surprise us, too." And that was what Edwin had done . . . what he'd been for her brother that day.

"Like . . . my father did today?" Stephen was too clever to miss the different meanings layered within her words.

Gertrude made to speak when two words reached out from all the others and held on: "my father." *Oh, God.* Why could she not have the strength that Cleo and Ophelia possessed? The one that made tears impossible. Gus knocked into her ankles, and she made a show of bending down to scoop him up. Stephen couldn't see her tears. He'd balk and then take flight. "Just like"—*Edwin*—"His Lordship did today," she said hoarsely. "He's not one accustomed to being amongst the world, and yet he went out twice today"—*at my request*—"for you." The marquess might hate her. He might treat her and her family with disdain and carry a seething resentment, but he'd always shown his heart to be open. He'd shown himself capable of great love, and a piece of her heart would forever belong to him for those gifts.

Her brother's throat bobbed. "If that's true, then why did he run and hide the minute we came home? He didn't take meals with us. Hasn't said a word since we returned."

"He has his reasons, Stephen," she murmured, absently stroking Gus's back. The grey tabby nestled against her chest. "I don't know what they were." She didn't know why seeing his former brother-in-law had brought about such a collapse in Edwin's emotional state that day. Was it simply the reminder of the wife Edwin had lost? Or was it more? "But I trust seeing your uncle had something to do with the reason he's been so . . . quiet since our return."

Stephen's lower lip quivered, and he clamped that flesh hard between his teeth. "M-maybe. But it isn't the first time he hasn't come around. When someone displays themselves, believe them. Isn't that what we say?" There was something faintly entreating there, in this child whom she'd raised since he was a boy new to Diggory's gang, fighting desperately to make sense out of two competing worlds and rationales. And it shattered her inside and out. Her arms curled reflexively around the warm bundle in her arms. Gus squirmed and then propelled back, jumping to the floor.

Gertrude sighed and moved closer toward her brother. "Our family has a way of speaking in absolutes, but that isn't the way of life, Stephen." Edwin had opened her eyes to that. "But I believe your father had his reasons for not coming for you these past weeks, and one day if you ask him, I'm sure he'll tell you."

His little body jerked, and he wrenched away from her. "Ask him?" He hissed. "If I ask him, it means I care. And I don't. Do you hear me? I don't." With that, he spun on his heel and took off.

"Stephen!" She surged after him. The little boy, however, was already gone, slipping off like the Shadow of Seven Dials, as he'd come to be known for his stealth. With a sigh, Gertrude started forward. There was a soft jingle, and from the corner of her eye, she caught a flash of movement. "No!" she gasped as Gus bolted.

Sethos. Blast this day to hell. Gertrude took off running, damning her vision that made it impossible to bring the small creature into perfect focus. "Stop," she hissed after the cat. How was it possible the day with Edwin and Stephen had gone from something magical . . . to this mayhem? Her skirts flew up about her ankles as she sprinted with the same steps that had guided her when she was running from the constables. "Get back here."

Sethos jumped onto the stair rail and scurried down. Gus bounded after him with long, leaping strides.

Her chest pounding hard, Gertrude quickened her steps.

The mouse continued his winding path lower, and then he disappeared over the side. Catching the rail, Gertrude leaned over and peered out at the white Italian marble. She made out a faint wiggling, and then . . . he was gone.

At last, Gus abruptly stopped in the middle of the foyer. With a wide yawn, he plopped down and proceeded to lick his paws.

Glaring at the troublesome cat, Gertrude hurried the remaining way downstairs. "I am disappointed." Her voice echoed around the soaring foyer.

"Meowww."

"We'll speak on this later," she muttered, and with determined footsteps, she went in search of Sethos.

Chapter 15

He'd been alone for so long.

After the conflagration that had left his family's ancestral London properties nothing more than a pile of tinder and ash, Edwin had dwelled in a new townhouse. There'd been no family nor friends around, only Marlow, an entirely-more-loyal-than-Edwin-deserved servant.

Edwin had let no one in. He had carefully built towering walls up, about himself and the townhouse he dwelled in, and lived contentedly, alone. Content to feel nothing for anyone or anything, he'd welcomed the gaping hole where his heart had once beat for his son.

There'd been no laughter or smiles or carefree games. Until for a fleeting instance in Gunter's today, when there had been all of that.

Then Charles had arrived, stiffly formal to Edwin and then looking upon Gertrude like she was Satan's helper. That unexpected, chance encounter with his former best friend and late wife's brother reminded him all over again that he had no right . . . to any of it. Misery, pain, and heartache were his only due.

These two days? They had been too much. *Too much.*

Augu—*Stephen*, Gertrude, his mother-in-law and father-in-law.

And now . . . Charles, who'd gone against his parents' wishes and helped his sister elope with Edwin. Edwin's repayment for that friendship and gift had been to fail to protect her as she'd deserved . . . because he'd been too busy avoiding her and the reminder of a love gone cold and the hatred that had grown in its place.

Hunched forward in his leather, wingback sofa, Edwin tugged at the strands of his hair, yanking slightly, feeling as mad as the world proclaimed him to be.

Grabbing the nearly empty snifter of brandy, he stared over the crystal glass to the fire that raged in the hearth. Those crimson flames bathed his face in heat, taunting him with an unneeded reminder of the peril they posed and the hell they had wrought.

He squeezed his eyes shut and allowed the memories of that day to come rushing back: him out at his clubs, partaking in drinks with gentlemen who'd been acquaintances at best. And yet, he'd hated being home when his son had slumbered. When Stephen slept and Lavinia was home from *ton* events, she had favored him with cold glances and thinly veiled insults and recriminations.

Coward that he was . . . selfish bastard that he was . . . he'd escaped those tense exchanges whenever he could. That night had been no different. He'd grown tired of the reminder that the woman he'd loved couldn't so much as stand the sight of him. Through those miserable days of their marriage, he'd accepted that theirs was a special kind of hell—a union that neither could get out of, no matter how much better it would be for them. That they were consigned to a marriage full of nothing but regret until death did they part.

Then death *had* parted them, and Edwin had come to appreciate what hell, in fact, was.

It was the pungent scent of smoke and ash and melted flesh; it burnt a man's nostrils and remained crisp in one's memory, long after the plumes of grey faded and new bricks were laid in place of the former conflagration.

He'd long ago accepted that his fate was to be hated. His own wife hadn't been able to stomach the sight of him. His own child despised him. His staff feared him. As such, he'd taken that as how it was for men like him. And he'd come to terms with his place in the world.

Until Gertrude Killoran.

She didn't cringe or cower in his presence but boldly challenged him at every turn to be a better man and father to his son. She didn't sneer at him but smiled and teased, and God help him, when he sat beside her this day, first at Draven's and then at Gunter's, he'd had a taste for a life he'd never known. One that he'd never thought to know, and certainly not with a Killoran of all people.

In just the short time he'd known her, however, she'd challenged everything he'd previously taken for fact. And now he didn't know which way was up or d—

A flash of white darted past the fireplace and then stopped . . . only to double back. Edwin followed the rodent as he pumped his tiny legs as fast as they could carry him before settling just beside Edwin's boot.

Like a damned family pet might.

Why, even the damned mice in his household were insane.

"Sethos." Gertrude's breathless voice sounded outside the library, and a moment later she came rushing into the room.

She held her palms out, feeling her way with her hands around the darkened room, and making himself go slow, he used the moment to study her.

He'd taken care to learn everything there was to learn about Broderick Killoran and Mac Diggory. The women who'd belonged to that gang had occupied less of his attentions. As such, he knew little about them. The married sisters had been ones he'd kept a closer eye on because of their presence amongst Polite Society and the influence they'd steadily amassed.

This woman, however—Gertrude—he knew next to nothing about. She was partially blind.

169

Had she been born so? Or had illness taken it?

And what must it have been like for a person on the streets to exist with that faulty sense? Just then, she flitted gracefully around the library; in possession of some innate knowing of which loose floorboard to avoid, she glided like a specter come to haunt. But a library was wholly different from a crowded street of London. What risks had she known, surviving out there with just one functioning eye? The idea of it hit him like a kick to the gut.

Edwin clenched his hands, and the leather button sofa crackled under those subtle movements. It was enough.

From her place at the opposite corner of the library, Gertrude straightened and faced him. "Edwin," she blurted. A splash of color filled her cheeks, and with the fire's soft glow bathing the delicate planes of her face, she was . . . *beautiful*. Unable to speak around the staggering weight of that silent admission, he remained seated, cowardly allowing her to cut a path back over until she stood before him.

"I trust it is not my company you've come in search of?" he drawled.

The minx cocked her head.

Lifting a brow, Edwin glanced pointedly at his feet. Gertrude followed his stare, and gasped. "You've found him." Sinking to the floor, she held out her palm.

The white rodent, like some devoted pup, scurried into his mistress's hand. A moment later, Gertrude placed him into her pocket. And at last, it made sense.

Let her go. She'd found what she was in search of, and there was nothing really for them to speak on. "So that is the reason for the pockets, I presume," he said instead.

Taking that as an invitation to sit, Gertrude settled herself comfortably in the folds of his sofa. She curled up like a contented cat and briefly contemplated the fire. "Not at all. Every garment should be fitted with pockets. They're really quite beneficial, you know. The more pockets one has, and the clever places one has them, the more one can store items. Particularly those one is wishing to keep from prying hands and eyes."

"I . . . see."

Her color deepened, and she immediately went . . . regretfully silent. She stroked that mouse resting within her pocket and stared into the dancing flames.

God, he was rot at this.

Conversing, striking up a dialogue, making others comfortable . . . he'd always been so very skilled at it all. Now every word that left his mouth was taken as an insult. Was looked at as if it contained layered meaning, none of which was kind.

When the truth was . . . her admission about her gowns had opened his eyes to a possibility he'd never considered.

Even textiles were a mechanism of self-defense to her and those in the streets. Gertrude's admission simply highlighted the ignorance and naivete he still carried all these years later. It didn't matter that Mac Diggory and his kind had invaded Edwin's world. Their evil had taught him much about the ugliness of the human spirit, and yet it hadn't opened his eyes to how the other half lived. Those outside the peerage and the *ton*, who didn't have to worry about protecting one's every cherished item from thieving hands. For if they did, there would be a constable to bring the pickpocket to justice.

He shifted, unable to look at her.

Yes, he was rubbish at . . . all this now—talking to people. All he did was make a person feel uncomfortable with his presence: Gertrude. His son. His staff. And perhaps he'd been silent for too many years, and that accounted for this need to continue speaking with her, as well.

Edwin tried again. "You have a mouse." He grimaced. Bloody hell. That wasn't even a question. It was a damned statement. Still focused on the flames, he knew the precise moment her stare moved to him.

"I do."

He waited for her to say something more. She would not make this easy, then. She'd insist that he feed his curiosity with questions. "It seems an . . . odd creature to take as a pet." Also not a question. "How did you come to have him?" There, he'd mustered one.

Gertrude drew her knees up to her chest and, reaching inside her pocket, fished the small creature out and then rested him atop the crest of her white night skirts. "He is an unconventional pet, isn't he?"

"Quite. But no less unconventional than naming him after an ancient Egyptian ruler."

She sat upright and excitement lit her eye, and his chest was filled with an unexpected lightness. "You know of him?"

"As a boy, I had a fascination with the ancient Egyptians. I wanted to—" A log shifted in the fireplace and sent up a fitting explosion of sparks and embers. His body jerked. *Do not think of it . . . do not think of it . . .* His entire body broke out in a cold sweat. Damned fires. After the conflagration, he'd not allowed them in his residence, not even in the dead of winter. Since his son had returned, however, Marlow had taken to ordering the rooms warmed and the hearths lit.

"You wanted to?" Gertrude prodded. That gentle encouragement brought his eyes open.

"What?" he said in blank tones. What had he been talking about?

Perfectly balancing the rodent on her knee, Gertrude scooted over until no cushions divided them. "You were saying that you had a fascination with the ancient Egyptians and wanted to . . . ?"

Share them with my son. I'd wanted to take him to museums and discuss the fascinating stories of those peoples . . .

"I wanted to know how you've come to name such a small creature after that ancient Egyptian leader," he finished, the lie lame to his own ears.

His own wife couldn't have been bothered with anything outside her social pursuits.

"Surely you know the mouse myth told by Herodotus?" She stared at him pointedly.

Actually, he didn't. "The extent of my knowledge on the Egyptians did not extend to those aspects of their culture."

Gertrude made a clucking noise with her tongue. "That is a shame," she chided, setting Sethos down on the arm of the sofa.

That mouse scrambled along the high back of the leather-button seating.

His lips pulled into a ghost of a smile that strained muscles still unaccustomed to that movement. "I trust you intend to give me a history lesson."

"Oh, absolutely," she vowed, settling into the seat beside him. And it was a distraction he welcomed. For having her here with him, sharing stories about . . . anything, kept him from giving in to the thoughts of the fire. "You studied Sethos's leadership, and so you know—"

"That he disgraced his army and found himself without one when Sennacherib invaded his country?" From the start, he'd expected Gertrude Killoran to be peculiar for the life experience she'd entered his household with. Just not in this way—a clever bluestocking who'd elucidate to him all the interesting stories and details he'd not gathered through the years. "I'm very familiar with his failings."

Her eyes went soft. Her lips parted. The air crackled around them. And he was riveted by the evidence of her adoration. His own wife hadn't even looked at him that way. Once she had . . . until she hadn't. And when only hate remained, hate was what had become all too familiar, and eventually comfortable. Only this was potent. This gaze filled with awe and appreciation and wonder over mere words to leave his lips. And he didn't know what to do with it. Or how to be around it. Edwin coughed into his hand. "Your story, madam?" he said, his tone gruffer than he'd intended and all he was capable of anymore.

She blinked enormous brown eyes. "My . . . ? Ah, yes . . . as I was saying, Sethos . . ." A pretty blush turned her cheeks a pinkish-red, giving her the look of an innocent, and her hushed murmuring cast a spell over him. And perhaps he wasn't still the naive fool who'd trusted a nursemaid whose speech had occasionally dissolved into Cockney, but Edwin believed the innocence before him. Or mayhap it was now that he craved that simplicity so very much.

"And he was promised divine succor would come to him," Gertrude was saying, her enlivened voice bringing him back to her telling. She scrambled onto her knees and shifted closer; her entire body became part of the telling, thrumming with a palpable excitement that was contagious. "The night before the battle, field mice chewed the quivers and shield handles of their enemies, who were disarmed and forced to flee." Gertrude deepened her voice, and when she spoke, she did so in feigned masculine tones. But God help him, they emerged as a low, husky contralto. "'And now,' says Herodotus," she boomed, her tones a siren's song that sucked him under her spell once more, and he didn't wish to break free. Later. Not now. "'There standeth a stone image of this king in the temple of Sethos, and in the hand of the image a mouse, and there is this inscription.'" Gertrude lifted a hand to the ceiling; the movement sent the loose belt at her night wrapper falling, and the fabric gaped open. "'Let whoso looketh on me be pious.'"

Impossible. His pulse knocked around loud in his ears. Her allure would have been safer had this draw been purely sexual, physical in nature. But it wasn't. It was her, brimming with energy and excitement and innocence, and he didn't want to shake free from the hold. "I've never . . . ," he whispered.

"Heard of it?" She flashed an endearingly cocky grin. "Some dispute the factuality of it."

How could she be so very oblivious to the fact that he'd been so upended in this instant? *Nay, you've been off kilter since the moment she showed up in your household, an avenging warrior to look after your son.* "But not you," he forced himself to say, because he had to say . . . *something.*

Gertrude chewed at the tip of her index finger. "I don't know," she finally conceded, the happiness dimming in her gaze, and he wanted to call his throwaway comment back and restore that bright light that had set him and this entire library aglow with some emotion other than misery. "There is historical proof attesting to the fact that the tale is of Egyptian and not Greek origins."

"That biblical account of when the Assyrian army was destroyed."

"Precisely," she murmured. "Those tales, however, fail to include mention of a mouse, and scholars say that the fact that the Egyptians did not deify the mouse as a godlike figure proves that it is a tale of fiction." Her expression wistful, Gertrude stretched her arm along the high back of the sofa. Sethos scrambled into her palm and promptly lay there. With steady hands, Gertrude drew him close to her chest and stroked the top of the rodent's back.

The minx could command even a wild creature, bending it to her gentle will. Just as she'd done with Edwin.

Over the top of that small white mouse, Gertrude's gaze held Edwin's, and he could not look away if this townhouse were set ablaze and his life destroyed once more. "But there was one mouse included in a monument, and so I prefer to believe in a history where those seen as valueless to society and unwanted are capable of some good that earns them even a bit of reverence."

Her. Edwin stilled. Along the way, she'd stopped speaking of Egyptian legends and started speaking of herself . . . and her place in this world.

Gertrude must have seen something in his eyes, for she hurriedly set the unlikely pet down and returned to her corner of the sofa. "I cannot keep him out anymore."

He attempted to follow that abrupt shift.

"Sethos," she clarified.

And he learned, despite these past years of snarling hate and simmering rage, he was . . . human, after all. For that creature mattered to her. She had a bond with the mouse, because she felt a kindred connection to it for her own circumstances, and he'd not be the one to sever those ties. "I'll not force you to get rid of him."

Surprise stamped her features. "You wouldn't?"

"I *won't.*"

Her expression went soft once more, and there was nothing weakening in his concession or his response. There was just a lightness in his chest that he'd not known in so very long.

"Thank you," she said softly. "I still cannot keep him out, though. He needs a c-cage." She tripped and stumbled over that word. "I've thought his place could be anywhere, and yet it cannot. It is dangerous for him here. I've a cat."

"You have a cat," he echoed dumbly. She'd been here just a short time, but still, he'd never seen that creature about.

"I actually have seven cats. Only one of whom is here with me." With every jolting word she spoke, he felt spun around. "And my mouse," she added after a moment's pause.

"You have a cat *and* a mouse living together? Out in the open."

"Yes. I thought I could teach them to live as companions, but I saw that relationship could never work, and so it is best for Sethos if he's at least safe." Gertrude sighed, and drawing her knees against her chest, she dropped her chin atop them. "Sometimes we think we know what is best, but we don't always." Again, she spoke in veiled meanings. "You didn't come 'round after we returned."

"I was otherwise occupied." That meeting with his brother-in-law had played out in his mind over and over again, and it had proven safer to retreat and contemplate all Edwin's own failings and what his reemergence into the world now meant.

"Because of your brother-in-law."

My God, how much she saw.

Edwin surged to his feet and wandered closer to the hearth; the blaze bathed his face with a loathsome heat that he forced himself to suffer through. He gripped the marble mantel and stared down into those flames. "Because of me." It was always because of him.

The leather groaned slightly, indicating Gertrude had moved. He felt more than heard her as she drifted over, standing just beyond his shoulder.

"He was my best friend and supported me in my match of his sister, my wife, when his own parents did not. And then rightfully blamed me when she was killed."

Gertrude made a sound of protest. "The blame was not yours. What happened belonged to the ones who took Stephen, and to Diggory." Her tones dripped with a seething hatred for that man so loathed by Edwin.

Edwin lifted his gaze slightly and stared at the crystal case clock atop the mantel, using that clear glass as a mirror to study the woman behind him. All along, Edwin had simply cast a net of hatred upon all who shared that bastard's blood and name. And until recently, never had he considered any of that Devil's offshoot would carry a like abhorrence for the man. He'd been so absorbed in his own past that he'd not allowed himself to see that mayhap they, too, had been victims, themselves gutted by Mac Diggory. "Blame belonged to me because I married a woman against her parents' wishes. I thought love could be enough. I thought her parents would come to accept our union. I was arrogant," he murmured, at last owning that failing. Edwin forced himself to face her. "I didn't think how Stephen's return would mean I'd have to confront . . . all of it." His voice emerged entreating. "I can't. I'm not ready." He never would be.

"You're not speaking just about your brother-in-law," she quietly observed.

No, he wasn't. He stood there in silence that Gertrude matched, not pushing him beyond that previous statement. "I'm mad." It was a phrase he'd uttered more times than he remembered about himself. One ascribed to him by society. And yet something, in speaking it now, to this woman, felt . . . remarkably freeing.

Her piercing gaze went through him, powerful in its ability to probe, and suddenly that ease dissipated and he wanted to call back his earlier pronouncement. "You're not mad. You're a man who has suffered greatly. Such grief would shatter any person, Edwin," she said, so pragmatic he could almost believe that illusion she spun.

"That night destroyed me." Unbidden, his gaze drifted back to the fireplace, and he lingered his stare on the orange-and-red flames there. "I'll never be the same man I was."

Gertrude covered his hand with her own, and his entire body went still. A heat greater than the blaze beside them scorched his palms. "You're right," she said solemnly. "You'll never be the same. Just as I'll never be the same from my experiences on the streets." She gave his fingers a light squeeze, as if willing strength into those digits. "What matters is we look forward and learn to live with, and find a semblance of peace with, our own demons."

He contemplated her words for a moment. "I once railed at what I first took for an insult," he said, bemusedly. "I lost my wife, my son, and my unborn child, and they'd shame me for my grief." His facial muscles spasmed. "Eventually, I came to accept society had in fact been . . . correct. I was mad." The misery over his losses and the memories of that night had rotted his brain until he'd come to not only freely accept but also, oftentimes, *embrace* his lunacy. "And then . . . it became something more."

Gertrude stared questioningly back. "A tool," he said, his voice gravelly. Edwin angled himself so that he was directly facing her. "It became a tool to protect myself."

She didn't blink. "From what?" she whispered.

From the world's disdain. From regret over all he'd lost. Grief had morphed into madness until it had become so interwoven with who he was there could never be any separating himself from it. He shook his head, unable to utter those truths aloud. "I can't see Charles," he said, flatly, ending the matter.

Of course, she'd never be content with that nonanswer.

"We're never ready, Edwin. We just do the best we can. But hiding away will not erase the past or help your future. And your future is with Stephen."

He closed his eyes. "I don't know how to be around him. I don't know how to be around anyone." Edwin slashed his spare hand through the air.

"And you won't know how to be around your son as long as you hide away from him." Gertrude gave his fingers a light squeeze. "Tell me this," she prodded. "Which felt most right to you today? Which felt best? Eating ices at Gunter's and playing a child's game with Stephen? Or hiding in your library and avoiding him for the remainder of the day?"

Edwin stalked over to the sofa and, presenting her with his back, sank into the folds of the chair. "I don't think I can face the world again." There it was, the realization he'd grappled with all day.

The floorboards squeaked as Gertrude drifted over. She sat beside him.

Collecting his hand in hers, she gave it another squeeze and drew it close to her chest. His fingers brushed her skin. He felt the steady, reassuring beat of her heart. "You just do it slowly. You do it with Stephen, and you do it for him. It is always about him."

She spoke as one who knew. Who'd made sacrifices for the boy and done so without question.

The heart he'd thought broken and empty stirred to life, and Edwin curled his hand around Gertrude's, twining his fingers with hers.

The air crackled between them. Or was that the fire raging in the hearth? It was all twisted, with reason having receded and leaving in its stead the stirring heat of her touch.

Gertrude darted the tip of her tongue out and dusted it along the seam of her lips, that innocuous gesture of nervousness erotic for what it conjured and implied: her awareness. For it was there. It had been there from the moment they'd first met. Desire flared to life, and this time he did not seek to quell it. He could not quell it.

"Edwin," she whispered, slightly breathless. Her chest rose and fell from the force of her rapid inhalations.

His throat moved painfully.

Release her. Release her for so many reasons: because of who she is. Because of what you wish to do. Because of what you will do, if she doesn't leave in this instant.

Chapter 16

He was going to kiss her.

As a woman who'd grown up on the streets and witnessed cruder acts than a kiss, Gertrude had come to recognize the moment just before a man embraced a woman.

In those instances, that discovery had been retained in a bid for self-preservation: know when, so one could flee. And she had fled before, for the basest beasts in the Dials didn't give a jot about a blind eye when it came to their animalistic urges.

She'd had two men who'd dared to put their mouths on hers and their tongues in her mouth before she'd nearly bit that loathsome flesh and knocked them to the ground with a knee to their groins. Those had been the only two kisses she'd known, both vile acts from ruthless thugs in Diggory's gang, who'd gambled . . . and accurately . . . that Diggory wouldn't give a jot about the blind daughter. From then on, Gertrude had carried nothing more than an apathetic view of those intimate exchanges between men and women.

Until now.

Edwin hooded his gaze, those thick black lashes sweeping down and obscuring his dark-brown eyes, but not before she caught the flash of hunger blazing from within their depths as they lingered on her mouth.

Gertrude's heart quickened.

For in this moment, with this man, nay, with Edwin, the Marquess of Maddock, she didn't want to flee. She wanted to know the feel of his mouth on hers. She wanted to know what it was to have him wrap his arms about her.

Someone groaned. Was it her? Or him? Everything was blurred.

And then his mouth was on hers.

Heat. A scorching-hot blaze that burnt on contact. His lips, hard like steel and soft like satin, melded to hers. Gertrude went still under the delicious onslaught of it, and then turned herself over to everything he promised.

Going onto her knees, she twined her arms about his neck, tangling her fingers in his luxuriant silken tresses. Angling himself on the sofa so that they faced one another, Edwin slanted his mouth over hers again and again, and she unashamedly met every bold touch of his lips.

He filled his hands with her buttocks and drew her closer to him so their bodies were flush with no divide between them.

A long moan spilled from her lips, that sound swallowed as Edwin slipped his tongue inside, touching it to hers, and she met it with abandon.

There was nothing sloppy or vile about this exchange. "Edwin," she groaned into his mouth, his name a plea and a prayer.

He responded by caressing his large hands over her, searchingly. He moved them down the narrow curve of her hips, her thighs, molding the fabric of her nightgown to her heated skin.

Then he reached between them and palmed her right breast.

Desire seared her veins, setting her afire from the inside out as he stroked and teased the puckered tip. "What do you do to me?" he rasped against her mouth between kisses. "You remind me what it is to feel and be alive."

That raw admission sent a new wave of emotion through her, and lest reality intrude with too many words spoken, Gertrude opened her mouth once more, allowing his tongue entry.

They dueled with their tongues, sparring in an erotic, heady battle that she gladly surrendered to.

She dimly registered him guiding her down; the cool leather crackled and groaned under their added weight as he brought himself to rest atop her. He caught his weight at his elbows; all the while, he never broke contact with her mouth.

He kissed her as though he sought to memorize the feel and taste of her. As if she were the only woman in the world.

And she, Gertrude Killoran, long invisible to all, felt what it was to be wanted and hungered for . . . and so very much alive because of it.

Edwin shifted, and she groaned in protest, fearing he'd break this kiss and shatter this most glorious moment of her existence. But he merely moved his weight onto his left side, freeing his hand so he could continue his previous exploration.

With expert fingers, he slid her wrapper off, shimmying the burdensome fabric off her shoulders. Next, he guided her nightshift down, so that the cool air kissed her skin; that juxtaposition of heat and cold sent desire shooting through her.

He lowered his head, and Gertrude held her breath; she did not move. She did not speak. She made herself absolutely still as he brought his lips to the crest of one modest swell.

Her eyes slid closed, and a shuddery sigh spilled from her as he took that swollen tip deep in his mouth, suckling, teasing.

An ache throbbed between her legs, and Gertrude released a long, throaty moan, wanton to her own ears, and she luxuriated in her womanhood. Embraced it. Thrilled in feeling what it was to be beautiful and wanted and—

"Gert? Where *are* you?" That child's voice piped through the doorway and had the same effect as a bucket of Thames water being tossed atop her head, as Diggory had awakened her when she'd been just a babe.

Edwin was on his feet in an instant. He had his garments in order and his cravat straightened, and then he was helping Gertrude to stand before she could make order of her thoughts through the desire cloaking her mind. And then horror came slapping at her senses, robbing her of that all-too-brief interlude of bliss. She looked to the doorway, dimly registering Edwin righting her nightgown and tucking the curls that had escaped her plait back behind her ears.

That sprang her into action. Fingers shaking, Gertrude grabbed up the forgotten wrapper and shrugged into it—just as the door opened.

A pair of shocked, wide eyes stared back. "You are here!" Stephen exploded. "I thought you'd come and try to—" He stopped. The little boy looked between Gertrude and Stephen.

"Stephen," she said lamely, fiddling with the latch at her waist. She took a step toward him. "What are you—?"

"What's going on here?" Suspicion better reserved for a man twenty years his senior fell across Stephen's gaze.

What was she doing here? What was she doing? Gertrude's mind raced beyond her passionate embrace with Edwin to the reasons that had propelled her here: Stephen, her mouse. Her mouse! She opened her mouth, but Stephen homed his rapidly wary gaze on her face.

She prayed the shadows concealed the guilty blush staining her cheeks. "You're flushed."

Bloody hell. Why was he so blasted observant? In a bid for support, she cast a sideways glance at Edwin and found him abjectly unhelpful.

"I lost Sethos."

"He's right *there*." Stephen jabbed a dirt-encrusted fingertip at Edwin. "Next to *his* hand."

As if on cue, Sethos scrambled onto his back legs and nibbled at the air.

Drat. "Uh . . ."

"We found him," Edwin intoned in a perfectly cool, composed noble delivery.

"Obviously," Stephen drawled, folding his arms at his chest. Looking like his father. Sounding so much like his father that Gertrude's heart turned in her chest. The suspicion in Stephen's gaze deepened.

Neatly sidestepping her brother's far-too-observant statement about her flushed cheeks, and in a bid to break the boy's scrutiny, Gertrude went and retrieved her mouse. "We were having a heated discussion," she allowed.

Which wasn't altogether untrue. There had been a discussion. And their exchange had been heated. Just not, however, in the ways she now presented them to Stephen.

Stephen came forward. "You were?"

"We were?" Edwin asked at the same moment. His son swung his sharp focus back his way. "That is, *we were*," he neatly supplanted.

Gertrude deposited Sethos into her pocket. "Indeed. We were speaking about the woman who'll be hired as your governess."

That statement had the expected and hoped-for reaction.

Stephen surged forward. "You found someone?" he demanded, and not allowing Gertrude or Edwin a word edgewise, he launched a steady flow of statements that saw his speech dissolve into an all-too-familiar Cockney. "Oi haven't seen anyone come here. Ya think to foist me off on just anybody so ya can be done 'ere and return back to the clubs?"

That charge hit like an arrow to the chest. "Do you think so little of me?" she asked, unable to keep the hurt from creeping in, even though it was a vulnerability that would only earn her brother's derision.

Except . . . Stephen just gave a little shrug. "I wouldn't blame ya," he said, moving between proper English and his Cockney. "But neither do I want you just going and leaving me here, either."

Gertrude stole another glance at Edwin. If his son's words landed a like mark in him, he gave no outward reaction. And yet . . . there was a tension to his facial muscles, a whiteness at the corners of his lips from one who sought desperately to reveal . . . nothing.

"Your sister is not one who'd simply leave you," Edwin said at last.

Breathless at that unlikely defense, her mouth fell open, and she sought to mask it.

"She is, however, one who'd be certain that we hire you someone who would be a good match for you as a person and student."

He knew that of her. After only a brief time together, the first exchanges of which had been laced with hatred and fury, he could speak so solemnly to her character.

And he knew her. His words revealed as much. She cleared her throat in a bid to rid it of the tight wad of emotion there. "Your father is right. In addition to our time visiting Draven's and seeing your new rooms readied, we have to also be certain that we give proper attention to your future governess." Which she hadn't given thought to until this moment. Because seeing Stephen settled comfortably in his surroundings had been the pressing concern.

"Fine," Stephen conceded, and then he swiftly shot another finger up. "But I don't want a stuffy snob."

Edwin lifted his head in acknowledgment. "Never."

"And I don't want someone who's going to faint or squeal or try to make me into someone I'm not."

Whoever was ultimately hired and charged with his education wouldn't make him into someone he wasn't, but rather, that young woman would restore him to who he'd once been. What could she say to him that wasn't a lie?

Edwin answered for her. "We wouldn't tolerate someone attempting to change your spirit, Stephen."

We. A single syllable. One word that twined Gertrude and Edwin as one. And it was pure madness, surely a product of a stolen embrace that had seared her soul, but had felt so wholly right.

Her brother nodded slowly. "All right, then. I'll trust you . . ." Then he added on a rush, "*Until* you give me reason not to."

It was an enormous concession from a boy who never made one.

"Fair enough," Edwin vowed.

Tears pricked at her lashes. And it was an equally significant concession made by a father scarred by treachery.

Stephen started for the doorway, then stopped. "You coming?" he asked Gertrude.

"I'll be along shortly," she murmured. "I wanted to finish speaking with Edwin." Which was also not an untruth.

He nodded and then continued on. After the door closed, she trained her ears on Stephen's faintest of footfalls, until they receded and faded altogether. With his absence, a sobering reality descended on the room: her purpose in being here. "We'll need to find and interview suitable governesses. For when I'm gone," she added.

Edwin rescued his snifter and drank the rest of it. "It is essential we do not rush the process. It matters more that Stephen has the right person."

"Yes." She smiled wistfully at him. Who would have imagined just days ago he'd utter those words?

Gertrude lingered. She should leave. Stephen was no doubt even now monitoring her absence. And yet, she waited. Wanting . . . something more. Uncertain what that was. When it became apparent after a long stretch that Edwin intended to add nothing else, she bowed her head. "Edwin," she murmured as she began to leave the room.

When she had the door handle in her fingers, she cast a last look over her shoulder. "Edwin?"

He lifted a blond brow.

"You spoke about the world being off-balance. But . . . setting all this to right, and including Stephen in the process, will help you find a semblance of normality." *How am I this steady?* How, when it spoke of her leaving Stephen behind and his education to another? If she could be honest with herself, she could admit she'd begun to enjoy life outside the hell and found joy in this household. Her mind shied away from that.

"Good night, Gertrude," he murmured.

Good night, which was really just another form of *goodbye*. "Good night," she returned, oddly bereft.

And as she took her leave, Gertrude could not rid herself of the feeling that everything had shifted this night, and despite her promises for him, nothing for herself would be normal, ever again.

Chapter 17

In the week that followed, Gertrude and Edwin settled into an easy existence. The rage that had simmered between them had receded, and in its place they'd forged a companionable relationship where they each worked with Stephen's best interests in mind.

They took meals together. Gertrude reported to Edwin on Stephen's progress with his lessons. They interviewed candidates for the position of governess and then discussed each woman's suitability to the post.

There was such an ease between them that Gertrude could almost forget that a blood feud divided them. She and Edwin had become unlikely friends.

In fact, so much had changed she could almost forget the explosive moment of passion shared in his library, late one night when all reason had fled and only desire had raged.

Almost.

Liar. You've thought of little else, since.

"We've already interviewed two candidates today," Edwin muttered, adjusting his cravat. He was all cool formality, perfunctory. No-nonsense. All business. And as such, he bore no hint of the one who'd been so overtaken with passion that he'd laid her down under him, framing her body with his elbows. "We agreed to two per day."

Heat prickled on her neck. How could he be so . . . unaffected after their embrace and just relegate them so easily to the role of employer and . . . and . . . whatever she was? How? When their embrace had been the singularly most breathtaking moment of her existence, and she'd felt at last what it was to be beautiful and desired.

"Gertrude?" he asked impatiently.

"Er . . . yes." Dropping her gaze to the leather folder atop her lap, she went through the pretense of drawing out the résumé of the candidate they even now debated. And a wave of shame battered at her. Here she sat, longing for some evidence of caring, when she should be wholly attending to the hiring process for Stephen's governess. Fighting back those pathetic ponderings, Gertrude composed her thoughts and brought her attention back into focus, where it should be—on Stephen. "Mrs. Upton's services have not been strictly relegated to the nobility," she explained, brandishing one page for him to read. Gertrude laid it out before him. "As you can see, she's had charges born outside the peerage."

Edwin picked up the sheet and proceeded to read.

"She's also dealt with children who've had . . . complex pasts."

"Not as complex as Stephen's," he muttered, directing that observation without inflection at the page in his hands.

Nonetheless, that statement landed like a physical punch she'd taken to the chest by one of Diggory's most lethal fighters. It had robbed her of breath and thought, knocking her square on her buttocks, until the stars dancing behind her eyes had lifted.

For despite the ease they'd settled into, the truth remained that her father had destroyed Edwin's life. And how much better a person he was than she or any of the Killorans, with his ability to set aside that hatred and allow her a say in Stephen's future. It left her humbled and hurting all at the same time.

Edwin lifted his head, and a frown grazed his lips. "What is it?" he asked with an intuition she would have never believed a nobleman capable of. They were all supposed to be self-absorbed, pompous bastards, unaware of the feelings or suffering of anyone around them. How narrow she'd been in her thinking.

"I believe you should give the young lady a chance," she brought herself to say. Gertrude was saved from having to add anything more by Marlow's familiar knock.

A moment later, the door opened.

"Mrs. Upton," he announced.

This was Mrs. Upton.

She was a breathtaking vision of English beauty personified. Her hair a flaxen blonde, her eyes a cornflower blue, and her cheeks a pale cream white, she was a sight.

"Mrs. Upton," Edwin called out, coming around his desk.

Taking that as an invitation, the young woman glided forward with the regal grace of a queen. "My lord," she greeted in singsong tones.

And oddly, Gertrude had a sudden inclination to cry. Governesses weren't supposed to be . . . beautiful.

Edwin turned to Gertrude. "May I present Miss Killoran?"

Belatedly, she came to her feet and hovered behind the leather wingback chair. "How do you do?"

Mrs. Upton dropped a perfect curtsy. "Miss Killoran, it is a pleasure." She spoke as though she meant it. And she wore a smile, to boot. A wide, generous one that bespoke kindness. Unlike the other dour-faced matrons who'd sat before them with fear riddling their eyes when they'd looked upon both Edwin and Gertrude.

And Gertrude, who'd led every previous interview, found herself at sea.

Edwin neatly stepped in. "Won't you sit?" After Gertrude sat, Mrs. Upton slid into the indicated chair beside her. "Perhaps you can begin by sharing your work history with us?"

As the young candidate enumerated her four years of experience, Gertrude listened on. Wanting to find fault. Selfishly, she didn't want to like her. It was wrong and piteous and humiliating to acknowledge, even to herself, but there was something . . . easier in imagining a grandmotherly figure left behind here with Edwin and Stephen and not . . . not . . . this flawlessly gorgeous woman who had full use of both eyes.

Edwin briefly slid his gaze away from Mrs. Upton. There was a question in his eyes. Gertrude forced a smile and then returned all her attention to the young governess.

When Mrs. Upton concluded her recitation, Edwin steepled his fingers and studied her over the tops of them with an unflinching gaze that would have had most any other woman cowering . . .

Not Mrs. Upton. She met his stare unwaveringly.

"And what of your experience with recalcitrant charges, Mrs. Upton?" Edwin urged.

A wry smile pulled at her lips, a perfect cupid's bow. "Vast, my lord. Most of my charges begin recalcitrant."

He narrowed his eyes. "And when you leave them?"

"They retain their spirit but are polite and respectful."

It was a perfect answer. She wasn't a woman come to crush children, but to shape them.

"My brother collects weapons," Gertrude blurted, and two sets of gazes swung her way. She cleared her throat and smoothed her palms down her skirts. "What are your opinions on . . . such a pastime?"

Mrs. Upton furrowed a perfectly noble brow. "It is my opinion that as long as he does not use those weapons to hurt or harm, then though unconventional, it is not uncommon. Most of my previous employers held on display ancient weapons, relics of some significance to their family. I trust Master Stephen's are significant to him in their own way."

Gertrude didn't move.

She was . . . "The One." The very candidate they'd been searching days for, and she also signified the end of Gertrude's time here.

This time, she didn't even attempt to speak through the ball of misery knotting her throat. When it came to hiring staff, Gertrude didn't have unreasonable standards. She was, however, attuned to the character of individuals in her family's employ and those who sought posts. As such, she'd known after seven days of nonstop interviews with possible governesses that the first fourteen candidates would never do. And the most recent woman seeking the post *would*.

Edwin stood. "Thank you, Mrs. Upton. At this time, I feel we're looking for someone with different experience for my son."

"I understand, my lord," the young woman said with perfect aplomb as she came to her feet. "Should you find you might benefit from my services, I am available to assist His Lordship."

What? Gertrude swiveled her head back and forth between them. What in blazes was happening? As much as she despised the idea of the beautiful Mrs. Upton with her experience schooling all manner of children remaining on while she left, neither could she simply just allow her to leave. Not when she would be the perfect governess for Stephen.

She scrambled to her feet. "But . . ."

Edwin withered that interruption to silence with a single glare.

Gertrude clamped her lips shut.

Mrs. Upton walked proudly from the room, shoulders back, turned away by Edwin just like the other women to come before her.

As soon as she'd gone, Gertrude shut the door behind her and waited.

And given every lesson she'd learned on the streets about the importance of private conversations, she restrained the words on the tip of her tongue and continued waiting until those footsteps receded altogether. "What is the meaning of this? Surely she is the one."

"No. She is not."

"What do you mean, 'No, she is not'?" Gertrude exploded, stalking across the room and planting her palms on the smooth mahogany surface of Edwin's desk, in what had become an all-too-familiar exchange.

"I meant . . . no," he said with an infuriating simplicity.

Interview, dismiss, reject . . . Repeat.

That had become the process she and Edwin had followed these past seven days, interviewing candidates put forward by the distinguished agency.

"She would never do," Edwin said, and with an air of "I'm done speaking on this; find another" that he'd struck before, he climbed to his feet and started across the room.

Gertrude stared incredulously past him. "And just why not?"

"Do I really need to tell you?" he asked in beleaguered tones as he came to a stop at his sideboard.

Beleaguered? He was beleaguered? Straightening, Gertrude perched her hands on her hips and stared after him. They had at last found a woman who'd suit Stephen, and Edwin had spared her no more than the customary fifteen minutes he had when interviewing all the ones before her? "Actually, I just told you that you do. So *yes*. You really do need to tell me why Mrs. Upton won't make a suitable governess for Stephen."

Edwin picked up a crystal decanter and contemplated it for several moments before setting it down. He reached for another.

She growled. He'd be this . . . casual?

The door burst open, and Stephen came rushing inside. He skidded to an abrupt stop. "We're going to be late." *Bloody damn.* Gertrude consulted the brooch timepiece at the bodice of her dress. They would be late to their meeting at Draven's. "Did you forget?" Stephen demanded.

Gertrude and Edwin spoke simultaneously.

"We did not."

Color spilled along Edwin's high, chiseled cheekbones, and as he took a quick sip of his brandy, Gertrude frowned. After days of meeting and discussing the qualities and characteristics of the governess Stephen would require, then debating the merits of each candidate who left, their thoughts had begun to move in an alarmingly synchronic harmony. It was a level of closeness she didn't know with even her siblings, and with this man it disquieted her all the more—for reasons she didn't care to consider.

"Are you paying attention?" Stephen snapped, giving the oak panel a shove that shook its frame and Gertrude from her reverie.

"I'm paying attention. Wait for us in the foyer, Stephen. Edwin and I will be along shortly." After Gertrude brought him around to bringing Mrs. Upton back for another interview. "We're just discussing . . . business."

Stephen alternated a suspicious stare between them. "You're fighting again."

Gertrude and Edwin spoke as one.

"Yes."

"We are not fighting."

She glared at Edwin. "We are not fighting," she repeated. And they weren't. Not really. Fighting had been the volatile display he'd put on when she'd first arrived and they'd been foes. Now they were two people working as a pair with Stephen's best interests and needs compelling them both. From the boy, an unlikely bond had been forged.

Stephen dropped a shoulder against the panel of the door. "Well? Which is it?"

Edwin set aside his snifter. "Very well. Your sister is one for semantics this day." *Your sister.* Warmth built in her chest at that admission. He'd been adamant at the beginning that Gertrude's ties to Stephen were false ones. In a short time, however, he'd acknowledged that bond he had every right to deny. "We are debating yet another candidate for the position of governess. Isn't that correct, Gertrude?"

She hurriedly sought to regain her footing and focus, not on the conundrum this man was proving to be but on the immediate issue before them.

Stephen's slender frame went taut. "And?"

"I do not believe this is a discussion to be had at this time."

Her brother tossed a withering glance her way. "Because I'm here?"

"Uh . . ." Unwittingly, her gaze went to Edwin.

The ghost of a grin on his lips, however, said she'd find no hope there. "Your sister was inclined to hire the young woman, and I invited the young lady to leave and suggested she look elsewhere for a post."

Stephen angled his head. "I don't see what the problem is with that."

"Mrs. Upton did not balk at the idea of your weapons collections."

"That supposed to impress me?" the boy asked bluntly.

"Exactly," Edwin said.

Gertrude shot him a glare and then presented her shoulder to him and directed her focus entirely to Stephen. "We are searching for an unconventional governess for you. Mrs. Upton—"

"That's a bloody rotted name."

"Hush. It's hardly her fault, the name she's been given." Gertrude tossed her arms up. "Furthermore, her name is irrelevant. What *is not*"—she directed that to Edwin—"is how she might or might not prove an adequate governess."

"And is that all we're searching for in my governess?" Stephen drawled with his father's droll tones. "Adequate."

"Precisely." Edwin toasted his son.

And Gertrude identified that slight lift of a glass, and the look that passed between Edwin and Stephen, as the precise moment her brother's loyalties shifted . . . or at least on the subject of his governess. It was a loss to her, when the Killorans didn't relish, tolerate, or accept defeat in any form. But in this . . . this moment between father and son, too long divided, she'd willingly concede, if only to see that fledgling bond grow all the more. She sighed. "Very well. That will be all the interviews for today. We'll meet with Draven—" Stephen let out a loud, excited whoop and bolted from the room. Alone once more, Gertrude looked to Edwin. "And then we'll return to the matter of finding Stephen a governess."

Chapter 18

Mrs. Upton *would* have made for an adequate governess.

Nearly an hour later, seated on one end of the sapphire-blue satin, checkered tête-à-tête chair and watching his son engrossed in his daily conversation with Draven, Edwin could admit that to himself.

At least in silence.

"I still do not see what the problem was with Mrs. Upton," Gertrude whispered from the other end of the odd seating.

"You would not."

And he did not. Most of the candidates to come before her had inspired the same unease in his belly that he'd ignored when Stephen had been a babe. The young governess Mrs. Upton hadn't caused that disquiet, and yet . . . something had kept him from capitulating.

Because if you hire her, it means Gertrude Killoran would no longer serve a purpose in your household.

Yes, he was as mad as the world took him for.

"Then, why was she a 'no'?"

God, Gertrude Killoran was nothing if not persistent. She'd not quit until she had an answer and the truth he could not give. "I don't know, Gertrude," he finally shot back in hushed tones. "I can't tell you why." Which was the truth. "Something about her . . . about the situation . . . did not feel right, and so I'm trusting that instinctual feeling that tells me that she was not the one."

For the first time since Mrs. Upton had taken her leave, that effectively silenced Gertrude. "I understand," she said quietly in tones that said she very much did.

Edwin took his gaze from Stephen and looked at the woman pressed against the curve of the odd chair they both occupied. He swept his gaze over her cheeks. "Years ago, I had reservations about the woman put forward as Stephen's nursemaid. My wife"—he stared beyond the top of Gertrude's head to the boy who had been, and would always be, his everything—"insisted that I disapproved because she had recommended the young woman for hire."

By that point in their union, their marriage had dissolved to a constant debate and fight about everything, from which social gatherings they would attend to who was hired to care for Stephen. "Had I trusted my instincts . . . ," he whispered to himself, and a memory intruded.

I said we're hiring her, and we're hiring her, Edwin. You merely want to control all decisions.

It is not that, Lavinia. There is something I don't trust . . .

Pfft. *You'd play the doting father. You, who visit your clubs and gaming hells.*

Edwin struggled to swallow around the wad that threatened to choke him with the weight of past regrets.

If only I'd not conceded the point. If only—

Gertrude's hand covered his own, drawing him back from the agonizing path his thoughts had crept down. He stared at their entwined fingers, hers the most unexpected of lifelines. "It wasn't your fault."

"It actually was all my fault," he said, unable to keep the bitterness from spilling into his admission. It was the first time in the whole of his marriage and then the tragedy that had unfolded after that he'd taken ownership of that fact out loud. "I married where I oughtn't."

She shook her head slowly. "I don't . . . ?"

"Oh, she was a lady. I was a lord. For all intents and purposes, it was a noble match that one would think any parent from the peerage would support."

"And yet hers did not?" Gertrude ventured.

He'd been arrogant enough to believe Lavinia's disapproving mother and father would come 'round because he was a nobleman . . . and their son's closest friend. How wrong he'd been on every score. "They saw the young man that I was: a rogue who wagered too much. Who kept outrageous hours and visited gaming hells and, as such, was undeserving of their cherished daughter. They launched quite a campaign to dissuade her. Whatever she wished for from them, she received. The one thing she could not, however, garner in all our years of courtship and marriage was their approval."

"What happened?"

"She wed me anyway," he said, stating the obvious. And it had been the end of her life because of it. "She married me, believing she could bring them 'round to accepting our love for one another." His lip peeled up in one corner in a derisive sneer.

A boom of laughter went up from across the room, interrupting Edwin's telling. They looked to where Draven thumped Stephen on the back. Laughing, his cheeks flushed red with amusement over whatever jest the pair shared.

As if feeling their stare upon him, Stephen glanced over. He lifted his hand in a little wave before returning his attention to whatever question the cabinetmaker was now putting to him. He bore little resemblance to the snarling boy who'd entered Edwin's household almost ten days ago. It almost gave Edwin hope that, in the years to come, they might forge something between them. When he'd never been able to maintain a bond with his son's mother.

"She loved you," Gertrude murmured, bringing his gaze over to her. "Her family disapproved of you and fought your suit, and yet, she chose you."

"And hated me every day thereafter because of it." The remembered pain of that had haunted him continuously over the years. That realization had left him splayed open, and even when the jagged sharpness of it had diminished, it had faded to a dull ache but remained. This time, the pain did not come. In its stead was a somberness to that admission. "And with good reason. I drove a wedge between her and the parents who meant more to her than anyone." That realization of their place in the order of her life had held true even with Stephen's birth.

And it had only intensified his own resentment for the young woman he'd once loved.

"Good reason?" Gertrude echoed. "Resenting you because her family disapproved? That isn't how love is supposed to be."

"And how is that, Gertrude?" He leaned closer, across the curve in the chair, dipping his mouth near her ear. The scent of her filled his senses, delicate and enthralling. "Patient and kind? Neither jealous nor boastful nor proud nor rude. It does not demand its own way. It is not irritable, and it keeps no record of being wronged. It does not rejoice about injustice but rejoices—"

"Whenever the truth wins out. Love never gives up, never loses faith, is always hopeful, and endures through every circumstance. Corinthians," she stated flatly. "Yes, that is precisely what love is and means. *All of it.*"

Clever bluestocking that she was, she would know verbatim the ancient words of the Bible. She knew everything from taming rodents to Egyptian kings and biblical texts.

"Are you laughing at me?" she demanded.

And he froze. *I'm smiling.* This time it had come so naturally, without a thought, and with him unaware of that slight twist of those muscles until she'd pointed it out. "Never, Gertrude."

Some of the tension left her narrow shoulders.

He shifted, straining closer, hanging on to the words that hovered on her lips.

"What your wife did at first? Standing up to her family despite their wishes for her? That's what you do when you love someone, Edwin," Gertrude said softly. "You love unconditionally and without a care of what the world says or thinks."

He chuckled. "I was once that innocent." Back then, however, he'd not seen that. He'd seen himself as a scoundrel. Life had schooled him on the fact that there were many types of innocence. He'd been naive of the ugliness that dwelled in a man's soul until Mac Diggory had burnt down his existence.

A little frown hovered on Gertrude's lips. "That is the first, and likely the last, time anyone would accuse me of being 'innocent' of anything."

Yes, he'd been of a like opinion. But that had been before. Before she'd revealed herself so very devoted to Stephen's well-being and future and happiness. Before he'd found that she was a young woman who'd make a rodent into a pet.

Gertrude rose and sailed around the tête-à-tête chair. She perched herself on the edge of his bench, stealing the corner. "You believe I'm speaking of a romantic form of love. Why? Because I'm a woman?" She didn't allow him a reply. "I've never been in love." She was better off for it. All love had left him was broken and empty. He'd not see Gertrude become that. "I've never known what it is to surrender so wholly to that emotion you knew with your wife." Did he imagine a wistful quality to her clear gaze? "The love I speak of, the kind where one will do anything, just to ensure the chance of happiness for another? Those are sentiments I understand, because I've felt them for my siblings. When you love, you do so with your whole heart." Gertrude thumped a fist against her chest, knocking that pearl-set brooch affixed there.

Edwin had never been loved that way. His parents had left his care to nursemaids and tutors and then happily sent him on to Eton and Oxford. When they'd died, within a year of one another, they'd been more strangers to him than family. His wife had been in love with the idea of being in love with him, but ultimately her parents' disapproval had trumped all.

His feelings and desires had been secondary. "Whether she loved me or not, she was still deserving of my protection." It was the most basic, primitive offering a husband could provide for a woman. "I *allowed* that nursemaid into my household. And if I hadn't, then even now . . ." He and Gertrude wouldn't be sitting there, watching on as Stephen designed furniture to hide his belongings in.

Gertrude covered his hand with hers and gave it a light squeeze, and he clung to that warmth that filled him, that human contact he'd been so long without. Only, there was something . . . more in her touch, too. Something terrifying that he couldn't explain. "We do the best we can in every moment that we have."

"Indeed," he murmured, "but it cannot erase the mistakes or regrets."

"No, it cannot. They'll always be there. But if we cling to them, we're living only in the past with no thought to the future."

Edwin again found Stephen. The boy knelt on the floor alongside an ornate carved mahogany bureau, deeply attending the cabinetmaker now giving a lesson on the compartments that had been designed into that piece. "I did not think of the future until you arrived," Edwin whispered. "I've dwelled in the past and didn't care what each new day brought." Because there could be no surcease from the suffering. Edwin looked to a silent Gertrude, needing her to understand. "This"— she followed his deliberate stare over to his son—"is all foreign to me. Caring about tomorrow and another person's tomorrow." His throat constricted. "And I do not know if I can be what he needs me to be."

Gertrude's clear, clever gaze lingered on his face. "That is why." Her words emerged a breathless exhalation. "That is why you didn't come for Stephen. It's why you didn't storm the clubs and demand to take him back."

A thousand denials sprang to his lips, but none slipped forward. Because they'd only be lies. Edwin briefly closed his eyes as his already unstable world shook all the more under him. *My God. She is right.* When the investigator he'd hired had first brought him the news of August's existence, he'd been besieged, first by hope and then by mind-numbing terror. That fear had dominated logic and reason, and he'd been unable to accept that which had been laid out before him—that his son was, in fact, alive.

He felt cut open and exposed before her, on display in all his vulnerability and weakness.

For there it was . . . the reason he'd not rushed to that hated club and ripped down the damn door to steal back his son—*because I'm a damned coward.*

He couldn't move. He couldn't so much as draw a breath through the shame of it.

Who was this woman, that she'd chipped away at the defenses he'd built and read the secrets he hadn't even known he'd carried?

"I don't . . . I can't . . ." Form a proper response. For there was none to give. He was at sea, as he'd been for too many years.

"You don't have to say anything, Edwin," she said in gentle tones he should take offense to, but that instead brought a desperately hungered-for calm. "There is no shame in how you feel. And Stephen and you can only both benefit from your sharing that truth with him."

"Tell my own son I didn't want to get him?" he asked, his tone emerging more sharply than he intended.

From across the room, Stephen and Draven glanced over.

Gertrude waited until that pair returned their attention to the bureau before discreetly covering her mouth to hide her lips and mute her tone.

"That's not true," Gertrude said with that dogged tenacity that shook him to the core. "If you didn't want him, you would have never hired Connor Steele. You'd not have given my brother Broderick an audience. And you'd not have demanded your son be returned to you."

How methodical and precise she was. It spoke to a woman wholly in control of her thoughts and logic when he struggled to make sense of anything anymore. "Stop," he said, his voice a hoarse command.

But she was unrelenting.

Gertrude scooted closer so their legs brushed. "You were afraid, Edwin. That does not make you a bad father or terrible person. It makes you human. Do you want to know, however, what does matter?"

He managed a shaky nod.

"What makes you a good, honorable father is that you call your son by his street name and not the noble one you gave him at birth. You are here now, when you've not left your household or wanted to leave your household . . . but you are here for him."

And when she spoke with that conviction, he could almost believe his worth.

"We're done!"

They looked up as Stephen skidded to a stop before them.

Seeing Stephen's cheeks flushed, his eyes bright and unguarded, Edwin felt the first stirrings of hope for who his son might become. Knowing any hint of vulnerability would crush all those sentiments, he smoothed his features and allowed brother and sister to speak.

"He has one more piece, Gert, and then my furniture will be all finished up." *My furniture* . . . that small but significant mark of ownership in a world he now shared with Edwin. *Oh, God.* Edwin struggled to retain a tight rein on the swell of emotion . . . and felt his control slipping.

Gertrude Killoran caught Stephen by the shoulders and said something to the boy, unwittingly allowing Edwin that much-needed moment to collect himself. It was a small victory, but any move away from his son's icy loathing was a triumph.

"We'll have to ask Edwin," Gertrude was saying, bringing him back.

Edwin blinked and stared over at the expectant pair.

"Stephen enjoys visiting Hyde Park," she said gently.

And just like that, the magic was shattered. "Hyde Park," he repeated dumbly. Those grounds favored by the nobles, the same ones he'd relished riding through every early morn, at this hour would be teeming with lords and ladies, gawking at and whispering after the Mad Marquess. "I . . ." *Cannot.* All this had been a struggle . . . but this? Mingling amongst Polite Society? This was too much. "I . . ."

Stephen's earlier enthusiasm faded, and that joy was like a bright light being extinguished. The boy jutted out his lower lip and looked away . . . but not before Edwin viewed the disappointment there.

Ah, Lord, he could sooner flay his own chest open than deny the boy. But then that had always been the way. He'd loved August more than anyone, with an intensity he hadn't known was possible, and that love had not diminished with time or by their separation.

"Very well," he croaked.

Stephen's head swung back, and joy paraded across his features.

And before his courage flagged, Edwin continued. "We can go to Hyde Park." He glanced across the room and found Draven, his arms full, approaching. "Soon." The smile slipped on his son's cheeks. "There is just one more matter of business for us to see to here." Ignoring the question in Gertrude's eyes, Edwin gave his full attention to the cabinetmaker.

Draven stopped before them. "It's completed, my lord, as you instructed."

Edwin peered at the peculiar creation; constructed of painted wood and metal, the odd contraption featured a metal caged wheel.

"What the hell is that?" Stephen asked bluntly.

"A cage . . . ," Draven answered, but then immediately clarified. "Of sorts, rather." The builder set it down at the center of the table for the trio to examine. "There's the main area over here which functions as a house of sorts." Resting his elbows on the table, Stephen leaned in and peered at the constructed piece. "Each level within contains a series of chambers and intersecting alleys."

"But what's it for?" Stephen asked, opening the little latch door. He stuck his right eye against it and then shot a look over his shoulder, up at Edwin.

Feeling Gertrude's piercing focus trained on him, Edwin struggled with his cravat, that scrap of white satin suddenly choking him.

The trio stared on. And he, who'd dealt with no one in so long he'd forgotten how to be around people, considered the door and escape.

Draven replied for him. "His Lordship wished for a cage . . . that wasn't a cage . . . for a rat."

Gertrude gasped, and unable to meet her eyes, Edwin studied the "cage that wasn't a cage" intently.

"A mouse," Gertrude whispered. Her full lips trembled, and she touched a hand to them. "It's for a mouse. You made me a mouse house."

And Edwin, cynical, scarred, and completely jaded by life, found his face going hot. Blushing. He was . . . blushing. "If you could please see the . . . cage delivered this afternoon, Mr. Draven."

As the other man nodded and stalked off, Stephen rolled his eyes.

"Seems like an awful lot of trouble for a damned mouse," his son muttered, hopping to his feet.

Sethos wasn't just a "damned mouse." He was a creature that mattered to Gertrude, who felt an unlikely connection to him, and because of that and other reasons Edwin could neither identify nor care to try to explain, he'd wanted to do this . . . for her. He didn't know why it had been so important . . . but it had. "Shall we be on our way?" he asked, wanting to end all further talks on the gift he'd had commissioned for Gertrude Killoran.

It's merely because she's helped ease Stephen's return. There is nothing more to my actions.

And as he, Gertrude, and Stephen made their way out of the shop and started for Hyde Park, it felt very much like he was lying to himself.

Chapter 19

Throughout her life, Gertrude's family had tolerated her peculiar interest in rescuing animals and giving them homes. But they'd never understood it. Nor, aside from the occasional pet of a cat or dog, had they tried to form any connection with those animals.

They were, to them, just that—animals offering nothing of any value.

All the while, they'd failed to see.

"You are quiet."

Seated on the grass alongside the Serpentine, she stared on as her brother tossed rocks out onto the placid surface in a bid to skip them. She laughed softly. "Who would have imagined you should be calling me out on silence?"

They shared a smile, a tender exchange that knew no divide between them. There was no pained past, only this newly forged bond that at the same time filled her chest with both an airy lightness and panic. For nothing good could come of it.

Soon, she would be gone, and he and Stephen would carry on, living their life without her. And by the terms of her family's arrangement with Edwin, she'd never see either of them again. Pain stabbed at her breast, sharper than any blade to pierce her skin during her years on the streets.

And suddenly, tears stung her lashes. In a bid to hide those blasted drops, she closed her eyes tightly and lifted her head skyward, letting the sun's rays bathe her skin in their warmth.

"You didn't like it?" That hesitant question brought her eyes flying open so fast she looked directly at the sun. When she glanced over at Edwin, she blinked several times in an attempt to rid the dark circle flashing there from her vision.

That diffidence from a man who never showed that emotion was a reminder of the lasting effects his sad marriage had left upon him. "No, I do not like it, Edwin."

A muscle jumped at the corner of his mouth.

Gertrude leaned close and knocked against him with her shoulder. "I love it."

He stiffened, and then a booming laugh filtered from his lips and filled the air around them. Nearby passersby gawked, and even with those rude stares, he continued laughing, his expression of amusement no longer as rusty as it had first been upon her arrival. "You're making light of me."

"Oh, absolutely I am," she said, not missing a beat, and he laughed all the more.

She smiled, unable to take her gaze from the relaxed planes of his chiseled cheeks, that high flesh suffused with color. And her heart continued on at a double-time rhythm.

When they conversed, there were no longer traces of bitterness or anger. Oh, those sentiments would never completely leave either of them. Life scarred one, and even as one healed, the wounds remained.

Stephen paused midthrow and shot them a look.

Gertrude waved him on. She didn't speak until her brother was fully immersed once more in his task. "It's not so very awful, is it?" At his questioning look, Gertrude discreetly gestured at the lords and ladies strolling along a nearby path. The couples averted their curious stares and hurried along. "As a girl, I always wanted to come here. To this end of London. I was certain the air must be cleaner and the roads safer because of the people who moved along them." And they were . . . in ways. "Several of the prostitutes employed by Mac Diggory were once actresses. They would tell me stories about the park and the gardens, and I couldn't believe that there was anywhere in London that looked like they described." She stretched her legs out so that the bottoms of her soles kissed the gravel path. "I was determined that I'd visit."

"And you could not while he was alive?"

She could pretend it was a statement he'd made and retain those most miserable parts of her past. After Diggory's death, she'd found a peace in focusing on the best moments she'd ever known with her siblings and life after the ruthless scourge of the Dials, and she'd deliberately fought off the ugliest of remembrances. But Edwin had shared the pain he'd known, and it would be the height of selfishness to take and not give. It violated the code she'd insisted on living by that her siblings had seen her weak for. "I could not while he was alive," she said softly. "People . . . men, women, children . . ." Her throat tightened. "His own children"—*me, I'm one of them*—"whoever lived with him, served a purpose. We were no different from the wheel of a carriage or the knife and fork to cut a piece of steak. We served a purpose, and it wasn't to know joy or love or anything but work." She'd been Diggory's daughter in the most primitive way, but she'd never been a daughter to him. Not truly. Until Edwin, she'd never before even witnessed that bond between a father and his child.

Edwin's fingers crept over, and he discreetly covered her hand with his own, the heat of his touch tingling at that contact. He gave the lightest squeeze, silently urging her on and supporting her through that telling. Moving away from the darker thoughts of Mac Diggory, she went on with her story of these grounds. "When I first started visiting

Hyde Park, it was after Dig—" She bit the inside of her lower lip and braced for him to yank his hand back, but he didn't. He stroked the pad of his thumb in a light circle along the inseam of her wrist, that caress enticing. It gave her the strength to complete that thought. "It was after Diggory was killed." She made herself say the rest of it. "I came here. It was early." She stared on wistfully as Stephen launched another pebble that promptly sank to the bottom, leaving a ripple of little waves atop the surface. "There was no one here. I heard birds." She chuckled. "I'd lived in London the whole of my life and had never heard a bird until Diggory died. It was so . . . peaceful." And she'd never believed there was a place where it could be . . . that. She'd never believed she could know that elusive gift generally reserved for the nobility.

Except Edwin had not been immune to the hell of the Dials. It had invaded his life and household and left him with indelible suffering that could never fully go away.

She lifted her gaze to Edwin.

He stared on at Stephen playing at the shore, like any other child. "He likes it here," he said hoarsely.

"He does. Oh, he resisted acknowledging as much at first, until he owned that love of this place. At first, we only came in the morning because no one was about, but then . . . I said, 'Never again.' Why should I hide away?" Gertrude tilted her chin toward one intently gawking stranger. "Why should I let them keep me hidden? Their scorn doesn't go away. Not for me." It would for Edwin. Soon the same peers who condemned him with their gazes, words, and whispers would recede until all that remained was a nobleman accepted once more amongst them. Gertrude lifted her gaze to his. "And you shouldn't let them keep you hidden away any longer, either, Edwin. Live your life again. You've nothing to be ashamed of." The dead Diggory did. The *ton* did. This man, a grieving father, did not.

"I still can't do it," Stephen yelled, stomping over and ending the exchange. He wedged his tiny frame between them. "They don't jump."

"Skip," she amended. "You want them to skip."

"Jump. Skip. It's all the same."

"Your sister has been instructing you on skipping stones?" Edwin asked.

"Tried to." Stephen opened his fist and dropped the pile of rocks onto the grass. "She's rubbish at it *and* skipping them."

"Thank you," she drawled, giving her brother a light shove with her elbow. He returned that bump with one of his own. "We've been working at it for three years now," she explained to Edwin. For all the lessons she'd managed to deliver on the proper way for him to speak, how to read, and complete basic mathematics, she'd been useless to learn and teach the simplest task a child should enjoy.

Tugging off his gloves, Edwin tossed them onto the ground, and with a bare hand he scooped up the previously discarded stones and pebbles. Head bent over that collection, he sifted through each. "Humph."

Stephen edged closer. "'Humph,' what?"

"Well," Edwin expounded, "it's simply that there is an art form to the whole stone-skipping process. Before one can successfully *accomplish* the feat, one has to have the proper object to hurl. Here. Hold your hand out," he instructed.

Gertrude sat on, afraid to move, afraid to breathe lest she shatter the moment unfurling between father and son. Her family had taught Stephen how to steal and survive, and the basic functions of society, such as reading and simple mathematics . . . but this is what they'd failed to provide. These simple exchanges that marked true joy in life. And he found it now . . . with his father, the only one who'd ever had a rightful claim to him.

"Feel that?" Edwin asked. "Slightly round, jagged. That one will never do." To demonstrate his point, Edwin picked it up and drew back his arm. Releasing it in a flawless arc, he launched the stone. It hopped once. Twice. And then sank.

"You did it!" Stephen cheered.

"Two hops. Now look at this one."

Stephen examined the next rock placed in his hand.

"Not too large. Not so small as a pebble. But feel the smoothness there?"

Rubbing the impending projectile between his thumb and forefinger, Stephen nodded.

"The smoothness of that helps it sail along the surface. Like so." Taking the stone back, Edwin tossed it.

It skipped. *One. Two. Three. Four. Five.* Six hops, rippling the waters as it went, before disappearing under the surface.

Stephen cheered, that jubilant cry earning more stares and sending several kestrels into flight. "That rock jumped six times."

"Now, you try it. First, let us find your stone."

Stephen dropped to the earth and proceeded to crawl along the shore, feeling around as he went. Unhesitant, Edwin went down into a like posture and searched alongside his son.

Just like that that, Gertrude lost every last corner of her heart to this man: one so capable of forgiveness that he'd allow Gertrude, daughter to the man who'd murdered his wife and stolen his child, a place in his household.

No.

It was impossible. She barely knew him. Had known him just under a fortnight. It was illogical when she was only practical, and yet . . .

Oh, God. I do. I love that he is a father in every way to his son. But it was far more than who he was with Stephen. She loved Edwin for who he was with *her.* For being a man who didn't doubt her because she was blind or a Killoran, but had instead allowed her a voice within his household and accepted her decisions when her own family had only ever questioned her.

On the heel of that realization came the sobering wave of misery.

There could never be anything between them. It didn't matter that she loved him. Her father had murdered his wife and stolen his son.

And not for the first time that day, she wanted to cry all over again. Only these tears were not the ones that had blurred her vision at Draven's establishment over the mouse house Edwin had commissioned on her behalf. These were crystalline drops of misery, and she wanted nothing more than to curl up into a tight ball and give way to that sorrow.

Edwin glanced up, that movement sending a blond curl tumbling over his brow, giving him an almost boyish look. He grinned, flashing a glimpse of who he'd been before his world had been torn asunder.

She clawed through the tumult to present a display of naturalness, forcing her lips up in a smile.

He lifted his hand in a wave. "Join us, Gertrude," he called, attracting another bevy of stares.

Anxiously, Gertrude glanced around. "Edwin," she said, giving her head a slight shake. "You can't."

"I can't what?"

"I think it's because you're calling her 'Gertrude'?" In equally negligent tones, her brother piped up. "Right?"

Gertrude briefly covered her eyes with a hand. Now would be the time Stephen chose to display a grasp on propriety. When she let her palm fall to her lap, she found a devil's smirk on her brother's lips that indicated he'd known precisely what he'd done by calling out his words about Edwin.

She pushed herself upright and stalked over. "Stop," she hissed.

"Why? We don't care what the *ton* thinks."

Yes, that had always been the way. And they still didn't. She did, however, care for Edwin. His and Stephen's reception amongst the *ton* was important to him, and therefore, it was important to her. "Your father does."

"No, I don't," Edwin said unhelpfully. "Not really." As if to drive home that point, he lifted his broad shoulders in a shrug.

Sweeping past Stephen, she drifted closer to Edwin and whispered, "Yes, you do."

"I'm certain I just indicated I do not."

"No," she said calmly.

"Didn't I? Stephen?" He directed that question over her shoulder.

"He did," her brother confirmed.

Splendid. Now would be the time this previously dueling couple should choose to be a pair. Contrary bastards.

"Go find some rocks, Stephen," she snapped.

And for once her brother did as she bade. After he'd wandered off to collect those rocks for throwing, Gertrude moved closer to Edwin. "Your reputation and how Polite Society view you is important to you. Our being here has already stirred the gossips." She had been born well outside his exalted station, but she knew enough of the world and how it operated to gather that his calling her by her Christian name would only add fuel to the fire of gossip burning its way through Hyde Park.

"I don't care, Gertrude."

"But you do," she implored.

"You've helped me see I care a good deal less than I believed. Now take a rock." He took her hand and pressed a stone in her palm, closing her fingers around it. How odd that a single touch should cast a series of flutters in her belly. "And show your brother how to properly skip it."

"Gert's giving it a try?" Stephen shouted from the off-beaten path he'd wandered down.

Edwin cupped his hands around his mouth and called back. "She is."

Gertrude winced. Passing lords and ladies stared baldly back. "Edwin," she pleaded.

"I thought you didn't care about the opinions of others."

"I don't, but neither do I wish to deliberately attract atte—"

Stephen raced over, and as he skidded to a stop, he kicked up dust and gravel under the heels of his boots. "Well, have at it, Gert," he urged. "What are you waiting for?"

With a sigh, Gertrude brought her arm back and let her missile fly. It sailed along the water's surface, hopping seven times before plummeting below. "There, are you happy?" she muttered.

Her brother let loose a triumphant cry on her behalf.

Edwin brought his hands together in a little clap that brought a blush to her cheeks. "Splendid, Miss Killoran. But I'd venture it was merely a lucky first chance."

She bristled. "I say not." Plucking another stone from his fingers, she released it and peered at the small plops it left upon the smooth lake.

"Eight!" Stephen cried, launching himself at her.

Gertrude grunted and pitched forward, knocking into Edwin.

Under the weight of both of them, he tumbled back, coming down on his buttocks with Gertrude laughing, sprawled atop him. Their bodies shook with their amusement . . . until the intimacy of their position hit her at once.

They lay with their bodies flush, her chest crushed to his.

Edwin's eyes darkened; the glint in their piercing depths radiated the burning heat of his desire. He slid his gaze to her mouth.

His thick, black lashes swept down, hooding his eyes. And the whole world melted away.

Gertrude's breath quickened.

He wants me . . .

"Maddock."

And just like that, that same person who'd intruded days earlier stole this moment, too.

They glanced up at the man standing over them.

Lord Charles, the Marquess of Tenwhestle—Edwin's brother-in-law.

Gertrude pushed away from Edwin and struggled to her feet. "My lord," she greeted, dropping a curtsy.

The gentleman slid her a brief glance, dismissing her before training all his attention on Edwin. "I . . . thought you might spare me an introduction."

The trio of adults looked to Stephen.

"Don't want an introduction." He spit on the ground, that saliva landing at the tips of Lord Charles's feet. "We're busy."

"Stephen," she said softly, giving her head a slight shake.

The marquess glanced down at his now-stained boots.

Gertrude stiffened, braced for an onslaught of outrage—that didn't come.

"I'll not intrude any more than I have," the marquess murmured, doffing his hat. "I thought I'd see if you'd join me for drinks at White's."

Edwin's mouth settled into a tight line. "I'm afraid I am otherwise engaged."

Gertrude gave him a sharp look. These two men had once been friends. Despite the resentment and heartache that had separated them, the marquess now sought to rekindle that friendship. Edwin needed that friendship. And Stephen should know his uncle.

"I . . . see." Lord Charles fiddled with the brim of his hat before returning it atop his head. "If you change your mind, you can find me there most evenings at ten o'clock." At Edwin's answering silence, the marquess looked to Gertrude.

Even half-blind, the hatred in his gaze reached out like a physical touch and burnt.

She took a step back under the intensity of it.

But then as quickly as it appeared, it was gone. "Miss Killoran," he murmured. "August," he offered to his nephew. Lord Charles's features twisted in a display of grief, and with that, he left.

Gertrude stared after him, following his retreat. Even in his absence a chill remained, and she rubbed her arms to ward it off.

"Can we return to the stone business?" Stephen whined.

And as Edwin, Gertrude, and Stephen continued on with their earlier efforts, the levity they'd known was gone as the other nobleman's presence lingered amongst them.

Chapter 20

Edwin's loathing of fire would always be there, but where he'd embraced a cold, empty hearth in the past, now he sat before the lightly blazing embers.

Yet another demon had been conquered.

And yet so many remained.

Cradling a snifter of half-drunk brandy in his fingers, Edwin stared into the amber contents.

His brother-in-law . . . his former best friend . . . sought a meeting with him. Once, that was all he'd wanted. Nay, he'd wanted that which he'd been undeserving of—forgiveness for costing Lavinia her life.

He and Charles had been as close as brothers, both scoundrels of London who'd reveled in their reputations and lived that carefree existence of rogues together. As such, Charles had possessed every reason under God's sun to reject a match between Edwin and his cherished sister. But he hadn't. He'd trusted that Edwin could and would do right by her.

You should have been the one who burnt in that fire . . . My parents were right about you . . . Lavinia was right about you . . . You are dead to me . . .

You are dead to me.

Those had been the last words ever spoken between them . . . until Charles had come upon him and Gertrude and Stephen at Gunter's . . . and now, today, at Hyde Park.

Where the former friend had requested that Edwin join him.

And less than a fortnight ago, as emotionally deadened as he'd become, Edwin would have gladly sent his brother-in-law on to the Devil . . . just as he'd done with Charles's parents. They'd blamed him . . . but no less than he'd blamed himself. His in-laws' opinion of him hadn't mattered. They'd always hated him. To them, he'd never been anything more than the contemptible cad who'd stolen their precious daughter.

Charles? Charles, however, had been altogether different.

His was the betrayal that had stung most. As such, it had been far easier to resurrect barriers insulating himself from the pain of having lost not only his wife and his son but also the friend he'd so desperately needed in those earliest, most agonizing days.

But now, the walls had been knocked loose.

By her.

Gertrude.

Gertrude, who'd challenged him when everyone else had feared him, who'd helped him to see the fears he'd carried, ones he'd not even acknowledged to himself—about Stephen and their life together as father and son—and likely wouldn't have come to terms with, without her forcing his eyes open.

You were afraid, Edwin. That does not make you a bad father or terrible person. It makes you human . . . What makes you a good, honorable father is that you call your son by his street name and not the noble one you gave him at birth. You are here now, when you've not left your household or wanted to leave your household . . . but you are here for him . . .

The irony was not lost on him. He'd hated her on sight, blaming her for the sins of her father. He'd snapped at her. Taunted her over her birthright and been cruel at every turn. With all that, she could have let him flounder with Stephen's reintegration into his life. She hadn't, however. She'd eased his son's way and helped Edwin accept that he was a father again.

She had proven the one who'd pulled him back to the living. Not his mother-in-law or father-in-law. Not his best friend and brother-in-law, Charles.

Gertrude had been the one. It was because of her that he'd learned himself capable of smiling and laughing again . . . and of being someone other than the scared, wounded beast hiding away in his townhouse.

His throat moved. She had set him and Stephen on a path together as a family and given him a gift for which he could never repay her. Edwin went still.

A palpable energy hummed to life within the room.

She's here.

He felt her presence before he saw her.

Gertrude hung back at the entrance, her arms wrapped about a grey tabby. "Hullo."

She would be here now. Conjured by his own thoughts of her. His need for her.

He was supposed to say something here. He'd not lost so much of the proper way to move about people that he'd forgotten as much, but neither could he form words on his lips.

The faint glow of the lit sconces in the hallway cast a soft light about her; her plaited hair hung over her shoulder, those strands, dark like chocolate, glimmering with shades of auburn. Had he once thought her plain? Hers was the bold beauty of Joan of Arc; fearless and spirited, it radiated from within her and made a man hungry with the need to hold her and that vitality within his arms.

"I didn't hear you," he said quietly, twirling his drink in a light circle.

She drew the cat almost protectively to her chest. "I've learned to move silently through the years."

"Because you were a pickpocket." It left him before he could call the thought back, words blurted out from one who'd forgotten how to be around people.

"I'll go," she said quickly, turning on her heel.

"No!" With a curse, Edwin exploded to his feet, splashing several droplets over the rim of his glass and onto his fingers. He set his drink down on the table beside him and rushed to the entrance of the room. "I didn't intend it as an insult." He stretched a hand out, even as her back was presented to him, wanting her to remain. *Needing* her to remain. Only knowing he didn't want to be alone . . . and that something in her presence filled him with a lightness he'd not known since long ago, back before his wife's love had turned to hate. "Please, don't go. Stay." His was an entreaty that a prouder man wouldn't have made. His pride had died long ago. She was going to leave. Poised on the balls of her feet, her whole body sang of flight.

Gertrude wheeled slowly back. She surprised him at every turn.

Burying her nose in the top of that deucedly lucky feline, Gertrude pinned him with an accusatory gaze that caused Edwin's heart to stutter in his chest.

In a short time, her opinion had come to mean something. He'd not have her believe he sought to disparage her.

"I didn't mean it as an insult. I wanted . . ." *To know.* Which was equally offensive, in asking her to speak about crimes she'd committed. It bespoke an insensitivity—him, a gauche noble curious about a woman who'd survived in ways he never had to or would have. Only it wasn't that. It was more. It was a yearning to know the secrets she herself carried.

"You wanted . . . ?" She drifted over, wafting those fragrant floral scents as she walked. "To know?" she put forward without malice.

He cleared his throat. "I . . ." Edwin glanced away. *Tell her no and let her either go on her way or enter the room so you might speak about safer topics, like tossing stones and Draven's recently completed furniture for Stephen.* Edwin opted for the truth. "I was asking so I might learn more about you."

Please, don't go.

That plea pinged around his mind.

Gertrude ruffled the cat—Gus—at the base of his neck. The cat purred contentedly. "I was, you know . . . a pickpocket," she clarified. Gertrude slipped past him and moved deeper into the room, so fleet of foot she'd left him and found a place at the center of the library before he'd even completely turned. Reaching out, he pushed the door closed, shutting them away.

Gertrude paused, taking in the panel before going on. "I hated it, but I was quite good at it." Her gaze grew distant. "Every time, my stomach would turn, and I was so certain this would be the time they caught me that I threw up before I went out." *Oh, God.*

He briefly closed his eyes, imagining Gertrude as a young girl, a smaller version of the woman who stood before him, living with terror.

"For five years I filched purses," she said softly, bringing his eyes flying open. "I was taller than the other children, and they doubted I'd be able to manage it, but Diggory . . . my father"—she wrapped that word in a hated sneer—"insisted I try."

"Because he knew you were capable." There was nothing this woman couldn't do. She would have been the same way as a child.

She laughed softly. "Because he said a child's only value was the number of pockets they could pick, and if I couldn't manage, then the constable would do away with me and he'd not have to worry about having another mouth to feed."

"He . . . said that." Her . . . father. The man who should have taken care of her and loved her had spoken so flippantly of forfeiting her life. A red haze of fury fell over his vision; briefly blinding, that rage throbbed within him, and a hungering took him in its grip to drag Diggory from the pit of hell he even now burnt in and murder him all over again.

"He wasn't really my father, Edwin," she explained, absently stroking a finger down one particular tabby stripe. "I mean . . . he was in the way that you and Polite Society so value, but those sentiments? Paternal concern? Respect for one's child. Love. Dedication. Pride. They don't exist for children in the streets. Not from parents. If one is lucky, one finds family in strangers or the bastards unfortunate enough to share the blood of those sinners."

Like she had.

Gertrude spoke quietly, in muted, disguised tones close to Gus's ear, and with her focus wholly trained on that grey tabby, Edwin freely watched her . . . unable to look away.

I condemned her for her connection to her siblings. Those women, that man . . . Broderick Killoran . . . they had been the difference between Gertrude's knowing only hell at Mac Diggory's cruel instruction . . . or having some sense of family.

Needing to move . . . needing a drink, Edwin went and rescued his previously abandoned glass and took a much-needed swallow.

He'd been wrong. On so many scores.

Do not ask . . . do not ask. You do not want to hear the answer . . . Regardless, the question left him anyway. "Why only five years?"

She cocked her head at an adorable little angle that sent her braid flopping over her shoulder.

"You indicated you were skilled, so why should he not have used you?" From the Devil Diggory had been, such a decision would have never been about concern for his child.

"I don't . . ." She shook her head. "I won't . . ."

She didn't wish to talk about it. Shivers of apprehension dusted along his spine.

Gus squealed and scrambled to get out of his mistress's arms. Gertrude released him and stared after the cat as he took flight, finding a place under the leather button sofa. Her fingers shaking, Gertrude picked up the hard-paste Sèvres porcelain statuette of a mother with her bare babe as she led him by the hand.

Edwin knew the very moment she'd forgotten his presence. A far-away wistful smile graced her lips as she trailed a cracked fingernail along the clasped hands of the jubilant young mother and child.

Edwin's heart buckled. And he wanted to call back every question he'd put to her. He wanted to put each back in a box, tucked away, and then carry it over to the still-burning hearth and let that blaze consume her pain until all that remained were ashes left in its wake.

"He loaned me out."

Edwin's mouth went dry. He didn't want to hear anymore. And by the way she dropped her attention back to the white porcelain statue, she was allowing him the ultimate decision, the decision on whether that statement and the story of her past went nowhere.

But yet, for her, he did want her to continue. Because just as she'd aptly gleaned about him . . . she needed to share. She needed to let those demons out, and he wanted to be the person there for her when she did. "What do you mean?" he finally brought himself to ask.

Gertrude stroked her thumb over the top of that white porcelain babe and directed her answer at it. "London is vast. The sheer size of it alone makes it too much for any one man to lay domination over. Diggory was just one gang leader, but there are many. He was the most powerful, and also clever enough to recognize he couldn't rule all of East London without help. He would loan me over to a rival thief to use. Diggory would receive a share of the profits, and Jake-O would pay a fee for using me." Her lips tipped at the corners into a heartbreaking smile. "He won twice, that way."

Edwin's legs carried him over. He stopped a pace away and, brushing his knuckles along her jaw, brought her gaze up to his. "What did he do?"

Gertrude drew in a shaky breath, and then with the same courage she'd shown since their first meeting, she met his gaze squarely. "He wanted more than the purse I'd filched one night." The muscles of his stomach contracted into a twisted mass of knots. "I insisted that wasn't the deal Diggory made with him. He tried to take it anyway." Bile stung his throat as rage briefly blinded him. Through his tumult, she continued on, so very calm when her every admission hit like a fist to the gut. "I knocked him out cold. I ran and didn't stop running until I returned."

His admiration for the woman before him swelled. Back when he'd moved amongst the living, a young rogue set loose on the *ton*, the ladies he'd kept company with hadn't given a jot about anything beyond baubles and balls. They'd been cherished and pampered, and they'd never had to fight to survive. And shamefully, he'd failed to see the world outside the one he dwelled in. While he'd caroused about the *ton* with Lord Charles, young girls like Gertrude had been fighting tooth and nail for their survival. Shame stuck in his gut.

"Don't look at me like that," she snapped.

"Like what?" How did she think he was looking at her? In wonder. Awe.

"Like you pity me," she said flatly, stepping away from him.

Edwin caught her by the upper arm, encircling that soft flesh in a light grip. "Never," he vowed. *"You are amazing."*

"I'm not," she said, drawing away from him. She scoffed. "If I were, I would have known Jake-O would have never settled until revenge was met."

And once more, he was reminded of how foreign the existence she'd lived was to him that he'd believed that to be the end of her story. It wouldn't be. Those streets were ruthless, and the men who served as kings over them ruled with cruelty and delighted in the suffering they inflicted. "What happened?" he asked, his voice hollow.

"Jake-O came 'round to see Diggory. It was the worst time for him to come. Diggory was always a ruthless bastard, but that day . . ." She shivered and clutched her arms close. "One of his thugs was in the middle of reporting on my sister for having freed another street urchin. Jake-O was insisting that I'd lost a purse promised him." As she talked, her words came more quickly. "Diggory walloped me twice in the face. A punch . . . right here." Gertrude laid her palm against her left eye. "One to atone for my mistakes against Jake-O, and the other here"— she motioned to her temple—"a message to Ophelia that if she helped others, her sisters would pay the price." Her voice quavered. "H-he said both matters were settled."

So that was how it had happened. She'd been left partially blind by that monster. He struggled to get words out. But there were none. Years earlier, he would have been the man with soothing murmurings. Now he could manage nothing more than three syllables: "Oh, Gertrude."

"I passed out. Everything went black, and when I woke up . . ." Her long, graceful neck moved from the force of her swallow. "Everything was still black in my left eye." She breathed slowly through her clenched lips. "The one good to come of it was that it was the last pocket I was ever made to pick. From then on, I was assigned the role of mother to Diggory's bastards. I looked after my sisters and the other children, and eventually . . ." Stephen.

It was because of this woman his son had survived. Had she not taken him into her care, none of the street lessons doled out by the others would have meant anything, for Stephen's soul would have withered. She'd kept that spark alive and allowed Stephen a path forward. "Thank you," he said quietly.

Gertrude gave her head a little shake. "I don't . . ."

Edwin cupped her cheek. "My son is alive because of you. He is able to laugh because you saw that he knew visits at Hyde Park and trips to Gunter's. You saved him."

A watery smile formed on her lips. "I did—"

He touched two fingers to her mouth, cutting off the remainder of her erroneous assumption. "You did more for him than anyone else . . . myself included."

All at once, the air sizzled between them, and he registered that his fingers still brushed that mouth he'd kissed a week ago. That he'd hungered to again take under his. He yanked his hand away and forced his arms back to his side. *Bastard. You are a contemptible bastard.* "I owe you an apology." She was deserving of many where he was concerned.

"For what?"

How did one who'd suffered as she had retain such a pure spirit? "I was a fool." He tossed back the remaining contents of his drink and then grimaced as it burnt a fiery path down the back of his throat. With a sound of frustration, he stalked to the sideboard and retrieved the bottle. Desperately needing another drink, he set his snifter down and went through the motions of pouring a glass. "All along I held you to blame. I placed crimes committed by another at your feet." The amber spirits brushed the brim of the glass and spilled onto the table, staining it with errant drops. Edwin stopped. "I was wrong about so much where you were concerned," he whispered. He gave his head a disgusted shake and made himself face her. She stood precisely where he'd left her, unmoving. Setting his glass and decanter down behind him, Edwin lifted his palms. "All along I've behaved as if I'm the only one who has known pain. As though I'm the only victim of Mac Diggory, when the truth was . . . you lived a life of suffering." While her life had always been one of drudgery and fear, Edwin's had been, until seven years ago, a charmed existence.

"No," she said emphatically, sailing over, and he was a cad for lingering his gaze on her delicate ankles as her skirts twirled about her legs. He turned away to take another long drink. Surely this yearning to tug that scrap of fabric higher and explore the length of her legs was a product of years of celibacy.

"You aren't allowed to do that, Edwin," she chided, and for a devastating moment he believed she'd gathered the improper wanderings of his mind. "We are so accustomed to measuring everything—rank, wealth, power—that we would do the same with degrees of suffering." Gertrude took his snifter and set it down hard, and then filled her hands with his. "What happened in your life, your losses and your pain and how *you* feel"—at that emphasis, she gave his fingers a firm squeeze—"is no less significant because of what happened to me in mine."

Any other person, man or woman, would have splintered long ago, and yet she stood before him resolute in her strength and convictions. "Thank you, Gertrude."

Gertrude drew his hands close to her chest. "Do not thank me. I should thank you for allowing me to come here and be with Stephen when you had no reason to do so."

"I didn't want you to remain," he agreed. He'd wanted to send her on to the Devil, with Diggory. Shame gnawed at his conscience. "I want you here now, though," he said, needing her to realize that everything had changed and she remained not out of an arrangement made upon her arrival, but because of the bond they'd formed. His gaze fell to their joined hands, pressed against the soft swell of her breasts, that most intimate joining that sent another wave of desire through him.

Her breath caught . . . or was that his own?

"And I want you, Gertrude," he whispered, stroking the pad of his thumb along the inseam of her wrist. Her pulse raced under that lightest caress . . . but she made no move to draw away.

That admission ushered in a heavy silence, one charged with desire and passion and a hungering to continue what they'd begun in this very room a week ago.

I want her . . .

But he wasn't as much the black-hearted bastard as he'd believed himself to be. Edwin disentangled his fingers from hers and stepped away. "You should leave, Gertrude, because if you don't, I cannot promise I'll be a gentlem—"

Stepping into his arms, Gertrude went up on tiptoe and kissed him.

Chapter 21

For the whole of her life, Gertrude had shuddered at the mere thought of any physical act between a man and woman. Having endured two violent embraces that had been stolen from her by men with liquor on their breaths and stinking of unwashed bodies, she'd come to view any act of intimacy as a vile, depraved exchange.

Everything, however, had changed. Because of this man.

Because of Edwin. Who, with one embrace, had shown her that kisses could be beautiful, and that even she was capable of passion.

Gertrude tangled her fingers in his hair, luxuriating in the silken texture of those tresses, and pressed herself against him, deepening their kiss.

Before she left him, before she left this place, she wanted to know everything there was to know about desire from him.

"Gertrude," he groaned, her name an entreaty.

To stop? She wouldn't. Nor couldn't. "I want you, Edwin," she breathed between every slant of her lips, and it was as though that wanton admission freed him.

Edwin filled his hands with her buttocks, cupping her through the fabric of her gown, and dragged her between the V of his legs. He deepened their kiss; parting her lips, he slipped his tongue inside and laid mastery over her mouth. Every stroke of that flesh against her was like a fiery brand, marking her as his, burning her with the heat of his passion. And she met every bold lash. Angling her head to better receive his kiss, Gertrude matched him desire for desire.

His manhood throbbed the evidence of his hunger for her, and emboldened, she lifted her hips in a bid to be closer to that tumescence.

He moaned into her mouth, that slight vibration thrilling.

Edwin kneaded her buttocks, sculpting that flesh with his hands, and then he was tugging up the hem of her skirts.

The night air kissed her skin, that cool a balm against her heated flesh. Drawing one leg up, Edwin wrapped it about his waist so that his shaft nestled against her womanhood, the only barrier between them and that most intimate of acts the soft wool of his trousers, and there was something so very forbidden in that, something so very erotic in all that separated them being a scrap of fabric, that her lust spiked.

Whimpering, she gyrated her hips, undulating them in a primitive rhythm as old as time. That action only teasing, it fueled the ache building deep within her core.

Not breaking their kiss, Edwin lifted her nightshift up over her hips, and sliding it above her waist, higher, over her breasts, he drew it off so that she stood nude before him.

He drew back, and she made an inarticulate sound of protest, but he stood frozen, motionless, his hooded gaze radiating a fiery heat as it touched upon every expanse of her exposed skin.

Drawing in a ragged breath, Edwin stretched a hand out and palmed her right breast.

Gertrude's eyes slid shut, and her head fell back as she allowed herself to simply . . . feel, surrendering to Edwin's touch and this moment, and all that it entailed.

He lightly rubbed the swollen nipple between his thumb and forefinger, mercilessly teasing the bud.

Perhaps there should be a modicum of reticence. Or shyness. Even a smidgeon of restraint. And there *would* have been had she been born to the same station as this man who now made love to her, but she hadn't. And so there was no shame or coyness. There was only an all-consuming yearning to continue what they'd begun.

Edwin covered that swollen peak with his mouth, and a hiss exploded from her teeth as he suckled at that flesh.

"Ed . . . mm . . . oh . . . please . . ." Her speech and ability to formulate thoughts dissolved with every pull. He shifted over to the previously neglected tip, laving it with the same glorious attention. *"Mmm . . . ,"* she moaned, urging him on, gripping his hair and anchoring him close. A wanton moisture built between her legs, and she bucked in time to his lips' efforts.

He slipped a hand between her thighs.

Gertrude cried out; her legs went out from under her, but Edwin caught her. Sweeping her up from under the knees, he carried her back to that leather sofa he'd occupied when she'd arrived a short while ago. A lifetime ago? Time had ceased to matter, and she existed within a vortex of nothing but primitive feeling.

Like she was a delicate treasure to be cherished, he set her gently down and then came up over her.

"Wait," she breathed, putting her palms on his chest, staying him.

He stared on, a question in his passion-laden eyes.

"I want to feel you, Edwin. All of you." She wanted to explore him the same way he now did her. Gertrude tugged his white lawn shirt from his trousers, freeing the article.

"There is no one like you, Gertrude Killoran."

And where he'd once hurled her name as the ugliest of epithets, now he wrapped it in a caress that only heightened her need for him.

Edwin effortlessly pulled the shirt over his head and tossed it at the back of the sofa. Sitting on its edge, he tugged off one boot. It landed with a thump. Followed by the other. He came to his feet, and her breath caught as Edwin's fingers went to the waistband of his breeches. Holding her gaze, he shoved them down until he stood before her, glorious in all his naked splendor.

His hips narrow, his belly flat, and his body lean, he resembled a specimen of masculine beauty she'd once observed on display in a sculpture at the British Museum. That nude of the ancient God of War, Ares, paled as a vapid display of manhood when presented with Edwin's vitality. And then, she lowered her gaze to the flesh between his legs.

Long and thick, it sprang from a thatch of blond curls; his shaft stood proud and flat against his belly. "Oh, my," she whispered. She was no innocent. In the streets, a person saw . . . everything. As such, the human body, male and female, had never been some great mystery or surprise. Or so she'd believed.

She'd never set eyes upon any person who'd rivaled this man before her in strength or beauty. She trailed her fingertips over the swath of muscles of his abdomen; they constricted under her touch. "You are so beautiful," she breathed, her touch urging him to rejoin her.

Edwin caught her hand, staying her caress. His eyes glazed with passion, he drew her palm to his mouth and dropped a hot kiss upon the place where her hand met her arm. "You are beautiful, Gertrude. You are magnificent in every way." And she, who'd accepted and even relished her plainness for the protection it offered a girl on the streets, with this man, and with his husky avowal, felt the beauty he spoke of.

"Gertrude," Edwin groaned, pleadingly, but ignoring him, she caught his hand and drew him back into her arms so that she could resume her exploration. She ran her hands down his biceps, and the sinew bunched and corded under her touch. The faint sheen of perspiration glistening upon his skin slicked the way, and she luxuriated in the feel of him.

Gertrude tentatively touched his throbbing shaft.

It leapt wildly.

Edwin hissed and grabbed her hand.

And for the first time since she'd initiated this moment, she faltered, as a wave of bashfulness and embarrassment overtook the previous glow of desire. "I'm sorry," she said, her voice thin to her own ears. "I—"

Edwin swallowed her apology with his kiss, and she melted against him. "You need never apologize to me, Gertrude. There is nothing wrong in any of this between us. It's my own weakness. I want to be able to give you the pleasure you deserve, and I'm dangerously weak from your touch."

A burst of warmth stirred in her breast at that guttural admission; he was weak with hunger . . . because of her.

Their bodies moving in a like harmony, she and Edwin came together; their lips found and devoured the other's. Their hands were everywhere, searching one another, learning and memorizing the texture of each plane and contour.

Edwin guided her down, and she went, wrapping her arms about his waist and taking him with her. Of their own will, her legs fell open, and Edwin slipped a hand between them.

She cried out, that sound of her desire reaching to the rafters and echoing around the room as he stroked her. He toyed with that sensitive nub, driving her mad, reducing her to a bundle of simple feeling that tunneled in that throbbing place of her womanhood. He slipped a finger into her sodden channel. "Edwin," she wailed. Tears pricked the corners of her lashes and mingled with a bead of sweat that dripped from her brow. She blinked it back, focusing on the pressure building at her core.

"That's it, love," he urged in hoarsened tones, his voice strained. "I want you to come."

And she wanted to go where he would take her. And then that endearment whispered in his husky baritone registered.

Love.

It was certainly a throwaway word, uttered in the throes of lovemaking, but Gertrude clung to it anyway. Wanting to believe it. Wanting to matter to him in ways that moved beyond sex and convenience. But if this was all he could offer, it was a gift she'd still gladly take from him.

Edwin slipped another finger inside her, and she keened his name as the ache within her grew, and she arched her hips, seeking something only he could give.

It beckoned. Promised. Enticed.

Gertrude lifted her hips frantically into Edwin's touch. She was close. So close to some seemingly unattainable end to the blissful sorcery he plied.

The chiseled planes of his face were a taut mask of restraint. "I've never felt like this before, Gertrude," he whispered, the weight of that admission piercing the blanket of desire he'd cloaked her in.

Then he drew his hand back, and she cried out in agonized protest.

But he merely shifted, laying himself between her splayed thighs. His manhood prodded the entrance of her womanhood, and he slid slowly into her, stretching her. Filling her. She moaned his name. "Edwin."

His length throbbed within her tight channel, a glorious pulsing that set her hips into a desperate, rocking movement.

"Don't." He squeezed his eyes shut. "I'm trying to go slow."

A single bead of sweat trickled down his cheek, and she wiped a trembling hand up and caught it. At that consideration, a wave of tenderness washed over her.

Edwin slid farther within her, and she bit her lower lip. He stretched her, and yet there was a gloriousness to the unfamiliar sensation, too. He found that sensitive nub with his fingers, wringing a cry from her lips; he continued to stroke her. Stirring her to a fever pitch where all logical thought fled and she was capable of nothing but feeling.

"Edwin," she pleaded, moaning his name, over and over, and then giving an agonized shout as he plunged deep.

Edwin swallowed her short cry with a kiss.

Her entire body tensed at the unexpectedness of that sharp stab of pain, and closing her eyes, Gertrude focused on the feel of him, his enormous length throbbing against her tight channel.

Edwin's breath came hard and fast. "I'm so sorry," he breathed against her temple. "I'm so sorr—"

Gertrude kissed the apology from his lips. Any regrets had no place on this day. He stilled and then devoured her mouth once more. Their lips mimicked the intimate joining they practiced even now.

And then, Edwin began to move within her. Slowly, at first. And with every slide and retreat, the discomfort receded, and the longing for some unknown gift he dangled swelled. It grew. The ache. The longing. Until her hips were moving in concert with his lunges, and she met every blissful stroke.

"Come for me," he pleaded, their bodies lightly dampened with a sheen from their desire that made it hard to grip him as she wished.

Gertrude wrapped her arms tightly about Edwin, hanging on, giving of herself, and taking what he offered. The pressure built, and she began to reach a crest that beckoned.

Panting, incapable of even the simplest utterance, Gertrude lifted her hips. She was so close.

She bit her lip. So close to some unattainable goal that, if she didn't catch it, would end her.

Edwin lowered his head, and catching the tip of one breast in his mouth, he suckled and milked.

Gertrude screamed out her release to the ceiling as Edwin pushed her over the precipice of desire that was a mix of agony and bliss all as one. She came in great big, shuddering waves. A heartbeat later he joined her.

Tossing his head back, he shouted, the primal cry ripped from his chest, and he withdrew. His seed arced over her belly, a white stream of hot, liquid essence.

And as he collapsed over her, catching himself on his elbows, Gertrude smiled.

———— ❧ ————

Sometime later, no doubt sometime soon, proper guilt would set in at his caddishness. Now, with Gertrude pressed close to Edwin's side, there was only an absolute rightness.

He'd had no right to the gift she'd given, but Devil that he was, he relished in it anyway.

"That was lovely," she murmured in dreamy tones.

He caught the delicate shell of her earlobe in his mouth and lightly kissed her. "Minx," he breathed against her temple.

Gertrude laughed lightly, that timbre still husky from her recent release.

Stretching a hand over the side of the sofa, Edwin fished around, searching for and finding his kerchief.

Gus butted his head against Edwin's hand. "On your way, you shameful ogler," he scolded, and Gertrude's laughter redoubled, that unrestrained, lighthearted mirth a balm to his once broken soul and spirit.

"He is shameful. Like his mistress," she tacked on.

Edwin gently cleaned the remnants of his seed from her person. He paused briefly and, glancing up, held Gertrude's gaze, faintly uncertain when she was usually unapologetic. "There is nothing shameful about his mistress," Edwin said quietly. "Nothing."

She smiled and lay back down as he cleaned her and then tended to himself.

When he'd finished, Edwin discarded the scrap. He caught Gertrude, wringing a gasp from her, and flipped onto his back so that she lay sprawled atop his chest. Her plaited hair slapped against his shoulder, those silken tendrils tickling him and stirring a grin.

"I must confess." She propped her dainty chin up and rubbed it back and forth along the faint whorl of curls that matted his chest. "I've heard much about lovemaking, and even . . . come across people doing that very thing." Her eyes went soft. "But I've never imagined it could be like this."

Despite the perils of East London, she'd retained her virtue and her innocence still.

Edwin stroked a palm in small circles over her back. "It's not always like this. More often than not, it's a purely physical exchange that somehow manages to leave a person feeling hollow after." Such had been the way even with his wife, who'd despised his touch from the night they'd consummated their impetuous marriage. No, the act had always been physical in nature, with raw emotion stripped from the exchanges.

Not with Gertrude.

His mind balked and shied away from that whispering.

"This didn't feel hollow," she said simply, laying her ear against the place his heart beat.

"No." His throat moved with the sea of emotions swirling within him. "This did not."

Gertrude picked her head up. Astute as she was, she would hear the unspoken admissions hanging there.

"Everything was hollow . . . until you. There was no purpose. There was no reason to smile or laugh. I was alone in every way a person can be."

She shimmied up his body until their lips brushed. "It's not because of me, Edwin." Gertrude touched a hand to his heart. "It's because of you. All of this is because of you. You could have very easily held on to your hatred at every turn, and you've not. I've done nothing. You've done all this yourself. You're in hiding no more, and you deserve to be out in the light."

Out in the light. It was precisely what he'd been since she'd stormed his household and taken up a place inside it. But to believe he could ever move amongst society as he once had . . . ? "You are an optimist, Gertrude Killoran." Edwin claimed another kiss. "But you're wrong," he said when he broke contact.

Mischief glimmered in her eyes. "I'm never wrong."

He chuckled. "No, I wager you're not."

The levity left her gaze. "Your life and Stephen's, together, will never be bleak. And you both have the ability to make it even fuller."

For one tick of the clock, he thought she spoke of them: of the three of them being a family together. *And I want that* . . . As shocking as that was after less than a fortnight of knowing her, he felt that yearning in his soul.

"Your brother-in-law wants to begin again with you," she said, stealing the brief interlude he'd allowed himself. "You have Stephen's grandparents."

Edwin gently rolled her off his body and then swung his legs over the sofa. "No." He stood, and just like that, reality intruded.

"They are his family."

"You don't know them." Nor would she want to. They'd treated him, one born of a like rank, as though he were the scum upon the cobblestones. They'd never see Gertrude's worth.

"They have a right to be in his life," she persisted, gathering up her nightshift. She drew it on, and as her slender frame disappeared under that decorous fabric, it signified an end to the all-too-brief interlude he'd shared with her.

"You don't know anything about it," he said tightly, rescuing each article of clothing.

"Then tell me," she urged.

"Tell you how they accused me of murdering my wife? Or should I go back further to the words of hatred they tossed about me when they learned Lavinia and I had eloped?" he asked sharply. "They destroyed our marriage."

"Your wife, in not standing up for your union together, destroyed your marriage. Her parents did not. Her parents haven't seen the man capable of great love."

Edwin wrestled his shirt overhead. "They can go hang," he muttered into the fabric. He yanked it down and grabbed his trousers next. He'd conceded enough points where she was concerned. This would never be a ground he budged from.

Gertrude lifted an eyebrow. "And Lord Charles?"

Damn her.

"He was your friend. He supported your marriage."

"He blamed me for her death," he whispered, collapsing onto the edge of the sofa.

Gertrude sidled up next to him and took his hand. "You blamed yourself and came to find forgiveness. It is not mere chance that we keep running into His Lordship. He wants to begin again with you, Edwin. You should allow both of you that."

"I . . ." Wanted that friendship again.

God, how could she see and know?

"I'd be bereft without my siblings." She stared at him with stricken eyes. "I . . . will be." Stephen. Her eventual departure.

His heart squeezed. *I'm not ready for her to go.* Nor was it because it would mean he and Stephen would learn how to be alone together, as a family. But rather, when she left, she'd steal a happiness he'd never thought again to know.

"You'll remain until a proper governess is found," he said crisply. Those were, after all, the terms.

It wouldn't be enough.

"We found one," she reminded him. "You should hire Mrs. Upton." Why did this feel like a goodbye? Why did it feel as though she was even now putting together the remainder of his life so she could go on her way?

Panic knocked around at his insides, rattling loose logic.

Edwin gnashed his teeth. Damn her. "She wouldn't do."

"You know she would."

"What is this about, Gertrude?" he thundered, surging to his feet.

She cowered, and he felt like the biggest bastard and his frustration only expanded.

"Do you want to leave? Is that what this is about?"

She shook her head. "I don't *want* to leave, Edwin," she whispered in heartbreaking tones that cut across his own fears.

Which implied . . . "You want to remain."

Gertrude wetted her lips. "I . . . do."

The energy drained from his legs, and he sank into the seat beside her once more. "You want to stay here," he repeated. No one wanted to stay. His own wife hadn't. Stephen didn't. This woman . . . did. It was foreign and unexplainable, and . . . also set joy seeping to the darkest, dormant corners of his broken self. "Then . . . stay."

A little snorting laugh shook her frame. "I don't know what kind of offer that is."

Edwin joined in. "I don't know, either." He crept his hand toward hers and claimed her fingers in his. "I just know I want you here, and whatever this is . . ."—this magic whenever they were near—"we'll figure it out . . . together."

Gertrude gave all her attention to their palms pressed together. "All right," she murmured, two syllables that brought his eyes closed and sent joy surging through him. "But on a condition . . ."

He went still. "No."

"That's the condition," she said with a finality. "Not Stephen's grandparents. That can come later. Lord Charles."

Join me for drinks at White's . . . You can find me there at ten o'clock most evenings . . .

Bloody hell.

"You stubborn minx," he muttered and spun, catching her quickly in his arms and startling a laugh from her.

"What are you doing?" she asked between breathless giggles as he trailed his mouth down the curve of her cheek and the sensitive flesh behind her right ear, and lower to her neck.

"Making love to you."

Her eyes formed perfect circles. "Again," she mouthed.

"If you'd rather I not—" Edwin made to pull away.

Gertrude caught him by the nape and guided him back. "I'd rather you did," she whispered.

And with volatile talk of his in-laws, or Lord Charles, and the prospect of Gertrude leaving forgotten, Edwin gave himself over to the joy of being in her arms once more.

Chapter 22

He'd been gone thirty minutes.

Gertrude stole a glance at the longcase clock in the corner of the library.

The squeak of metal as Sethos ran in the cylinder creaked gratingly, loud on her frayed nerves.

They should be meeting even now: Edwin and his former best friend, still his brother-in-law. She absently stroked Gus, who rested against her side, this time finding little comfort in the loyal tabby's downy softness.

What if she'd set him up for failure? What if even now Edwin and Lord Charles were coming to blows—

Stephen stepped into her line of vision.

He cleared his throat. "Gert . . . you are looking . . . *nice.*"

"I'm looking nice?"

"Yea . . ." Stephen yanked at his collar and then caught her watching him. He stopped. "Like . . . not ugly. Almost pretty."

Her lips twitched at that most typical of little-boy compliments. "Thank you," she said dryly. She narrowed her eyes, taking in his dark, threadbare garments, those clothes of the Dials he'd not worn in more than ten days. He was up to something, and she well knew what it was. "Absolutely not."

Her brother stomped his foot, proving how much a child he still was. "I didn't *say* anything."

"You didn't have to. I know you. I know what you want, and I know where you are not going."

"I want to see them. It's been a fortnight."

It had been just fourteen days, and in that time, her entire world had been turned upside down. Trust had blossomed between her and Edwin. She'd not go and shatter their new bond by violating the terms of their arrangement. Not even if she herself also wanted to see her family . . . all together.

"You want to see them, too," Stephen surmised, as good a reader of her as she was of him.

"That's neither here nor there." She scooped up Gus and stood, marking an end to this discussion. She'd need to see Marlow had footmen stationed at every entrance, because when her brother had in his mind to do something, not even God himself could barter with him. "One of the conditions of my remaining here with you is that I honor the agreement struck with your father."

"But that was before," he whined, rushing into her path.

"Before what?"

"When my father hated you."

My father . . . Her arms sagged, and with a feline squeal of worry, Gus leapt from her arms. Once more, he'd called Edwin his father, recognizing that relationship that he'd been so adamant on denying.

Her heart wept from the joy of it. She wanted Edwin here. Wanted to share that gift with him.

Stephen clutched her forearm in his shockingly strong grip, giving it a shake. "But he doesn't hate you anymore. Now he likes you, and when a man likes a woman like he likes you, he lets her do all kinds of things."

She blushed. "I'm just a woman in his employ."

He snorted. "I'm eleven years old, but I ain't a damn lackwit. I knew when Broderick was lusting after Reggie, and Adair was hot for Cleo. I—*oomph*." Stephen glared around the hand she'd slapped over his mouth.

"That is not appropriate, Stephen," she hissed.

"Ainf 'propriate howf he's looking atchyou."

"Bloody hell," she gasped as he sank his teeth into the fleshy portion of her palm. "He's not looking at me any way." He'd been discreet. They'd both been discreet. Hadn't they? Except . . . she cringed . . . an eleven-year-old boy had noticed the pull between her and Edwin.

"Well, he's not looking at you *nowwww*." Literal as only a child could be, Stephen pointed his eyes at the ceiling. "He's out doing fancy nob things. But he looks at you, and you know it."

Yes, she knew it. Her body still thrummed with the memory of his every stroke last evening. But that her brother knew it? Gertrude curled her toes so sharply the bottoms of her feet ached. "He isn't," she said belatedly, and made a show of looking for Gus.

Then Stephen's eyes went wide. "Not like *thaaaat*, silly. Not like the patrons at the club used to eye all the whores, but you know . . ." Color filled his white cheeks. "Like how Adair watches Cleo. All soft-eyed." He slackened his features, his jaw falling agape and his eyes going soft, and for all the horror of having her secrets uncovered by the boy she'd raised like her own son, a laugh bubbled up from her throat.

"He doesn't look at me like that." She wanted him to. She ached for the "I want you" he'd uttered last night and for his appeal that she remain to be more than sexual, to instead be the bond her brother had mistaken it for.

"Trust me, he does." Stephen beamed. "And so he'd forgive you anything, including taking me out," he cajoled, bringing them back to the earlier quest that had prompted his analysis of her relationship with Edwin.

"I'd not break my word, Stephen." Nor would she betray Edwin's trust. Gertrude stepped around him, retrieved Gus from under the leather sofa, that place he'd taken to making home. "This discussion is over."

"Please, Gertrude," Stephen called out on a tremulous whisper, a plea that brought her up short.

Keep going. If you don't, you'll waver . . .

But she'd come to view this boy as the son she'd never bear, and she could no sooner ignore that entreaty than she could pluck out her one working eye.

Gertrude forced herself to face him.

Stephen folded his hands together as if in prayer, holding them up. "Please. I miss them." Tears flooded his eyes, ripping at her heart. "D-Don't look at m-me like that. I'm not c-crying," he rasped, and yet the tears poured down his cheeks. "I-I just want to see B-Broderick and Cl-Cleo and O-Ophelia. I want to see them all." And then he, this life-hardened little person who'd not cried since his earliest days in Diggory's gang, dissolved into heaving sobs that shook his frame. At last, he let down the mask of invincibility he'd donned and surrendered to his emotions.

She was across the room in three strides and had him in her arms. Stephen collapsed against her, and she drew him closer. "I-I miss th-them," he wept into her shoulder. His little hands formed fists at her chest.

"I know," she said gently, laying her cheek atop his head. Gertrude smoothed her hands over his back the way she once had to urge him to sleep when he was younger.

"N-no, you don't know. N-not really. S-soon you'll go and return t-to Broderick and R-Reggie, and you'll see Cleo and Ophelia all you want, and I'll never see them, Gert. Never."

And I'll never see Edwin. Her tears fell freely. "You've been happy here." *Both of us have.*

"I-I have," he said, when in the past he would have offered a lie or curse, or worse. "I don't h-hate him like I thought I would."

No, because how could he? Edwin had allowed Stephen to retain pieces of his past and had sought to build a relationship with him: visiting Gunter's and Hyde Park, joining Stephen at Draven's to oversee the construction of his furniture. "He's a good man," she whispered.

And if it were possible, Stephen cried all the more, until his voice grew ragged and hoarse, and the front of her gown was soaked from the copious tears pouring from him. He cried until his tears dried up and heaving sobs shook his frame.

"It's all right," she soothed.

He pushed away. Avoiding her gaze, he dragged the back of his sleeve over his nose. "But it's not, though. How about just Cleo, then?"

Just Cleo.

Bloody hell. "I can't," she implored, needing him to understand.

"But he won't even find out. You and I will go and return before he even gets back from his fancy club."

"You don't know that."

It was a misstep. She'd faltered, and Stephen latched on. "We'll be quick. We don't live far from Cleo. We'll visit and return, and we're from St. Giles, Gert. St. Giles. Do you truly think a nob could find us sneaking about?"

No, she didn't. Not most nobleman, but Edwin, with his acuity and rapier intelligence, wasn't one to be underestimated. *And if you take Stephen without his permission, and he finds out?* Gertrude caught the inside of her cheek between her teeth. He'd never forgive her. *Or mayhap he would.* "I know you want to go now, Stephen. But we can't. I promise, we'll ask him," she hurried to assure him.

He stretched his hands out. "If you ask and he says no, then he'll have guards on me and you."

Yes, he would.

It was not Broderick her brother asked to see.

She felt herself wavering.

"It's just Cleo."

Was that her or her brother speaking in this instance?

"He owes me a favor, Gert. I want it to be this."

"You put the favor to him, then, Stephen." But Gertrude couldn't be the one to go against him.

"Nope. That ain't how it works. He conceded at Gunter's. I won. If we're discovered, I'll claim this as my request."

"And if we aren't discovered?"

Stephen flashed a half grin. "Then I'll steal me another favor."

She sighed. "Oh, Stephen. I'm so sorry. But I cann—"

"To hell with you, and to hell with him, then." He spat on the floor in an explosive display he'd not shown since Hyde Park. It served as a reminder of how far he'd come in his long road to healing, but how much more he needed to travel and how fragile he still was—and mayhap would always be. "I asked, when I've never done so before. I'm going anyway, whether or not you're with me." And this time, he stomped off.

"Stephen!"

He continued his march.

"Fine! I'll do it."

That brought him to a quick stop. Her brother, however, still made no move to face her. Gertrude glanced to the door, mindful that there could be servants passing by, and dropped her voice to a hushed whisper. "I'll join you." Because ultimately, at the end of the day, Stephen would find a way out of this household. Not a single one of Edwin's servants would be a match for keeping him here. And if Stephen went out, there would be no one to watch after him.

He whirled around. "You'll do it!"

"On a condition. I'm telling your father when we return." He'd understand. Two weeks ago, he wouldn't have. But Edwin was no longer the same spiteful person.

"Tell him what you want." His smile widened, dimpling his cheeks. "Now let's go."

A short while later, with Gertrude changed into black skirts and Stephen at her side, they slipped out the unattended servants' entrance, and she prayed Edwin would understand her decision.

Entering the famous doors of the most exclusive and oldest club in London, it was as though Edwin had stepped back in time.

Back when he'd been first a young bachelor and then a newly married man, Edwin had spent hours upon hours at White's, and never had he felt this cloying panic threatening to choke him the way it did now.

A hushed silence, one Edwin would have believed impossible for the peerage, fell over the club.

What am I doing here? Leave. Turn and go . . .

It would be so simple. He needn't even collect his cloak from the butler stationed at the famed double black doors. He could run and keep on running until he was home with Gertrude and Stephen and the world made sense the way it did whenever they were near.

As he walked with purposeful strides, cutting a path through White's, the stares of men he'd once taken drinks with and sat across a gaming table from followed him. Men who now swiveled in their seats, their horrified gazes burning into his back, enough to leave a mark.

No jovial greetings were called out as they'd once been. No invitations for him to join. Edwin had made this walk many times before. Never, however, had the path to this particular table felt longer.

His belly churned, and while he wanted to flee, Gertrude's voice slashed through the unease.

You've done all this yourself. You're in hiding no more, and you deserve to be out in the light.

At last he reached it.

Edwin stopped at this table he'd spent countless nights at. All previous visits to it, however, had been effortless, with him not awaiting an invitation, simply grabbing a chair, tugging it out, and seating himself. Servants had rushed over with a glass in hand for the regular patron . . . joining his friend. "Charles," he finally greeted his brother-in-law.

Charles sat motionless, a forgotten snifter poised halfway to his mouth, frozen in his fingers. And then . . . he seemed to jerk back to the moment. He jumped up, sloshing his spirits around his glass. He set it down, forgotten. "Edwin," he greeted on a whisper. "You came."

Not the "get the hell out of here—I was merely taunting you" response Edwin had feared.

"Yes," he said lamely, wishing for the camaraderie they'd once shared. The jovial laughter and bawdy jests between two who'd been as close as brothers.

"Won't you sit? Please." Charles motioned to the empty chair that Edwin hadn't even realized he'd grabbed on to and now had a death grip upon.

A liveried servant, hovering in the wings, came over . . . then stopped. The young man glanced uncertainly from the owner of the table to Edwin's still-tight hold on the chair.

All this, how very . . . foreign it all was. How peculiar it all felt.

The buzz of whispers generated around White's swarmed his ears, like the hive of bees he and Charles had knocked loose from Edwin's family's country estate as boys.

Charles's brows came together.

You're in hiding no more, and you deserve to be out in the light.

Edwin forced himself to release the chair and stepped back.

The servant rushed to draw the seat out for him, and as Edwin slid into the comfortable folds and a glass was set before him, he forced a wry grin. "I forgot the whole expectation that we can't manage to even seat ourselves."

And just like that the tension broke.

Charles laughed, and retrieving his glass, he lifted it in salute. "Indeed." Setting his brandy down once more, he proceeded to pour a snifter for Edwin. He pushed it across the table.

It was an offering.

An olive branch.

And bloody hell—before a room of strangers, servants, and once friends, Edwin's throat flooded with emotion. Desperate for a drink, he gathered it and took a long sip. When he'd finished that swallow, Edwin contemplated the dark contents of the fine French stock. "I . . ." Gertrude had convinced him not even one day ago that he needed this reunion to occur. He'd resisted at first, and then he saw the truth in what she'd said . . . He'd known he was coming from that moment. He'd ridden his mount through the fashionable end of London. Strode up the steps and through the whole of the club, and hadn't given a single proper thought to what he should say.

Simply being here had represented the impossible task.

He'd believed that . . . and he'd been wrong.

Finding any appropriate discourse with his best friend was the greatest struggle . . . and had he fixed on that before his journey here, it was likely a road he'd never have traveled.

Charles cleared his throat. "I'm happy you decided to join me."

It was more than he deserved. "I thought about not coming," he confessed, at last lifting his gaze. "I felt everything that needed to be said had been years ago." When Lavinia had perished with her and Edwin's babe, and Stephen also had been lost.

"There's always more to say," Charles said in grave tones. "There was never closure."

No, there had been only raging fury and explosive agony. "Is that what this is about? Closure?"

A strained smile ghosted Charles's lips. "No. It's not about that. We were friends." He paused and stared briefly into his drink. "Best friends."

"Brothers until we die, Edwin! First—"

"Egads, what are you doing, Charles?"

"I'm cutting my palm. So we have a blood bond. We'll be . . ."

"Blood brothers," Edwin murmured.

"You remember that?" Charles stared past Edwin's shoulder, his gaze distant, his eyes seeing that same long-ago memory. "A friendship that will not break. A devotion no one can ever shake. No person shall . . ." His words trailed off, and reality forced its way back in.

"Come between us," Edwin made himself say for the benefit of both their remembrances.

"I blamed you," Charles said suddenly, unexpectedly. "And I was wrong."

Edwin stiffened. Of everything his brother-in-law might have said, those had certainly not been the words Edwin had thought would leave his lips.

Charles dragged his chair closer and, dropping his elbows on the table, framed his face so that the people to the left and right of them were shut out. "I needed to blame someone. It was never you. It was the rotted luck to bring into her employ that Devil in disguise. It could have been anyone."

Only, it hadn't been. It had been Edwin. Lavinia. Stephen. And another tiny babe who'd never entered the world.

A boy or girl, Edwin had never known and never would because of one ruthless act of violence committed against them. Had she been a little girl, one Stephen even now would be a protective older brother to?

This is too much . . .

Nothing these past years had destroyed him—this would.

"How is August?"

What . . . ? His head foggy, Edwin glanced over, having forgotten the man across from him.

"August?"

Charles frowned.

"My son. He is . . ." What was he, exactly? The answer he would have given Charles two weeks ago would have been very different from the one he considered now. Stephen now laughed and smiled and didn't speak about splitting his stomach open or, worse, returning to Broderick Killoran's clubs. But neither was the child one Charles would recognize or know how to speak with. "Stephen is settling in." There, that wasn't untrue.

"Stephen?" his brother-in-law asked, confusion heavy in his gaze and query.

A dull heat climbed Edwin's cheeks. "That was August's name when he was kidnapped. He's faced so many changes, I thought it would be easier for him if he were to retain the name he's gone by these past years."

"You changed his *name*?"

"*They* changed his name."

"And you've kept it."

Edwin searched for judgment in Charles's expression, for God knew it was all there in those four syllables. This was a mistake. He made to stand.

With a shake of his head, Charles tossed back his drink in one swallow that strained the muscles of his throat as they worked to down those spirits. When he'd finished, he grimaced and gave his head a shake. "Who's to say what's the right way to do *any* of this?" he muttered, and that calm forgiveness kept Edwin there. "They don't prepare one for how to deal with this tragedy."

"No, they don't."

"And one never is really happy again after it," Charles whispered.

Yes, that was true. Again, that had been the case, but for Gertrude. She'd shown him that it was all right to live again . . . and that it was wrong for him as well as Stephen not to find happiness once more.

And I want it with her . . .

On the heels of that was another long-accustomed sentiment he'd come to know around Charles—guilt.

"Your parents want to see him." Edwin searched his friend for some outward reaction.

"They've told me as much." His brother-in-law grabbed the bottle of brandy and refilled his glass. "I told them it wasn't their place to force a reunion, and perhaps in time there could be something, but you'd decided that this is not that time," he murmured, topping off Edwin's glass.

So that had *not* been the impetus behind Charles's sudden appearance, a peace brokering so Lavinia's family might have access to Stephen. Made a cynic by life and all its misery, those suspicions had been there at the back of his head.

"Will you send him on to Eton?"

An image flashed to mind of Stephen attending that school with distinguished boys of his same station, except so wholly different. He'd bloody them senseless. Nor could any good come from their own relationship as father and son if he were to send the boy away. "I don't think that is wise." Edwin picked up his glass. "Not at this time. Mayhap one day." Or mayhap never.

"Governesses and tutors, then?"

"We are in the process of finding one that might be a good match for him." *You should hire Mrs. Upton . . .*

Charles quirked a brow. *"We?"*

Edwin started, and cursed his loose tongue.

"Miss Killoran."

The air stirred around them like the dangerous charge right before a lightning strike. That name, Gertrude's familial one, had once inspired a like response in him. "She's a good woman."

His brother-in-law stared back incredulously. "A good woman?" he whispered, surging forward in his chair. "Her family kidnapped August. Killed my sister." *My wife.* "Your second babe. And you'd say she is a 'good woman'?"

Just like that, the fragile truce fractured. Yet neither could he, in good conscience, blame Charles for that volatile response. It was a realistic one that he himself had had, and he still would have been mired in his hatred for Gertrude had he sent her away weeks earlier. "She took care of him. She kept him safe. And she is attempting to ease his way back into my household." A task that he would have never accomplished without her assistance.

"And then she'll go?"

I don't want to leave, Edwin . . .

"And then she'll go."

The narrowing of his brother-in-law's eyes indicated that he'd heard the hesitation there. A sad smile formed on hard lips. "You were always more trusting than was safe. And you're trusting still. That woman . . . her blood is that bastard's. She cannot be trusted."

"You're wrong," he said automatically, and never had he more believed those two words.

"Am I?" Charles shot back. Once more, he dragged his chair closer. "But what if I'm not, Edwin? What if this is all some other ploy to steal him right back?"

At the back of his mind, for the first time, suspicion stirred.

What if that was the only reason she wished to stay? So she could be closer to Stephen?

As soon as the traitorous thought slipped in, he batted it back.

"I trust her." And he wanted to go. Wanted to leave his club and all the icy stares and whispers and return to her side. To listen to whatever peculiar bit of information she was in possession of, or join her and one of those unconventional creatures she'd made pets.

Charles exhaled slowly through his clenched lips. "I heard the pause there. Mark my words, she isn't to be trusted. Blood will tell, and hers flows with that bastard Mac Diggory's. She's as evil as her father."

They were condemnations Edwin himself had uttered, too many times to remember. He'd been of a like opinion since he'd uncovered the treacherous act committed that night. Everything, however, had changed.

Fury pulsed in his veins. "You don't know her."

"I don't want to know her," Charles barked. The whispers around White's grew to a frenzy. His brother-in-law grabbed his snifter and took a drink. "I didn't ask you here to discuss a Diggory." Reaching into his jacket, he withdrew a folded sheet with the marquess's seal upon it. He tossed it across the table, and the page landed next to Edwin's drink. "I wanted to host you and August as guests for dinner. My parents won't be there," he rushed to assure. "But I want to know my godson."

That's what this was about . . . Charles wished a reunion with him and his nephew. Edwin picked up that invitation and tucked it inside his jacket. "You want to know Stephen," he murmured.

"I want to know August. That"—he jammed a fingertip at the surface of the table—"is his name, Edwin. Not *Stephen*. Not *Killoran*. August. My God, man, how can you cede any part of your son to that family?" he implored.

Edwin pushed back his chair. "This was a mistake."

"Because I'm being honest with you?" Charles challenged. "Because I'm trying to protect you and my nephew?"

Because my judgment has been so flawed. Because I trusted where I oughtn't too many times, which has brought me to this point in my life. And yet, he'd not have anyone looking after him like he was a damned babe, and certainly not the former best friend who'd been absent since Lavinia's death. "I do not need protection."

His brother-in-law arched a brow. "Just like you and Lavinia didn't require it seven years ago?"

The barb found its intended mark.

Charles pounced. "This sudden weakness . . . does it have anything to do with Gertrude Killoran?"

"It's not your business," he gritted out.

Charles's eyes rounded with horror. "My God, you *care* about her. A common street rat, thief, and murderer—"

Edwin shot a hand across the table and gripped his brother-in-law by the shirtfront. "Not another word," he whispered. "Do not mention her name again."

Silence blanketed the club, and the prickling along Edwin's nape brought him back to the moment. He abruptly released Charles. The other man fell back in his chair. "I understand the reason for your hatred; I shared it. But I've come to know Gertrude Killoran, and she is nothing like Mac Diggory."

Edwin turned to go.

"Edwin . . ." *Keep walking.* There was nothing left here to be said between them. Charles was too mired in his hatred to see reason. So why did Edwin stop? "You might resent me in this instant . . . but you'll see I'm right about her. She is not to be trusted."

And with that ominous warning reverberating in his mind, Edwin left.

Chapter 23

After the initial "Good God, what in 'ell are ya doin' 'ere," hurled in Cleopatra's Cockney, had come a series of swift and very tight hugs from a sibling who'd never been given to any expressions of warmth . . . for both Gertrude and Stephen.

Positioned in the corner of her sister's parlor at the edge of the floor-length windows overlooking the London streets below, Gertrude alternated between watching that pair deep in discussion and stealing nervous glances outside.

And then at the clock.

They could not remain long.

As it was, they'd been here almost forty minutes. If Edwin's meeting with Charles proved a disaster, or if Edwin could not face the *ton* after all, he'd be home and likely find out that they were missing.

He might not notice. He'd have to be looking for her upon his return. And why should he?

Because you made love last night? Because he brought you pleasure you hadn't believed possible, over and over?

A blush scorched her entire body, blazing a path from her toes to the roots of her hair.

Cleopatra chose that inopportune moment to glance her way.

Gertrude jerked her attention to the window and prayed for her skin to cool. What a pathetic fool, waxing on about what she and Edwin had shared. What *had* they shared? A virtuous lady would have had the naivete to believe that having made love as she and Edwin had signified intimacy greater than the physical act itself. But Gertrude was anything but an innocent young miss. The world she'd dwelled in had proven that sex was just another physical urge as common as eating and sleeping.

Only, it hadn't felt that way. It had felt like something so very much more.

Her brother-in-law's tall form reflected back in the visage of the crystal windowpane. She gasped, having been so absorbed in her musings that she'd failed to hear his approach. He'd been stealth of foot, but she never, ever failed to hear anyone coming upon her.

"I'm sorry to startle you," he murmured.

"You didn't. I was . . . woolgathering," she confessed, which wasn't a lie.

"You snuck off with him."

For one horrifying moment that left her dizzy, she believed he spoke of a different "him." "I didn't sneak. I don't know what—" Adair gave her an odd look. *He's talking about Stephen, you ninny.* Why should Adair Thorne or . . . anyone gather that Gertrude had gone and fallen in love with the least likely person? *Say something. Say anything.* Her mind whirred. "Oh." She winced. That is what she'd managed? Bloody useless, she was. Mac Diggory had proven correct after all. "I suppose one might call it sneaking," she finished lamely, which only ushered in a fresh onslaught of guilt.

Adair leveled a stare on her, one that delved deep and saw too much.

Her cheeks burnt all the hotter. Why, oh, why hadn't she, with the life she'd lived, lost the damned ability to blush? It was the curse of her pale-white English cheeks.

"I wanted to thank you," her brother-in-law said in grave tones.

She fiddled with the fine lace trim along the edge of the curtain. "I didn't do any—"

"You did. Despite the marquess's clear warnings, you knew Cleopatra's grief at never again seeing Stephen, and you made that reunion happen." And risked so much along the way: her trust with Edwin. Her siblings' establishment, should Edwin find out and exact revenge as he'd promised.

He won't do that. He wouldn't. But if he found out . . . nay, *when* he found out, he very well might toss her out on her arse and destroy her family along the way.

Gertrude's stomach turned. In her mind, she'd rationalized her decision to come with the truth that Stephen had been determined to go, regardless of whether she'd gone with him. In accompanying him, she'd merely ensured he was safe journeying to Cleo's. Would Edwin, however, see it that way? For the first time since she'd resolved to go with Stephen, misgivings reared in her mind. She and Edwin had forged a deep bond, but that relationship hadn't and would never extend to her family. *Or mayhap it could . . .* That tantalizing hope whispered forward. Gertrude shoved the thought aside for now. "We have to go," she said insistently. She stole another glance at the clock. Forty-six minutes. "We've already stayed longer than we should have." Forty-six minutes too many.

"Yes." He held a hand up, staying her before she could go. "You managed to bring my wife the one thing I've been unable to secure," he interjected gruffly. They stared over at Cleo and Stephen side by side on the sofa, engrossed in whatever topic they now spoke on. "She's been listless, silent." His features contorted. "Sad."

I know what it is to want to drive back another person's misery. "I am happy that she and Stephen will have this goodbye that they were denied, but it cannot happen again. This meeting insisted upon by our brother? It's wrong to his father, and it's wrong for all of us to go against those wishes." Edwin had already proven that with time he was capable of great forgiveness. It was not, however, their place or right to make that determination for him. "If you'll excuse me?"

"I've just one more question . . . Has he been in any way unkind to you?"

Gertrude stared quizzically up, and the glint in his eyes that promised death registered. Edwin. He was speaking of Edwin. "No. His Lordship has been nothing but kind," she promised, warmed that this man who'd once been her family's rival should be so devoted and concerned after her well-being. It spoke to the depths of his character that he should feel that loyalty, given the fact that Gertrude's own brother had attempted to destroy his hell and Stephen had actually succeeded in burning down his clubs.

But then, that is what love did to a person.

"Gertrude?" her brother-in-law asked, concern in his question.

Footsteps sounded in the hall; with her heightened hearing, she'd always detected those steps moments before her siblings, who were skilled in different ways.

A moment later, the door burst open with such force it bounced back and nearly slammed Ophelia in the face. "Stephen," she rasped, her husband, Connor O'Roarke, appearing just behind her. With a cry, she sprinted across the room, knocked Cleopatra away, and launched herself at Stephen.

The little boy grunted, and where he'd once have chafed at those displays of affection, now he wrapped his sister in a tight embrace. "Ophelia!" he cried out.

"I came as soon as I received word," she wept against Stephen's spindly chest in a display she never would have made before her marriage to Connor. Her middle sister also had been changed by love.

Gertrude stared on at brother and sister. She'd devoted her entire life to Stephen and his upbringing. She'd sought to give him skills beyond the ones involving a weapon or acts of treachery and deceit. In short, skills that would always be seen as useless in St. Giles. As such, she and Stephen had never formed the bond he shared with Ophelia and Cleopatra, one forged in both friendship and love.

To him, Gertrude had been a bothersome motherlike figure who didn't have anything of real meaning to offer. Oh, she didn't doubt he loved her, but their relationship had been . . . different.

From over Ophelia's shoulder, Stephen opened his eyes, and his gaze collided with Gertrude's. "Thank you," he mouthed.

Her heart swelled, and all the reservations she'd felt in coming here, all the worrying that had followed their late-night flight to Cleopatra and Adair's, fled.

She returned a tremulous smile that quickly wavered. The quarterclock chimed another reminder. "We have to go," she said back, silently.

He nodded. "I know."

With a maturity better suited to a boy ten years his senior, Stephen was the one to break that endless hug with Ophelia. "We've got to be going." He stepped out of her arms and, stuffing his hands into the pockets along the front of his midnight trousers, rocked on his heels. "I wanted to say hello and . . . and . . ." *Goodbye.*

Gertrude swept over, and catching his hand, she gave it a light squeeze.

Stephen's little fingers clutched hers tight.

Cleopatra and Ophelia exchanged a look.

"We'll escort you back," Ophelia said.

Gertrude was already shaking her head. Impossible. "We can't risk being discovered." She'd speak to Edwin and own what she'd done this night and hope he understood, but to bring her family 'round?

Her youngest and most obstinate sister growled. "I ain't letting you two go back by yourself."

"We got here by ourselves, and we'll return the same way. We do not require a nursemaid," Gertrude said tightly.

Shock pinged around the room, reflecting back in the eyes of her siblings and their spouses. Yes, Gertrude, as her sisters had known her the whole of her life, had never questioned their authority or decision-making. No more. Now she'd make her own decisions, without interference.

"It isn't safe," Ophelia said gently.

"Because I'm blind?" Gertrude shot back.

Ophelia couldn't hold her gaze. "I didn't say that."

"You didn't have to. None of you ever directly stated as much . . . to my face." But the truth had always been there, implicit and understood. She looked first to Ophelia and then to Cleo. By their guilty, hangdog expressions, they, as she'd suspected, made her vision . . . or lack of, the reason for their overprotectiveness . . . and the limitations they had placed on Gertrude. Only Edwin had never doubted her capabilities simply because she had lost vision in one eye. "I'm not in need of your protection. I'm a grown woman who lived the same life that all of you did." Including Connor and Adair, who fell back, allowing Gertrude and her sisters their long overdue talk.

"We look after one another," Cleo said tightly. "It is what we do."

"Yes, we do. But you have both been permitted the right to choose." Gertrude turned her palms up. "Can't you see, can't you at least own, that those decisions always belonged to you? I never had a say . . . My opinion never mattered."

Ophelia made a sound of protest. "That's not true."

"Isn't it?" Gertrude shot back and then glanced to Cleo. "Isn't it?" She took a deep breath. "I'm not condemning either of you. I allowed you both to stand in the de facto role of big sister. I ceded my rights." Because she'd ceased believing in herself. Living with Edwin . . . taking a stand on behalf of her brother, had inadvertently proven to also be a stand for herself. "I'm not doing so any longer. I moved into Lord Maddock's with Stephen. I reasoned with him. I came here with Stephen. Those were all my decisions." Gertrude lifted her chin in that defiant manner each of her sisters had proven masters of. "And I'll walk out of here." And take that hired hack she'd paid to wait. "Just as I entered, with Stephen, and alone."

The room stood in a silence so vast the drop of a pin could be heard.

Small fingers clenched hers once, twice, a third time. Gertrude glanced down at her brother. The pride glimmering in his eyes filled her. She winked once.

He returned that little gesture, and then his grin faded, replaced with the usual pugnacious set to his features. "We're leaving this place . . . together. I trust her."

I trust her.

Oh, God. That evidence of his trust in her, after all these years, was too much.

Tears stung her eyes and blurred her vision. And lest her family see and take that for the weakness it was in the streets, she made a show of adjusting her cloak.

Cleopatra broke the impasse. "Very well. Ophelia, Adair, and I won't follow you." She flicked her chin in Connor's direction. "He will. At a distance," she hurried. "He's different from us, in the marquess's eyes. Mad Maddock hired him."

Gertrude and Stephen spoke together.

"He is *not* mad."

"He *ain't* mad."

Every set of eyes swung to her and Stephen.

Fiery blush on her cheeks be damned, she'd not allow her siblings to disparage Edwin, not when Mac Diggory and an unwitting Broderick had been to blame for Edwin's retreat from the world. "He is not mad," Gertrude repeated, daring a room full of London's most notorious street toughs to challenge her. "He's been fair and kind to Stephen and me—"

"And we won't have you talk about him." Stephen slammed a fist warningly against his open palm.

"Very well, then," Cleo said, the only one who saw the way things now were. Through her wire-rimmed spectacles, a suspicious stare met Gertrude's gaze.

Or mayhap . . . she saw entirely too much altogether.

Gertrude cleared her throat. "Come on, Stephen. We have to go. One more goodbye."

In a whirlwind of hugs, Stephen went around the room hugging each sister, and in a sign of how much he missed life in St. Giles, he even hugged their former foes and the men he'd spoken with open loathing about. Moments later they were gone, their carriage rattling through the streets of London.

Stephen sat silent and small in the corner of their hired hack. He reached for the curtain, but Gertrude stayed him. She shook her head once.

He let that fabric fall and sighed. "You think he'll let me see them again?"

"I don't know," she said simply, not pretending to misunderstand.

"He's seen you ain't bad."

"You 'aren't,'" she corrected out of a lifetime of serving in the role of tutor.

"We're talking about *you*, Gert."

"I know. I was merely indicating that—" His eyes twinkled. With a quiet laugh, she nudged him with her elbow. "Scamp." Throwing an arm around his shoulders, she drew him close. "I don't know if he'll allow it. I like to think he will. I like to think he's come to see that the Killorans aren't the Diggorys, but I also know it might take him time."

They didn't speak the remainder of the ride through Hanover Square. When they reached the intersecting street that emptied out into Grosvenor Square, Gertrude knocked hard on the roof, twice.

The driver immediately drew on the reins, bringing the conveyance to a stop. Not waiting for assistance, she opened the door and urged Stephen out ahead of her. Drawing the hood of her cloak closer about her face, she caught the sides of the carriage and climbed out. Stephen waited at her side as she handed over another small purse with the agreed-upon fare for the ride and wait. Then, hand in hand, she and Stephen found the shadows, that St. Giles art form, and wound their way through the streets.

"Do you like him?" Stephen asked quietly, breaking the rule about silence and stealth in nighttime travels.

Gertrude missed a step. "Do I like . . . ?"

"My father. The marquess."

"I do," she said simply. "He's kind and wants what is best for you and is trying to be a father and *oomph*—" She glared down at her brother, who'd given her a sharp jab. "What was that for?"

"I don't mean 'like him' like that. I mean . . . you know . . . like him like Cleo likes Adair and Broderick likes Reggie and Ophelia likes Connor. You know, where you want to have his babies and"—he puckered his lips and made smooching sounds—"*that* kind of like."

Oh, God in heaven. Of all the people she'd ever thought of having this conversation with—mayhap her sisters, Reggie—never had she dared consider she'd be having it with Stephen. She wanted the cobblestones to open up and swallow her whole before continuing this discourse with her brother.

"*Oomph.*" Glowering at him, Gertrude rubbed at her wounded side. At this point she was going to be sporting a nasty bruise. "Do stop hitting me."

Taking her arm in a surprisingly strong hold, Stephen brought her to a stop. "You aren't answering."

"I . . . I . . ." Gertrude briefly closed her eyes. "I do," she breathed.

"I knew it!" Stephen exclaimed, jubilant, his voice echoing around Grosvenor Square. Somewhere in the distance, a dog barked.

"*Shh,*" she whispered, pressing a finger to her lips. "Come, let us—"

"Turn around real slow. 'And over yar purse and fancy jewels." That coarse, guttural Cockney cut across her orders.

Cockney that had no place in these parts. *Bloody hell.* Caught unawares. And mistaken for a lady in these parts, which would be the likeliest assumption, given the people who dwelled here.

Careful to avoid sudden movements, she turned. "Oi'm afraid ya've come to fleece the wrong pocket," she said, easily slipping into her original East London street tones to match the masked stranger before them.

The thief gave no outward display to that revelation of her station. "Don't care if yar a lady or not. Yar fancily dressed, and ya got jewels there." He brandished the tip of his blade in a manner meant to threaten. He pointed it at her breastbone, to that place her brooch dangled.

Automatically, her fingers went to that piece, a gift from Broderick, special because it had been the first gift anyone had ever given her. She shook her head. "I can't," she whispered, her disavowal reflexive.

"Put yar knife down," Stephen growled. "Or I'll split you open."

"Careful," the burly man warned almost gleefully. "Or Oi'll cut 'er."

And he would. From the corner of her eye, she caught Stephen, his entire frame poised, braced for the fight. She gave her head a slight, imperceptible shake, willing him to not draw his weapon. The minute that happened, situations always dissolved into a street fight, and in her skirts as she was, she'd be useless to him. "You can have it," she said in the same calming timbre she reserved for the skittish cats around the Devil's Den. Holding her palms open so the pickpocket could see them, she moved her fingers slowly to her chest, and not taking her attention from the blade trained on her, she unfastened the cherished piece and tossed it lightly on the ground at his feet.

He made no move to retrieve it.

"Now the knife. I want that fancy jeweled piece strapped to you."

How . . . ? Gertrude gritted her teeth.

"Over my dead body." Brandishing his knife, Stephen flew forward.

The brute spun and turned his weapon on her brother.

"Stephen!" she cried, launching herself in front of him.

Their assailant immediately swiveled.

Stephen's cry echoed around Mayfair. "Gertrude! Watch out!"

Gertrude turned her head in time to catch the flash of a silver blade. Gasping, she leapt out of the way, sidestepping the brute of a man barreling down on her. His mask had slipped, revealing the harsh, angular planes of his face, marked and scarred from too many knife fights. He took another swipe at her. Her heart pounding, Gertrude lunged back. "Run," she rasped, giving Stephen a push, propelling him forward.

And God love him for choosing to obey her. Stephen took off running, and she started after him. Her chest rose and fell hard; both fear and exertion set her heart to pounding a fevered rhythm. They weren't far. She recognized the familiar pink stucco residence leading to Edwin's townhouse. So close. They were so close. Her entire body burnt with the intensity of their assailant's gaze. As Gertrude stretched her legs, she damned her cloak and skirts, encumbrances that hadn't hampered her as a young thief but now slowed her escape.

She stumbled and came down hard on her hands and knees. Agony radiated from her palms up her arms.

Stephen cried out and doubled back.

"Go," she screamed, shoving to her feet.

The masked stranger was almost upon her. Fiddling with the dagger strapped to her lower leg, she drew it out. Connor O'Roarke came flying from the shadows.

"Go," he thundered, taking down the assailant.

The pair wrestled, rolling for domination. Her stomach climbed into her throat. *Ophelia.* She could not leave—

"Go now," he bellowed, managing to bring his opponent under him.

And that sprang her into motion. Stephen stuck a hand in her face, and she took that small palm.

She had to leave for him.

They continued running, their steps slower from their efforts. Gertrude concentrated all her attention on Edwin's doorway; it beckoned, called her forth, and gave her strength. Ignoring the stitch in her side, she pushed herself and Stephen onward.

Bloody hell, how in blazes was she going to explain this to Edwin?

Chapter 24

After his meeting with Charles, there had been only one place Edwin had wished to be.

He wanted to be there with her and thank her for reminding him that it was all right to live again. She'd shown him that the crimes he'd held himself guilty for . . . didn't belong to him. Not truly. Those acts against him and his family had been carried out by another—just as Gertrude herself had been innocent of wrongdoing.

Stalking through his townhouse, Edwin made his way with purpose.

It was late and improper, going in search of a young woman living in his household. Even if she was like a sister to Stephen and serving in the role of temporary governess, a gentleman had no reason or right to, but there it was. Anticipation built around his chest, this lightness filling every corner of him, buoyant and joyous. Upon finding the library, that place she made her own each night, empty, he climbed abovestairs.

A chambermaid coming down the hall in his direction paled.

Whistling a cheerful ditty he used to belt out when drunk with his university chums, he called out a greeting. "Hello."

The girl opened and closed her mouth several times. "M-my lord," she returned and dropped a curtsy as he passed.

Edwin reached Gertrude's chamber and knocked once.

And waited.

It was late. He could, and certainly should, wait until the morn to speak with her. He'd always been selfish, however.

Edwin rapped again.

As the seconds ticked by, he strained his ears for some hint of sounds within her chambers, some shuffling of her quiet footfalls, the whispery whir of fabric as she donned her night wrapper.

And it was the third rap . . . the third one, when unease crept in. It was a traitorous sentiment for a woman who'd given him no reason to doubt her.

Nonetheless . . . there was no shaking that fear. It was the same, hated disquiet that had gripped him when a melee had broken out at the entrance of White's and one of his servants had stormed the clubs, violating the code expected of servants to tell him his entire life had been consumed in a fire.

His palms slick with sweat, Edwin grabbed the door handle. It gave easily, and he pushed the panel open. Working his gaze quickly over the rooms, he determined in short order the realization that sat like a stone in his belly—she wasn't here.

He tried to make the muscles of his throat move so he could swallow.

You're being a fool. She never goes to bed at this early hour.

Still, the doubts had taken hold and magnified so that logic ceased to exist. How many times had he trusted before, and how many times had he been betrayed? His wife. His best friend. The nursemaid who'd kidnapped his son.

Not Gertrude. She'd proven only devoted and loving, and yet what if he'd made yet another costly misstep?

Edwin spun on his heels and took off running for his son's rooms. His feet pounded a path along the floor that matched the chaotic beat of his heart.

Not bothering with a knock, Edwin tossed open his son's door and stormed in.

Oh, God.

The bed, turned down, remained untouched.

Empty.

"No," he rasped. Impossible. There had to be another reason for Stephen and Gertrude's absence. Mayhap they were in the kitchens. Or somewhere else.

Edwin staggered back several steps, until his back collided with the mattress. *Oh, God.* He threaded his fingers through his hair and yanked. This was his hell. He'd lost his son all over again. He'd trusted where he shouldn't. The lesson long ago should have killed all trust and cemented the evil in people's souls, and yet it hadn't.

Stop. Stop.

There had to be a reason. They had to be safe.

They . . .

A tortured moan spilled from his lips. It was that prayer and hope of long ago, alive still, all these years later.

Shoving to his feet, he took off running. "Marlow," he shouted, his voice booming off the corridor walls. "Marlow!"

And devoted as when he'd first found Edwin in the streets, drunk and praying for death, his butler was there.

"My son. Gertrude."

His brow creased in confusion, the younger man shook his head. "I don't—?"

"They aren't in their rooms."

All the color leached from Marlow's cheeks.

Oh, God. No. Edwin's legs went weak under him, and he shot a hand out, catching the wall to steady himself. "I want my horse readied," he bellowed, and took off running. "I want Bow Street called." Marlow struggled to match Edwin's pace. "I want Runners here now. I want her found, and I want my son back," he thundered as he raced through the hall.

From the front of the townhouse, furious shouts emerged. Calls for Marlow. For Edwin.

"My lord," Marlow was saying over and over, yanking on his arm.

The world whooshed through Edwin's ears.

With a thunderous, incoherent shout, he took off for the din that grew louder with every step he took. "Summon the damned constable," Edwin bellowed. He reached the top of the landing, and a wave of relief so strong, so potent and gloriously wonderful, overtook him that he couldn't so much as breathe.

He was here.

With her.

They were both here. In the middle of his foyer . . .

Gertrude in her cloak. And Stephen . . . in his threadbare garments. They were here. Both of them. Relief snaked through him.

And then he registered his son's attire.

"Where in blazes did you go?" he shouted, taking the steps two at a time, nearly tripping over himself in his haste.

Stephen took a step closer to his sister, and she rested a hand on the little boy's shoulder. Edwin only gnashed his teeth at that protective gesture.

Furious with himself for doubting her. Furious with her for having given him reason to do so.

She stared at Edwin with pained eyes, stricken ones.

She'd heard him. It was stamped there in her features. By God, he'd not feel guilty. She'd gone off without a word, without asking him or telling him . . .

And yet, despite his resolve to feel no shame for his response, he did. It clawed at his gut.

Without so much as a word for him, Gertrude returned her focus to Stephen. Whatever she said was too hushed, near silence that Edwin, an interloper once more, could not make sense of.

"I asked you a question," he said in steadier tones. The servants around them jumped as if he'd bellowed that statement. Gertrude, however, remained stoic, unaffected. She'd been the only person in all these years to not shrink in fear from him. "Did you defy my wishes and bring him to your family?" he asked, his muscles tightening in fear of her answer.

The already grey pallor of Gertrude's skin went white as parchment.

And he knew. Betrayal. It wasn't the first time, but this cut the sharpest. Edwin sank back on his heels. "You lied to me," he whispered, the evidence of her treachery striking like an arrow. He'd believed they'd formed a bond, one where he could trust her. He'd confided in her. And all along she'd set out to deceive him. Yet again, his judgment had proven so very flawed.

"Leave her alone!" Stephen barked. "She didn't do nothing wrong," Marquess." He hurled that title that one day would belong to him as though it were an insult.

Marquess. That was all Edwin was again. Just like that, the tenuous bond between them broke, and they were restored to that same adversarial role.

"Enough." Gertrude clutched at her sides like she'd run a great race. "Stephen, go to your rooms," she whispered.

His son stepped around her, complying when he only ever resisted Edwin's requests or overtures at a relationship. It was petty and pitiable, but envy at the ease of their relationship sluiced through him. Edwin seethed. "Did you take my son when I expressly forbade it?" And when she remained silent, he slammed his fist onto the nearby foyer table. "Did you?"

Stephen drew his knife and pointed it at Edwin. "Oi ain't leaving ya alone with 'im," he promised, slipping back into his Cockney.

That only sent another healthy wave of fury jolting through Edwin. "By God, I asked you a—"

Gertrude swayed on her feet, and Stephen instantly dropped his dagger. It clattered noisily upon the floor, forgotten, as he wrapped an arm around her waist, keeping Gertrude upright.

Stephen paled. "You're hurt," he whispered. "Did he get you?"

Did he get you?

And consumed by his earlier rage and panic, Edwin now looked on, noting those details that had previously escaped him, the drawn lines at the corners of Gertrude's mouth, the agony pouring from her eyes.

Edwin dropped his gaze to where Stephen held her. And the earth shifted from under Edwin's feet. The dark shade of her muslin cloak had previously obscured that bright stain soaking the left portion of the fabric.

Stephen drew his hand back and cried out. "You've been stabbed."

"Oh, my god," Edwin whispered. She'd been stabbed. "Oh, my god." It was a litany that poured out of him, over and over. Incoherent and irrational. "You are hurt," he said dumbly, his voice hoarsened. Bleeding. That was blood marring her garments. *Her blood.*

I'm going to be ill.

"I'm fi—" Her lashes fluttered.

He was across the foyer in three strides. He caught her to him as she collapsed.

"Fine," Gertrude finished the lie she'd been determined to utter.

"Get a damned doctor," Edwin shouted, sweeping her into his arms, and she went unprotestingly, and panic swelled. Gertrude was never compliant. And certainly not when he was shouting out directives. "Water. Bandages. Clean linens," he croaked out order after order in fragments. Taking the steps two at a time, he bounded up the staircase. Her door still hung ajar from when he'd stormed inside earlier. When he'd allowed himself to believe that Gertrude had performed the same act of treachery as that nanny and made off with Stephen.

As he set her down on the untouched bed, shame burnt through him, and he fought it back.

There'd be time enough for that later. Nothing useful could come from that emotion—not now. For now . . . Gertrude was hurt. His focus belonged there. "Where are you injured?" he asked hoarsely, already reaching for the clasp at her throat. His fingers shook so badly, he couldn't get a proper grasp on the clasp.

"I have it," she said, her voice weak, and terror threatened to spill over and consume him. Ignoring her protestations, Edwin made another attempt at the hook, and this time it gave way with a slight click.

"Let me see," he murmured, removing the article. He tossed it down on the floor and urged Gertrude to lie down.

This time, she didn't resist.

He struggled to draw a breath, but it lodged somewhere between his chest and throat. "My God," he whispered. A crimson stain marred the entire left side of her gown and had begun to spill over across the middle. Or what if she'd been stabbed there, in the middle of her belly? An animalistic moan tore from him.

"I've been injured far worse," she said with her usual pragmatism, but this time her voice was so very threadbare, so faint.

It sprang him into action. Mindful of her wound, Edwin rolled her slowly onto her opposite side. "I need to see it," he said, talking himself through each action to keep from giving in to an all-consuming panic. "And apply pressure." He started at the row of buttons down the back of her gown.

"You need to cut the fabric. Get my dagger," she whispered. "It's strapped to the bottom of my left leg." She doled out those instructions, methodical, one who'd been so injured before and tended like injuries herself. And all over again, he felt wholly useless, unable to protect those in his care.

Edwin lifted her skirts, and finding the jewel-encrusted dagger, he unsheathed it.

"Start at the top and work it down the middle," Gertrude managed in between labored breaths. How was she so calm? Instructing him on how to tend her wound, when any other person, man or woman, would have been reduced to a sobbing heap of panic and pain. There wasn't another woman like her.

Edwin's fingers shook as he cut away the fabric of her dress. Her chemise followed. And when he at last had the garments removed, the room dipped and swayed.

He briefly closed his eyes.

Her skin was soaked from the gash that continued to seep copiously. Gertrude lay sprawled upon a crimson blanket of her own lifeblood. Yanking off his cravat, he pressed the article to her side and applied pressure. Blood immediately soaked through, staining the useless cloth.

I'm going to throw up.

"Goddamn it, where in hell is the doctor?" he thundered. Grabbing at a pillow, he tugged free the white linen case, and made another make-shift bandage from it. *She cannot die. Please, not her.*

"That bad?"

"Worse," he directed at the wound commanding his attentions.

And God love her, Gertrude began to laugh. That clear, bell-like expression of her amusement immediately died. A little moan spilled from her lips.

"Tell me what I can do," he entreated. He'd give anything to ease her pain.

There was a lengthy pause, the silence so long and pronounced that, for one agonizing moment made from terror, he believed she'd died. Edwin yanked his head up, forcing himself to look at her.

"I want my family."

And in that instant, he discovered something far greater than the hatred he'd carried all these years—his regard for this woman.

Edwin shouted once more, this time calling for the unlikeliest of guests to his household—the Killorans.

He'd fetched her sisters.

It was a request she'd have wagered her very life he would have declined, and yet he hadn't. That sacrifice, however, allowing the Killoran clan inside his household, was wholly at odds with the man who'd been shouting down the household with calls for a constable.

He hadn't trusted her. He'd believed her capable of harming Stephen. Nay, what was worse: for everything they'd shared, for the bond they'd struck and the intimacy that had passed between them, none of it had mattered. In one instant all that had been erased, and she'd been presented with the truth: Edwin would never trust her. Not truly. And she might love him, and he might have cared for her, but there could never be any relationship when one person so doubted the honor of another.

A single tear fell down her cheek, followed by another, and another.

The doctor drew the needle through her side.

"You're doing splendidly, Gertrude," Cleopatra praised, giving her fingers a light squeeze. "He's nearly finished."

Her sister would construe those tears as weakness over her injury. This time, however, Gertrude preferred that underestimation. She welcomed it, for it prevented either of her sisters from asking probing questions she didn't want to answer.

"What happened?" Ophelia pressed from the spot she occupied at Gertrude's other side.

Cleo shot her a look. "We'll talk when she's able."

"There's questions that need answering," Ophelia persisted.

"And she'll answer them later. Not now. This isn't the time."

They'd heard nothing of what she'd said earlier. Her sisters still sought to make decisions and determinations for and about her. "I can talk," Gertrude said tightly, and winced as the needle pierced her skin. God, how she'd always despised sewing a person's flesh up and having her own done. The sensation of that piece of metal traveling through one's skin, and the drag of the needle. Her stomach roiled.

"Did you recognize him?"

In between the hurt of Edwin's mistrust, she'd sought to identify the masked attacker . . . to no avail. "I didn't."

"Connor caught him and is in the process of . . . interviewing him now."

Interviewing him. Gertrude shivered. She well knew in St. Giles what that entailed. "His mask slipped loose enough that I saw him. He's not a patron of the club. He's not a previous employee, and he's not one of Diggory's rogue gang members." Those ruthless men and women who continued to surface, seeking retribution for some imagined crime against the greatest criminal.

"So . . . a foreign adversary."

"You're assuming he wanted to harm me. He sought my valuables."

"Stephen said you handed them over and he made no move to take them."

And through the mayhem and action out on the streets of Mayfair, for the first time that incongruity hit her. He hadn't tried to collect the brooch. He'd simply left it there.

She sat upright and promptly gasped as she pulled in the opposite direction of Dr. Carlson's efforts.

"Easy," he soothed.

"He knew about my knife." Gertrude resettled herself against the mound of pillows and cushions the doctor had arranged at the start of the process.

"Did you flash it?"

"No." She shook her head frantically, this time ignoring the pain. "I didn't reveal that I had it. I didn't draw it." He'd known.

Which meant . . .

"It's someone who *knows* you're a Killoran," Cleo finished that thought, her brown eyes grave with the implications of that revelation.

"It doesn't necessarily mean that," Gertrude put forward, even as her gut intuition—which had saved her and her siblings countless times—screamed that there was more to that meeting on the street.

"It usually does, though," Ophelia pointed out. "Connor will send one of his men to serve as a watch."

"I don't need a watch." They were imagining bogeymen where there were none.

"Are you certain of that?" Ophelia countered.

Except . . . Gertrude wasn't certain of *anything* anymore.

A pall fell amongst the sisters, and the only sound to fill the room was the softest whisper of Dr. Carlson drawing his needle through Gertrude's injury.

Gertrude troubled her lower lip between her teeth, concentrating on that slight discomfort to keep from focusing on the drag of that needle. After Dr. Carlson had passed the thread through her flesh, she allowed herself the breath she'd been holding.

"Breathe in slow through your nose," he murmured, his baritone so very soothing it served as another distraction. "Then release the breath slowly through your lips. Focus on your breathing." He went back to his masterful sewing. Gertrude squeezed her youngest sister's hand.

"He seemed upset," Cleopatra noted, and she welcomed that distraction.

To the contrary, Stephen had displayed his usual strength, one that she wished he didn't have to rely upon so often. For no child should be required to be strong at all times. "He handled himself perfectly. He ran when I said to and did not remain for the fight." That brashness which had always been Stephen's weakness had not been there.

Her sisters exchanged another glance. "Not Stephen," Ophelia clarified. "She's talking about the Mad Marquess."

Gertrude's patience with that callous insult they continued to level at Edwin snapped. "He's not the 'Mad Marquess,'" she bit out, then squeezed her eyes shut as another rush of pain burnt along her side. "He's a father who desperately loves Stephen and who has done nothing but attempt to make life more comfortable and familiar for him, and I'll not have you disparage him."

That effectively silenced a pair who were never given to backing down from a debate or discussion. And if it fueled further questions, so be it. With his lack of faith in her, he might as well have ripped out a piece of her heart. But regardless of Edwin's distrust of her motives this evening, she'd not cast aspersions upon his character, and she'd not begrudge his having become the man he had, not after the losses he'd suffered.

"Try not to move," the doctor said needlessly. "I'm nearly finished. There," he murmured, cutting off the thread and tying the last stitch. "You'll need to keep the wound clean, to avoid infection."

Cleo frowned. "What does that do?"

"There are some schools of thought that any dirt near the open wound can lead to infection, which could poison the blood and kill a patient."

"If that were true, then the three of us would have been dead long ago," Ophelia muttered.

"As that is true, you three should consider yourselves very fortunate," he drawled, a little twinkle in his eyes. With that, he took himself off to the workstation several maids had set up in the corner of Gertrude's temporary chambers. Pouring a pitcher of water, he proceeded to wash his hands.

Ophelia spoke in hushed words that barely reached Gertrude's ears. "Very well . . . *Lord Maddock*, then." And that was the belated moment Gertrude realized she'd stumbled directly into another trap, and for a second time that night. She'd revealed her hand. "Let us speak about Lord Maddock."

Blast and damn.

"What is going on there?" Cleo asked bluntly.

"I don't know what you are talking about." Gertrude shot a glance toward the doctor, still wholly absorbed in his cleanup, and sent a pointed look in his direction. "Furthermore, this is hardly a conversation to be had with strangers about."

Ophelia snorted. "Come, we don't have much time here. We were invited to see that you are well, and then he's going to toss us out. So do not think to drag out the time on the hope that you can avoid answering."

Damn her sister for being too clever by half. "There's nothing there."

"If that were true, then that would have been the first thing you said instead of pointing to the good doctor there."

Another fair and accurate point, and also further proof that she'd never mastered subterfuge in quite the same way her sisters had.

"There's nothing to say," she whispered. "He resents us for having stolen Stephen, and he can never, ever forgive that." His explosive outburst had reached her in the foyer; she'd heard his fear, seen his mistrust. For the illusion she'd allowed herself—the illusion they'd both allowed themselves—there could never be anything between them. Not really. Tears clogged her throat, and she struggled to swallow around them.

The mattress creaked slightly as Ophelia settled herself on the bed close to Gertrude, offering a shield from Dr. Carlson. "And . . . it's important that there is forgiveness between you."

It was a statement, not a question. Nonetheless, Gertrude nodded.

"Oh, bloody hell," Cleo whispered, sinking onto the opposite side. "You care about him."

Gertrude bit down on her lower lip and shook her head.

Cleo slid her eyes closed. "Oh, bloody, bloody hell. You *love* him."

Gertrude dropped her gaze to her lap and offered a slow nod.

Ophelia made a pitying sound. "Gertrude." How odd that one's name could be delivered as nothing more than a chastisement.

"I know." Vehemence ripped that whisper from her. She knew precisely the folly in what she'd done here—falling in love with the last man she should. A man whom she could never have anything with. Not truly. Gertrude stared at the mural overhead. "I know," she repeated. "It wasn't supposed to happen. But it did. So quickly. He made a mouse house for Sethos, and commissioned all new furniture from Draven, and sat through all of it while Stephen designed those pieces, and—"

She was rambling. "I'm a fool."

Her youngest sister sighed. "Yes. Yes, you are. But then, we all do foolish things. I fell in love with our rival."

"And I fell in love with the man investigating our family," Ophelia piped in.

A half laugh, half sob spilled from Gertrude's lips, and she instantly cringed as pain radiated from her injury. "Those are different. What Diggory did to Edwin . . . to his family . . ." Could never be forgiven.

Ophelia caught her fingers. "I know . . . it sometimes seems like the odds against one are insurmountable. But . . . Diggory also killed Connor's father, and . . ." Tears glazed her sister's wide, luminescent eyes, giving her a haunting look. Or mayhap the better word was . . . *haunted.* "He did"—hatred poured from her slender frame—"horrific things to his mother. And there was forgiveness between us."

A fledgling hope stirred where there should be none. And then died.

. . . Summon the damned constable . . .

"This is different," she said with a shake of her head. "Connor never doubted you. He didn't hold you to blame for Diggory murdering his family." Her throat closed, and she struggled to get words through the emotion choking her. "When Connor's adoptive father orchestrated your downfall, Ophelia"—one that had seen Ophelia thrown in gaol— "Connor went toe to toe with his father, the earl, who despised you. He fought for your honor and married you anyway. He battled the Earl of Whitehaven and anyone else who'd done wrong by you." Because that is what one did in a relationship: they trusted, defended, and loved. Unlike Edwin . . . Her shoulders sank. "Edwin has only ever blamed me and our family." She'd deluded herself into believing that the friendship they shared and the bond far greater than friendship, which had grown between them, were enough. They would never be. He hadn't trusted her. And that was what hurt most and meant there could be nothing between them.

"But . . . mayhap it's not different?" Cleopatra put forward hesitantly.

Mayhap it's not . . .

When had her sisters become the hopeful optimists of their trio? Gertrude smiled sadly. "He believed I took Stephen." Her sisters cringed. "Precisely." Somewhere along the way, the roles had reversed, with Gertrude becoming the one who saw struggles as insurmountable. "I'm a realist," she said quietly as the young doctor finished packing away his supplies.

"Very well." Ophelia glanced at her wound. "Then you also know, given the circumstances—the peril you're likely in and the lack of a future with the marquess—you cannot remain here indefinitely."

Actually, she did know that. As Dr. Carlson had sewn her up, she'd come to the sad realization about her and Edwin's fate. "I do." And as several maids came forward to gather up the bowls of bloodied water, Gertrude knew that what she had to do must come sooner rather than later for all of them—Stephen, her, and . . . Edwin.

It was the logical, rational decision. One that, given Edwin's lack of faith in her, should be easy . . . and yet as the servants and doctor gathered up the supplies, she was besieged all over again with the dratted urge to cry.

Chapter 25

Edwin wore a back-and-forth path along the hall outside Gertrude's rooms.

The doctor had been in there for nearly—he paused and consulted his timepiece for the tenth time—fifty minutes. Dr. Carlson, the doctor who'd arrived with Gertrude's sisters, Cleopatra Thorne and Ophelia O'Roarke, had been in there for nearly an hour. In that time, Edwin had strained his ears for some hint of cries or screams or . . . anything through that heavy oak panel.

Edwin resumed his frantic pacing.

Nothing.

There was nothing.

Which was surely a promising sign. Had Gertrude been on the verge of death, there would have been some sounds from her . . . or her sisters.

Or mayhap there wouldn't have been sounds from her. Mayhap that silence was in fact an ominous sign that the knife wound she'd suffered had pierced an organ.

Edwin stopped abruptly. *Do not think of it . . . do not think of it . . .*

And yet, the haunting image slid in: Gertrude drawing slow, shallow, labored breaths. Her bleeding uncontrollable.

Dread scissored through him, crippling. Nothing could happen to her. He'd be lost, and this time would remain adrift. *I love her. I love her for her strength and her sense of right and her ability to have emerged triumphant and filled with a lightness and optimism in life and love and trust, despite the hell the world has visited upon her.* Nay, her own father had brought that suffering into her life. He was going mad. Edwin dragged a shaky hand through his hair. She had saved him. And he'd repaid that gift with the ugliest doubt.

Footsteps sounded from within the bedchambers, and he straightened.

But no one exited.

With a growl, he resumed his march along the carpeted floor.

"They're tough."

He'd been pacing in silence so long, dwelling in the miseries of his own tortured mind, that it took a moment to register that those words belonged to someone.

Edwin glanced over at the quiet-until-now figure of Adair Thorne. Positioned at the doorway across from Gertrude's, his arms folded at his chest, the slightly taller, burlier man looked back. Stephen stood alongside the other man . . . who would be his uncle.

"The Killoran women," the notorious gaming hell owner murmured.

"A street rat with a knife won't bring any of my sisters down," Stephen said, puffing out his chest like a proud papa. And then his gaze flitted over to Gertrude's door. His lip trembled. "It can't," he whispered.

Thorne dropped a hand on the boy's shoulder and squeezed. "No one has looked after Gert's animals. She'll be worrying after them. Would you be able to do that so when the doctor finishes, I can assure her that they're cared for?"

Stephen brought his shoulders back. "Clever thought, Thorne. I can do that." He started to go and then hesitated. "You'll send word . . . when they are done with her?"

"I will," the other man vowed and watched as the child darted off, disappeared around the corner, and then was gone.

How easily some other man had eased Stephen's worrying. It should have been Edwin, but the role was still new to him. He was still relearning his way around being a father. In the past, he would have been riddled with fury and frustration. Gertrude, however, had taught him there was no shame to be had in refinding his footing in the world.

"They are, you know . . . tough. The boy is right." Thorne grimaced. "Your son," he corrected, "is correct. A Killoran isn't going to be felled by a thug in the streets."

How confident the other man was. "Would you be so calm if the roles were reversed between Gertrude and Mrs. Thorne?"

The sandy-haired proprietor contemplated that for a moment. "No," Thorne admitted. He arced a single brow. "But *Mrs.* Thorne also happens to be my wife. And what exactly is your relationship with . . . *Gertrude?*" The layer of steel attached to that latter word, a name, contained an icy threat.

Edwin had said too much. Terror had made him careless. "Forgive me," he said curtly, and resumed pacing.

Quiet descended between them yet again and was even more welcome than before.

"Do you care about her?" Thorne wouldn't be the sort content to let the matter rest. "My sister-in-law," he clarified, as though there could be some other woman they possibly spoke of.

Yes, Edwin cared about Gertrude . . . but he also loved her. It was a revelation still too new and terrifying to reveal to *anyone*, especially this stranger from the Dials. "I do," he said, hoarsely, unable to look the other man in the eyes.

Thorne released a long sigh. "My apologies. I've been there."

Edwin abruptly stopped, facing the other man. "Where?" he pleaded. Needing someone, anyone, even if it was a bloody stranger, to help him make sense of . . . all this. *Any* of it.

"Spending my life hating someone only to find that she is the one person I cannot live without."

So the other man did know something of it. A great deal of it.

"I made a blunder of it . . . today," Edwin admitted, shame stinging his cheeks with color.

"Then fix it," Thorne said flatly.

"You don't even know what I did." His tongue felt heavy in his mouth, and he couldn't force out that tale of his guilt.

Thorne narrowed his eyes on him. "Did you hit her?"

He recoiled. "Good God, no!" The denial ripped from him. Edwin's shoulders sagged. "But I . . . hurt her all the same."

"Make your atonement, but there ain't place or use for self-pitying."

How very direct these people were. Having lived amongst Polite Society, who prevaricated and danced around anything and everything, those responses were wholly foreign to Edwin.

The door opened, and a row of servants filed out. Edwin caught sight of the bowls filled with bloodstained water.

Bile climbed his throat, and he rushed to the young doctor, who followed the maids and closed the door behind them. "How—?"

"The wound has been stitched," Dr. Carlson cut in and then continued with an accounting of Gertrude's injury. "The knife did not strike any organs. The edge of the blade sliced through her side. Had the tip of the dagger punctured the flesh, I'd have a very different report on the young woman and her prognosis."

"Thank God."

Did that exhaled prayer belong to him or Thorne?

With a swift word of thanks, Edwin rushed around the doctor and let himself into Gertrude's chambers.

Three pairs of eyes met his: two brown, one blue. Two accusing . . . and one . . . empty.

And that emptiness cleaved him in two. Her anger and outrage would be far easier than the blankness there. Edwin folded his shaking hands behind him. "You are well?" he blurted.

Gertrude nodded slowly. Still silent. Condemning without any words required. She looked to her sisters, who took that unspoken command and filed past him.

Cleopatra Thorne paused when she reached him. More than a foot smaller, she had the height and size of a child, and yet—she touched a finger menacingly against the corner of her right eye. "Careful," she said. "Or I will end you," she finished in barely there tones meant for his ears only.

He bowed his head.

The Killoran sisters lingered a moment more and then exited, leaving Edwin and Gertrude alone.

Clasping his hands behind him, Edwin remained rooted to the floor. He cleared his throat. "Stephen is seeing to your animals." Her expression softened, and he hated that the credit for her response belonged to the thoughtfulness of another man. "Your brother-in-law . . . Mr. Thorne had the thought for him to see to them."

"Oh."

One syllable containing so much disappointment.

"Is there anything you need?" he asked quickly. "Anything I can do or provide or—?"

She shook her head. "No. I'm fine. Thank you for allowing my family to come."

"I do not require your thanks."

How wooden they were. This awkwardness unfamiliar and hated. *And it's all because of me . . . I created this where there was lightheartedness and warmth.*

"Gertrude, I—"

"I heard you," she interrupted him. His entire body stiffened. "Earlier, that is." Gertrude plucked at the lace trim of her coverlet and attended her fingers as she did. "You called for the constable. You wanted me found." She stopped that distracted gesture and lifted her head, meeting his gaze squarely. "You thought I took him."

So much hurt bled from her gaze and words that his chest ached. "I wasn't thinking," he said dumbly, his words meaningless to his own ears. "I wouldn't have—" He inwardly cringed. What was he to say there? *I wouldn't have had you tossed in Newgate?* God, what a failure he was as a man.

"Yes, well, I believe that is the point." A sad smile curved lips that had only ever turned up in those joyous expressions of mirth. *I want those back. I want that laughter and happiness.* "I can't stay here."

His heart skipped a beat, stopped altogether, and then resumed a frenzied knocking in his chest. "Yes, you can. Or would you rather return to your family and convalesce? Then you can come back when—"

"That's not what I mean, Edwin," she said gently. "You know that."

Yes, he did. But he'd wanted to hope that she spoke of something different than leaving and never returning.

Edwin stormed across the room and made to sit at her side. The bandages wrapped around her middle creased the fabric of her nightshift. He dragged over a nearby chair and sat. "I panicked. I came back and found you gone—"

"And believed I'd stolen Stephen. Edwin," she entreated, "you were calling the *constable* on me."

"I don't know what I was thinking." He'd allowed his past and past prejudices to blind him, and he'd atone for it, as Thorne had urged, if Gertrude would but let him. He had to make her see reason.

Gertrude reached for his hand, and he made to take hers . . . but then she drew those long fingers back, denying him that gift. Instead, she twined those long digits together, in a lonely hold. "But that's just it, Edwin . . . in the moment, you didn't see"—*what we shared?*—"anything but who I will always be to you. Diggory's daughter."

"Don't say that. It isn't true. I made a mistake. I'm owning that mistake, but please don't let it be the reason you leave," he pleaded. "I want you to s—"

Gertrude pressed her fingers against his lips, silencing him. "It's *not* a mistake to feel what we feel. You were always entitled to your anger and resentment, Edwin." Goddamn it, why should she be so accepting of his betrayal? "I shouldn't have taken Stephen out. I know him enough that when he sets his mind to something, he'll not be deterred. I followed him to protect him."

She'd been looking after his son, and Edwin had questioned her actions and motives. "I was going to tell you, though."

"I should have listened. I should have trusted that there was a reason you were gone." But he hadn't.

That truth hung there, damningly, unspoken, and more powerful for it.

"I don't care about any of that. Not anymore." This time, he grabbed for her hand and clung to her.

She didn't draw back, and he took hope in that. Her next words, however, killed that sentiment.

"You did, and that doesn't just go away because you're suddenly worried I might be hurt."

"You *are* hurt."

"I'll be fine." There was a finality there that spoke to the double meaning. She was leaving.

"But Stephen . . ."

"He'll be fine with you. You'll both be fine together."

"Not now," he said bitterly. "Not after this." Nor could Edwin blame his son. He quite hated himself enough for the both of them in this instance. He was going to lose her. "I love you."

It was harder to say who was more stunned by that pronouncement. Her lips parted.

"And I'm not just saying that to keep you here. I love you. I want a future with you."

Joy lit her eyes and brightened her precious face, radiating a pure light that knocked away all the agony of this night. And then . . . it was gone.

"Oh, Edwin," she said, pityingly.

He winced.

"Sometimes . . . love is not enough. Your marriage was proof of that."

He gritted his teeth with such force pain shot along his jawline. "What my wife and I shared . . . was nothing like what we share. So don't dare confuse the two."

"Isn't it, Edwin?" she challenged. "A relationship without trust will only die, and I love you—"

"You love me," he whispered, joy suffusing his chest.

"But I can't remain here and watch that grow to hate when you realize you can't separate me from my past . . . from our past," she said over his interjection.

"We didn't have a past." And now, with her wish, they wouldn't have a future.

"You had one with my father."

"Don't do that." Edwin shoved back from his seat with such force the chair tumbled over and clattered noisily upon the hardwood floor. "That man wasn't a father to you."

She gave him another of those sad little smiles. "*I* know that."

That insinuation found its mark. *I'm going to lose her.* And suddenly Edwin found himself wishing he were still the man he'd been long ago, who'd been capable with words, who'd held an ability to charm. After his marriage, all his trust in himself and his ability to be with people had been flipped around. He swiped a hand over his brow. "I have made so many mistakes in my life, Gertrude." Too many to account for, but every one of those errors had brought him to this failed moment in his life. "I married my wife, believing our love was enough to conquer all."

Gertrude hugged her arms to her chest. "It should have been, Edwin."

"But it wasn't." Something told him, with this woman, bold and loving and loyal to her family, it would have been enough. "Nor did my mistakes end there." Restless, he moved over to the window and stared unseeingly out at the streets below. "I allowed my wife to select a nursemaid. It was a decision that went against my better judgment, and still I let her make the ultimate decision." And it had cost him so much. Everything.

Or . . . almost everything. Had he not lost all, he'd not have found everything in Stephen and with Gertrude.

"You wanted to believe the best in the woman your wife wished to hire. There is no shame to be had in hoping for the best in people," she said quietly.

He faced her once more. "No, but there is shame when that decision cost my wife and child their lives," he said, needing her to understand. Because mayhap if she understood, she could see all the reasons he struggled to trust . . . *anyone*. "Even my best friend, who'd stood by me in my marriage, came to believe me a murderer."

A smile so sad it broke his heart all over again turned her lips. "I am not those people, Edwin."

"I know that," he said quickly. "I do."

"Do you?" she returned. "Do you *really* know that?" she asked without any malice or inflection.

This could not simply be the end between them. The light he'd known with her and because of her couldn't just go out. Not when it would plunge him, along with his son, into eternal darkness.

"There is nothing I can say, then," he said flatly.

Gertrude hesitated, and then she shook her head.

"All right, then." He inhaled slowly through his teeth, concentrating on breathing. *How am I still standing?* How, when his damned heart was breaking? "So . . . you are leaving."

She nodded. "I have to. I think . . . we both knew we were merely playing at pretend. There could have never been anything more between us."

He didn't believe that. He wouldn't. "You're wrong."

"I'm never wrong," she said, their words an echo of the night they'd made love. *Was it really only just yesterday?*

"This time you are, love."

Gertrude laughed softly. "Oh, Edwin." His name, spoken as a goodbye.

How am I so calm? He was going to lose her. Nay, he'd already lost her the moment he thundered for a constable. But what had he really offered her before this? He hadn't told her he loved her. He hadn't offered his name or respectability. And worse . . . he hadn't trusted her.

"Please stay," he begged, all out of pride where this woman was concerned. "At least until a governess is found."

She troubled her lower lip in that endearing manner he'd come to know spoke of her indecision.

Then, proving himself a bastard yet again that day, he pressed with the one reason she'd never refuse. "For Stephen."

Gertrude closed her eyes briefly. "Very well. Until we find a governess. And then I'm returning home."

Home. The gaming hell she'd grown up in and wished to return to.

Afraid she'd change her mind, he nodded. "Let me gather Stephen so he might see for himself that you are well." Edwin turned to go, and then he stopped. "I need you to know . . . all my doubts . . . my inability to trust? It isn't because of you or Diggory or your family, Gertrude," he said hoarsely. "I need you to know that. The mistrust that led me to question you? It was only because of me."

Tears glazed her eyes, crystalline drops that wouldn't fall but illuminated the sadness in their depths.

Edwin lingered, waiting for her to speak, and when no reply was forthcoming, he made himself leave. To give her the space she needed—for now.

He had until a proper governess was found to prove himself worthy of Gertrude and give her a reason to stay with him long after that.

Chapter 26

Meoowwwww—Meowwwww—Meowwww—Meow.

"And I was saying . . ."

Meow.

Through that cacophony of feline calls, the latest candidate for the post of governess struggled to finish her sentence. The greying woman cleared her throat. "As I was saying . . . *achoo*."

Meowwww.

"Bless you," Gertrude said automatically after the seventeenth sneeze from the prospective candidate.

From around her rumpled white kerchief, Mrs. Beckett glared at the collection of cats wandering Edwin's offices. "I cannot do this. Not for any—*achoo!*"

"God bless you," Edwin and Gertrude said simultaneously.

Collecting her cane, the older woman stood and let herself out.

"choo—" The door closed, punctuating that final sneeze.

"God bless you," they both called after her.

"Well, I say she'll not do," Edwin chimed in almost cheerfully as he dragged the tip of his pen over the governess's name. Hopping up from his chair, he went, made himself a brandy, and returned to his desk. "I've always said one cannot trust a person who doesn't like cats."

"In fairness, Edwin, there are . . ." Gertrude did a quick count of the various assortment of cats scattered about the room. "Ten. Ten cats in here." In the week since she'd been injured and resumed her daily activities with Stephen and finding him a proper governess, Edwin had made it a point of filling the house with whichever stray or mangy tabby he'd found lurking around his residence. "And that isn't counting the ones you had fetched from the Devil's Den."

"*Pfft,*" he scoffed, coming to his feet. "And here I thought you appreciated cats." She'd hand it to him. That muscle didn't tick at the corner of his eye the way it usually did when any mention of her family or the Devil's Den came up.

There was the faintest thread of hurt.

So that was why he'd done it. The protective walls she'd resurrected trembled slightly. "You've brought them here because of me."

"I don't mind them," he mumbled, so like a boy caught with his hand in the biscuit jar that she found herself smiling.

"Ten of them?"

The door burst open, and Stephen came tripping inside. "She wasn't the one. She—" Several cats bounded toward him, and he darted left and right to make way for the feline exodus. "What in hell is this? You need to stop bringing cats in, Gert. This is too many. Too many," he muttered, stepping around a particularly fat, lazy cat sprawled on his back.

"I didn't bring these particular ones in," she felt inclined to point out.

Stephen glanced over at his father. "*You're* rescuing cats now?" he asked, picking his way over to Edwin's desk. He sprawled into the chair previously occupied by Mrs. Bennett. "You've been spending too much time together." Stephen made to speak, and then understanding dawned in his too-clever gaze. "You're doing it because you think she likes them."

Color filled Edwin's cheeks, and Gertrude had her confirmation. "Yes . . . well . . ."

He was doing it because he knew she loved rescuing animals. "Stephen," she scolded.

"I'd rather not talk about your"—his mouth twisted like he'd sucked a lemon—"*feelings* for one another." Her entire body went hot. "Did you find me a governess?"

Gertrude and Edwin spoke, together.

"We're closer."

"No."

Tipping his head, Stephen alternated his stare between them. "Well? Which is it?"

"No, we have not," Gertrude amended, shooting an unrepentant Edwin a scowl. "But we are closer to finding one."

Stephen snorted. "Either you have or you haven't."

"Precisely my point," Edwin chimed in. Lifting his glass, he saluted the boy.

Father and son shared a commiserative look. In her time here, Edwin and Stephen had learned to be a pair; their relationship, though not wholly healed—if it even could be—had evolved. With each day, the anger was being replaced by the deepening bond between them. It highlighted the fact that the great urgency in her being here was no more.

One of the new strays recently taken in—Fat Cat, as she'd taken to thinking of the enormous tabby—waddled over and made an attempt to climb into her lap. She eyed the creature, who might or might *not* actually be a stray, and took mercy on him. Gertrude scooped him up and, using his soft fur as cover, buried her face against him to keep from giving in to tears: those of happiness . . . and selfishly, of regret for what could never be. "Mrs. Upton is the one," she finally brought herself to say, setting down Fat Cat and picking up her folder of notes for the candidates they'd interviewed.

Stephen pumped his legs back and forth. "The only one who doesn't mind if I have weapons and isn't trying to change me . . . right away?"

Her skin burnt from the feel of Edwin's gaze on her. Gertrude nodded. "Correct. And she isn't trying to change you."

"She will," he said without his usual belligerence . . . so much of that fury, the one that had lived within him at the Devil's Den and on the streets, having waned.

Stephen had gone from living a life where card games and freely drinking drunkards and brawls and prostitutes were the norm. All that had been replaced by trips to Hyde Park and Gunter's and a furniture-maker's shop. He belonged here. In time, he would completely heal. She saw that now. "I suspect she won't, and if she does, then your father will find a governess worthy of you."

Stephen ceased swinging his legs and leveled her with a hardened stare. "You're talking about leaving."

"I was not talking about it."

"Thinking about it, then?"

Gertrude focused her attention on Fat Cat.

Edwin answered for her: "She is."

She braced for the usual display of resentment and hostility.

"You miss the clubs?"

Except only curiosity tinged her brother's question.

"Do I miss the clubs?" she repeated, contemplating her answer. She'd not really given much thought to the Devil's Den. She'd understood that returning to the only place she'd called home was inevitable. The hell represented that which was familiar . . . but it was not a place she longed to spend the remainder of her days . . . and yet . . . she would anyway. "I miss Broderick and Reggie," she murmured. "And the staff. The guards. MacLeod. But I don't miss it, Stephen." She needed him to know that, to find peace in appreciating his new life. And her soul proved as black as Diggory's, for she was riddled with envy that Stephen should stay and she would return.

"Humph," Stephen muttered noncommittally. "I miss playing cards and the other boys."

"I'm sure your father will allow Ned and Beatie and the other children to visit?"

"Of course," Edwin replied, not missing a beat, and blast it all, Gertrude lost her heart to him all over again. How many other noblemen would allow common street rats and known thieves . . . and worse . . . within their residence, all to bring one's child happiness?

"Oh, this arrived," Stephen said, pulling an official page from his jacket front. He tossed it at Edwin.

Were he horrified at having that seal split and the private contents of a note read, Edwin gave no outward indication. He merely gathered the page, read the contents, and then tucked it away. "Thank you."

That was . . . it? What had been written there? Gertrude sat upright, feeling as she had for so long: the person on the outs, trying desperately to wedge her way in.

"We going?" Stephen asked as Gertrude remained on the fringe, an outsider in the conversation between father and son.

"I haven't decided."

In the past, she might have been submissive enough to not interject where it wasn't her place. She was no longer that meek woman who let the world continue around her, without her. "What is this?" she asked, putting that question to Edwin.

Stephen answered for him. "Lord Charles invited us to dine this evening. My . . . uncle."

"Haven't decided?" Edwin and his former best friend had met at White's, and then he'd retreated once more, to oversee Stephen's future alongside Gertrude. She'd known him just a month, but she knew Edwin enough to know he wanted a relationship with his brother-in-law. "Well . . . you have to go," she insisted.

"I don't have to do anything," he said in crisp tones only a man raised from boyhood knowing his birthright could manage with such coolness.

Gertrude bristled. "Very well, *my lord.*" Edwin thinned his eyes into narrow slits. "Then you should *want* to."

"One time, I did. I no longer feel that same impetus."

"But . . ."

Edwin stood. "If you'll excuse me? I've business to see to."

"You're leaving," Gertrude blurted.

"I've a meeting," he said.

"Forgive me." She hopped up, sending Fat Cat scrambling. He landed on his feet with a loud thump and emitted a long meow in protest. A meeting? What manner of business did Edwin have to see to? He was a marquess, but he'd not been out in years before their arrival.

"I'll leave you to your lessons. Stephen." Edwin bowed his head.

The boy waved.

As soon as Edwin had gone, Stephen shot a foot out, kicking her in the shins.

She grunted. "What was *that* for?"

"Because you're wanting to leave, and you have every reason to stay."

Every reason to stay: Stephen . . . Edwin. They were her every reason: her brother, whom she'd loved with the love a mother surely felt for a child, and Edwin, whom she loved in ways she'd never believed she could feel for a man. He kicked her again. "*Oomph.* It's complicated." Gertrude darted out of the way to avoid another connection between her leg and his well-placed toe.

"Complicated, my arse. It's easy enough for a child to work through."

"You've never identified yourself as a child," she teased.

"Don't try to distract me. He *loves* you."

Her heart leapt. He loved her. That euphoric joy rapidly deflated. Sighing, Gertrude gathered his hands close. "You just want me to stay, Stephen, but even when I go . . . you'll be fine."

He yanked his fingers back. "This ain't about me."

"This isn't about you," she unconsciously corrected.

"Precisely. It's about the both of you. He loves you, Gert. And you love him, and so I wish you'd both get on with it and get married."

Gertrude glanced around the room. "It's not that easy."

Her brother ticked off on his fingers. "You get married. You live together. Have some babies. Yes, it is that easy."

Have some babies . . . which only conjured images she'd never allowed herself to have: of a tiny babe who belonged to her, cradled in her arms. And that imagined babe, with its golden hair and slight cleft in his chin, bore a remarkable likeness to Edwin.

"You like babies. Make some with my father and get on with the rest of your lives."

Make some . . . ? Strangling on her mortification, Gertrude pushed her chair back and stood. "It's more complicated than that. And furthermore"—she pointed at him and wagged a finger—"I'll have you know 'having some babies' isn't as easy as you make it out to be." She'd helped several of the prostitutes over the years who'd come to Broderick, seeking employment with babes in their bellies, deliver those children.

"Making them is."

Gertrude slapped her palms over her face. "Oh, for the love of all that is holy."

"I'm just saying he loves you."

"Sometimes love isn't enough," she cried, that pronouncement ringing around the room and reverberating back the misery of that statement. Hugging her arms around her middle, Gertrude held herself. "There has to be trust, and your father . . . he cannot completely trust me."

"He made a mistake," her brother said flatly.

"You . . ."

"Heard that?" He rolled his eyes. "I heard you two jabbering on. Thorne fetched me and told me to come see you. You were with my father."

My father. How very much her brother now owned those words. Any other time, her heart would be singing with the happiness of that. She winced. "It's not polite . . ." She let that useless lesson on decorum die. "Stephen, I love him, but I can never change my parentage. It will always be there between Edwin and me."

Her brother kicked his chair and sent it tumbling over. "You're being stubborn. You talk about . . ." He pitched his voice to a falsetto. "I can't ever forgive him, we'll never be able to trust one another . . ." Stephen returned to his normal gravelly timbre. "Because . . . why? He was mistrustful when he returned to find us gone? Well, I have something to tell you . . ." He stomped across the room, backing Gertrude up as he went, until her legs knocked against the sofa, stopping her flight and tumbling her into the squabs. "You did violate the terms you struck with him."

"Because you were going to go without me." And she'd have seen him safe at the cost of anything . . . including her relationship with Edwin.

"That's neither here nor there. You went along, and given what happened to my mum and me"—oh, God, it was the first time he'd ever claimed the late marchioness as his mother; tears filled Gertrude's eyes at that breakthrough—"he had reasons to be mistrustful. But he loves you, and he wants to do right by—" He drew back. "Good God, are you *crying?*"

"No." Yes.

"Humph. Listen, Gert . . ." Stephen gripped her shoulders. "All I'm saying is, I burnt down Thorne's club, and he forgave me."

"That is different."

"Not the way I see it. My father *defended* you. That's why I like him, and that's how I know he doesn't blame you and really wants a life with you."

What? Gertrude creased her brow. "I don't know what you're—"

Letting out an annoyed sigh, Stephen tugged several pieces of jag-gedly shorn paper from his jacket. "Here." He slammed them into her palm.

Gertrude read the top page, and her breath caught. "What is this?" she whispered.

Mad Marquess Defends the Daughter of His Wife's Murderer...

Gertrude frantically skimmed her gaze over the page. "... *clear to all that Lord M has made Gertrude Diggory-Killoran, or whatever name the street rat goes by, his lover...*"

"You were too busy convalescing, but that was in the papers while you were hurt. Lord Charles was saying some nasty stuff about you. My father defended you. Said Lord Charles didn't know you." Stephen's gaze bored into her. "He defended your honor."

"Oh," she whispered, her voice a soft, breathy exhale. She worked through the small stack of paragraphs from the gossip sheets. Her heart fluttered. Before all of Polite Society, and the people whose opinion had mattered to him so much that he'd gone into hiding, he'd spoken up on Gertrude's behalf. He'd defended her...

She let the pages fall to her lap.

And then come back to discover she'd violated his trust.

"You're missing the point if you're feeling guilty." Stephen wrinkled his little freckled nose. "Or you're feeling guilty about the wrong thing. Point is, he loves you, and you love him, and everything else you can figure out... after. Now I'm done with you."

"Stephen," she called, but her brother was already across the room and out the doorway.

"Oh, and another thing," he shouted, doubling back. He glowered at her. "He's bringing all these animals, some that I suspect aren't even strays, into the household to make you happy. Swallow your pride, or we're going to be overrun with them soon."

Meowwww.

She opened her mouth, but Stephen was already gone.

Alone, Gertrude forced herself to reread the gossip her brother had clipped out. The vile comments about her past and parentage rolled off her, those insults ones she'd long become accustomed to . . . except from Edwin. His opinion had mattered . . . and it still did.

But what if her brother was right? What if she and Edwin could, just as her sisters had with their spouses, move beyond their pasts and have a future—together?

Chapter 27

Properly dressed in matching black wool breeches, dark jackets, and midnight waistcoats, Edwin and Stephen stood in the foyer, awaiting the carriage to be brought 'round.

For all intents and purposes, they were any other father and son of the peerage.

And since Gertrude had joined the household and helped put together that broken relationship, that is really what they'd become.

"I hate this. It's bloody stifling," Stephen groused, jerking the snowy-white cravat at his throat. "It's choking me."

"It's because your valet tied it too tightly," Edwin murmured. "Here. Put your arms down. Robins has an appreciation for the elaborate. This one is called the l'Irlandais," he explained, untying the intricate knot.

Stephen's face pulled. "The earl of . . . what?"

Edwin paused in his efforts. "The l'Irlandais. Unless you want something intricate, complicated, and sure to choke you? *Never* let him tie your cravat like this. Remember, your valet answers to you. If you don't set expectations of what you want, you'll get what he wants." He grinned. "And trust me, you do *not* want this."

"What do I want?" Stephen mumbled, making himself absolutely motionless as Edwin removed the silk cravat.

"You?" Edwin brought the opposite ends of the silk scrap crossing over the other. "That's for you to decide. Me, I prefer something relaxed. Something that's"—he winked—"not choking me. You might ask him for the Maratte tie or the à la Bergami. Both aren't fussy and won't cut off your airflow. There," he murmured, assessing the simple knot. "How is that?"

Stephen moved his head back and forth, turning his neck experimentally. "It's . . . as good as can be expected for what I'm wearing."

"Yes, I hear you there," he muttered, and Stephen broke out into a belly laugh that shook his little frame. Slapping him on the shoulder, Edwin joined in.

The joy of that shared mirth washed over him, healing, cathartic, and so bloody perfect.

Everything was perfect.

Almost.

He felt her there. Her presence could fill any room.

She hovered at the balustrade above, overlooking the foyer with all the regal elegance of the queen whose name she bore. Her dark curls drawn back in a loose arrangement, several strands hung about her shoulders like an auburn waterfall, and hunger stirred to life, a need to again have her in his arms as he'd had more than a week ago—

Stephen gave him a discreet nudge.

"Gertrude," Edwin called up belatedly.

"Ed . . ." She glanced to Marlow, hovering off to the side with Edwin's cloak in hands. "My lord," she revised.

My lord. That proper form of address that strangers and people divided by formality were expected to adhere to.

He wanted to live with her at his side, where he was only ever "Edwin" to her, and where propriety mattered not at all because their relationship was all that did.

What was she thinking? The divide that had sprung between them stretched far greater than the physical distance, even now. He couldn't make sense of her smoothed features or clear gaze.

An awkward pall fell over the foyer.

Stephen broke that impasse. "We're going out."

At last, Gertrude pulled her gaze from Edwin's. "Indeed?"

His son yanked at his lapels. "Taking care of gentlemanly business."

"I . . . see," she said, all the while seeing nothing at all.

"We had that invitation from Lord Charles. To dine? Not sure why he wants to dine with me, but—"

Edwin cut him off with a slight shake of his head. "Too much," he said from the corner of his mouth. It was too much.

Stephen scowled. "Either way. We'll be off soon, and you can take care of the cats taking over this place."

Gertrude's eyes flared wide. "You're going to meet Stephen's uncle."

Heat splotched Edwin's cheeks, and he adjusted his cravat.

"You're messing it," Stephen muttered, and Edwin stopped.

Taking the rail, Gertrude swept down the stairs, with Master Brave trailing close behind her like a dutiful servant.

Gertrude stopped when she stood a pace apart from Edwin, close enough so she could meet his gaze, but even that distance was too great. Edwin devoured her with his eyes. *I want her close, in every way.*

Stephen rushed to scoop up the cat, but with its feline agility, he dodged the boy. Laughing, he took part in a chase around the foyer.

"You're taking Stephen," she said softly.

"We're going out," he confirmed.

Gertrude reached for him, and then her gaze caught on the waiting footmen. Her arm wavered, and then she let it fall forgotten to her side. He yearned for that touch, to hold her, to have her touch him, in any way.

"I'm . . . proud of you, Edwin. It is the right decision . . . for both of you."

He moved closer, Stephen's calls to Master Brave echoing around them. "Who is to say what is right, Gertrude?" he returned in hushed tones. "You speak so often of 'what is right.' But what does it mean? You and Stephen committed theft." The color bled from her cheeks. "But you did it to survive. You did it so that you had food in your stomach, and so that monster didn't hurt you. So . . . can those acts have been 'wrong'?"

"I . . . I never thought of it in that light."

"No, you didn't. Just as you automatically assume that me resuming a relationship with Lord Charles is the right decision. And why? Hmm? Because we were once friends? People change, and we are both different people. Just as you are a different person."

Marlow cleared his throat. "The carriage is readied, my lord."

He held a hand up. "Stephen, would you wait for me in the carriage?" Edwin called, not taking his eyes from Gertrude.

"I'm taking Master Brave for the carriage ride," Stephen returned, his statement more a directive as he scooped up the cat and hurried through the doors held open by Marlow.

Gertrude briefly studied the toes of her slippers. "Is this because of what he said about me?"

She'd gleaned the incendiary words about her splashed across the gossip columns. Rage lanced through him, as fresh as when Charles had dared besmirch Gertrude's name at his private table at White's. He forced himself into a calmness he didn't feel. "Look at me, Gertrude. It is because of what it said about him when he chose to say those things about you. How did you—?"

"Stephen showed me the papers," she murmured.

"He should not have," he clipped out.

Gertrude shrugged. "It doesn't change what happened or what was said about me."

"No, but neither can any good come from you knowing . . . what you know."

Edwin dusted his knuckles down her cheek. She leaned into his touch, and a thrill of masculine satisfaction went through him. She wanted him still. Her love, however, was what he wanted. What he needed. "Answer me this, Gertrude," he said in hushed tones for her ears alone. "Why should you care whether or not I renew my friendship with Lord Charles? Hmm?"

"Because that friendship was once important to you. It is a relationship that is fractured, and if you nurture it, you can put it back to rights and find happiness where it once grew."

She wanted that . . . for Edwin? Knowing, and yet still supporting his friendship to the man who'd disparaged her. She was deserving of someone capable of that selflessness . . . and he wanted to be that man for her. Because of her. "There is not a more gracious, honorable woman than you, Gertrude Killoran," he whispered. Cupping her about the nape, Edwin closed his mouth over hers.

She melted against him, all heated warmth and perfection, and not a hint of the reservations that had sprung between them. He kissed her as he'd longed to since they'd spent the night making love in his library. She parted her lips, allowing him entry, and he swept his tongue inside.

Marlow cleared his throat. "My lord?" he said on a scandalized whisper.

Edwin reluctantly broke that kiss. "I love you," he said quietly.

Her breath caught, and she fluttered her hands about her chest.

Leaving that declaration at last spoken, Edwin accepted his cloak from Marlow and swept outside.

Waving off assistance from the servant positioned at the doorway of his carriage, Edwin pulled himself inside.

"Did you tell her?" his son asked before Edwin had even settled onto the opposite bench.

"Which—?"

"That you love her," Stephen clarified when the door had been shut behind them. The carriage rocked into motion, drawing them onward. "You were supposed to tell her you love her."

These were sorry days indeed when a reformed rogue such as himself required guidance on winning the heart of a woman. "I did. I told her."

"Poetic-like? Lovey words? Did you call her Queen of Your Heart or Dear Heart . . . or *anything*?"

"I . . ." Edwin yanked off his hat and tossed it down next to Stephen. "I . . . it might have been abrupt. I might have just said it." He grimaced. His son was right. Gertrude deserved far more.

"Like you blurted it?" His son released a beleaguered sigh. "You're rubbish at this, Father."

Father. There it was, that address his soul had ached to again hear from this boy's lips. Something stung his eyes. Something that felt very much like . . . tears. He smiled through that swell of emotion his son would only reject. "Yes, well, I used to be much better at it."

Stephen glowered at him. "You didn't need to be good at it then. You need to be good at it . . . now. For my sister."

"Yes, I know. I'm trying to be a man worthy of her."

"Try harder," his son shot back.

As the carriage rumbled along the quiet streets of London, Edwin stared wistfully over at his son. "Someday, Stephen," he began quietly, "you are going to be a wonderful big brother." And in his mind's eye, he saw that child . . . a little girl with her mother's courage and laughter and wit. Gertrude. The child was Gertrude's in every way.

"I ain't going to have any more siblings if you don't figure this out." Pulling back the curtain, Stephen pressed his forehead against the windowpane and stared out.

"Stephen?"

Hi son peeled his gaze away from the window.

"I . . . I know you wondered why I didn't come to you. I was afraid, Stephen." It was an admission that would likely earn only his child's derision, but Stephen's need for the truth outweighed Edwin's pride or the pretenses the boy expected him to keep up. Gertrude had opened his eyes to his need to share those reasons with Stephen. "First, I was afraid to believe it was truly you, and then after? You were a stranger, and I didn't know how to be around you." Stephen's eyes fell to his lap. "Look at me, Stephen."

The boy hesitated, and then he slowly lifted his head, meeting Edwin's gaze. "I thought you didn't want me because of all the bad things I've done."

Oh, God . . . It was a prayer and an entreaty in his mind. "Stephen, we have *both* done some truly awful things because of the circumstances we were in." He reached for his son's hand. "But perhaps that actually makes it easier for us to know one another and accept one another."

Stephen stared at his outstretched fingers a long moment before placing his palm in Edwin's.

Reflexively, Edwin's fingers folded around the smaller, callused one. Emotion threatened to overwhelm him. "I have *always* loved you," Edwin said hoarsely. "*Always.* I wanted you. And when I learned you were, in fact, alive . . ." Tears clogged his voice, making it impossible to continue. He swallowed several times. "The joy of that was second to nothing, not even the moment they first placed you in my arms."

Stephen's mouth quivered, and even in the darkness of the carriage, Edwin caught the sheen glazing the boy's eyes. His son dragged the back of his sleeve across his nose. "That . . . is good to know." A smile formed on Stephen's lips. *"Father."* As if embarrassed, Stephen drew his hand back and, scrambling over to the side, stared out the window.

They didn't speak the remainder of the ride, but where tension had only throbbed between them, now they moved with a companionable silence.

In the crystal pane, Edwin studied every emotion that paraded over his son's face: impatience . . . excitement, and then, as they reached their destination . . . joy.

It was a reaction he would have once resented. No longer. Gertrude had shown him there was room enough for the many who loved Stephen to be in his life.

"We're here," Stephen whispered. He lurched for the doorway and pushed it open.

From the establishment across the way, a cacophony of ribald laughter and the din of distant conversation spilled out.

Stephen jumped down, landing on his feet with the agility of one of Gertrude's cats. "Come on!" he called, sprinting ahead.

Edwin lingered in the carriage. What had seemed . . . easy, this journey to the last place he'd sworn he'd ever step foot within, kept him immobile. He'd spent the past so many years resenting everything about this man and this place. *I cannot do it . . . I cannot . . .*

Stephen stopped on the bottom step of that long-despised establishment and cast a questioning glance back. "You coming?" His query emerged hesitant.

His son expected him to falter, and that was what allowed him the strength to grab his hat, climb out, and follow along silently after him.

Twisting the brim of that Oxford, Edwin swept his gaze over the darkened streets of the Dials. The stale scent of horse shite and refuse hung on the air; it was a heavy stench that filled a person's nostrils and turned their stomach.

These were the streets Gertrude had called home. The ones she still did and, if he failed to win her, would. Whereas during his life he'd known only material comforts and ease. Having failed to see how the majority lived left him with a learned-too-late shame.

Edwin climbed the steps where Stephen waited.

An eager little hand darted out and knocked hard, with a man's strength.

An instant later the door burst open.

The bearded, scarred guard, near a height to Edwin, glanced his way first. "Ye ain't a member," he noted in a thick Scottish brogue, and made to shut the heavy door in his face when he dropped his gaze. "Master Stephen!" he cried, grabbing the boy by the shirtfront and pulling him into a bearish embrace.

"MacLeod!" Stephen exclaimed, returning that hug.

Edwin hovered there, an interloper on a reunion of two with an ease and a clear love.

The guard abruptly set Stephen down and looked to Edwin. "Ye brought company," he said flatly. Hooking his fingers on the waist of his breeches, he flashed the metallic cut tucked there.

"Stand down, MacLeod. I'm looking for Broderick."

"In his offices."

"We're here to see my brother."

And with that statement, his son slipped his hand into Edwin's and led him on through a crush of bodies.

Cheroot smoke clouded the dimly lit hell, overflowing with patrons. The betting tables were filled with an eclectic mix of fancily dressed noblemen, street toughs in tattered garments, and scars enough to make the man MacLeod appear smooth of skin. Scantily clad women moved throughout the hall with drink trays raised on their shoulders.

Everything about this place oozed the sin of the Devil's Den it was professed to be. And Stephen moved through it like one who'd been born to it, the eventual king of this empire, and that would have been his place. And mayhap, one day, if he so chose it, it still would be.

They reached the back of the clubs, and two guards, standing with their arms folded at broad chests, stepped aside and let them pass. "This way." Stephen tugged him abovestairs and then stopped at an unassuming door. He rapped once.

When there was no immediate call or even the faintest hint of sounds within that room, Stephen rocked back and forth on the balls of his feet. Excitement poured from his tiny frame.

Stephen knocked again, this time harder.

"I'm busy." That booming voice pierced the heavy oak panel.

MacLeod cupped his hands around his mouth and leaned close to the door panel. "Ye've a meeting," he called, a grin on his hard lips. He looked down at Stephen and gave him a wink.

"I don't have any appointments. Tell him to schedule one and return later," Killoran ordered.

"Careful. If I leave, I might not come b—"

Footsteps pounded on the opposite side of that door, and the person on the other side of it wrenched it back with such force he nearly ripped the panel from its hinges.

Broderick Killoran.

A half-mad, overjoyed glint in his eyes, the proprietor reached out and yanked Stephen into his arms.

"You're crumshfing me," he mumbled into the tall, wiry man's shirt-front. Stephen still wrapped his arms around him and held tight.

"Stephen," Broderick whispered, pressing his cheek to the top of the boy's head. "Stephen. Stephen." It was Edwin's son's name, a litany . . . a prayer, on some other man's lips.

"Stephen!" Reggie Killoran sprinted over and wrapped the pair in her arms. MacLeod slunk away, and Edwin was left hovering, an outsider once again.

That display of love and devotion so intense, Edwin stared on. Where was the rage that had sustained him after his family's murder and the discovery that his son had been kidnapped? Where was the burning hatred? It had been a part of him so long, and yet there was none of it. Rather, there was a peace in knowing that for all the struggle and strife Stephen had known, he'd survived and been . . . loved by Gertrude's family.

At last, Broderick Killoran looked over.

And reality intruded in that interlude.

Killoran set Stephen down. "My lord," he greeted tersely. He said something in his wife's ear. The young woman nodded and made to leave. Killoran stayed her, and drawing her back, he raised her fingers to his lips and brushed a kiss along the knuckles. The pair shared a long intimate look, one Edwin knew a good deal about. Not from the wife who'd hated him more than she'd ever loved him . . . but rather, from Gertrude.

Edwin stepped aside so that Mrs. Killoran could exit, and then he entered.

For all intents and purposes, he might as well have stepped within any gentleman's Mayfair offices. From the gleaming mahogany furnishings to the ornate gilded frames that hung about the room, Killoran had fashioned the head of his kingdom with an elegant taste and attention to detail.

"Stephen," Edwin murmured, "if I might speak alone with . . . Mr. Killoran."

Killoran's gaze took in everything: Stephen's quick nod and his hasty flight, and then the door closed behind them.

"Would you please sit?" he asked quietly, gesturing to one of the high-back wood chairs across from his desk.

Wordlessly, Edwin came forward and took that indicated seat.

And found himself alone for only a second time with the man who'd given the orders which had seen Edwin's son kidnapped. Setting his hat down, he pressed his gloved fingertips together and spoke without preamble. "I learned Stephen was kidnapped three years ago. At that time, the investigators didn't know who was behind that act. And I hated the nameless stranger who took everything from me."

Killoran stiffened. "I would have you know, I would have you hear it from me . . . until I draw my last breath, I will forever regret the pain I've visited upon you." He swiped a hand over his jaw. "Though meaningless, I offer you my apologies. I thought I was doing good. I believed I was giving an orphan a home, but instead, I brought all of this upon you . . . and us."

Yes, he had. That was the only detail Edwin had clung to these years. He ignored that apology. "When Steele discovered your role in Stephen's kidnapping"—when Edwin himself had at last accepted that Stephen had been found . . . alive—"it gave me something concrete . . .

someone real to hate. You were the cause of all my suffering. You killed my wife. And unborn child. You took my son."

The proprietor's throat moved in the slightest, infinitesimal sign that he'd heard those words . . . and that they'd affected him in some way.

"And therefore, it was all too easy to plot your demise and plan ways with which to shatter you as I was shattered." Edwin touched his gaze upon every corner of this man's kingdom. The wealth fairly dripping from all the baubles and furnishings. The evidence of Killoran's pride and power. All this, he'd wanted to tear down. All this, he could tear down. And a short while ago, he would have been able to. Before Gertrude. He was no longer that same man driven by revenge. "I cannot do that anymore," he said quietly, looking back to a stoic Killoran. Nay . . . "I do not want to do that anymore."

Killoran's blond brows drew together with a seasoned suspicion. Crossing his arms nonchalantly at his chest, Gertrude's brother kicked back the legs of his chair. "Why?"

Yes, a man who'd survived in the Seven Dials and led these streets as a kingpin would have reason to be wary.

"I'm in love with your sister."

"My . . . ?" Killoran's chair tumbled back. He shot his arms out in a futile bid to catch himself before he crashed to the floor. To no avail.

A smile ghosted Edwin's lips, and coming to his feet, he leaned over the surface of the desk and found the proprietor, the seemingly unflappable street tough, sprawled on his buttocks, a dazed glint in his eyes. "What did you say?" Killoran demanded, jumping up. He grabbed his chair and set it to rights. He made no move to sit.

"I'm in love with Gertrude," Edwin repeated. He drew in a breath. "I'm asking her to marry me." And this time, when he spoke of a future between them, he'd come to her without hatred of her family the greater barrier dividing them. "And I'd like there to be peace between you and me."

Chapter 28

Gertrude should be overjoyed.

Tonight was the culmination of a hope she'd carried for Edwin and Stephen: that the two could find peace and a new beginning with Stephen's other family and Edwin's once best friend. And yet, seated with the menagerie of animals in Edwin's library, never had she felt more alone.

For despite Stephen's wish that she'd remain and Edwin's insistence that she do so until a suitable governess was secured for Stephen, the reality of it was, she wasn't needed here. Not really. Not as she'd been three weeks ago. Not even as she'd been needed here a fortnight earlier.

A memory flickered forward, of Edwin as he'd been with Stephen a short while ago, adjusting the boy's cravat and teaching him the proper knots and the preferable way to fold them.

There had been such a paternal devotion and love in that simplest of acts, she'd fallen in love with him all over again. For Edwin wasn't, and never had been, just an absentee sire. He'd not had Diggory's ruthless soul. No, Edwin loved his son so completely, so deeply, with a devotion that took her breath away. The kind that she'd believed fictional, existing only on pages of the novels she'd picked up over the years.

That exchange she'd watched as a silent observer long before either Edwin or Stephen heard her arrival had solidified one truth . . . a truth that should make her happy.

Everything had changed. Edwin and Stephen had found footing as father and son and were on their way as a family.

And I want to be part of it with them. Nor did that yearning come from the need to be close at hand to her brother, which she of course did. It was, however, Edwin and a place in his life that she craved.

Their relationship, from the beginning—all the decision-making over Stephen's current circumstances and future, deciding upon the best person to task with his care—all of it had been made in partnership. There had been no one person fully in control and the other meek and accepting of those decisions, as had been the case with Gertrude and her family.

Edwin had been the first person to truly entrust responsibility to her, and never had he doubted her.

"Until you gave him reason to," she whispered into the quiet. And he'd been the one who'd begged her pardon. He'd owed her no apologies for his response that evening. She'd been the one who'd let that serve as the barrier to a future. She groaned. What had she done? He'd professed his love and offered her a future with him, a future she ached for. And she'd let her fears dictate her decision. "I'm a fool."

Gus yowled on her lap.

"Oh, hush, traitor." She gentled that chastisement with a stroke between his ears.

As if taking that as room to encroach on the rival cat's territory, Fat Cat waddled over and attempted to jump onto her lap.

Gus batted at him.

"Be kind," she scolded. Giving her a long look, Gus leapt down and sauntered off. Reaching for Fat Cat, she lifted the affectionate creature. "There is love enough to go around for all of us."

Energized, Gertrude sailed to her feet, adjusting the burden in her arms. My God, she'd been a hypocrite. Schooling Edwin on forgiveness and beginning anew, while she'd not held herself to that same standard.

Fat Cat wiggled in her arms, fighting for his freedom, and she lowered him to the ground.

Why . . . why . . .

Her sisters . . . Stephen . . . they'd all been correct—there could be a future with Edwin. There would—

She stopped.

All Gertrude's senses went on alert. The faintest tinge of smoke lingered in the air.

Smoke?

A shiver of apprehension snaked along her spine. "Don't be silly," she murmured into the quiet. With long, brisk steps, she made her way to the door, and with every step taken, that metallic bite thickened. She pressed the handle and stepped outside.

A stream of servants, their arms filled with buckets, came barreling past.

Gertrude gasped, knocked against the wall. "What—?"

"Fire," Reggie's brother rasped.

A buzzing filled her ears. Terror and horror and panic all rolled together, to keep her frozen motionless to the floor, utterly useless in the face of that warning.

Fire. That weapon used by Diggory to destroy so many lives, homes, and futures. Edwin. His family. Then Stephen, the grand arsonist who'd set blazes throughout London . . . including at Adair Thorne's club.

No. Her palms slicked with moisture. Not fire. Not here. Not again.

Marlow's mouth was moving. He was saying something. Gertrude tunneled her vision on his mouth. What was he saying?

He clapped his hands close to Gertrude's face, snapping her out of the daze, and the din of the household came whirring back. "You have to leave now," he barked as another stream of servants came barreling past, in their haste and panic sloshing the water in their buckets, losing that lone precious resource to battle any blaze.

"Leave," she repeated dumbly.

Marlow made the decision for her. Catching her by the hand, he tugged her down the hall, keeping them close to the walls, to permit the servants a clear path to the fire.

"I can't," she cried, digging her heels in. "The animals."

"Miss Killoran!"

With his cries of protest trailing her wake, Gertrude bolted to the library. She scanned her gaze frantically around the room. Searching. Where in blazes were they? *Bloody hell.* Never more had she despised her reduced vision. Dropping to the floor, she crawled around.

"Please, Miss Killoran," Marlow implored.

"I'm not leaving them." Any of them. She'd brought them into this household, and she'd certainly not leave a single one to perish.

Cursing a stream of surprisingly inventive curses, Reggie's brother joined Gertrude on the floor. "Here's one." He reached under the sofa and made to grab the tabby hiding there.

The cat hissed and dug its claws down his hand.

Shifting course, Gertrude scrambled over and sent a prayer skyward. Gus and Fat Cat, the two feline adversaries, lay side by side. "Keeping one another company, I see," she drawled, reaching first for the more easygoing of the cats. "Here." Gertrude deposited Fat Cat into Marlow's arms. "Now you." She held her palms out, and Gus slinked out, his head ducked. "How very brave you are," she cooed.

Struggling to a stand, Gertrude took off running with Marlow close at her heels.

"Where was it set?" she called over her shoulder.

There was a lengthy pause as they wound their way through the corridors around frantic footmen.

Gertrude glanced back. "Your rooms," Marlow said quietly.

Her rooms? She missed a step and hurriedly righted herself. The attack on the streets of Mayfair a week earlier. Her family's suspicions. Nay . . . it was no mere coincidence. There was no such thing. Someone sought to harm her. But why? And who? And . . .

They reached the foyer, and Gertrude skidded across the smooth marble foyer.

The door hung ajar with young maids and the children in the household streaming out. She joined that haphazard line. As soon as she was outside, Gertrude rushed over to the nearest maid. "Here." She dropped Gus into the young woman's arms.

"Miss?"

"Miss Killoran!" Marlow shouted after her. "Where are you going?" he wailed, his cries following Gertrude as she raced back inside and abovestairs . . . toward her rooms.

*　　＊　　＊*

It was the unlikeliest of carriage rides Edwin had ever taken or would ever take in his life.

Across from him on the bench sat Broderick Killoran and the man's wife. Stephen had crammed himself between the pair. To the left of Edwin sat the diminutive Cleopatra and her sister Ophelia.

Out of the corner of his eye, Edwin took in the eclectic mix of guests he'd assembled. Tense. Laconic. Suspicious. Every pair of eyes in the carriage bored right through him.

They were certainly not a chatty lot.

Which was all well and good, given that he'd really forgotten how to speak to anyone . . . except Gertrude and Stephen.

"You're in love with my sister, then?"

The smallest of the Killoran sisters broke the stonewall.

"I am," he said quietly.

Ophelia dropped her hands onto her lap and leaned across the carriage to better peer at him. "Not so sure how much we can trust you, given your . . . history."

"*Our* history. One does not exist without the other," he put forward smoothly.

She held his gaze. "Exactly."

"Be quiet, Ophelia. He's all right," Stephen chimed in. And every last stare trained on Edwin now shifted to his son. "What?" he muttered. "He is. Lets me keep my weapons and got on fine with Draven. We eat ices at Gunter's. And . . ." Stephen scowled. "I ain't defending him anymore. You have my word. Take it."

That avowal dared anyone to question him. And wisely, no one did.

The carriage continued its slow roll through the crowded London streets. Where the ride to Killoran's and then each respective sibling's residence had been brisk, now the roads were clogged with slow-moving conveyances. They reached Curzon Street and were forced to a stop behind the row of waiting carriages.

It was a level of traffic . . . foreign. Except in rare cases, when there was a cause for it.

Disquiet stirred.

There'd been another long row of like carriages. Nearly seven years ago.

"What is going on here?" Cleo muttered, tugging back a curtain. "One of your fancy neighbors having a ball?"

"Father?" Stephen ventured hesitantly.

Their conveyance rocked into motion, resuming its slow roll.

Stop.

Edwin gave his head a clearing shake and glanced out as they neared the townhouse. "It is . . ." His heart slammed to a stop.

"Fire," Cleo whispered.

The crimson flames illuminated the street, in a bright glow of false daylight. Streets flooded with gawkers who'd come to watch the blaze as it tore apart—

"It's our home," Stephen whispered.

Edwin dimly registered Broderick Killoran's fierce growl. "Is this your revenge?" He reached for Edwin, but Edwin was already out of the carriage. "Is this why you brought us here?" he shouted after him.

He landed hard on his feet, stumbled, and took off running.

"Mad Marquess strikes again . . . ," a stranger was saying as he raced by.

God, no. Not again. Not again. Not again.

Those two words rolled around his mind, a prayer, an entreaty to a God he'd ceased believing in, but he would now sell his soul to the Almighty or the Devil himself. It couldn't be. *Not her. Not her. Please . . .*

A sob ripped from him. He couldn't survive this. He wouldn't. Not if she were taken from him.

In unison, Gertrude's family shouted after him, "Maddock!"

Edwin's lungs burnt from the fear and exertion, and he stretched his strides. With a thunderous roar, he parted the crowd lined up before his burning townhouse. Servants. His servants. *Oh, God. Let her be here.* He went down the row of maids and young male servants, their arms laden with . . . cats.

They were carrying cats.

And for the first time since he'd caught sight of the blaze, hope swelled within him. Edwin searched and searched . . . and did not find her.

He caught the nearest footman. "Where is she?" he hissed. Terror darkened the boy's eyes. "I said, where is she?" Edwin cried, giving him a shake.

The pale servant, his cheeks stained with ash, stretched a trembling finger out.

Edwin followed that point . . . and the earth fell out from under him.

"No," he whispered. Stumbling back, Edwin gripped his hair and yanked the strands.

Someone rested a hand on his arm.

He jerked back, half-mad, or mayhap the complete madman the world had rightly taken him for.

Cleopatra stared up at him with such terror radiating behind her wire-rimmed spectacles.

Edwin took off running once more. This time, he stormed the residence. Grey smoke filled the foyer, clouding the air around him, making it impossible to see so much as five feet in front of him. Using a rote remembrance of this place, he scanned the area.

Where would she be? Where . . . ?

Just then, Marlow came rushing down the stairs, a metal cage . . . nay, the Mouse House bouncing awkwardly against his side as he ran. "My lord," he rasped, choking fitfully.

"Gertrude?"

"Her rooms. Rescuing the ca—" Edwin was already taking the stairs two at a time before the remainder of the words left the mouth of his man-of-affairs.

By God, after he kissed her senseless, he was going to shake her mad. Cats. She'd gone after cats?

That was just one of the reasons he loved her. Loved her so hopelessly. So desperately. And he would spend the rest of his damned days proving himself worthy and showing her that they belonged together. Edwin reached the landing and raised an elbow to his mouth and nose.

Thick smoke choked off all attempt to gasp a clean breath. He squinted and, through the thick of it, attempted to gather his bearings. "Gertrude?" he thundered, charging toward her rooms and colliding with her. A torn strip wrapped over her mouth and nose in a makeshift mask; over the tops of them, reddened eyes; one of them revealing shock.

"Edwin," she whispered, her voice ragged and muffled all at the same time.

The weight of relief nearly brought him to his knees.

"Are there more?" he yelled through the fire's roar.

She glanced at the cat in her arms and then shook her head. With that confirmation, he scooped her and the cat in her arms up.

"I can walk, Edwin."

Ignoring her protestations, he cradled her close, wanting her near, needing to assure himself that she was alive and in his arms. They reached the marble foyer and Edwin continued running, and the crisp London air slapped at them. He didn't stop until he reached the opposite end of the street, where the crowd was thinned.

As he set her down, Gertrude dissolved into a paroxysm of coughing.

And his panic resurfaced.

"You're hurt," he croaked.

She stood. "I-I'm fine."

Soot stained her cheeks. The hem of her gown had been charred black.

He took her by the shoulders. "I thought I'd lost you," he rasped. "Never, ever put your life at risk. And certainly not for any bloody cats."

She hugged the cat close. "Well, it's hardly my fault. If you hadn't brought me an endless stream of nonstrays, I wouldn't have—"

Edwin kissed the diatribe from her lips. Her kiss was a homecoming. And he took strength from it.

She was safe. And that was all that mattered. A sob tore from his throat, and he forced himself to break that embrace. "I love you, you daft woman. If something were to happen to you, I—"

Gertrude pressed her fingertips to his lips. "I love you," she whispered, tears glistening in her eyes. "Marry me."

He opened his mouth. "What?"

"I want you to marry me, Edwin. I thought of what you said, and you are right." Going up on tiptoes, she placed a callused palm against his face. "The past does not have to define us. We could begin again, as a family, and I want that with you . . . if you'll marry me. We'll sort out every complication that comes with it, but I just want a life with you."

Edwin gritted his teeth. Bloody hell, he couldn't even do this correctly. "This was *my* proposal, madam."

Gertrude cocked her head. He glanced pointedly over her head. She followed his stare and gasped.

The Killorans stood in a neat row with Stephen at their center. "It was intended to be a surprise. You were so adamant that I have Charles in my life because he was part of my past, but I want you and your family to be part of my future. I went to gather your family tonight. I wanted them to come 'round so that we could begin again and find peace with them and—"

Releasing the tabby in her arms, Gertrude hurled herself at him.

Edwin grunted and staggered back. His arms automatically folded around her. The pungent scent of smoke and fire clung to her hair, and he breathed deep of it anyway.

"I love you," she cried.

"I love you, too." Resting his cheek on the crown of her tangled curls, Edwin simply clung to her, hanging on tight. From over the top of her head, he found Stephen.

His son nodded slowly, approvingly, and then winked. "Slightly better," he called out.

Edwin grinned.

"My lord?"

He stiffened as that stranger's voice cut across the moment.

Edwin and Gertrude faced the tall, darkly clad figure. He had a hand about a balding, pockmarked figure.

"My name is Clark Hughes. I was employed by Mr. Steele to watch over your residence. This man was the one caught."

Edwin peered, seeking some indication that the man was familiar.

"He claims he was paid a sizable sum by a Lord Charles to set the fire."

Edwin's eyes slid closed. "No."

The rotund thug in fraying garments wrestled against the investigator's hold. "Oi ain't paying the price. He wanted it lit. Said scare her. I brought you the one really to blame. Lock him up."

Hughes jerked the other man's arm up sharply, wringing a scream from him and effectively quelling the remainder of whatever words he intended. "I'll come around after he's been properly escorted, to . . . discuss further the situation with Lord Charles."

Edwin nodded blankly.

That was what this had been. Each attempt on Gertrude's life had been an orchestrated plot, carried out by the former best friend he'd spent years both resenting and missing.

Gertrude slipped her fingers into his. "I am so, so sorry, Edwin. I know he was . . . will always be a friend to you."

"He was," he said, staring off after the departing pair: one man a ruthless killer, sent at his boyhood friend's request. "But that time of my life, Gertrude? Is over. You are my friend . . . and now family, and . . . I'd form new relationships with your brothers and sisters."

"I love you." Another sob ripped from Gertrude as she launched herself into his arms, and as the Killoran clan came forward with his son laughing between them, Edwin found what he'd been yearning for, a gift that this woman in his arms had given him—forgiveness.

Epilogue

In a way, Edwin had come full circle.

He stood in his office, braced for the arrival of the same pair who'd demanded entry into his household just two months ago.

And yet . . . at the same time, everything had changed. *Everything.* This time, he was not the man riddled with hatred who'd been twisted into an empty shell of a being after his late wife's murder and his son's kidnapping. In the time since Gertrude had entered his life, she'd changed him, in every way. For the better.

Otherwise, he wouldn't be waiting as he was now for the last people in the world he should wish to see. Standing beside the windows, those curtains, once closed, now drawn proudly back, Edwin searched the busy Mayfair streets.

The gleaming crystal pane reflected the barely suppressed tension that thrummed through him.

What am I doing . . . ? I thought I was ready. I believed I'd found a way to a place of forgiveness.

I was wrong. I was—

Gertrude came to stand next to him; as usual, her remarkably quiet footfalls masked her approach until her arm pressed against his.

Edwin glanced down and forced a smile out of a calm he didn't feel. However, he couldn't get any casual response past tense lips.

Her eye glittered with concern, and she passed that probing stare over the planes of his face. Of course she'd see past that false grin. His new bride was too clever. She'd always seen too much. It was, however, that insight into his soul that had seen the fear that had allowed him to embrace the role of madman society had assigned to him.

"Are you all right?" she asked quietly.

Edwin and Stephen answered at the same time. "Fine."

Only Edwin's assurance, however, rang with any real conviction.

As one, he and Gertrude glanced over to where Stephen sat perched on the leather button sofa. His tiny frame all but hung from the edge, indicating the child was one wrong word or move away from bolting.

The grey tabby he stroked on his lap was likely the only thing that kept him where he was.

His son was unnerved.

Then this was a power play. An all-too-familiar one. A battle waged with the intention of reminding Edwin that he was powerless. Once that would have sent him into a familiar rage.

Gertrude slipped her fingers into his and gave a light squeeze.

Edwin stared down at their joined hands.

Setting aside his earlier disquiet, burying it for the sake of his son, Edwin faced Stephen. "There is no point in you waiting about until company has arrived—"

"I'm not worried about your meeting," Stephen muttered, red-faced. "There's nothing to worry about, Father." That promise Stephen made . . . was for Edwin. Nor did it come with the previous derision or hatred that had first greeted Edwin after all their years apart. Now there was a concern that staggered Edwin from the beauty of it. He cleared his throat of the lump there.

"If you'd rather find Oliver—"

His son was already sprinting for the door.

Stephen slammed it hard in his wake.

"And I'll summon you when they arrive," Edwin finished dryly as the door shook in its frame.

"You do know in sending him off with Oliver you've risked them getting lost in some mischief or another," Gertrude drawled. Stephen, having missed his closest friend at the Devil's Den, had called in his "favor" from Edwin and asked that Oliver come live with them. Without hesitation, Edwin had agreed to take in the orphaned child, and they'd given the boy a new home.

"There is no point in having Stephen wait about for a meeting that should have taken place thirty minutes ago." Tension rippled through him. Thirty minutes he'd been kept waiting. Cursing, Edwin stalked over to the sideboard and made himself a brandy. How dare they? Whatever tension there was and would always be between Edwin and them, Stephen was the one who ought to be put first—by each damned adult. Outrage on his son's behalf pulled him back into one of his older furies. "I'll rescind the bloody invitation. I don't want them here. I never—"

Gertrude rested a hand on his sleeve, and nothing more than her touch managed to end the diatribe and free him from his anger. "This is the best for all, Edwin," she said softly. "It's not about, and never was about, winning or having the upper hand. It is about finding peace."

Peace.

Before Gertrude had stormed his household and stolen his heart, he'd have scoffed at the very idea of it. Peace, for a man such as him?

She, however, had shown him the meaning of that word and that the gift was one Edwin was deserving of.

He set his untouched brandy onto the sideboard. "I love you, Gertrude." She'd restored him to the man he'd been. Nay, she'd made him better in every way.

"I love you, too." A smile curled the corners of her lips at a mischievous angle. "Even with your outrageous temper."

His throat moved. "I don't deserve you."

Gertrude scoffed. "Don't be silly. We are both better for having one another, Edwin." Her lower lip trembled. "My life was incomplete until you."

Leaning down, he took her lips under his. With a sigh, Gertrude instantly melted against him; her body fit so perfectly to his. She twined her arms about his neck, and their mouths met in a tender union. And Edwin gave himself over to the homecoming that he always found in her kiss: the warmth, the love, and the joy that were a tangible part of her effervescence.

A sharp rap cut across that too-brief embrace.

He stiffened.

"They are here," she said softly, disentangling her arms from him.

"They are here," he echoed dumbly. Edwin's mind went blank, and then thoughts clamored within his head. Of course they were here. *You invited them, you arse.*

Because of your wife. Because she'd opened his heart and mind to the truest meaning of forgiveness.

"What if it is a mistake?" he asked hoarsely. He'd made so many errors before. Costly ones.

Gertrude smiled. "It is going to be all right," she promised.

He caressed his gaze over her serene expression. How sure she was. And smiling. "How in blazes are you smiling?" Awe pulled that whisper from him.

His wife took his face between her ink-stained palms. She went up on tiptoes, raised herself until their eyes met. "Because this is a new beginning, and new beginnings are good for the soul." His awe of this woman and his love for her swelled, leaving him buoyant. Despite the hard life she'd lived on the streets and the suffering she'd known, she had not lost that part of herself.

The servant at the other side of the panel knocked once more. As one, Edwin and Gertrude stared at the oak panel.

"I'll offer a hint, Edwin," Gertrude said on a teasing whisper. "This is where you admit our guests."

Our guests.

Those two words were what allowed him to see through with this meeting. They were partners in life and through everything. That was just another piece of his life that this woman before him had changed . . . he was no longer one dwelling in a self-imposed exile. And as long as he had her at his side, he could do anything. "Enter," Edwin called over.

Quint Marlow opened the door. "His and Her Graces, the Duke and Duchess of Walford."

Edwin gave the man, more friend than servant, a pointed look.

The other man nodded and rushed off.

The regal pair swept forward, only as he'd never, in all the years he'd known the pair, seen them. Hands clasped together. That small detail presented them not as Edwin's adversaries but as a devoted husband and wife, each taking support from the other.

The duchess staggered to a stop. "What is this?" she hissed.

"Pamela," the duke murmured.

She ignored him. "You did not say that woman would be here."

That woman. Edwin's hackles went up, and icy rage coursed through his veins. Gertrude touched his sleeve. "It is all right." She spoke in nearly inaudible tones that barely reached his ears.

"It is not all right," he gritted out.

"I'll not meet with you while she's here, Edwin." The Duchess of Walford's voice came out slightly pitched.

"Pamela," the older woman's husband said in soothing tones. The remainder of his words were lost to the distance between them.

"No . . . ," the duchess was saying.

The Duke of Walford's quiet murmurings filled the room, punctuated by the periodic denial from his wife.

"I want them out," Edwin said, not moving his lips as he spoke.

Gertrude angled her body, presenting her back to the pair, shielding them from seeing her lips move. "They lost their daughter at my father's hands, Edwin."

"You'd forgive them for treating you so?" he demanded on a hushed whisper.

"I at least understand it," she countered. "As you should attempt to."

What manner of woman was she that she should forgive so readily and accept the anger that had been directed her way over the years, because of nothing more than the blood in her veins? *I was that narrow-minded once.* It was only because of Gertrude that he'd come to see people . . . and himself . . . in a new light. He clung to that recently imparted lesson and forced himself to face his former in-laws with that in mind.

The duke and duchess had gone silent. They stood shoulder to shoulder, with their hands entwined, facing Edwin and Gertrude. "Shall we sit?" He motioned to the pair of leather wingback chairs that sat opposite the button sofa.

The duchess pursed her mouth and then, withdrawing her fingers from her husband's, gave a snap of her skirts and swept over to the hearth. Her husband followed at her heels with a dutiful obedience Edwin once would have mocked but now understood.

After Gertrude claimed a spot on the sofa, Edwin slid into the folds of the seat beside her.

"Would you like tea, Your Graces?" Gertrude ventured with the aplomb of one who'd been greeting peers just a smidge away from royalty all her life. His appreciation for her swelled tenfold.

"This isn't a social call," the duchess snapped. "We're only here—" The lady's husband covered her gloved palm with his and gave a slight shake of his head.

There was a pleading in the duchess's eyes, and as they conversed in their own unspoken language, Edwin found Gertrude's hand within his.

The duke cleared his throat. "Forgive us—"

"I do not need you apologizing for me, Tremaine. And certainly not to these people," his wife snapped.

"These people, as you refer to them, are also the reason Charles wasn't hanged for attempted murder, Pamela," the duke reminded her. "I'd remember that . . . that . . ." His father-in-law glanced to Gertrude and made another attempt to get the remainder of his words out. "Edwin's wife."

"You'd take their side," the duchess hissed, her eyes bulging in her face, highlighting the gaunt, pale cheeks. Life had aged the duchess. She was a pale shadow of the once vibrant leading hostess she'd been.

But then, she'd lost her beloved daughter and now . . . Charles to his imprisonment.

"At any time Edwin might be less magnanimous toward our son, Pamela. I'll have you remember that," the duke said somberly.

The duchess's body arched forward like she'd fly off in a rage, but then she sank back to her heels.

And Edwin found himself, for the first time since he'd married Lavinia and discovered the depth of her parents' hatred for him, connecting with his mother-in-law. Her suffering was one he could understand as a parent, and he pitied her for it.

"Your Grace." Gertrude directed that murmuring at the older woman. "Neither myself nor Edwin have any intention of altering the decision we came to with regard to Lord Tenwhestle."

"The decision was my wife's," Edwin said bluntly for the benefit of the duchess. "If I'd had my way, Charles would now be living in the Tower of London for his role in trying to coordinate the murder of my wife. As it is, the fact he's been sent to Cornwall and lives still, you have my wife to thank for."

"He lives with a magistrate on house arrest forever, for a crime he is not guilty of. I don't believe for one moment my Charles has the blood of a murderer in him." The duchess's lips trembled, and averting her tear-filled gaze, she dabbed at her eyes.

His Grace bowed his head. "My wife and I thank you."

"Is that why you've insisted upon a face-to-face meeting?" the duchess spat, and when she looked back, the earlier evidence of her tears had vanished. "Do you seek our thanks for the fact that Charles is in some godforsaken corner of England and will never be afforded the life he deserves because of his rank?"

That is what the peerage believed, his in-laws included—that a nobleman's life and luxuries were ones they were deserving of, and there was never a thought to those men and women who survived and worked. Women such as Gertrude, who'd been proud to build the fortune she and her siblings had with nothing more than strength, skills, and a need to survive.

"No, that is not why I've asked you here," Edwin said quietly. *Do not do it . . . You're making a mistake . . .* He felt Gertrude's gaze and glanced to her. She gave him a small smile and then nodded. And he found the strength to continue. "I have resented you from the moment I married Lavinia and you treated me like a monster for nothing more than loving her."

His in-laws stiffened.

"You treated me as a villain and made me one with my late wife. And I hated you for that. Now?" His throat swelled with emotion, and when he managed to get words out, they came thick and gravelly. "Now I appreciate what it is to be a parent and want everything in the world for one's child. I could have tried harder with the both of you. I could have tried to have peace instead of baiting you at every turn." Knowing his former wife and his in-laws, Edwin didn't believe there would have ever been any different outcome. But he could have attempted to make peace.

The older couple exchanged a look; in their eyes was the wariness of a pair fearful they were even now stepping into a trap. "And we could have certainly been a better father-in-law and mother-in-law to you," the duke acknowledged, his face contorting with grief and regret.

"We did nothing wrong, Tremaine," his wife protested.

"We didn't do anything right, though, either, Pamela," the Duke of Walford said with such firmness the duchess's cheeks went red. "We also should have welcomed you into our family, instead of blaming you for a decision that was as much Lavinia's as it was yours. And for that?" The duke bowed his head. "I will be forever regretful."

"I don't want to fight with you anymore," Edwin said, and there was something so very freeing in that admission. "I invited you here because regardless of how we felt or feel about one another, the truth remains our lives were forever intertwined the moment Stephen was born." The duchess's mouth pulled at that name, different from the one she knew and used. Only she did not fight him on that score, and Edwin went on. "I'm allowing you to have a place in Stephen's life . . . if you wish it."

A sob escaped the duchess. "Is this a game?" she cried.

"No game," Gertrude said softly.

Almost on perfect cue, the door was opened, and Stephen entered. His previously immaculate sapphire cloak and tan trousers, now wrinkled and stained with bits of mud, spoke of a child who'd managed to find mischief before he'd arrived.

Everyone came belatedly to their feet. The duchess was the last to rise.

Stephen wrinkled his nose. "I don't need any of that nonsense," he muttered. He pushed the door closed behind him and lingered at the entrance of the room before catching his sister's gaze.

Gertrude stretched a hand out, and the boy came bounding over, past the duke and duchess, and took up position on the other side of Gertrude. "The duke and duchess have come to visit," she murmured, brushing a suspiciously damp strand away from his brow.

She narrowed her eyes, and Stephen ducked his head. There'd be questions enough about his shenanigans later. "Won't you say hello to His and Her Grace?"

"Grandmer—" The duchess pressed her fingertips to her mouth, stymieing that desperate request.

Stephen shifted. "Hullo," he mumbled under his breath.

"Perhaps you'd like to speak to one another a short while?" Gertrude suggested; Stephen's permission for such a meeting had been set long before this one had been put into motion. His willingness to grant the visit was just evidence of how very mature he was, and how much the Killorans had helped shape him as a young boy.

When no one immediately responded, Stephen glanced up at Gertrude, a question in his eyes . . . along with a hint of relief and hope.

"We would love that very much," the duke whispered. He held a shaking hand out toward his grandson.

Stephen hesitated, and then a moment later, he sat before the older couple.

Edwin and Gertrude wandered over to the corner, allowing the trio some space in which to talk. All the while, Edwin's gaze remained locked on his son, searching for any hint that they'd offended him or hurt him.

"It is going to be fine, Edwin," Gertrude whispered, looping her arm through his. She rested her head against his sleeve.

"What if it's not?" he shot back in an equally quiet voice. "What if they can't accept him for who he is? What if he's hurt? What if—?"

"We cannot necessarily prevent Stephen from hurting, Edwin," she said softly. "We can only be sure that we'll be there to help him if and when he is hurt. But this time? I don't believe it will be one of those moments." The duke had shifted over to the seat next to Stephen and was displaying a handful of mints he'd tucked away in a silver case as long as Edwin had known him. Whatever Stephen said earned a booming laugh from the duke, and he turned the entire container over to the boy. "See?" Gertrude asked, lightly squeezing his arm.

He lowered his head so close their brows touched. "I do see. I see you've made me a better man. I see what happiness and love is. And now"—tears pricked at his lashes—"now I see what forgiveness is. I love you, Gertrude."

She caught her trembling lip between her teeth. "I love you."

And with an unexpected bark of laughter from Stephen that rolled together with that of the duke and duchess, Edwin held tight to Gertrude's hand and let go the last shred of hatred that had held him ensnared.

He was free.

About the Author

Photo © 2016 Kimberly Rocha

USA Today bestselling, RITA-nominated author Christi Caldwell blames authors Julie Garwood and Judith McNaught for luring her into the world of historical romance. When Christi was at the University of Connecticut, she began writing her own tales of love. She believes that the most perfect heroes and heroines have imperfections, and she rather enjoys torturing her couples before crafting them a well-deserved happily ever after.

The author of the Wicked Wallflowers series, which includes *The Governess*, *The Hellion*, and *The Vixen*, Christi lives in southern Connecticut, where she spends her time writing, chasing after her son, and taking care of her twin princesses-in-training. Fans who want to keep up with the latest news and information can sign up for Christi's newsletter at www.ChristiCaldwell.com or follow her on Facebook (AuthorChristiCaldwell) or Twitter (@ChristiCaldwell).